Praise for The Alliance Series

OCEAN'S GODORI

An Indie Next Pick
An Amazon Editors' Pick
A *Shelf Awareness* Best Book of the Year

"*Ocean's Godori* navigates the space lane blazed by Becky Chambers and James S. A. Corey, but it manages to arrive at some exciting new destinations."

—CHARLIE JANE ANDERS,
Washington Post

"Space. Murder. Romance. Tradition and technology collide in this impressive debut, perfect for fans of *Gideon the Ninth*."

—B&N Reads,
"Our Most Anticipated Books April 2024"

"Buckle up because this sci-fi will take you to places you never expected. Its plot moves with keen precision. The page-turner will bring readers to the edges of space while tackling the age-old questions of who we are and what we are here for."

—Debutiful

"*Ocean's Godori* is dark and dreamy and thrilling in a *Blade Runner* kind of way, but with an expansive love that thrums underneath the surface in the tradition of Becky Chambers. More, please."

—YUME KITASEI,
author of *The Deep Sky*

"The real strength of the book . . . is in the relationships between family and friends, the living and the dead, and the ways these threads of connection motivate and inform characters. This is an entertaining debut with satisfying cultural-background details for the characters and the world and plenty of room for development."

—*Booklist*

"Full of slow-burn romance, tense negotiation, and close shaves. Every scene builds suspense and illuminates fascinating themes of exploitation, privilege, and identity, all held together by a sweet found-family narrative. Ambitious and heartwarming, this is a treat."

—*Publishers Weekly*

"Fun, full of both heart and plot."

—*Kirkus*

"With its quirky band of spacefarers, this will appeal to fans of high-concept, high-appeal space opera."

—*Library Journal*

"A space frolic with a disgraced pilot, her ragtag crew, and unexpected allies. Cho's writing is tender and careful, a moving exploration of the human capacity for compassion and friendship in a brutal future. I can't wait for the next installment!"

—JULIA VEE, author of the critically acclaimed *Ebony Gate*

TEO'S DURUMI

"*Ocean's Godori* is such a thrilling, moving, transportive ride that, by the end, we were dying for more. We were overjoyed that Elaine was ready to continue Ocean's story with *Teo's Durumi* and go on an ever-evolving adventure with this ragtag crew we have already come to love deeply. As ever, Elaine takes us on a twisting journey that further expands on her haunting themes around grief, memory, and sacrifice, bringing us breathlessly to the end of a story we'll never forget."

—LENA WAITHE, RISHI RAJANI, AND NAOMI FUNABASHI, Hillman Grad Books

"No one alive writes sci-fi like Elaine U. Cho. Yes, her futuristic worlds are as expansive as her wild imagination, yet her unforgettable characters are cozy, sensual, and crackling with irrepressible human spirit. Once again, I found myself breathlessly rooting for Teo, Ocean, and the rest of the Alliance crew as they navigate treachery, conspiracy, and romance in the stars—epic on every level!"

—JUSTINIAN HUANG,
author of *The Emperor and the Endless Palace* and *Lucky Seed*

"As a writer, Elaine U. Cho's gifts are many—breathless action sequences, consummate world-building, and page-turning plot chief among them. As a genre fan, Cho filters the oddball crew of a *Firefly*, the swagger of Buck Rogers, and the sweep of *The Fifth Element* through the lens of her Korean heritage to create a work unlike anything before it. Reading *Teo's Durumi* reminded me why I fell in love with sci-fi."

—AARON JOHN CURTIS,
author of *Old School Indian*

"Like *Ocean's Godori*, *Teo's Durumi* is daring, delightful, and undeniably romantic. There's grace, deft and dance-like, to the car chases, the hijinks, and the high-stakes showdowns. As Teo, Ocean, and their unforgettable found-family crew navigate threats both tangible and internal, Elaine U. Cho never neglects the world-saving significance of an outreached hand, a shared meal, or a quiet drive."

—SYLVIE CATHRALL,
author of *A Letter to the Luminous Deep*

"Without a moment to catch our breath, *Teo's Durumi* picks up right where *Ocean's Godori* left off. The thrills and chills of nonstop action belie the profound questions on capitalism, colonialism, caste, family loyalty, and identity formation upon which the wildly inventive, cinematic plot is built. All this, and two achingly steamy love stories, make for a delicious, thought-provoking, can't-put-it-down read."

—ALICE STEPHENS,
author of *Famous Adopted People*

Also by Elaine U. Cho

Ocean's Godori: The Alliance, Book One

TEO'S DURUMI

The Alliance, Book Two

ELAINE U. CHO

HILLMAN GRAD BOOKS
A zando IMPRINT
New York

The characters and events in this book are fictitious. Any similarity to real persons, living or dead, is coincidental and not intended by the author.

Copyright © 2025 by Elaine U. Cho

Translation of verse from the traditional Korean folk song "Ieodo Sana" by Chong Hee Woo. Copyright © 2024 by Chong Hee Woo

Zando supports the right to free expression and the value of copyright. The purpose of copyright is to encourage writers and artists to produce the creative works that enrich our culture. Thank you for buying an authorized edition of this book and for complying with copyright laws by not reproducing, scanning, uploading, or distributing this book or any part of it without permission. If you would like permission to use material from the book (other than for brief quotations embodied in reviews), please contact connect@zandoprojects.com.

Hillman Grad Books is an imprint of Zando
zandoprojects.com

First Edition: August 2025

Design by Neuwirth & Associates, Inc.
Cover illustrations by Jee-ook Choi

The publisher does not have control over and is not responsible for author or other third-party websites (or their content).

Library of Congress Control Number: 2025936023

978-1-63893-365-6 (Paperback)
978-1-63893-229-1 (Hardcover)
978-1-63893-230-7 (ebook)

10 9 8 7 6 5 4 3 2 1
Manufactured in the United States of America
LBK

For Sam.

Thanks for changing my life for the best by saying hello.

RECORD OF VON KENT, XENOBOTANIST

38.04.16

We're approaching Artemis base on the Moon, and as it seems our strange time on the Pandia is coming to a close, I figured I'd jot down some thoughts. Not for posterity—Phoenix has made it clear that once we leave his ship, we can never speak of his crew or our time together. This is, understandably, to protect his team, which is currently wanted by the Alliance. For so-called raiders, though, they've been particularly hospitable to us.

I'm handwriting the note rather than logging a voice memo or leaving a digital print, so it will be easier to destroy it. Also, I did want to organize my thoughts to better remember them, and isn't handwriting a pleasant, severely underrated pastime? I used to scribble in diaries when I was younger and start off my voice memos with a gruff "Captain's Log," but it's a bit embarrassing to look back. It's much easier to believe I'm writing a letter to a dear friend (even if that dear friend is a figurative future self!). So, hello, dear friend and reader.

To begin, I'd like to introduce the Alliance crew that I am a part of: the *Ohneul* crew, although we can be only loosely called that now, as the physical *Ohneul* ship no longer exists.

This is particularly distressing to its captain, **Dae Song**. The *Ohneul* . . . well, to say it kindly, had seen some better days. And Dae . . . well, I have always been told that if you cannot find anything kind to say, it's best not to continue. But she did love her ship very much, and in some ways I think she has tried to do right by its crew. She served for a time on a ship with Ocean's older brother, earlier on in their Alliance careers, before he passed away. I think this is what influenced her to take on Ocean some years back, when the Alliance ships that would welcome her were few (or otherwise nonexistent).

Ocean Yoon is our XO and pilot, and she's happiest when she's behind the wheel. What can I tell you about Ocean? She was born on an island off Jeju and her mother is a haenyeo leader, but Ocean probably wouldn't want you to know that. She was sent to Savoir-Faire when she was young to become a Diplomat but dropped out . . . but she probably wouldn't want you to know that either. I believe she joined the Alliance after her brother died, and again, I find I'm being indiscreet . . . There's actually very little Ocean would want anyone to know about her, least of all that although she seems quite cold, I've found that to be merely exterior.

Next, **Margaret Thierry**, also known as Maggie, who can be described by her variety of interests and talents. She's an engineer and cook, and would love to tell you the difference between Schubert and Schumann. Her exuberance has buoyed us through many a crises, and currently, she's putting together snacks for our regular movie night with the combined *Ohneul* and *Pandia* crews. Neither of us are Alliance members; we're both contract workers, but Maggie signed on to take in some of the solar for experience. She wants to open a restaurant back on Venus with her

x   ELAINE U. CHO

spouses after this. Or a garage? Maybe a combination garage/eatery? I'm not certain Maggie's decided.

Haven Sasani, who prefers to go by his last name, is the newest member of the *Ohneul* and is quite conscientious with his reserved demeanor. I imagine this suits him in his role as a Mortemian, those who practice funeral rites and are well versed in death culture across the solar. It seems Sasani's close to his father, and he plans to return to Prometheus to take up his Mortemian duties after his stint with the Alliance. Currently, he's our highly skilled medic, and although he may come off as rebuffing your attempts at conversation, I personally think he's shy. I get the feeling, too, that he may not have always been treated kindly due to his Mortemian role.

Teophilus Anand is perhaps the newest newest de facto member though. You might recognize the Anand name from the tech conglomerate that dominates the solar and has a partnership with the Alliance. Teo (he feels "Teophilus" is rather stuffy and imposes a distance) is the second son of that, well, speaking of lofty words, I suppose some would call it an empire. Maybe we should say was the second son, as recently, his parents and his older brother, Declan, were tragically murdered. The situation has sobered Teo, but I wouldn't have you believe that the headlines that labeled him as "frivolous" or "philanderous" or any such nonsense were ever true. He may not show many people, but he's one of the most thoughtful folks I know.

Oh, I suppose I should talk a little bit about myself! **Von Kent**, xenobotanist. To be frank, I followed Ocean onto the *Ohneul*. We had served on the *Hadouken* together before . . . in any case, Ocean and I go back a ways! I'm afraid I don't have very many interesting qualities. I'm engaged to a wonderful woman, Sumi, who serves on another Alliance ship. And I suppose I could talk to you about my algae? ~~They're really fascinating specimens! Did you know that algae, unlike most plants, actually thrive~~

~~from being placed under external stress like microgravity and create anti-oxidants and~~ Well, I just caught Maggie reading over my shoulder, and she said that no one cares as much as I do about algae. But I take heart in knowing that I have files upon files written on the subject if Maggie turns out to be wrong.

I guess that brings us to the ship we're currently on, the *Pandia*, which is led by the intrepid <u>Phoenix</u>. The Phoenix, you might ask? Yes, the very same raider who's infamous across the solar and on all those wanted posters. I must say, though, I've seen some of those videos captured of him, and I used to think he gave off this air of a cartoon villain. In person, he's calmer, congenial, and caring of his crew. Not to say he doesn't thrive off attention. He came in the other day to read poetry to my plants—and whether that's because he agrees with me that it helps them grow or because he likes performing, I dare not say.

<u>Gemini</u> is Phoenix's right-hand man (although I've heard him refer to himself as Phoenix's left hand, *mano izquierda*, at times). I confess he's an enigma to me. He met Phoenix in Guatemala, and they've been together since. He's the one who has put together the different iterations of the *Pandia*'s crew over the years, and Phoenix trusts him enough to leave it completely to him (so perhaps he operates as both of Phoenix's hands sometimes?). One might say he's responsible for the *Pandia* and *Ohneul* colliding, as he's been trying to recruit Ocean to their team. So if nothing else, he's a very good judge of character. He has a soft step, and I've been startled more than once by his silent appearance.

<u>Cassiopeia</u>, or Cass for short, is another member of Phoenix's crew who gives off a gruff front. But I heard that she saves all her money from the *Pandia*'s exploits and sends it home to her family on Mercury. Three younger sisters and one younger brother! Anyway, she's the only one of Phoenix's crew who wasn't scouted and brought on board by Gemini. She

had been following Phoenix for years (he hails from Mercury as well), and begged to join them.

   <u>Aries</u> is the older brother of the group. He doesn't talk very much, but it's best to pay attention when he does! He's like the reticent character in a serial who finally speaks in the last episode to dispel pearls of wisdom. He has the intimidating aura and mass of a bodybuilder, but he claims he just does accounting for the *Pandia*.

   I confess I've only caught glimpses of the *Pandia*'s final member, <u>Lupus</u>, and usually against the glow of a monitor (or three). Gemini says Lupus is an NYC kid who got caught hacking into the library database. They're soft spoken, and you might be surprised to hear that out of all the Ohneul crew members, they get along best with Maggie. I hope to get to know them better, though, and they're giving a little presentation to introduce tonight's film of choice!

   But before I close, I fear I must give some space to those responsible for bringing our crews together. I speak, unfortunately, of <u>Corvus</u> and his team members. Corvus has some connection to Phoenix from the past, but we know him primarily as the one behind the deaths of Teo's family. He has some other nefarious design that's unclear as of yet, but he has long since harbored resentment against the Anand family and Anand Tech for draining Mercury of its resources. It seems that he has come into money and resources of his own, allowing him to enact his plan, which includes:

   <u>Hadrian</u>, who is currently impersonating Teo's older brother, Declan. He has some sort of suit that has allowed him to completely take on Declan's appearance. Even knowing the truth, I've found it impossible to discern that he's an impostor. Hadrian as Declan is claiming not only to still be alive but also that Teo is the one who killed their parents. I can't imagine what Teo must be going through.

__Amell__, who sounds like a rather unpleasant character all-around, and a fanatic follower of Corvus. He also used to work with Phoenix back before their ideologies and methods diverged.

And __Emory__, a woman who operates a powerful augmented suit. Ocean, Phoenix, and Gemini had a run-in with her and Amell on Mercury and were severely outmatched. Also, whatever you might say about Corvus, he has very devoted and faithful followers.

Anyway, enough of that. It doesn't seem right to end on such a note, so I will say that although the circumstances that brought us all together have been unfortunate in many ways, I am still grateful to have met the people on this ship. These may be small joys—donning face masks (avocado and manuka honey, now that we've run out of the sheet masks Maggie got in Korea) while watching the latest episode of Cemetery Venus. But we must take our joys when we can, don't you think?

Until we meet again,
Von Kent

ONE

THE LAST TIME Teophilus Anand arrived on the Moon, he was primarily concerned with the complex calculations of partying, food, and soju.

This time, Teophilus—known to his friends as Teo—supposes he should be processing how many times he's come close to death today, but he's distracted by how *drafty* the hangar is. Large spacecraft garages aren't known to be cozy, but velvet drapes could improve the impersonal encasement of metal and concrete. They'd at least soften the harsh light streaming through the glass panels of the side windows. Their building, Hangar B, is one of several on this base, but it has the capacity for only four or five ships because of the enormous, Olympic-grade pool at one end.

An enormous pool into which his best friend and ace pilot, Ocean Yoon, crash-landed the *Pandia* a little more than an hour ago. That was after she had destroyed nearly a whole forest of priceless sonamu, specifically cultivated for this area of the Moon, by flying the ship through them. And after they were chased by Corvus helming another spacecraft, hell-bent on destroying them.

So, back to those hypothetical velvet drapes. Underneath the windows, Koreans in austere white hanbok methodically sweep wide swathes of water into the grated drains at the edge of the pool. Even if the facility is designed precisely for this type of training exercise, they probably weren't expecting the real-life demonstration that threw spectacular tidal waves. Seonbi are known to be stoic, but Teo doesn't think he's imagining their pinched expressions as their large brooms chafe the floor.

The chill of the room isn't just from the severely practical aesthetic, or the water lapping at the edge of the pool. Guards are stationed all around the space, and Teo wishes he could chalk it up to his usual vanity, but he suspects they're all watching him. Which might or might not have to do with the small, vaguely inconvenient fact that he's wanted for murder. It doesn't help that Teo's always found the Seonbi to be a judgmental lot.

Korea won over the Moon last century, a huge gain in that it was considered a stepping stone to the rest of the solar. They chose to erect their tenth seowon here and this city, Artemis, is symbolic of the old melding with the new. As Koreans advanced into space, they wanted to honor the past by redefining their culture with the Seonbi, who are virtuous scholars dedicated to preserving Korea's history. Despite common belief, the Seonbi don't belong to the Alliance; they've always kept apart with their seowon to educate their own. But that doesn't mean they'll hesitate to hand Teo over to the Alliance at the first opportunity.

Teo rubs at his arms and is about to ask whether anyone else feels uncomfortable when a voice booms out, its volume amplified in the space of the garage.

"I can't wait to tell my spouses about this landing!" Maggie Thierry says brightly. "And the teamwork! Ocean, you have to tell Naya that I *can* be a good team player! She won't believe me otherwise."

Maggie's several meters away, but her voice pierces right into his eardrum, bulldozing all other thought. Teo relaxes as Maggie spreads her arms. She could be holding court on her throne of an overturned bucket she apparently assumed that the Seonbi didn't need. She doesn't seem to mind that the court consists only of Lupus and Von Kent sprawled before her. Ocean sits slumped against Teo, who keeps himself from shifting on his feet so as not to disturb her. Ocean rests her head on her bent knees, appearing dead to the world, but Maggie doesn't bat an eye at the pilot's non-reaction.

"Lupus, I've mentioned Naya to you, right?"

Lupus calculates, ticking off their fingers. Teo takes the opportunity to study them as their hood slides back from their cap of silvery-gray hair. He's seen the technician only a few times in actual daylight, rather than in the shadowy recesses of the *Pandia*'s computer room, and he's rarely seen them converse with anyone outside of their own crew except for Maggie.

"First wife?" Lupus asks.

"No, my first partner was Gunner. Then we married Naya," Maggie corrects. "When I was first working at her café, you wouldn't believe how angry she was when I yelled 'Hot! Behind!' at her. But that's what I'd always been taught to say when handling hot plates! How was I supposed to know? She made me come up with something else."

Lupus blinks slowly. "What do you say instead?"

Maggie places her hand on Lupus's shoulder and says solemnly, "I'm on your side."

"I like that," Von announces, which is a generous indulgence as even Teo, who's only been on a ship with Maggie for a week or so, has already heard this particular story four times.

As Maggie launches into another oft-handled story, Von crab-walks over from the center of the room to Teo and Ocean. "Ocean, do you think we're jake now?" The xenobotanist's hair is a puff of anxiety, ready to be blown away with someone's wish.

Artemis is behind a protective shield—one that requires approval for entry—but still, there's very little guarantee of their safety on the Moon. Teo's not certain where Corvus and his crew escaped to after they failed to shoot the *Pandia* down, but that's trouble for another day . . . although Teo has the feeling that that day isn't too far off.

Ocean stirs enough to say, "I think it's complicated."

She pats Von on the head, and her hand remains there as she closes her eyes again. Teo doesn't know if she's already dropped off to sleep, but Von's eyes go round and he adopts the posture of someone afraid to breathe. Teo carefully lifts Ocean's hand to free Von from her inadvertent trap. Von beams at him before scurrying back over to Maggie's circle.

Teo keeps hold of Ocean's cold hand. She's always had bad circulation. He rubs it, but not abrasively enough to rouse her. Whereas Maggie's buzzed from the adrenaline of helping land the ship, Ocean's completely sapped. No wonder, after that display. Teo's seen her fly, seen her drive, but not her diving and flitting through space like just now. For so long, she's been a bird with clipped wings, trapped in her Class 4 ship. And through the missiles fired and the barrel rolls today, through the terror that tasted like metallic finality in his mouth, Teo hadn't been able to help the ache in his chest at Ocean's easy, uncontrolled joy.

"Get some rest, Hummingbird," Teo says. "I'll wake you when things are moving again."

The Seonbi have kept the group waiting for an hour without any explanation. Teo would have thought the group of historians and scholars would be above such an uncomfortable tactic, but he suspects it's not the Seonbi who are making the decisions here. Rather, it's a specific Diplomat.

A Diplomat who is almost certainly observing them right now. As always, Teo automatically tabulates the surrounding cameras. The ones above the doors to the right of the hangar are obvious. But he can guess where the others might be installed, even in a vast space like this with such high ceilings, based on where the guards are stationed.

The *Pandia* crew is in a conference of their own by their ship now, which has been pulled out from the closer end of the pool. The battered, dripping vessel has large gaping windows, seemingly bewildered by its impromptu bath. The *Pandia* is a prizefighter who has won at a steep cost. Its members are far enough that Teo can't judge the curve of their murmurs. Close enough that Teo is caught by the easy movement of the tallest one as he runs his hand through what might be the most famous, or infamous, head of hair in the solar, the gold flecked with red and light brown.

Phoenix, a raider known for the Uranian Looting of '37, the practically mythical Naked Saturnian Fiasco, and the Mercury Murders, nods along as his second-in-command, Gemini, says something. Phoenix, Gemini, Cassiopeia, Aries, and Lupus. All constellation aliases that hide the true identities of the outlaw crew. Cass scowls, which isn't far from her default, at least where Teo's concerned;

she's a true Mercurian and hates both the Alliance and Teo's family in equal measure. Aries, the *Pandia*'s usual pilot, squats at the edge of the pool as he dips a hand contemplatively into the water.

Dae strides in front of him at that moment, stuck in her claustrophobic pacing pattern. Every time she veers too close to the *Pandia* group, Cass glares at her, but the Alliance captain is caught up in her own muttering. She's probably trying out various narratives to present to the top brass that will explain why her ship, the *Ohneul*, was blasted to pieces. The Alliance is neither forgiving nor great at listening. Worst case, they'll clap her in prison. Possible, though, they'll expel her, which is just as good as landlocking her since the Korean space agency dominates so much of the solar. Not that Dae would entertain the thought of an alternative space career; for Koreans especially, if it isn't the Alliance, it isn't worth mentioning. You become the sort of dinner topic that your parents avoid.

Maggie and Von have it easy in that respect—they're contract workers, with Maggie planning to go back to Venus to open up a restaurant with her spouses, and Von forever caught in the grind of algae research.

The same might be said for the last member of the former *Ohneul* group, Haven Sasani, although unlike Teo, he prefers for people to call him by his last name. The Mortemian leans against a wall not far behind Teo. Dae had hired Sasani to be the *Ohneul*'s medic, and he told Teo that his plan was always to return to Prometheus, the modified Saturn moon he grew up on, after his time with the Alliance was done. He's slim and tall, with dark hair and even darker eyes that flicker to Dae passing him before he's back to not paying attention to anything in particular. At least that's what Teo thinks until Sasani straightens.

Immediately after, the doors across the hangar bang open. The *Ohneul* and *Pandia* group goes silent as one. The only people who don't react are Maggie, who keeps chattering away, and Ocean, who remains fast asleep against Teo's leg. A band of Koreans enter, with one particular Diplomat at the head of four soldiers in brightly colored jeonbok. The Diplomat has the usual silk-hybrid uniform, this one in pale green. It has a weight to it so it doesn't flutter with his movements, but it's designed so that your eyes follow the line of the folds without realizing where the billows could be hiding items. Teo's palms itch, and it's a nostalgic feeling, this wanting to sketch out a design.

This is the Diplomat who facilitated their Artemis landing via the *Pandia*'s video comm, all while they had been battling Corvus's ship. He has pale skin and black hair slicked back into a topknot. He had joined the call after the first Seonbi on the transmission refused to open up Artemis's shield to let them in. While the Diplomat had also been inclined to let Corvus destroy them, Teo had offered him information on what happened to the Seonbi Embassy that got murdered on their way to Mars. Teo, as the sole survivor of the crew that was escorting them, is the only one who can give him that information. He'd asked the Diplomat to let them into Artemis and hold off on alerting the Alliance.

The guards split up to either side of the Diplomat, and he heads for Teo. Out of an ingrained habit, Teo slides his feet apart, hands behind his back in the Alliance stance. But the Diplomat ignores him and plants himself in front of Ocean.

"It's been a while, Ocean," he says.

Teo should have woken her up beforehand; this is the very definition of moving. When Ocean's steady breathing doesn't change, Teo gently squeezes her hand. It's only then that the Diplomat deigns to notice Teo, his gaze traveling from their clasped hands up to Teo's face. But then Ocean stirs and peers at the Diplomat. Ocean's not the greatest at remembering faces, and Teo recognizes her customary blankness that hides the mental sifting of placing someone, figuring out which stage of life she might have known them during.

A flicker of distaste ripples across the Diplomat's expression, like a stone being thrown into a deep lake. "Oh, come on. Seriously?"

Comprehension dawns on Ocean's face. "Park Joonho." She presses her fingers into Teo's palm in a reassuring gesture before she releases his hand and explains, "We were at Savoir-Faire together."

Diplomat Park's eyes crease into crescents, but when he tilts his head, he looks like nothing more than a predator assessing its prey.

"We weren't just there together, Ocean," Diplomat Park says pleasantly. "We were steadies, until you dropped out. Or did you forget that too?"

Ocean opens her mouth and Teo can immediately tell she's about to say something along the lines of *Kind of* or *Actually, yes.* But then her mouth clicks shut, which, snarky ex-steadies aside, is probably the best tactic when you've dove through the Moon's shield, busted up a generous amount of their property, and might need to be on the good side of their Diplomat. Not that it matters, because the damage has been done.

"Aigo." Dae sighs.

But Diplomat Park only raises an eyebrow. "Out of practice, Ocean? Well, I'm glad you're not dead, just . . . in interesting company." His scan grazes over the rest of them. "What would your umma think?"

Ocean's in the middle of rubbing her eyes, rolling her neck for cricks, but she winces at the Diplomat's question. Diplomats generally deal only with one another, but the stereotype is that they're always coldly tabulating every word and inflection. Ocean once said that after just a week at Savoir-Faire, you couldn't help but be sensitive to every motion, every word that was said or unsaid. You fixated on what other people were thinking and feeling. All so you could manipulate them.

"Teophilus Anand, would you come with me?" Park asks.

"Where are you taking him?" Phoenix speaks up.

When Park turns, Phoenix runs his hands through his hair, flicking it in a definitive motion. Teo's heard the crew call it the "Phoenix Toss," even seen them take turns imitating it. This is neither the time nor place, but Teo goes warm.

Park has already placed his hands back into the folds of his uniform. Interestingly, Diplomat Park wears the sleeveless jeonbok of a Seonbi over the usual Diplomat outfit, marking him as a hybrid Diplomat/Seonbi. Meaning he's studied as a Seonbi as well as graduating from Sav-Faire. It's an extreme accomplishment for someone his age; it speaks to his talent . . . and his ambition. Artemis has only a few Diplomats—it's a small jurisdiction, but it's a unique position in that the Seonbi are so fiercely apolitical that they tend to leave everything in that sphere in the hands of these representatives, which is why the selection process is so strenuous.

"I wouldn't be so hasty to attract attention," Park says, his tone bored. "I believe the current bounty on your head after the Circe jaunt last autumn is one hundred and fifty thousand marks. No one has ever even gotten sight of your ship, so that's valuable intel on its own. Whatever could we do with that?"

"You'll want to think twice before you use that information," Teo cuts in.

Maggie mutters about frying pans and fires.

"Everyone would be better served," Park says, "if they considered their own interests. I certainly am. As of right now, no one outside these grounds knows you are here. That can change very quickly, and I control that. So, again, Teophilus Anand, would you please follow me to the other room for questioning?"

"He shouldn't go alone," Phoenix interjects again.

"You act as if you have any power," Park says. "Who's going to go with him? You?"

"He still owes me marks," Phoenix says. "Our business isn't done."

Five hundred thousand marks, to be accurate, of the original million. Teo has already paid off the first half, but he still owes the second, which was supposed to be transferred once Phoenix safely delivered him here. Phoenix meets Teo's eyes steadily. Teo should have hammered out an actual contract, defined what "safely" meant. He wants to say something about that, or actually, what Phoenix specifically means by "business" because there's the matter of what was going on in Phoenix's bedroom before they were interrupted by Corvus, who if we're speaking of ex-steadies, was Phoenix's . . . Teo yanks the brakes on that runaway train.

"I can assure you he'll still have the facility to conclude your business after we're done, but I'll allow him to bring someone along to our meeting," Park says. "Teophilus?"

Park directs that annoying eyebrow arch at Teo, and Teo understands immediately; this is a test. His first thought is to choose Phoenix. But bringing in the high-profile raider will only heighten tensions. Ocean could be an asset since she knows Park, but judging from Park's well-aimed jab about her mother, that's a double-edged sword. Ocean turns her head a fraction away from Teo as if she heard his thought. If he were worried about being manhandled, then he would probably take a *Pandia* member for backup, but he doubts that's a real concern. No, Park wants to prove he's who he says he is, and he needs another sort of assistance.

"Sasani," Teo says. Sasani, who's been slouched, jerks at hearing his name. "Will you come with me?"

He's barely spent any time with Sasani, with any of them really except Ocean, but Sasani pushes off from the wall.

"Haven Sasani. The Vulture." Park's lip curls momentarily. He appraises Sasani as he disdainfully asks Teo, "Are you certain?"

Mortemians are at best ignored by most in society, but typically maligned, as if their association with death and funeral rites has soiled them. Teo doesn't need to explain anything to the Diplomat, but if he thought Park would listen, Teo might start with how Sasani gave him a cup of water at the makeshift funeral he created on the *Pandia* so Teo could mourn the death of his parents and brother, although he'd been far away from the actual, excessively televised rites. How Sasani's voice bolstered his own when they were reading the *Bhagavad Gita*. Or how Sasani's hand on his back had been the pressure he needed to release all his tears. But Sasani's already walking forward to stand by Teo, as if he wasn't just insulted to his face.

Park sighs. "Then, please follow me."

He leads them back the way he came, to the far right wall under the glass windows. The four soldiers split to hem in Teo and Sasani, as if there's any real danger of them escaping with the pool on one end, and a heavily guarded hangar entrance on the other.

The front two soldiers open the doors and stand to the side, while the back two soldiers follow them through the door and into a long hallway lit by unpleasant fluorescents.

The temperature drops a few degrees the moment Teo steps in, and he clenches his teeth against the first involuntary chatter. The rigid carpet muffles the timbre of their marching, and their boots track in the water from the garage, mottling the gray fabric. A guard stands in front of elevator doors at the end of the hallway, but they stop halfway down at another pair of doors. Park places his palm against a side panel and they slide open.

"Search them," Park says before he enters the room.

Teo is so thoroughly patted down, he bites his tongue. He can't remember the last time someone touched him *there*. Or *there*. And—what exactly do they think he could hide *there*? But when he attempts to exchange beleaguered looks with Sasani, he sees the guard tasked with searching Sasani is at a loss. He's frozen in position with his hands out, and the whites of his eyes are showing.

"What are you waiting for?" Park asks from inside.

"I don't—"

"Do you want me to search him for you?" Teo asks. "I'd be happy to put my hands on him."

Park comes out with a pair of gloves, handing them to the reluctant guard. "Use these. Then go sanitize yourself after."

"Excuse me?" Teo gasps, but Sasani merely holds out his arms as if he's waiting to go through security at a shuttleport.

"We would be more comfortable if you wore gloves too." Park holds out another pair for Sasani.

"*I* would be more comfortable if—" Teo starts before Park cuts him off.

"Not everything in this solar is about you, Teophilus. And isn't this why you chose to bring the Vulture? You wanted a distraction."

The Seonbi guard has pressed his lips together and his whole face contorts in a grimace as his hands graze over Sasani's body, as if he's sinking his hands into sewage. Sasani's blasé demeanor tells Teo, *If this is what you wanted, then this is what I'm here for.*

Teo goes hot then cold. He needs to make good on subjecting Sasani to this. "I find I'm enough of a distraction on my own."

Park studies him. "I suppose we'll see about that."

TWO

HAVEN SASANI HADN'T thought anything could be more uncomfortable than the cold hallway they passed through, but he's proven wrong the moment they step into the room. It would be flattering to call it utilitarian, with its gray concrete walls and bare table in the middle. Underneath a framed unified Korea flag on the back wall, the arrayed cabinets somehow give the impression that they want to slam Haven's fingers in their metal drawers. The room has the same ghastly neon lighting from the hallway that maintains the permanent vibe of a flashbulb bursting.

The ambience is bad enough already, but then as Haven goes to sit next to Anand, Diplomat Park stops him with a hand.

"You'll remain standing, of course?" the Diplomat remarks.

This is Haven's first time on the Moon, in Artemis, but he's heard it's an especially tough assignment for Mortemians, given how conservative the Koreans are here. The tech isn't the only thing that tends to be outdated. Not that Haven's surprised, after his reception at the Alliance during space training. Asking Haven to wear gloves seems downright civil compared to the passive aggression of immediately wiping down anything he touches. They'll probably deep clean this room after he leaves though.

Kent had once apologized for trying to hug Haven, wanting to be respectful of the Mortemian's space. But Diplomat Park's reaction is much more familiar to Haven, and reacting to it is like getting back on the seat of an extremely unpleasant bike.

Anand protests right away, saying Haven shouldn't be treated like a servant, but that's a generous assumption. He's not being treated like the hired help; he's being treated like an *other*, someone who should be kneeling on the ground while his betters are in chairs.

"I don't mind," he assures Anand.

"You *should*," Anand snaps at him. He orders Haven to sit, and nearly takes the head off the guard who tries to remove the cushion from the chair. It makes him oddly grateful, and then mortified to be grateful for the basic, decent right to sit anywhere.

"Please elucidate why we shouldn't throw all of you in prison," Diplomat Park says.

Park's every motion gives the impression of unnatural smoothness, as if he's practiced for hours in front of a mirror. His inspection of Anand makes his earlier conversation with Yoon heartwarming by comparison.

Is he the one she went on that Japan trip with? During Haven's first genuine conversation with her, she admitted that she maybe had feelings for that particular steady, but probably not the right ones. Yoon with her sharp, mocking eyes. Always wary, always considerate in a way that some have interpreted as having *too much* noonchi. She and Park could be cut from the same

TEO'S DURUMI 15

polished glass. Haven has always been drawn to the little nicks, though—the scar through her eyebrow, how she smiles with a lift in one side of her mouth. But in other ways, she's unwavering—resolute as she shielded him from bullets. Resolute as she told him matter-of-factly that she had killed and would do it again.

That moment had been their severing point.

"I'm not guilty of anything," Anand says, interrupting Haven's thoughts. He then amends, "Well, anything that deserves imprisonment."

"You were seen murdering your family in cold blood."

Haven can't help the pang of pain at the callous remark. He's avoided the macabre broadcast of Anand's doppelganger stabbing his parents, which is still being streamed and dissected constantly. The public fascination with the Anand Tech leaders has made it irresistible fodder for many, but Haven hopes Anand, at least, has kept himself from watching it.

Anand's face reveals nothing, though, as he replies, "There's footage of Martians murdering the Seonbi Embassy and the *Shadowfax* crew in cold blood too. But we both know how easily images are manipulated, don't we? You let us land in Artemis because you already suspected they weren't Martians; you about admitted as much on our transmission. I was on the *Shadowfax*, and I can tell you what actually happened to the Seonbi."

"The ship attacking you just now wasn't an Alliance charter," Park ventures. "Nor was it a Martian vessel."

"No. The attacking ship was our common enemy. They were trying to eliminate us to get rid of evidence."

Corvus's intent had been to turn the *Pandia* into a "*raging inferno*," in the words of his follower. But on the comm link,

Corvus had let out an anguished cry when the *Pandia* had shot back at his ship, as if *Corvus* had been the one betrayed.

"How did you end up on that raider ship? And with the *Ohneul* crew?" Park asks.

"When I fled the *Shadowfax*, I directed my escape pod to the *Ohneul*. Ocean Yoon was on it," Anand says. "She was where I knew I'd be the safest." He leans forward on his elbow. "Park, you of all people get that, right? You were lovers and all."

Haven stiffens at the same time Park's eyes flash.

"I don't 'get' that sentiment at all," Park says coolly. "You went to Alliance member Yoon's ship, even though she's just an XO, even though she was demoted from a Class 1—"

"Someone's been keeping track of their ex," Anand cuts in. "She got demoted because of me. Maybe you've already seen the report of the *Hadouken* incident, which apparently is not that hard to get a hold of. So, I ended up on the *Ohneul*, and then a contract was sent out to eliminate that ship because I was on it. That's where the *Pandia* came in. They rescued us and destroyed the *Ohneul* to throw off our pursuers. They agreed to deliver me here on the Moon."

"And why would the raiders help you?"

"Out of the goodness of their hearts? Or I suppose it may have had something to do with the exorbitant amount of money I offered them."

"If you're really you, then why don't you find asylum with Declan Anand? Or would your brother not believe you?"

"He would," Anand says, and a clench shivers in his face. "If he were alive. The man you see on the net is a fraud. Someone is impersonating him, like someone impersonated me while they killed my parents."

TEO'S DURUMI 17

It's a lot to take in, but Diplomat Park only considers for a few moments. "I merely have your word to go on," Park says. "I hope you can appreciate my skepticism."

"What do you propose?" Anand asks. "If I had a deus ex birthmark I could show you, I would. I wouldn't divulge any company secrets my father passed down, but I was never important enough for those anyway."

"Rather than a birthmark that's easily replicated . . ." Diplomat Park leans forward. "I'd rather gauge your emotions."

Anand scratches his temple. "So this is where the real test begins?"

"Were you close with your family?"

"We got along."

The tenor of their voices is relaxed, and Park and Anand could be conversing over a casual tea, if not for how still they are. Absolutely still except for one thing—Anand holds his trembling hands under the table. Haven all but stops breathing to remain unobtrusive.

"Did it bother you that your older brother was the primary heir of Anand Tech?"

"He was educated and trained for it from birth," Anand says. "I felt bad at times that all the duty was foisted upon him."

"If he was trained to take over the Anand Corporation, what were you trained for?"

"For drawing attention."

"Explain, please."

"No publicity is bad publicity. My family grew and expanded Anand Tech, and in between those spurts, I got into scraps. Nothing too scandalous ever, but enough to make the tabloids and to paint my parents as beleaguered. It humanized them."

"Is that what they told you?"

"We fell naturally into our roles. All the world's a stage and we all have our parts to play."

"You never wanted more?"

"You mean, did I ever think, *Hey I should kill off my family and seize all that power?*" Anand slouches back in his chair and Haven sees Park note that, how he's ready to pounce on anything as a tic, a give. Haven had also been about to shift in his seat, but he stops.

"I wouldn't have known what to do with it."

"But you wanted to."

Anand's face is impeccably smooth. "Did I?"

Does Park actually think that? Or is he saying it to make Anand react a certain way? And what *is* the correct way to react? Haven's head hurts.

"Then why did you join the Alliance? Was it what your father wanted?"

"I find Koreans to be particularly attractive." Anand gives a suggestive smile.

Haven flushes. How would Yoon have reacted to that? Anand flirts the line of impropriety and truth, and Haven's found he can't be sure how sincere Anand is unless Yoon's around to respond.

Anand drops the smile as if it's been pulled by gravity. "I think I surprised my father when I enlisted, and maybe that was part of the reason why I did it." He taps his shoulder. "It was a solid strategic move. Anand Tech benefits from its close relationship with the Alliance. What better way to exemplify that than for one of the Anand children to serve the Alliance?"

"But not Horangi Command School, the more prestigious choice."

"I'm not cut out to lead," Anand says. "I hope you'll excuse my impertinence, but what is the point of all these questions?"

"Like I said, Teophilus. Emotions." Park doesn't blink. "To ascertain whether you are a complete person, rather than someone in your shell, pretending to be you."

Anand says wryly, "Maybe I was never complete to begin with."

"What did you first think when you heard they had died?"

Anand glances over at Haven, bringing him into Park's radar.

"I felt . . . lost." Anand's last word is hollow in a way that suggests a deep, dark cavern. Haven keeps himself from moving toward him.

"Even though they used you?"

This time, Haven twitches, but Anand shakes his head at him.

"We used one another. I used my brother to cover a multitude of my sins. My father used me in the way he knew best, and I used my mother's unceasing forgiveness to excuse my own actions or inactions. And then that network of guilt, or whatever it is that families have for each other, that was gone."

Anand reveals his hand to snap his fingers with the last word. He glances at it, as if surprised to find that it's still shaking.

"Maybe that's not how everyone's families are," Anand says. "But I loved them, for all my faults. And to think the last thing they saw was me with a knife, to think they thought I was the one before them, repeatedly plunging that knife into their bodies . . ."

He hunches over, and Haven has to resist resting his palm on Anand's back. Haven presses the heel of his hand into his own sternum instead to forestall his rising grief.

"Well." There's an odd note in Park's voice, but his expression is closed off. "It would be troublesome if the Alliance found out we secretly took you in. Although, to be truthful, they have done scarcely anything since our Seonbi were killed, other than accuse the wrong people and bring the Koreans to the brink of an interplanetary war."

"I was a part of that uselessness," Anand says slowly. "Like I said, I was tasked with protecting the Seonbi, but I turned tail. I've never been good with responsibility, but I thought this would be a good place to start."

"Crash-landing here," Park says.

"I like making an entrance," Anand says. "At any rate, we do share a common, ruthless enemy. One that can appear and sound like anyone." Anand gestures to Haven. "Sasani, can you tell them about the chemical compounds you found when I was retrieved by the *Ohneul*?"

Haven spreads his gloved fingers on the table, surprised enough by Anand's request that he forgets himself. Park's focus goes directly to that motion. But the way he tries to pass off that automatic disgust as a careless movement steadies Haven.

"As you may recall from the footage, members of the *Shadowfax* and the Seonbi Embassy were hit with tranquilizer darts, as well as sprayed with a substance before they were set on fire," Haven says evenly. "The flame accelerant itself was composed partially of linseed oil, partially of a combination of some molds to increase the rate of heat generation. The linseed oil came into play, I believe, to aid in their clothing soaking up the melted fat of their bodies, to achieve combustion."

Park has closed his eyes. His chin dips down toward his collarbone.

"Lim Eunkyeong. Oh Haneul. Choi Hwanhee, Cho Gina, Kang Min, Park Minkyu." Haven's convinced that the reason why Park allowed the *Pandia* to land on Artemis was how Anand had recited the names of the Seonbi Embassy members who died on the ship. Not just easily, but as if they were names he kept close to him, names that he whispered to himself at night.

Anand nods at Haven, but Haven lets Park sit for a breath. He softens his voice as he continues, "The remaining tranquilizer in Anand's body wasn't enough for me to fully analyze, but I believe it created a soporific and euphoric sensation."

"So," Park says quietly. "They didn't even have the option of expressing their pain."

He keeps his eyes closed, and he reminds Haven of Yoon again, how she'll bring her hand up to hide her face. Anand gives him a few moments before he speaks again.

"Don't you want to know who did it?"

Park opens his eyes. "And you hold that information, is what you're saying?"

"I do." Anand tilts his chair on its back two legs. "But I won't give it freely."

"You would bargain this for your own gain?" Park asks.

"I'd be of little use rotting away in prison," Anand replies. "We can help each other."

Park drums his fingers on the table again. "I will be frank with you, Teophilus."

Haven sincerely doubts that.

"If either the Alliance or the government gets involved, then whatever happens with you will have solar reverberations. It's in both of our interests if your visit here is as quiet as possible, which I think was also your original intent."

"Aren't you the government?"

"Often. But let's say, not in this case. I like the idea of calling on you for a favor in the future."

"Me?"

"You. Alliance members. Phoenix and his crew. I'll let you go and all the witnesses here today will keep quiet at my behest. But remember: I'm the one who allowed it to happen," Park says. "So yes, we have a deal. Please proceed."

Haven doesn't like the idea of owing anyone, but he doubts Park really cares much about him anyway.

Anand drops the chair's legs down again. "The people behind this are a small group led by a man named Corvus. He's a Mercurian son of scientists from Venus, who were killed when they decided they didn't want to serve the government's agenda anymore. The group's fervor borders on religious. They're well funded, well connected, but I don't know much beyond that." Anand taps the table. "One of them, as I said, is pretending to be my brother. They intend to destroy Anand Tech, but it seems they're also targeting the Alliance for its relation to Anand Tech. It's possible the Seonbi were caught in the cross fire. Equally possible that Corvus has some plan to go after you next."

"Mercurian . . ." Park muses. "Anand Tech and the Alliance don't have a good relationship with Mercury."

"No, not at all. Phoenix suspects that Corvus wants nothing less than total annihilation."

"Sounds dangerously close to the ravings of a zealot." Park purses his lips. "I haven't heard the name Corvus before, but I'll investigate." He pauses briefly. "How much are you planning on telling Jang Yeonghui?"

While Haven's parsing the unfamiliar name, Anand clearly hesitates. And that extra second is significant enough for everyone in the room to register it as a mistake.

"Who's that?" Anand asks warily.

"Oh, please," Park says, drenching those two words in smugness. "I pulled the records on recently approved passes to enter Artemis, and imagine my surprise at finding who had requested one for a particular ship ID. Jang and her father have visited your father for business several times. The sugar trade, if I remember correctly."

Anand rubs his face. "She didn't really want to get involved with the Seonbi or any Diplomats."

"I imagine harboring a wanted criminal wouldn't look good for her," Park says. "But was there a purpose to your rendezvous, or were you only using your connection with her to enter Artemis? I wouldn't say this is an . . . intelligent location if you want to hide."

"I was planning on following a few different threads here," Anand says neutrally.

"Let me get this straight," Park says. "You embroiled the *Ohneul* in this conflict by landing on their ship, which led to it being destroyed. You paid the *Pandia* to drop you off here so you could do . . . what? Your own sleuthing? Plot revenge? While once again implicating the *Ohneul* and the *Pandia*?"

"No." Anand shakes his head. "I never meant—"

"You might posture all you want, Teophilus, but your father dealt with the politics. Your brother had savvy too. What do you know? Clothes, idols, how to spend marks lavishly. How to involve people in your mess."

A muscle in Anand's jaw flexes and unflexes as he falters. "We were supposed to part ways here. I don't want them to get into trouble because of me."

"Any more than they already have?" Park asks. "You follow your *threads* then, and hope that they lead you out of a labyrinth rather than to its minotaur. But I think it would be best to separate all of you as soon as possible. I can arrange for the flights to charter the *Ohneul* members home."

Despite Park's acid tone, Sasani's heart thumps at his words. Once he's back in Prometheus, he can put this brief, strange chapter of his life behind him. He folds his hands in his lap and weaves his fingers together tightly. They're trembling like Anand's.

"What about the *Pandia*?" Anand asks.

"They can do what they want," Park says.

"Really?" Haven blurts out, interjecting for the first time.

Park barely flinches, but at this point, Haven realizes that's the equivalent of someone rearing back. Haven might as well be a child butting into an adult's conversation. Or rather, a cockroach that shouldn't speak, but is a repulsive oddity when it does.

"I have no use for the bounty money," Park says. "He's wanted by the Alliance, and while I don't care to be on their bad side, I don't overcare about being on their good side either. As a Diplomat, I'm above it all. So long as Phoenix doesn't cause a ruckus, he is of no concern to me. But I'd prefer the *Ohneul* members return to Earth intact."

"Oh, about that," Anand says. "Ocean's staying with me."

Park halts. "Why would she do that?"

"I guess because I involved her in my mess?" Anand leans back in his chair. "But do you know what intrigues me?"

The corners of Park's lips tighten. "Why would I care what—"

"You must have recognized Ocean right away when you hopped on the call. But instead of granting us amnesty and allowing us easy access, you made the smallest possible opening in Artemis's shield for her to squeeze the ship through."

"It had to be a small opening, or Corvus's ship would have flown through right after you."

"Oh, *please*," Anand says, drawling out the two words. "You challenged Ocean, but the best way to rile her up is when she's behind a wheel. You should've known her better than that."

Park's eyes harden. "I thought I did."

Unsettlingly, Haven understands that sentiment. Park rises, his chair scraping harshly. Haven and Anand also get up, but Haven's first to the door. He hesitates at the panel.

"Please don't." Park slaps his hand on it to open the doors for them. Anand's hiss of disapproval parallels the sleek slide of the door opening, but Park's already swept by the two of them with a rustle of hanbok. Somehow, even in that narrow space, the Diplomat avoids brushing against Haven.

As he exits, Haven sneaks a peek to his left, where the guard who had to pat him down earlier was stationed. But a new guard with overbright eyes peers back instead; likely the original guard is shuddering in the shower now, scrubbing down his skin after having to "touch" a Mortemian. The patina of sweat on the new guard's face is at odds with the frigid temperature of the hallway. The guard's attention slides past Haven just as he sees that the man posted at the elevator at the end of the hall is slumped over. A bright smear of red trails down the wall behind his prone form.

"Kang, what—"

To the right of their door, Park bends over a guard slouched on the ground. He was the one who patted down Anand earlier. Park's head jerks up, his eyes wide.

"Watch out!"

Haven twists in time to see the new guard lunge toward Anand, a knife arcing down.

THREE

OCEAN YOON HAS always been better at reading other people than herself. The group left in the hangar has gone back to their own conversations, but the air is stilted. Teo's meeting with Joonho will determine what happens to them. Ocean's not worried; Teo's always been more capable than he lets on. Besides, he has Sasani with him.

The *Pandia* crew on the whole is more relaxed. Either because they don't much care about endearing themselves to the Seonbi, or because they're used to getting themselves in and out of jams. Aries and Cass have taken off their shoes and rolled up their pants to sit at the pool's edge. Hurakan leans against the wall nearby, giving off a nonchalant air, but Ocean has never known him to not be paying close attention to everything. As if in answer to that thought, Hurakan nods at her before going back to his covert surveillance.

She rolls his name around in her mouth. Although he had told her before that she could use it rather than his moniker of Gemini, she hadn't tried it out until today. Out of all the other *Pandia* members, she's only learned Phoenix's original name, Garrett. But the name Phoenix much better suits the raider, and he has a clear preference for it.

It's Phoenix now who affects a smile and a looseness to his pacing, but Ocean identifies his meandering path for what it is. He's drifting away from their group and closer to the doors that Teo, Sasani, and Joonho went through. It's a relaxed enough jaunt that the guards unconcernedly observe him come within tossing distance. Regardless of Phoenix's manner, it would be foolish not to be wary of him, but Ocean's not in charge of them.

Then, muffled yelling comes through the doors. The two flanking guards swerve as the doors slide open. Joonho stumbles out.

"Guards! Help!"

They move, but Phoenix is already hurtling forward, diving through the doors first. Ocean's on her feet and running. She pulls out her gun, swiping off the safety. To her side, Dae fumbles for the bonguk geom at her belt. Ocean distantly registers that as a mistake. Dae might be more comfortable with her sword, but the close-range weapon will be useless.

Teo comes flying backward from the hall, slamming to the floor and skidding across it. Ocean's heart stutters, but he lifts his head. Though his mouth is agape, he's seemingly unharmed. A whirlwind of limbs tumbles from the hallway. Phoenix grapples with a guard. A blade slices through the air. Joonho is yelling, his shouts muddled. More guards hasten toward them, but they were stationed at the edges and are too far away. The people fighting are too entangled. No one can get a good shot in.

Except maybe Ocean. She drops to her knee, searching for an opening. Hurakan dashes up from behind her and when he goes past, he pivots. They lock eyes and he points to his left bicep. Then he flips around to run forward full tilt. Ocean is re-aiming her gun when Dae screams at her.

"Ocean, don't shoot!"

Dae's desperation pierces Ocean. Ocean's shoulder twitches. Then she sees Sasani crouched at Teo's side, staring at her. All the blood has drained from his face and his dark eyes are so open and wretched that it's a knife to her gut.

Ocean pulls the trigger.

The shot rings out, and Dae flies forward to tackle Ocean. They collide and Ocean falls back, her head smacking the floor.

"Stand down! Stand down!"

Ocean cranes her neck, dodging Dae's flailing limbs. Hurakan took advantage of Ocean's shot to throw the guard flat to the floor. Blood oozes from the guard as his knife spins on the ground. The hangar guards surge forward to charge Hurakan too, but Joonho steps in front of them, waving his arms.

"It's Guard Lee! He tried to kill Teophilus!"

Hurakan wrests up Lee, shoving his limp body to the guards. Dae sucks in a breath like a sob. Then Lee jerks upright, his face contorted. He screams and jerks against the guards' hold. As he strains, the wound from his left arm flings blood.

"You—he's just—" Dae splutters.

Ocean shoves Dae off her. Her leg is still stiff from where it was shot on Mercury, and she stands with difficulty. She jams her gun back in its holster, clipping it down. When she clicks the last button, she unwittingly bites metal into her skin.

"Did you think I was going to kill him?" she asks coldly.

"I . . . He was a Korean, I didn't want . . ." Dae's still stunned, sprawled on the ground. "Isn't that what you were . . ."

"I don't miss, Dae."

Ocean almost asks *Did you think I wanted to kill them?* because Dae's thinking about another time Ocean pulled her gun. During the infamous *Hadouken* incident her first shot severed a finger, her second severed a life. Then the next shots systematically mowed down a line of raiders. Dae must have read the report; it seems like everyone has.

Past Dae, Teo sits up, and his hair is as mussed as his expression. Sasani keeps his head ducked, his face drawn and tight as he tends to him. It gives Ocean a one-two punch: relief followed by a far more unpleasant thud. But she's quickly distracted by the scuffling of Lee, the would-be assassin, as he struggles wildly against the other guards.

"*Die*, Anand. You should all *die*." Foam, spittle, and venomous words all fly from Lee's mouth.

The words chill Ocean, and it takes the combined strength of a few guards to contain Lee as he screams. When he spots Teo, he hurls himself forward, and even though Teo's far enough away, he scrabbles back.

"He said we'd become one." Lee laughs hysterically. "He promised we'd destroy all of you."

"Who promised?" Joonho asks sharply.

Lee's giggles rise in pitch. His jaw gapes wider than Ocean thought possible, as if it's about to unhinge. The guards drag him away. Ocean strides over to kneel next to Teo. His hands are shaking.

"You jake?" she asks him.

"Oh, you know," Teo says wearily. "The sheen wears off the first time someone tries to murder you." Then he says, "It was a good shot, Ocean."

His quiet words give her a strange weightless feeling; a swoop in the stomach as if she missed a step going down that she can't register as either pleasure or pain, just an unsteadiness.

"Yoon," Sasani says, bringing her attention back to him.

Somewhere down the line, Ocean will replay this moment to examine his tone. Doing that now will just open herself up to the hurt of how much his conviction matched Dae's. But she can't complain; this is exactly what she had wanted when she told him about the *Hadouken* in their last conversation.

She nods perfunctorily. "I'm fine too. Maybe check on the others?"

Sasani doesn't answer right away, but from the corner of her eye, she sees him rise. Phoenix and Hurakan are sprawled just behind them. Joonho confers with a few guards, and next to them, other uniformed men rush in and out of the hallway with covered stretchers. Ocean takes Teo's hand.

"I'm good. Really," Teo says. But he lets her press her palm against his clammy one.

"Phoenix, may I?" Sasani's voice comes from behind them.

Ocean can picture Sasani reaching for the emergency kit he always keeps inside his med officer's uniform. He'd already had gloves on when he was next to Teo, but they were different from his usual Alliance-grade ones.

"Wanna hold hands, Sasani? It's awfully forward of you, but I don't mind." Phoenix's voice is bright, but then Ocean hears a sharp strike.

She turns to find Phoenix massaging at his forehead, and Hurakan with his hand still in flicking form. "Not the time, Phoenix."

"I must be rubbing off on you," Teo says.

"I can think of worse things," Phoenix replies.

It's then that Ocean notices the red splatters leading up to them, and how Phoenix cradles his hand in his lap, blood welling in his palm. Teo goes still next to her.

Teo sputters, "Is that . . . How—"

"It's mostly cosmetic," Phoenix says mildly as he surrenders his injured hand to Sasani. He *tsks* as Sasani cleans it.

"The guard must've been talking about Corvus, yeah?" Hurakan asks. He tilts his head at Ocean and Teo, inviting them into his ongoing conversation with Phoenix.

Phoenix nods as Teo says tightly, "I've barely been on the Moon an hour, and he's already got someone trying to kill me."

Someone touches Ocean's shoulder, and she angles her head up to a pair of light-brown, assessing eyes.

"Somehow, this lifestyle suits you better than I thought it would," Joonho says.

Ocean stands to face him. She hasn't missed this at all, the mockery always hinting at a second or third meaning. "There's a reason why I dropped out of Sav-Faire," she says. "Diplomat Park."

"There was a lot of speculation." He waits a couple beats, but she doesn't really have anything to add. His lips pinch together.

Hurakan sidles up to them. "I'd love to chat with that guard. Lee, was it? Has he worked for you long?"

"Yes, Lee," Joonho says. He smooths his eyebrows with his thumb. "He has been with us years. Which is unfortunate."

"When did Corvus recruit him?" Teo asks tersely. Then he shakes his head. "It would have been easy for Corvus to figure that the Seonbi helped us get into Artemis. You control the shield, after all. But who else is he connected with? Was Lee the only one? We can't underestimate his reach."

"Nor his hatred of you," Joonho says dryly.

"I told you so," Teo says, unbothered. "In any case, you're no longer secure."

"If he has that much influence, he probably has eyes elsewhere," Joonho says. "We'll house you at our seowon."

Out of the prying eyes of others, and kept hidden like a secret until Joonho can find use for them. Joonho's traits are filtering back into Ocean's head against her will, flavored with the bitter taste of her time at Sav-Faire.

"Thank you for your offer," Teo says, although it's clear it was anything but. "But I'd like to consider other options."

"You don't strike me as someone with options," Joonho says.

Teo ignores that, though, and asks Phoenix, "Do you have your comm on you?"

Phoenix holds up his wrist to Teo, and Ocean catches Teo's slight hesitation before he undoes the comm at the raider's wrist and swipes up for a dial pad.

"Who are you calling?" Joonho asks.

"Corvus isn't the only one with connections," Teo says as he walks off. From several paces away, Ocean hears a sappy "Yeonghui, *darling*, yes, it's me. Well, I'm afraid our plans may have shifted a little, and . . . Oh, where am I now? Well, that's a funny story . . ."

Joonho turns to the group when the exchange wanders off too far to be overheard. "I told Anand this in our meeting, but I'll work on chartering all the *Ohneul* members back to Earth. If you prefer to go elsewhere, you should let me know now." He raises an eyebrow at Ocean.

"Maggie might want to go back to Venus." Ocean scans the group. Other than Hurakan and Phoenix next to her, the rest of the *Pandia* is by the pool. Dae's gone back to Maggie and Von, who are huddled together. "But I think Von's heading back to Earth?" She raises a hand to beckon him over, but a soft voice arrests her in mid-motion.

"Excuse me," Sasani says. "If it's not too much trouble, could I get a ticket back to Saturn?"

Ocean's hand jerks, but she disguises the movement by dropping her curled fingers to examine them. Cracked nails, fissures in the beds, and a familiar callus that's hardening on her index finger. An old tattoo of a crane in flight stretches back from the finger to the rest of her hand.

"A seat to Saturn will cost quite a bit more than ferrying you down to Earth with the others," Joonho says.

"I'm fine with a ticket to Earth too. I can find my own way to Saturn from there," Sasani says.

Joonho sniffs. "I'll see what I can do."

"Well, that's settled," Teo says as he walks back over to the group. "My old friend Yeonghui has a place for us to stay."

"I don't think that's wise—" Joonho starts.

"Are you going to detain us, Diplomat Park?" Teo cuts in.

Joonho presses his lips together. He could, but Ocean suspects that it's no small feat keeping this information limited as it is. And keeping them against their will, not to mention hidden from the other Diplomats, might be near impossible.

"I thought you said that she didn't want to be involved with the Seonbi," he says.

"Oh, I think it's too late for that," Teo says. "You made that clear when you called her out earlier."

"Well, at least let me provide a cadre of guards—"

"Really, Diplomat Park, you think assigning Artemis guards on us would be *wise* after what just happened?" At Joonho's frown,

Teo says, "but we'll certainly take you up on your offer of arranging flights to take the *Ohneul* members back home. And in the meantime, we could all use an escort to Yeonghui's estate. I don't think we should take public transportation."

Joonho's face is placid, although Ocean's sure he must be internally seething. It's a concession on both their parts—Joonho to allow Teo and the others out of his grasp; Teo to let Joonho know where they will be staying. Ocean sighs. Maybe Teo should have been the one to go to Sav-Faire and not her.

"Very well," Joonho says. "Eleven of you, all told?"

"I believe I'll part ways with you here, so you don't need to count me in the tally," Sasani says.

This time, Ocean's nails embed themselves in her palm before she relaxes them. This is what she wanted.

"What?" Teo blurts out. "Where are you going?"

"My father told me about a Mortemian commune near Artemis," Sasani explains. "He wanted me to visit if I had the opportunity."

"Ah . . . Well, let's get you a ride to wherever you're going anyway," Teo says. "Surely you can do that, Diplomat Park?"

"There's no need—" Sasani starts.

"And I'm sure," Teo says menacingly, clamping his hand down on Joonho's shoulder, "that it will be a very pleasant, very luxurious ride?"

Joonho's eyes crease as he smiles. "We are nothing if not solicitous."

There's a weighted pause, and Sasani shifts on his feet. Teo shares his politician's smile to match Joonho's. "Marv."

"Thank you," Sasani says. "I'd like to inform Captain Song and the others as well, so if you'll excuse me."

He matches eyes with Ocean, and she ricochets her gaze away.

Teo steps close to her. "Do you want to see him off?"

"Me? Why?"

Teo pats her on the head. "I will then, Hummingbird."

• • • • •

They say to never visit Korea in August, but Teo had forgotten how closely Artemis hews to Korea's environment, down to the humidity of its late summer. It's an oppressive weight that no amount of aircon can fight because once you step outside, you're entering a swamp.

Teo sits on the front steps with Sasani, tenting his shirt to fan himself as they wait for the car Park's arranged. When exactly was Phoenix stabbed? Teo had come out of that meeting room, had heard Park shout. Then that knife had streaked down. Where was his Alliance training? Where were his combat skills? Instead, he could only desperately fend off the guard before Phoenix came barreling through the door.

"It was very impressive." Sasani leans back on the steps, much more relaxed now than Teo's ever seen him, as if in reaction to the somewhat tense events of the day. His long form sprawls across several steps, his legs stretched out before him. Flat shadows cross the orange light on Sasani's face. His eyes are closed and his head is back, throat exposed to the sky. The closest guards are at the top of the steps, giving them some privacy, more or less.

"I don't know how Phoenix got in there so quickly," Teo agrees. And for what? He'd gotten stabbed because of Teo. Misery shrivels Teo's insides.

"No," Sasani says. "I meant you, in there with Diplomat Park."

"It was a very personal meeting," Teo says regretfully. "I ended up giving Park ammunition for the next round."

"You held your own."

Teo wonders how Declan might have handled it. Or his father. But Sasani regards him seriously, with a dignity that belies his age. Teo should mistrust the easy phrase, like the rote ones that have lost meaning over multiple uses. *I'm so sorry for your loss.* But he finds himself grateful that Sasani believes the words, at least.

"Thanks for your assist," Teo says.

"I was only a witness, really."

"You talked about the science of it," Teo says. "But, more than that . . . I suspected he'd wear me down. I needed someone to help keep me together."

Sasani props his elbows on the step behind him. "Anand . . ." He trails off. "Other than very tense meetings with Diplomats, you don't always have to have it all 'together.'"

Teo barks out a laugh that sounds more wrecked than he wants. "I do, just for a little more," he says. "I need to . . . I need to make up for . . ." He rubs his eyes, trying to ward off the weariness.

Sasani asks quietly, "Do you really think your parents believed you were responsible for their deaths?"

Even if Teo just talked about it, the jangled wire of his body quivers. "I never gave them any reason to believe in me."

Sasani shakes his head. "That can't be true."

"Oh? You want to tell me about my family?" Teo asks, but it lacks bite.

"No," Sasani says, "but I have grown to know you a little. And I think you would have given your parents reason to trust in your goodness."

Teo draws in a breath, lets it expand in his lungs. But it doesn't ease the painful suffocation there. "I haven't . . . lived my life well," he says. "I've thought a lot about what you said about living generously. And how I don't have to stop wanting to do better for my family even though they're dead."

Sasani waits for him to go on. Teo likes that about him. He doesn't say *And?* He doesn't try to fill in the blank for you if you trail off.

"I've thought a lot too about your question about how I could honor them. It might be a good compass for a while," Teo says. "For now, that means atoning for my failures. Which I figured could start here."

"It's not a bad beginning." Sasani hesitates. "But . . . Anand, it might be good to think about how to live for the living too."

Easier said than done. "A Mortemian is telling me to live for the living?" Teo smiles at Sasani. "Your father must be proud."

Sasani's body relaxes. "I think he would be."

Teo would never have associated that bonelessness with his own father. He says easily, "Good. That's great." He fastens his smile in place.

Sasani searches Teo. "We don't have to talk about this."

"What do you mean?" A tear slides down Teo's cheek. He puts his hand up to it, startled. "I'm—" His fingers are wet. "I don't understand."

Sasani's eyes soften. "You don't have to."

"No, that's not what I mean." Somehow the tears are still falling. "I'm not—"

He's cried in front of Sasani before, but Sasani tilts his chin up to the sky again as if giving Teo that small modicum of privacy he so desperately needs.

"No, you're not," Sasani agrees, although he directs his words upward.

Teo doesn't know what Sasani's agreeing to, because he can barely keep his own thoughts together, but the gentle tone opens the floodgates. There's no shame in crying, but Teo fights it, squeezing his eyes shut as he calculates how close the guards are and how much they can actually hear.

"Well," he says, and then has to try again when the word comes out strangled. "Well, that's enough of that." He dabs at his eyes. If he rubs them too much, they'll be red, and then Ocean will know he was crying. He needs a distraction. "How's your fiancée?" Teo asks. "I'm sure she was happy to hear you're alive."

Sasani doesn't respond right away, probably surprised at the non sequitur. Teo gives him time to adjust, but after a few moments, Sasani drops his chin.

"She's not my fiancée anymore."

Teo's mouth shapes an O without any volume before he composes himself. "Is that . . . recent?"

"Last night," Sasani says.

"Did she . . . Did you . . ." Teo scratches his temple. That's not what's important. "Does anyone else know?"

Sasani's answer holds a hint of surprise. "I think . . . Gemini knows? He monitored my call."

Teo wants to shake him. As if he cares whether *Gemini* knows. Questions burst into his head. But Sasani has so kindly not said anything about how Teo's eyes became a fountain of tears without warning, and Teo should try to return the favor.

"Breakups are never easy," he says in what he hopes is a measured, yet sympathetic tone. When Sasani's head whips around, Teo says with mock offense, "What does *that* look mean?"

TEO'S DURUMI 39

"Nothing! Just that you—" Sasani gestures at Teo helplessly. "Weren't you dating the actor Kim Minwoo? You must have had lots—I mean . . . Have you not?"

"I'll take that as the compliment you meant it to be," Teo says. "I've been in a few serious relationships. Didn't work out. Obviously. And to answer your question, no, the Kim Minwoo date was a publicity stunt, but—"

A car pulls up on the pavement before them and a Seonbi steps out the driver's side. "Vulture Haven Sasani?" she asks from the bottom of the steps.

Teo could spit at the emphasis on *Vulture*, and he's about to correct the woman, but Sasani straightens.

"Yes?" Sasani asks.

"I am here to escort you."

"Thank you." Sasani asks Teo, "Could you please extend my thanks to Diplomat Park? He didn't have to."

Sasani doesn't owe any thanks to anyone, Park least of all. Teo stands, brushing off his pants. "Call us when you want a ride to join us at Yeonghui's estate, all right?"

Sasani doesn't answer, and Teo has a sudden premonition.

"I mean, you'll have to coordinate with everyone to go back to Earth together. I'm sure you don't want to *stay* in Artemis."

"No, but I'm not intending to go back to Earth," Sasani says, almost apologetically.

Teo stops short of grabbing Sasani by the shoulders again. "You're telling me this *now*? You're leaving?"

The Seonbi next to the car clears her throat and Teo couldn't care less about her convenience, but Sasani ducks his head apologetically before turning to Teo.

"I'm sorry. I—" Sasani gathers himself. "I always knew I would return to Saturn. But . . . I truly wish you well."

Another pithy saying that Teo would normally ignore, except damn Sasani and his sincere eyes. When Sasani raises his hand, it's with regret and a finality that Teo doesn't like one bit.

"I have a lot more crying to do in front of you, Sasani!" Teo calls after him.

Sasani's not able to respond to that, though, because the door closes shut.

FOUR

NO MICS, NO cameras. Teo sweeps the place once they arrive. It has nothing to do with whether he trusts Yeonghui or not; she might not even know she's being surveilled. Jang Yeonghui always accompanied her father when he had business with Teo's. The two progeny had been included in those rather instructive dinners, until Teo's father had deemed that they were going over his son's head. Teo's never been particularly close to Yeonghui, but he wanted to find answers in Artemis, and the avenues in had been slim to none. If nothing else, they had both commiserated about their patriarchs.

He's sorry to have involved her, but it's the lesser of two evils if the other option is staying under Park's thumb at the seowon. More than that, though, is the fact that she believed him when he called her up out of the blue and explained what had happened.

"I knew you didn't do it," she had said on the comm.

Tears pricked his eyes. Could it be that easy? But as Yeonghui prattled on, her words had fallen over each other in her eagerness to offer her assistance and he had, despite himself, felt some misgiving. Shouldn't she be running screaming in the other direction? He tried to squash it though; how could he wish for more people to have faith in him if he couldn't trust anyone else?

When Yeonghui had proposed a place to hide out, he expected some sort of secluded safe house, not her family's private vacation estate on the Moon. It's one of many they have across the solar. The Anands have only two homes: a penthouse in Seoul and a lavish estate in Mumbai. His father had deemed anything else an extravagant boast, and he might as well have been talking about this mansion. Teo and the others arrived to find the place abustle: servants removing sheets that protected the furniture from dust, airing out the rooms, and already cooking up a veritable storm. So much for being a fugitive.

Yeonghui hasn't even arrived yet, but their group wasted no time settling in. While Teo did his check, everyone else ran around snagging rooms, claiming spots in the shower queues.

Phoenix and Teo are now seated at the long table in a front receiving room, and Ocean leans against the wall next to Gemini, who's on the lookout from the window seat. Teo has the feeling he's more suspicious of the front guards than anything beyond the gate. Cass and Lupus have taken posts around the room, while Aries sits in a chair next to the doorway.

Beyond this group, Von's reading poetry to the plants he moved into one sunny room, Dae's soaking in a tub, and Maggie probably hasn't moved from the pantry where she fell to her knees after witnessing the abundantly stocked shelves.

"Do you anticipate any trouble from Park?" Phoenix asks Ocean. "Will he keep quiet?"

"I think what he told Teo was the truth. He's always liked having more information in his pocket," Ocean says.

"Do you know the other Artemis Diplomats?" Gemini asks, his legs bent up on the seat with him. He touches a finger to the curtain to peer out.

"I didn't keep in touch with anyone after I left."

"No class reunions?" Phoenix asks lightly.

"For Sav-Faire?" Teo snorts. "That's asking for trouble. They couldn't end a night without figurative and literal backstabbing. And an interplanetary war."

"I think poison was the weapon of choice at the last reunion they attempted," Ocean says thoughtfully.

Phoenix laughs, but when he's the only one to do so, his chortle fades. "Wait, really?"

"They weren't guarding the punch bowl closely enough," Teo says. "I'm surprised you didn't hear about it. Wiped out half that year. Caused a dearth of Diplomats for a while."

"Rumor is it was an underclassman who wanted to clear the market," Ocean says. "But they were never able to prove anything."

"Fun."

This last rejoinder is from Gemini, and Teo swears his mouth curls up just the slightest bit. That's disturbing.

"So, we watch our step around the Diplomat," Cass says. "Great. What's our timeline, Phoenix?"

Teo's stomach clenches. They're all waiting to hear back from Park about the arranged flights home, but the *Ohneul* members will probably be here for a few days while Park ensures that the flights are secure. And once the *Pandia* is ready to fly, its crew will also depart to leave Teo and Ocean on their own.

"There is the small matter of our transportation." Phoenix runs a hand through his hair. "We may be landlocked for a tick."

"Mea culpa," Ocean says.

"Not at all," Phoenix says as Teo's opening his mouth to say something along the same lines. "A damaged ship is very small payment for our lives."

"I can pay for the repairs," Teo says. "And I can pay extra to get it done quickly." It's the least he can do.

Phoenix's expression goes blank. "You can take it out of your original payment."

"That's all right," Teo says. "Consider it a bonus."

"We'll take it out of the original payment," Phoenix says firmly. "You don't even know how much it will be."

"There's very little I can't afford," Teo says. "No matter how much it is, I—"

"I don't want to owe you anything," Phoenix cuts him off.

The words die in Teo's mouth and he presses his lips together. The rest of the room is quiet, and their exchange sags like a hot wad of shame tangled with confusion.

"Make sure you bring Maggie with you to the body shop," Aries says calmly. "She'll know if they're fleecing you."

"Yes, good point," Phoenix says, as if he hasn't steamrolled over Teo's body with his rejection. "In the meantime . . ." He hesitates and then continues in a businesslike tone, "We'll make the best use of our time here. And we should talk about what happened today."

For one delusional moment, Teo thinks Phoenix is talking about what happened in Phoenix's room on the *Pandia*, how Teo had pushed Phoenix down on the bed and . . .

"One question is whether Lee is actually a Seonbi guard member," Gemini says, not missing a beat. "And not someone in disguise, using a deepfake suit."

Teo blinks. And blinks again to gather himself. Right. "You mean, whether an actual guard was turned, or whether one of Corvus's men infiltrated the guards?"

"It was a sloppy job," Cass says. "I would have gotten you in your sleep. Not tried to attack you when there was security on the other side of the door."

"Thanks," Teo says.

"No prob."

Teo shakes his head. "There has to be a way to detect a suit," he says. "It's obviously been good enough for Hadrian to fool everyone into thinking he's Declan, but there must be a flaw."

"Cass?" Phoenix asks.

Cass shrugs. "I mean, sure. But I'd have to get my hands on one to work out the tech."

"Lupus?" Phoenix says, "We're going to do some digging. I'm sure Corvus has left some traces. We'll start with Mercury. And let's set up some search parameters so we're monitoring comms, the net, whatever we can get our hands on for any signs of his movement." He nods at Aries next. "Aries?"

"Finances?" Aries confirms. "Yeah, he has to be moving money. And a lot of it. I'll see what I can find."

"Wait. Slow down." Teo holds up a hand. He says to Phoenix, "You . . . you said before that you couldn't help me against Corvus."

"He should have known better than to threaten my crew," Phoenix says. "I've forgiven him much, but there's a limit."

Teo shivers at his tightly controlled tone.

"He doesn't strike me as quitter," Gemini says. "I, for one, don't relish living the rest of my life looking over my shoulder."

"This has nothing to do with helping an Anand," Cass says. "We're going to hunt down Corvus before he decides to hunt us down."

"But if we end up clearing Teophilus's name as a result?" Gemini throws to Cass.

"Well," Cass sputters. "That's fine, I guess. But that's not why *I'm* doing this."

Teo hears a rumbling and realizes it's Aries chuckling. "We talked it over at the hangar," he says. "The enemy of my enemy is my friend."

Across the room, Ocean shares her trademark smile at Teo, with one side of her mouth lifting.

"Well . . . thank you," he says quietly.

"Just to reiterate," Cass says. "We're not doing it for *you*."

"Typical Anand," Gemini scoffs. "Making it all about him."

Despite their claims, a wave washes over Teo, dizzying him. He shields his eyes. He's *not* rubbing them because moisture has built up.

"Getting back to the matter at hand," Gemini says. "Phoenix, you're going to have to do some digging of your own."

Phoenix bites his thumb. "Yes, I know," he says. "I can check contacts from back when I worked with him."

"Contacts . . ." Lupus says as they type away. "Other people like you who were part of his team?"

Phoenix bends over his hand again, and he traces the edges of the bandage before he answers, "No one else *used* to be part of his team. If you wanted out of Corvus's team, well . . . there was only one exit door."

TEO'S DURUMI 47

"But you left," Lupus says, their fingers not missing a beat.

"Right," Phoenix says. "About that."

Unexpectedly, Phoenix meets Teo's eyes from across the table. The black pain there makes Teo want to reach for him. Maybe Phoenix hadn't given him over to Corvus, and you'd think that two ships shooting at each other would wrap up the loose ends of a severed relationship, but Teo doesn't think it's that simple. It never is.

Teo clears his throat. "I have a few leads of my own to follow while we're here in Artemis."

"Speaking of," Gemini says. "How well do you know this Yeonghui person?"

"You mean, do I trust her?" Teo says wryly, "I barely trust myself these days. But I don't think she's worse than any other spoiled, entitled heir." He thinks about it for a moment. "Or better."

"But she trusted you," Phoenix says. His tone is carefully neutral. "She believed you right away, you said. You must be close."

Teo taps his shoulder. "Or she might have some other angle. People always take care of their piggy banks until they need the marks."

Phoenix winces. "Teophilus . . ."

"Keep your friends close, enemies closer?" Lupus says.

"Keep your enemies close enough to strike is how I see it," Cass says and stretches. She walks to the door and cuffs Aries on the shoulder. "Are we good for now? I called dibs on the shower next."

"Lupus and I have a lot to do," Aries says, tugging Lupus by their hood.

Ocean pushes off the wall. "I probably need to free the servants in the kitchen from Maggie's terrorizing."

"I'll come with you," Gemini says, finally moving from his rock-steady position, the curtain whispering as he lets go of it.

Oh no, this is not happening. Teo moves to rise from his chair too, but Ocean places her hand on his shoulder as she goes past, applying the gentlest pressure. She flicks her gaze back at Phoenix and to him, as if he didn't already glean the reason for the room's all-too-convenient speedy exodus.

Teo attempts an "Ocean, you did good earlier."

"You did too," she says. And then adds, "Your parents would have been proud."

Teo blinks furiously as she leaves. He's already cried today; surely he hasn't replenished his body's tear supply. It's almost enough to distract him from the situation she's left him in. Phoenix sits across from him, the sunlight cutting a line between their hands on the persimmon wood table. Bright. Dark. Phoenix in the light, while Teo sits shrouded in shadow.

"You don't have to do this," Teo says.

Phoenix has gone stiff again. "You're stuck with me. For now."

Teo hesitates, then says quietly, "Don't you mean that *you're* stuck with *me*?" When Phoenix averts his gaze, Teo continues because they might as well address the elephant in the room. Well, actually, not even just in the room, but currently sitting on Teo's chest. "Didn't you kiss me because you thought you'd never see me again after today?"

Phoenix's blue eyes flash back to him. His mouth opens and then closes. Teo tries not to let that hurt.

"Don't worry," he says breezily. "I'm used to being used."

Even as he says it, Teo can vividly recall Phoenix's lips on him, Phoenix's wrecked voice in his ears. He snuffs that out, so all that remains is the bitter taste in his mouth.

"Teophilus," Phoenix replies quickly. "That's not what was happening."

TEO'S DURUMI

But Teo doesn't want to hear the pity in his voice, nor whatever pithy explanation he's going to conjure up.

"I get it," he says harshly. He stops, moderates his tone. "I can't say I'm not guilty of it either, Phoenix. I'm very good at not taking things seriously."

He'd seen the way Phoenix drew to Corvus like a moth to a flame, their bond undeniable. Their relationship had been forged on mutual belief and respect, something profound and significant.

"Teophilus . . ." Phoenix falters. "Is that really . . ."

"Did you ever think about going back to Corvus?" Teo asks to the floor.

Phoenix lets out a long breath. "I'd be lying if I said I didn't," he says. "But it would have destroyed me." Phoenix taps the table, more a movement borne of thinking rather than to get Teo's attention. "I loved him too much to stay. And I think he loved me enough to let me go. I don't know."

Teo's feelings toward Corvus are complicated enough without this. Lupus had shared files with Teo of pictures of the two together—Phoenix with his hair shorn short, an intensity to his bearing, the pale Corvus, lit from some fire within. But now, although Phoenix sits in the sunlight, he looks deflated. Wan. Teo wonders when the last time was that Phoenix and Corvus saw each other, what sort of plans they made together in their shared hatred of the Anand family.

"Why did you save me today?" Teo asks. "You got hurt because of me."

Phoenix flexes his wrapped hand. "I wasn't really thinking."

Ah. Of course not. Always playing the hero to whoever might be in trouble.

"With instincts like that, I'm surprised you've survived this long," Teo says. "Isn't it common sense to get out of a knife's way?"

Phoenix doesn't answer for a while. "But you were in the knife's way."

Teo finally does raise his head at that, ready to seek out whatever meaning, whatever tone Phoenix intended to impart with those words, but he only catches Phoenix's profile, as he looks out the window Gemini was at.

"I think that might be Jang Yeonghui at the gate now," Phoenix says.

Teo gathers the thoughts windmilling in his mind. "What makes you say that?"

"She looks like one of yours," Phoenix says. He faces Teo again. Resigned, now. Diminished in some other way Teo can't place.

A knock comes at the front door. But god help him; Teo has no idea what he'll do or say if they ever do circle back to their conversation.

FIVE

JANG YEONGHUI'S HANBOK is black and gold. She has a gold binyeo in her hair, the bird at the end curved up to the sky, its jeweled eye twinkling in the light. She could be hosting a lavish dinner party rather than sheltering fugitives. She actually has a separate building for her dining and kitchen areas, one that's connected to the main mansion with a long, exquisitely tiled pathway. Giwa tiles form the roofing of the walkway, and Ocean heard Aries murmuring that the blue in the paint was a nod to the traditional Korean royal palaces, which featured the color of the sky to pronounce the king's communion with the heavens.

Now presenting their sixth course, eleven servants come into the room so that they can serve the individual dolsot bibimbab simultaneously to the table members. As Ocean peers to either side, she finds their choreographed movements while they mix the rice bowls uncanny instead of impressive.

Teo says blandly, "I thought we talked about being . . . discreet."

Yeonghui blinks at him. "Whatever do you mean? My family avoids Artemis this time of year, so you don't have to worry about them showing up. Our hanok may be air-conditioned, but the climate in Artemis is beastly during the summer. Anyway, I promise it's extremely private."

"I hadn't realized that private included this many staff members," Teo replies.

Yeonghui sips from her wine. "Teo, you should remember from our dinners. A person's power is only secure if they can trust the help."

"But this is a big secret to keep," Teo says. "I'm a murderer."

Their table goes quiet. Ocean glances at the servants, but all of them have directed their eyes downward. Yeonghui puts a napkin to her mouth, carefully patting her lips.

"Allegedly," Teo finishes.

"You'd never," she says calmly. "And if you did, I'm sure you had good reason."

Ocean's fairly certain Teo's never had a relationship with Yeonghui, fake or otherwise. A fake relationship would be too politically fraught, and a real one she would have known about. Teo scratches his temple, which Ocean knows is his tic for buying time. But he's saved from responding to that somewhat astonishing statement.

"You'll probably want to save that for the kongjuk," Youngui says brightly to Phoenix, who's holding up a spoon. Her suggestion holds the perfect balance of innocence and condescension.

"Right," Phoenix says, placing the utensil back on the table.

Ocean catches just the slightest tightening of Teo's eyes. But it wouldn't do for him to antagonize their host, especially since she's being trusted to keep quiet about them. Ocean picks up her kongjuk spoon and uses it to scoop a kkakduki from the dish between her and Phoenix. The bright-red radish cube slips off and spins on the beautifully lacquered table between them.

"Oops."

Phoenix's eyes crinkle, but Yeonghui speaks up to address Ocean, much to her dismay. "I had no idea you knew Diplomat Park from Sav-Faire. What was your elective?"

"My elective was dance." Ocean keeps herself from rounding her shoulders.

Ocean doesn't really care for the wine that's being amply poured into everyone's glasses, but she applies herself liberally to the dolsot bibimbab. The rice at the bottom is perfectly crisp, the marinated vegetables fresh, and the beef juicy. She tells herself she's only here for the food.

Yeonghui explains to the table, "Savoir-Faire requires everyone to focus on an elective. Diplomats are supposed to be well versed in the arts. It makes them well rounded and cultured. Good conversationalists."

Yeonghui has the open manner of explaining so that everyone's on the same page. But Ocean senses the contemptuous undercurrent. It makes her food taste metallic, and she has to fight the automatic rising of her hackles.

Yeonghui holds out her wine glass, and a servant immediately glides forward from the wall to refill it. She expertly swirls the glass on the table, her fingers splayed down on its base. The servant backs into their position again.

"What was Diplomat Park's elective?" Yeonghui asks.

Ocean has to dive back into the memory banks, past the last few weeks that have taken up a lot of her hard drive, back beyond the years at the *Ohneul*, the *Hadouken*, and the years at the

Alliance's Yong School, until she reaches the time spent with Park Joonho. His sense of style hadn't been nearly as developed back then.

"Piano," she says finally.

"Oh," Yeonghui says approvingly. "He certainly has the hands for it. But I suppose you'd know more about that, wouldn't you?"

It's the kind of dig one would sneak in at Sav-Faire. And unexpectedly, Sasani comes to mind. If he were here, the tips of his ears would have reddened and he'd have rubbed the back of his neck, while he struggled to keep his face completely composed. The surprise of that thought hits her harder than anything else, almost making her double over.

Ocean pushes out, "Joonho always said he took up piano so he wouldn't have to join the orchestra. He wasn't a team player."

Yeonghui leans forward. "No, but none of the Diplomats are, are they? But at least Joonho is Korean. It's a pity he's the only native Diplomat that Artemis has. How can we expect them to take care of us if they're not *of* us? Granted, I don't know Joonho well, but I'm well acquainted with Diplomat Randlett, who was a few years above you. He always makes Sav-Faire sound like a glorified boarding school." Bitterness trickles into her words. "While Diplomats learned Chopin, I learned on hand from my father. Don't you think we had our own relevant schooling, Teo?"

"Sure, experience is the best teacher," Teo says. "But we never had any opportunity to rub shoulders with people outside of our circles either."

"And who do you think goes to Sav-Faire?" Hurakan scoffs. "How much did it cost a year?"

"I really don't think I could have gotten a better education than from my father." Yeonghui ignores Hurakan. "Teo, I'm sure you feel the same way about . . . well, have I mentioned that I'm so sorry for your loss? But don't you think he'd be happy to see the two of us together like this?"

"My father . . ." Teo trails off. He clears his throat and tries again. "My old man . . ."

Sometimes, Teo is perfectly fine. But Ocean knows how there's no rhyme or reason to it. It can be easy to talk about whom you've lost, and then the next minute it can feel like glass crushed into your skin.

"It's very good wine, isn't it?" Ocean asks. She ignores how Hurakan's eyes go right to her very full, very obviously untouched wineglass, but Yeonghui attaches on eagerly.

"Oh yes," Yeonghui says. "It's Teo's first night here, so we went through some trouble to get a '16. Not a great year for Artemis generally, except for its wine."

"A '16, huh . . ." Teo swirls his wine, and Yeonghui leans toward him before he continues, "I've found the different regional qualities of the land provide such unique tastes. I'm more about mouthfeel, myself."

"Are you now?" Yeonghui's eyes widen before she recovers. She asks with a coy smile, "And what kind of mouthfeel do you prefer?"

Despite the fact that Yeonghui isn't a Diplomat and never went to Sav-Faire, Ocean thinks she would have enjoyed it. But the whole performance is interfering with Ocean's enjoyment of her food.

Teo tilts his head. "It depends on my mood," he says. "Sometimes I like it velvety smooth and other times I like it rough."

Phoenix shifts next to Ocean and a wave of pity washes over her. She had hoped that whatever conversation he had with Teo after they were left in that front room would diffuse the tenseness . . . but it's been a while since she's seen Teo act out like this. No matter how many tabloid pictures Phoenix has seen or articles he's read about Teo's philandering, it's entirely different to witness it up close.

Yeonghui's lips tremble, but her smile widens and holds. "But about that wine—"

Teo knocks back the rest of his glass. "Where are we going for round two?"

"Where—round two?" Yeonghui falters.

"Last time I was in Artemis, there was this great rock café. What was it called? Cool Ranch Norito. I don't remember *anything* from that night, which"—he winks at Yeonghui—"is the mark of a *fantastic* night, don't you think?"

"I . . ." Yeonghui swallows. Her tone is strained. "Teo, I don't think you should be . . . at a bar?"

"Why not?" Teo asks blithely.

"You're . . ."

It unfolds just as Ocean's witnessed dozens of times before. The drop in the face as someone realizes how foolish, how useless Teo really is. That all their sycophantic effort is never going to get them anywhere. And again, as it's happened so many times, Ocean's heart sinks even if this is exactly what Teo intended.

Yeonghui straightens and gulps down her glass. She shoves it to the side for the servant to repour. "Teo, you're *wanted*." Her voice is no longer sparkling nor vivacious. The hand at the base of the newly filled wineglass shakes. "You shouldn't go—it's *dangerous*."

"Oh, yes, I suppose you're right," Teo says absently.

Yeonghui deflates in relief. She takes a hurried gulp from her wine before rearranging her face again. "Well, this is all very exciting." Her voice is overbright as she turns from Teo. "I mean, I had *no* idea that when Teo said he'd be dropped off at Artemis, it would be by the famous Phoenix."

Phoenix offers Yeonghui a languorous smirk as if he's taken in more wine than he has. He tosses his lustrous hair in that infamous Phoenix Toss.

"That was the point, sweetheart," Phoenix drawls.

Ocean has to keep from slumping in her seat. Honestly, he and Teo are perfect for each other.

"How ever did the two of you meet?"

"We met beard to beard," Teo murmurs and Phoenix stiffens.

Yeonghui ventures, "But Teo, your father . . ."

Ocean now recalls Park's musing voice as he asked, "*What would your umma think?*" Striking at a person through their parents' expectations is somehow so easy, and yet so lethal. Ocean hasn't yet learned whether it's a specific poison you can inoculate yourself to.

"I'm very grateful to you, Yeonghui, for opening this place to us," Teo says. "But speaking of dangerous, I wouldn't want people to know you're consorting with either Phoenix or me. It might be better that you stay away from the estate, especially since your family is known to usually avoid it during the summer. Where *are* you staying currently?"

"I had business just outside Artemis," Yeonghui says faintly. "But Teo, I really don't mind—"

"No, no," Teo says firmly. "I couldn't do that to you and your reputation. And what would you do without your servants? I wouldn't dream of depriving you of them."

"N-no," Yeonghui says. "On that, Teo, I absolutely insist. How will you get by without them?"

"How would we ever," Hurakan mutters.

"Are you worried about them bothering you, Teo?" Yeonghui's forehead furrows. "They have their own quarters in a separate house and they won't be in your space."

Ocean suspects it's less that they'll be *intruding* and more that they'll be *listening in*. She reads the bare wrinkle in Teo's forehead before he bows his head.

"Then, I'm very grateful, Yeonghui. Really . . . for everything."

"Of course, Teo." Yeonghui grasps his hand on the table fervently. "I just . . ." She peeks over at Phoenix. "I want you to be *careful*."

As if whispering loudly means that Phoenix won't hear her. Phoenix, on his part, fluffs up his hair as if that really is all that's on his mind. Down the table, a much happier tableau isn't caught up in this conversation; Dae, Von, Lupus, Cass, and Aries are fixated on Maggie's demonstration of how to *properly* mix the dolsot, oblivious to the servants behind her who just did it. Ocean regards the cold remains of hers, forgotten while she was concentrating on this conversation, sifting falsehood from truth.

And then, she thinks of a pair of serious eyes that regard her carefully, take her words at full value, and wait patiently for anything she might have to say.

"Oh, I'll be careful, Yeonghui," Teo says. "I know I've always been an easy mark."

SIX

CORVUS COUNTED HIS breaths. His heart was pummeling him. His ribs might rupture from the pressure. *Calme.*

If he was telling himself that, it was probably already too late. He was spiraling. It's hard to stay composed when you have a gun pressed to your temple.

"What made you think you could come in here"—the metal dug into his head, and Corvus bit his lip so hard that it drew blood—"steal from me, and get away with it?"

Corvus sucked the blood into his mouth, savoring the coppery taste. *Calme.*

"Answer me!"

Corvus was shoved to the floor. He coughed. Blood splattered onto the tiles. He squeezed his eyes shut, stars sparking in the dark of his eyelids. He hummed a refrain under his breath. A snatch of a melody his mother always used to sing to him. *Il y a longtemps . . .*

Once he was sure he had it under control, he opened his eyes to the sneering man who loomed over him. Corvus pushed himself up to a sitting position and wiped his mouth with the back of his hand, leaving a smear of red.

"It's so clean." Corvus gestured around them. White-tiled floor that slanted down toward a drain in the corner. Otherwise, the room was completely bare. Painfully bright. "How many people have you punished in here?"

The man's eyes widened. "What was that?"

"You lounge in your office, day after day, while other people drag themselves to your mine for backbreaking work. You remain spotless, while they coat their lungs black. Treacherous conditions, laughable pay, and for what?"

Corvus rose slowly to his feet. He pretended to sway, as if he was groggy. When he straightened, he made sure to stumble a few steps to the right before shaking his head.

"You . . ." He said and shook his head again. Crossed and uncrossed his eyes to sell the bit. "You have the chance to repent though. You're in a position of power. You're a Mercurian, like me. Don't you think you should help other Mercurians?"

Bradford would get up so early that the light hadn't yet crept its fingers into the sky. He would touch Corvus's head before he left, always. If Corvus was aware enough, he'd rest his hand on top of Bradford's gnarled, hairy one that dwarfed his. Corvus had always kept himself from asking if Bradford even saw any of that sunlight before taking the shaft down into the mines, before the world closed over him. When Bradford came trudging back at the end of the day, the darkness trailed even in his thick eyebrows, coating the white hairs. How long had he experienced that pitiless blackness before he died, crushed under its weight?

The man laughed as he holstered his gun. He pulled out two gloves from his jacket. He punched his hands together and they expanded and lit up green. Power gloves. The sound of them charging up made Corvus's mouth water. It was an expensive sound.

"You're right; we're Mercurians," he said. "So you and I know that I'm not the problem. This pattern has been ground into us for years. And if I don't comply, then I'm the one in the mine."

Everyone who grew up on Mercury knew how it was. That didn't mean it had to stay that way. Corvus had stalled enough. He took in the man before him. Luxurious suit jacket, shoes polished to a spit-shine gleam, an expensive haircut that had to be constantly maintained, and that premium tech on his hands. And still . . .

"I pity you," Corvus said.

The man snarled as he whipped his green comet of a fist. Corvus ducked, but didn't account for the second fist uppercutting into his stomach. His ribs groaned. Cracked.

Behind the man the door slammed open.

"Stop right there!"

Corvus was flat on the tile again, but the words weren't for him. The man swiveled around to the person whose presence filled the doorway. Shaved head, but Corvus knew that when it was grown out, it would be golden blond with strands of red like sun-ripened wheat.

Garrett's bright-blue eyes met Corvus's. Garrett's shoulders sank before a gangly, dark-skinned youth shoved past him.

"Corvus! What did he—"

With a roar, Amell leaped at the man. They both went down, slapping the ground so hard it vibrated Corvus's wrecked bones. He clenched his jaw, bracing himself to get up, until a hand crossed his vision. Corvus grasped that familiar palm and was launched upward and into Garrett's arms. When Garrett squeezed, Corvus couldn't help but groan. Garrett immediately pulled back. He tilted Corvus's face.

"Was this really necessary, Corvus?"

"You tell me," Corvus said. "Did you get it?"

Garrett sighed as he dropped his hand. "I don't know that the end always justifies the means." At Corvus's eyebrow raise, he rubbed his shorn head. "But yes, we got the access codes. Your diversion and Hadrian's voicework did the trick."

"How. Dare. You. Touch. Him." Amell punctuated each word with a punch, each staccato so precise, it imprinted a picture in Corvus's mind even though the scene was unfolding behind him.

"Amell, enough," Corvus said.

Amell dropped the man. "So now what? We kill him?"

Garrett blanched, but Corvus put a hand on his shoulder. He walked to join Amell.

"Please. I have a family," the man moaned.

"So did I," Corvus said.

"And me too," Amell growled. "How do you think my *father* ended up in the hospital and—"

Corvus put up a hand, and Amell's mouth snapped shut even if his face contorted. Corvus crouched in front of the man. "If you had kept your gun in hand, you might have had a chance. But you have a reputation for enjoying the physicality of your brutality. You lost the moment you pulled out those gloves." Corvus extended his palm and Amell placed a knife into it. "But I appreciate the allure of taking care of something with your own hands." He held up the knife to the light. What would it be like if he plunged it into the man's stomach and dragged it all the way . . .

Past the knife, Garrett's expression was strangely frozen. Corvus shrugged and dropped his knife hand. He rested a palm against his ribs as he stood over the man.

"You broke three of my ribs," he said. "Amell will break three of yours. It's only fair."

He barely finished his words before Amell set on the man, his blows fast, hard, and accurate. The man bellowed, and Corvus sheathed the knife into his belt.

"I thought..." Garrett started, and then stopped. "Never mind."

Corvus seldom gave Garrett the full power of his gaze; he used that sparingly. But now, he put a fingertip to Garrett's chin, redirecting his attention from the sheathed knife. Corvus cupped Garrett's face, and Garrett leaned into the touch.

"If we don't hurt him, he won't learn," Corvus said. "But he doesn't deserve to bear the weight of Anand Tech's sins."

That was only partially the truth. The other part of it was that Corvus had an inkling of how the man would be punished by his superiors. Cast down into the depths of the very mining facility he used to run. Made to taste that acrid fear as he realized that at any time, it could collapse just like the one in Penelope had, taking Bradford's life. But he didn't need to expound for Garrett, who was still a little too soft.

"Amell, tie him up," Corvus commanded. "And grab his gloves. I want to dissect the tech." As Amell scuffled behind them, Corvus stroked Garrett's cheek. "You and me. We're going to change the solar."

Garrett placed his hand over Corvus's. "You and me."

Corvus.

An unexpected, sharp crack breaks Corvus's recollection in two. It sounds like bones breaking. Immediately, Emory is at his side, her suit powered up and a gun out. But before him, Amell lifts a bent knee to show a crushed snail shell, a slick swipe of entrails.

"That's . . . a bad omen." Emory shudders.

"Shut up, robot," Amell snarls.

It's been several years since that sweep of the mining official's office where they drained that company's marks. Corvus heard that the official didn't live very long once he was demoted to work the mines. Amell's no longer an awkward lanky youth and has filled into a massiveness that's only matched by his rage. He has an ugly white scar gracing his lip.

And Garrett is no longer with them, nor does he go by that name.

Corvus squashes down the remnants of that memory. This isn't the time to mourn. He pulls on his glove and focuses on Amell kneeling before him. This glove has been molded to his hand, and although it's his first time using it, it glides on like butter. All of his research, all of Alessa's money, has funneled into this moment. Whatever Hadrian is setting up for them in Korea, whatever they've accomplished up until this point, is meaningless if this doesn't work.

Would it have been more convenient if they could have eliminated Teophilus Anand? Certainly. He's proved troublesome, but there are other, more time-sensitive matters to deal with. Corvus set a testing schedule for his latest invention that he intends to adhere to. After their clash with the *Pandia*, they had fled the Moon and entered the Earth's atmosphere. Although they'd been afraid of pursuit, none had come, which Corvus supposes he could have guessed from the nature of the Seonbi. They would rather not get involved, even if it means letting him loose.

"I'm not going to lie," Corvus says to Amell. "I think this will hurt."

Amell's hands are laced together as if in prayer. He has dressed himself in a long white robe. But still, he quivers. He has good reason to; all evidence points to his demise. He is, after all, the one who procured the bodies for Corvus to test the first stages of this device on. Like a gravedigger or attentive vampire hunter pouncing on recently deceased miners. And he was the one who burned those bodies when those tests went awry. But Amell's devotion, ultimately, has always been about his faith.

Their temporary hideout is austere, and this inner basement room, while well lit, is cold and bare. But Amell chose this room for its asceticism.

"I'd never make you suffer something I'm not also willing to suffer," Corvus says. "And I hope it is some comfort that whatever you experience will soon become a part of me."

Amell licks his lips, and Corvus can almost taste the salt of his sweat. But they all committed to this long ago and Amell is merely the first. It has nothing to do with the fact he failed to destroy Garrett's ship and crew. That he was witness to Corvus's last conversation with Garrett before the latter definitively cut the comm line. Garrett will come back to him, eventually. If this works, Garrett will see what Corvus has been reaching for this whole time. It'll remind him of what they were reaching for together.

"Have you heard back from Alessa?" he asks Emory.

"She's in Artemis," she responds. "She'll update us."

"Make sure you keep checking in on her," he says. Alessa is useful, but can be . . . somewhat of a loose cannon.

He flexes his gloved hand. It has some of the same makeup as the deepfake skinsuit, which Hadrian has proven to be unstoppable in.

Hadrian, who has always had a particular gift for molding himself into other people. And now he's taken the shape of a politician, the spoiled first son of a tech magnate, and one of the most powerful men in the solar. Even easier for Hadrian to impersonate when the people closest to Declan Anand had been ripped away; and any discrepancies could be relegated to the grief of losing those people.

Alessa had had her time in the deepfake suit too, although she wasn't nearly as skilled at it. Then again, she'd only had to imitate Teophilus Anand in a coma for the most part. And to imitate him waking from that coma in a wild rage to murder his parents. That hadn't been difficult for her at all.

Corvus developed both the skinsuit and this glove, but the glove has a completely different purpose. The skinsuit alters what people see with their eyes. It separates them from the truth. This glove is about stripping away illusions, about seeing each other truly. It will force Anand Tech to face everything they've done wrong. It will bring the solar together.

Unfortunately, certain . . . aspects of the glove meant that he couldn't test this final stage without a human subject. A living one, this time.

"Are you nervous?" Corvus asks Amell.

"No."

"If you're lying, I'll know soon enough," Corvus says.

"Corvus." Emory steps forward. "Let me do it. It's dangerous. You shouldn't—"

"Stand back," Amell snarls. "Do you think I want to do this with *you*?"

"You think we should risk Corvus then?" Emory asks shrilly.

Amell's hackles rise. "You're not even *human*," he growls. "You're half robot. It wouldn't do any good."

"Amell," Corvus says sharply, "surely you haven't forgotten how many times she's saved your life, including the last time you saw Garrett in person."

Emory's right arm is indeed a biological construct that Corvus fashioned for her. Not that it matters; right hand or left. The glove's reversible, but that's far from the point. Emory skitters backward with a whir of her joints, but her wounded expression is aimed more at Corvus than Amell. Corvus would normally reprimand Amell more stringently, but Emory serves as a reminder of Amell's failure, his lack. Amell's aggression is ratcheted even higher than usual, with his sweat popping out of his skin. Besides, if all goes to plan, Corvus will soon convince Amell in a different, more effective way.

"Emory, your turn will come." Corvus only has to say a word, adopt a slightly different tone, and she always backs away, this time stopping short of dropping to a knee. "But now, it has to be Amell and me."

Corvus directs his attention back down at Amell, who has his head tilted up. "Once I touch you, you'll always be with me."

Corvus thinks about Garrett on their call, his hair grown out now to a burnished gold, although his eyes are the same anguished ones. He wonders what version of himself exists in Garrett's mind, what Garrett could possibly think of him. When they were together, he had thought they could conquer the whole solar. When they had slept next to each other, his hand curled in Garrett's, he had thought he couldn't ever be more complete.

But then Garrett had left. Like Corvus's parents had died and left him. Like Bradford.

"I'm sorry," Amell bursts out. "I failed you."

"Is this outcome a failure?"

"No." Amell shakes his head furiously. "But I wanted to do more for you."

"This is not the end, Amell," Corvus says.

Corvus presses his palms together, his right hand gloved and the left hand bare. The glove activates, lighting up blue. The points on the glove's interior prick Corvus's fingertips and his palm, and then they sink into the nerve endings there. He squeezes his eyes as they do. It stings, but it's the least of what will come.

"Do you remember what you said when I asked you to join me, Amell?" Corvus says, eyes still closed. It's hard to keep his voice even, but he breathes in through his nose and out through clenched teeth.

"I said I would never leave you."

"And you never will."

Corvus pictures his handpicked four, his inner circle. Hadrian, a wolf in sheep's clothing. Emory, the most willing of servants, his right hand. Which he supposes makes Alessa his pillar, his left hand of darkness. And Amell, who has been with Corvus since Mercury, who believed in Corvus long before Corvus did himself.

Corvus puts his hand to Amell's forehead and then pushes down. Immediately blue lines flow out from his glove and drill into Amell. His jaw drops down and he screams. His head jerks backward, but Corvus is attached to him now and his hand only moves with him, and—

Corvus is

Amell is

flowing

eyes/lights/flickering, passing like coruscant glimpses in the water.

Memories Amell could never consciously conjure up are being drawn like iron fillings gathering around a magnet, like a silver splinter impaling Corvus's mind.

Amell is *weightless as he's thrown up into the air by strong arms, stronger than he is, stronger than he'll ever become.*

And then *those arms hooked up to an IV, the pulse of an electronic heart somehow supposed to stand for his father's vitality, those arms withered and disused and grasping at his.* Amell weeps, screams at the unfairness of it.

Amell is still screaming, his throat scraped and stripped, and because Corvus can't control it, can't control the flow of himself or of Amell or of what is shifting or slipping where, Corvus opens up too, exposed and bright.

Corvus is *sitting on a desk, legs swinging back and forth, while his parents work around him. His mother, beautiful and pale, her blond hair loose, and he loves the smell of it all around him. His father, tall, taller than he is, taller than he'll ever become.*

Then *Corvus is being shoved under the desk and he can't see anything, can't hear anything*

but fragments of words. Wails. The sound of jagged tearing, the slop and splatter on the ground. The coppery overwhelming stench of—

Corvus gags. He's never told anyone about this memory, but it's unfurling within him—is it only in his mind, or is Amell seeing it now too?

Not that the question matters because nothing separates them anymore.

Amell's knee skids forward and he leaves a wet trail of slime and it opens another memory in Corvus—

"*Hey, kid.*" Corvus raises his head along with the child in his mind's eye, as if triggered by a muscle memory connected to strong emotion. "*Your parents must be worried.*"

Corvus wipes his nose, and the silvery mucous trail delineates his shame on his sleeve.

"*My parents are gone.*"

Sympathy flickers in the stranger's eyes. His eyebrows are bushy, blond and silver tufts. "*Aw hell.*"

With his last iota of strength, Corvus forces himself past that. He pushes forth his thoughts, his powerful emotions for Amell. He shares exactly what he has thought of Amell all these years. No filter, no deceit. Amell sees all the judgment, all the small gratitudes Corvus has harbored.

They're able to share in this last memory together:

Amell kneels before Corvus. Corvus is a haloed saint before him. Corvus's promises swell in him.

"We'll pay this back to those who did this to you."

Corvus looks down at Amell's bent head. A stalwart knight, his talisman that proves he's been right all along.

"I'll never leave you."

Emotion rushes into him with this binding of life to life, this promise to each other.

Corvus wrenches his gloved hand away. Amell slumps to the floor. Corvus stumbles back, colliding with a chair. Amell's eyeballs are rolled back, his body just a shell now.

"Corvus!" Emory's arms come around him.

Corvus can't stop the tears from spilling. He doesn't know if it's because of the strength of Amell's memories or the strength of Amell in him he's so painfully, vitally, thankful for.

"Are you all right?"

She's been repeating the question over and over. Beautiful Emory, who has always believed she was broken and that he came to fix her. But once they achieve their mission, she'll understand how he sees her too.

"I'm not merely all right, Emory," Corvus says. He brushes the hair off her cheek. "I'm becoming perfection."

But as he says that, another memory—his? Amell's?—slips into his mind.

"*Corvus isn't the devil.*"

"*No. He's the morning star.*"

He spasms and darkness overcomes him.

SEVEN

"HI, UMMA."

Ocean doesn't know how to have this conversation, but she couldn't keep putting it off. The silence stretches out for so long that Ocean thinks she made a mistake, that she didn't dial home. Like a coward, she kept her video off, so she stares at her bedroom's white wall as her ears strain. Is it wrong to hope it didn't connect?

"Eung, Ocean-ah," her mother finally says. She sounds weary. "Dae umma called to tell me that you're headed back to Earth soon. Why did I have to hear it from her?"

A hard block forms in Ocean. Dae, who is so close to her moms, and probably called them as soon as she could. It makes this conversation that much harder.

"Umma . . ." Ocean swallows. "I'm not coming home right away."

"What? You almost died. We *thought* you died. Dae is coming to visit her family. If your captain can take time off, then so can you."

Ocean had promised Teo she was sticking with him, whatever that would entail and for however long. But that's not something she can tell her parents, not when the solar thinks Teo's a murderer, and not when they don't know that their daughter has ever even talked to an Anand.

But a small part of her withers at her mother's tired voice. Ocean might say *I thought you might be happy I was alive* if she didn't fear the retribution. Twenty-seven years old, hasn't lived at home since she was eight, and still her mother is always able to diminish her.

"Nah jweo." She hears the wrestling and then her father comes on. "An dacheosseo? We didn't get any details and the Alliance wasn't giving us answers."

"Appa, gwenchana." Ocean hastens with, "We couldn't contact you, we were in danger—"

"Ocean-ah, we're so grateful you're all right. After what happened with your brother, we couldn't . . . we thought . . ." He pauses before he adds, "Please forgive your mother, you have to try and—"

Ocean hears more tussling and her mother blares into her ear again. "Ocean, come home."

Her heart leaps, and she pictures her mother opening the door where a hot meal will be waiting for her on a low table. A comforting bubbling jjigae, the bracken she has picked and washed with her own hands, the tightly packed kimchi.

"This nonsense has gone on long enough," her mother says harshly.

The portrait snaps inside Ocean, crackling into splintery pieces that pierce more keenly when she tries to breathe.

"Come back home, and we'll decide what to do with you."

If they had gotten a call that Hajoon was actually alive, her parents would have broken down with joyful tears. But with her...

"You were so proud of Hajoon oppa when he joined the Alliance," Ocean says abruptly, without thinking.

"*You're not Hajoon,*" her mother hisses.

"I know that! Don't you think I know that?" How could she not know that when she still remembers how her mother bragged to the members of her haenyeo clan when her son became an Alliance pilot? How her mother cried at Hajoon's Alliance award ceremony? Ocean's words are coming out loudly. They're tumbling out too distraught, too emotional, too *much*. "You wouldn't let me dive with you, but this—This—" *This was an escape but it's more than that now* she wants to say. She wants to say *I didn't know how to keep Hajoon close.* She wants to say *I was drowning.* Ocean can only manage, "I wanted something that was mine. Something I could claim."

But what she can never say is *I wanted to be claimed.* Can she somehow convey all her earlier certainty, how weightless she'd been in space? This is the first time, in so long, that she has even tried to offer something vulnerable and true to her umma.

"What are you talking about? Micheosseo?" Her mother laughs and somehow that hurts worse than anything.

"Why don't you hear me?" The struggle to explain exactly what she means, what she feels, funnels into this.

"What is there to hear?" her mother asks. "I have always known you are heartless."

Something thuds into Ocean, overtaking everything. No glass shards in her heart. No feeling of having ripped out her heart to offer it up still beating and raw. No, because she has nothing in her chest. Instead, she's left with a faint, tinny hum in her ears.

"What's wrong with you?"

Some of Adama's last words float to the surface of Ocean's mind. It wasn't the first time she'd heard that sentiment. How funny that her ex-steadies and her mother view her the same way. And who would know her better other than the people she's let in closer than anyone else? Teo named her Headshot even before meeting her, but it's perhaps the most accurate nickname of all.

Is this why her umma didn't want her to be part of her haenyeo after all? Not that she thought Ocean didn't belong, that she wasn't Korean enough, but because when it came down to it, Ocean lacked something crucial.

"You went to the Alliance and you—all those people, you—how could you . . ."

Her mother can't even say the word, doesn't even want to speak about something that Ocean did with her own hands. But she's not the only one because Ocean can see Dae's face, Sasani's distress, not that she needs that reminder because she's never going to forget that when she was forced into a situation where she acted without thinking, she killed other people. She was that person. She is that person.

"Hajima yeobeo," her father says from the back, but Ocean's done.

"I'm not coming back." Distantly, Ocean's pleased with how even her voice is.

"Don't be childish."

"I have something else I need to do."

"Ocean-ah, please. Come back home. She's upset, you have to understand . . ." Her father this time.

"I do understand." That's the problem. "Don't try to call me. I'll call you."

Ocean puts a hand up to her nimbus to cut the line. Then she activates privacy mode so it won't receive any incoming calls. She focuses on the walls so hard that even if they weren't white, that's all she would see. The chair's wooden arms stick to her sweaty skin. She can't think, she can't think. She doesn't care.

There's a sharp rap at her window and Ocean starts. It's ajar, but she slides it all the way open. Hurakan's head comes down. Even hanging upside down, she can tell he's studying her face.

"Wanna join me?" His head disappears, and he dangles his arm down from above.

Ocean puts a foot up on the sill while she grips his arm. He pulls her up through the window, and then helps her clamber onto the roof. She inhales the clear night air as she does, filling her lungs with something other than that tightness.

Ocean peers cautiously over the roof's edge. There's no light to see by other than the ones from the bedrooms below. Earth is a slim crescent of blue in the night sky, which means that anyone looking out from there is seeing an almost full moon.

"Do you like high places?" Her voice is naturally smaller out here with the outdoors buffering her rather than the walls closing in on her, but she loathes the strain in it.

He glances at her, and the motion has more form than the features on his face. "I'm more comfortable higher up. It's suffocating in that house."

"Sometimes, it's suffocating everywhere," she says. She grips her arms briefly before letting go. "I wish we were *doing* something." But admitting that leaves a stale taste in her mouth. *Doing something.* As if she's only good when in action, with someone to point a gun at.

"Lupus will find a lead soon. They're good at that." Hurakan picks up a wine bottle and holds it up to her. "You want some? It might make you feel better."

She opens her mouth to . . . do what? Deny it? It's a reflexive motion, and his smile is a flash of teeth in the darkness.

"Suit yourself," he says, and then takes a swig of it. Then he stands and dances too close to the edge of the roof. Her hands are sweating vicariously, and he laughs lazily. "You're not going to stop me?"

"You know your limits better than I do."

"That's such an Ocean answer." He stretches a leg over the edge. "But I've had *so* much to drink."

She frowns and he laughs as if he can see it. Maybe he can. He always seems to glean more from the darkness. She says, "I thought you didn't like drinking."

"I don't," he says, then takes another swig. "Like I said, it makes people sloppy. And it makes me . . ."

Hurakan holds out his arms to the sides as he steps forward, like someone proving they can walk a straight line after they've had too much to drink.

"I don't like drinking, but the information is useful," he says as he inches closer. "The right wine, the right fork to use. It's a code that gets you into certain circles." She expects him to about-face again, but he keeps walking closer and closer until he's right before her. "But it's not really any more useful than knowing which ribs to slide a knife in between if you want to reach the heart."

Hurakan presses his palm against Ocean's ribs, and she smells the wine's sweetness on his breath, sees his slitted eyes. The flutter on her skin could be from his fingers or her pulse, and then Hurakan slips away. He takes a few steps and then trips. Ocean lurches forward to nab him, but he meets her outstretched hand halfway.

"Gotcha," he says, enfolding her hand with his. He laughs again. Then hiccups. He puts a hand to his mouth and crouches down, placing the bottle beside him. He tugs down Ocean, so she sits next to him. Her shoulder settles next to Hurakan's and her body relaxes. She makes her breaths even and audible and eventually, Hurakan matches her.

"Phoenix did imply you couldn't hold your drink," she says.

Hurakan dips his head, ruffling his hair. "This is Phoenix's fault, you know. And Teophilus's."

"Oh, really?" Ocean's surprised to find a thread of amusement in herself.

"After that display at dinner, Phoenix went on and on about *mouthfeel* and *Nebbiolo* and I couldn't let him drink alone." He interlaces his fingers with hers, reminding Ocean that they're still holding hands. His is cool, devoid of emotion. But then again, Ocean's never been good at reading touch. She's always been far more aware of its lack, or its proximity. He asks bitterly, "Do you think Phoenix really gives a damn what spoon is the 'correct' porridge spoon? Last week he wouldn't have." His voice drops. "Is Teophilus going to break Phoenix?"

"I don't think he intends to," Ocean says carefully. Whatever Teo has led people to believe, he hasn't been attracted to many people.

"There's no such thing as an equal exchange, I know that." Hurakan's thumb glides over their knuckles. "Is this bothering you?"

Ocean thinks that over. "No."

"I'm a big supporter of people making their own mistakes," Hurakan says. "I just . . . wanted better for him."

"Better than Teo?" Ocean keeps her voice even, but she can still hear the warning in it. She catches the gleam of catlike eyes scrutinizing her. "What's so great about Phoenix?"

"What's so—" Hurakan sputters. "This is *Phoenix*. Steals from the rich and gives to the poor. Orphans love him. Titans fear him."

Ocean can't help but laugh. "You make him sound like Hong Gildong."

But Hurakan hasn't stopped. "When I met him, he was like a supernova in my life. I didn't think it was possible for someone to be that *good*, I thought—" He stops abruptly and hunches over. "I shouldn't drink."

Maybe it's not about Teo after all. "Does he know how you feel about him?"

After a slight pause, Hurakan says, "Felt. I love him in a different way now. And, no." He flattens his palm against hers. "He never mentioned Corvus, but it was easy to figure he was mixed up in a bad relationship. He's been gun-shy as long as I've known him."

Ocean considers Hurakan's hand in hers again. "Hurakan," she says as she pulls her hand away. "Maybe you deserve to be on the better part of an unequal exchange for once."

Hurakan laughs softly. "But not with you, is that what you're saying?" His fingers reach out for her hand again. "Don't worry about me, Ocean. I'll ask you again, does this bother you?"

Again, she considers his fingers against her skin. It sparks nothing in her. She wonders if she could make herself feel something.

"No," she says.

"Well, I find it comforting. We'll leave it at that." He moves on casually. "You know, when Phoenix and I first started this . . ." He waves a hand vaguely. "He asked me to take someone out. And I said, 'Yeah sure, how should I kill him?' Because that's what I do, Ocean, what I'm good at, and I figured that's why he wanted to pair up with me."

It had crossed her mind, the idea they would want her because her sordid past fit in with their ways. But that was before the run-in on Mercury, before she saw the two of them working together.

"And then?"

"He laughed." Hurakan tries for a chuckle, but it doesn't quite form. "Because he was setting me up on a date. He wanted me to scope out this guy, see if he'd fit our team." He lifts their entwined hands and his breath ghosts over their fingers, but she's more focused on his words. "Phoenix has been teaching me the worth of changing a little at a time. Of changing others too. If he was able to teach me that, then I wonder what he could do with you."

Ocean's had a gun pointed at Hurakan's head before, and Phoenix's. And yet, the two of them have trusted her implicitly. Phoenix even trusted her enough to move the barrel of her gun to his forehead.

"I wonder that too," she says.

Hurakan releases her hand then and rises to his feet. "You'd go to the ends of the solar for Teophilus," he says. "I think everyone knows that. But what about after that, Ocean?"

"Are you recruiting me, Hurakan?" she asks.

"Always, Ocean." He taps his bicep. "Thanks for picking up on this. I think we made a good team in the hangar today, yeah?"

Ocean puts a hand to her chest, rubs against the pang there. "Yeah," she says softly.

His smile is the glittering curve of a knife's edge before he reaches out and brushes her ear. "Why haven't you asked for your earring back?"

That takes a moment. She feels her left earlobe, which is still bare. "I don't mind that you have it," she says. "You're keeping it safe."

His hand goes to his ear, a shape moving in the darkness like Peter Pan's shadow wreaking mischief on its own. She can't see it, but she knows the wing earring there is the pair to the one in her right ear.

"I'm glad we match," he says. "Should I get you a new earring? We could get another matching set. Or I could get us matching rings?" Ocean only stares at him flatly, and he laughs. "Just a joke, Ocean. Nongdam. Like you said, I know my limits. And . . . I've had way too much to drink for tonight. Any more and I'll need to sleep on the roof. I'll help you down through your window."

When she's back in her room, his head hangs upside down in the window again.

"Lupus picked the movie for tonight, so it'll probably be old. Just warning you."

"You're not going?"

"No," he replies. "But you should. Von's worried about you."

That's another conversation she needs to have. And soon.

"I think I will."

When she's at the door, though, he speaks up. "The roof's always a good place to come clear your head, Ocean. If you ever need it again, I'm willing to share."

When she turns back to the window, he's already gone.

EIGHT

THE DRUM BEATS and Haven places his heel down. The drum beats again, and a wailing piri picks up the tune. Haven flicks up his wrist and the jijun flutters. As he waves it to the side, the strips of hanji rustle in the air and he continues his steps, moving always in a circle. The movements are usually improvised, but the circle remains the most important part of the Korean shamanistic dance, representing the cyclical nature of birth, death, and rebirth.

The ssitkimkut is a purifying shamanic ritual, meant to cleanse the recently deceased and to comfort the living. Traditionally, it is led by women, but then again, traditionally, it was led by Koreans. Instead, Mortemians surround him, each playing a role. To his right, the drummer's arm lifts, showing off an overlay of feathers inked on his forearm. Next to him, Farah sings out, leading a lament for those close to the deceased, praying for his safe journey. She has her neck tattooed, like Haven's father. But while his father has the white and brown feathers of a Himalayan vulture, she has the white feathers etched over a black backdrop that stretches up to her jaw, emulating a slender-billed vulture.

Haven spreads the jijun with one arm. The paper object represents money offered for passage to the underworld. Haven hops up on one foot. He has always loved dancing. The combination of the purely physical—this, the sweat tracing a path down his face; this, the slide of his toe on the ground; this, the strain of his muscles as he stretches out to the sky—with the intangible—this, his heart soaring up to the heavens; this, the grief that stamps his foot down to the pounding of the drum and the heaviness of the singing; this, a feeling of being made clean in a way he never experiences anywhere else. And this, this ritual that coalesces the physical and spiritual.

The Mortemian behind him draws a bow across the strings of the kayakeum. Haven's momentarily distracted from his spin when beyond him, he recognizes the flowing green robes, the translucent black hat. Seonbi Park sits on the side, stone-faced.

The song ends and Haven exits the stage as another Mortemian takes his place in the middle. The Mortemians who serve Artemis are trained to perform the traditional Korean funeral rites, and although on Prometheus they ascribe to sky burials, the ssitkimkut is one of the practices that Haven's well versed in. Farah perhaps took that for granted, given his father's affinity for the Alliance.

Fortunately, his father had called ahead at Dunian, because his arrival at the small Mortemian commune caused no small amount of concern at first, given his appearance, even after or especially since he explained that he hailed from Prometheus. But Farah is an old friend of his father's.

Haven winds down the side path behind the shrine to take his break. As he grabs a water bottle from the table, someone speaks in Korean behind him. When he turns around, the friendliness on the woman's face dissolves.

"Ah," she says in Common. "So you are a Mortemian, after all."

He supposes that from behind he could pass as a Korean. The woman doesn't elaborate, but Haven's well acquainted with the look-over she gives him. He lets it glance through him even if his insides want to coil up, like he did when he first shook hands with Farah and wondered if she also felt the stark difference of their skin tones against each other.

Haven bows his head. "My name's Haven Sasani. I am visiting the Mortemian commune here from Prometheus. Farah, their leader, asked me to take part in today's rites." A group of them had traveled from Dunian to perform this funeral for the deceased and his family.

She starts. "Haven . . . are you . . ." She draws forward, but then halts. Better to keep a well-defined distance. She drops her voice. "Did you come here with the *Pandia*?"

"How—" Haven bites his tongue.

The woman's red lips spread into a wide smile. "My name's Jang Yeonghui. But how strange that I didn't see you with the others a few nights ago?"

Haven bows again. "Thank you for taking in . . ." He stops there and he's glad he's still facing the ground. ". . . my colleagues," he finishes before straightening. "Are they . . . settling in well?"

"Quite well, I should think," she says offhandedly, managing to both answer his question and to leave him extremely dissatisfied.

He clears his throat. "Are you here to pay your respects to Lee Taekwan?"

"Yes, his family is connected to mine. His mother is beside herself," she says, but before Haven can offer any condolences, she adds, "although I suppose you're connected with him as well." She waits demurely, but when he doesn't prompt her, she lowers her voice again. "Did you not recognize him?"

"I did not prepare the body," Haven says politely. "That wasn't my role today."

"He was a part of the guard for the Seonbi," she says. "But the last time you saw him, he was attempting to take the life of our mutual friend."

Haven remembers the knife flashing in the air, the screams, but more than that, the way Yoon had pulled out her gun so naturally. He brings his attention back to Jang. The last time Haven had seen Lee, the man was being dragged away by the other guards.

"I didn't realize—" he starts to say.

"That he had died? I was rather surprised at the news," she says. "Last I heard, he was being questioned by Seonbi Park."

Ssitkimkut are usually performed when someone dies before they are ready to accept their death. All he had been told was that this Seonbi guard died while in service.

"But I guess you know as little as the family does," she says. "What's the point of this ritual," she asks, "if it's performative?"

"Performative?" he repeats.

"Do you know what I like about Artemis?" she asks. "There aren't any cuckoo birds."

He's lost the thread somewhere and has an urge to repeat her words again, to clarify. He clamps down on it.

"Artemis has many carefully fostered flora and fauna, selected by the Korean government. Some of it had to do with maintaining an ecological balance. Some of it had to do with what's essential to Korea. Do you follow?" When Haven doesn't answer, Jang lifts an elegant finger. "Like the cicadas. Do you think you can properly call it a Korean summer if you can't hear them?"

Haven shrugs. Not that it matters what he thinks.

"They introduced many birds too. But not the great spotted cuckoo. That bird was accidentally introduced to Korea centuries ago, along with many of its ilk. It's a brood parasite bird. Do you know what that means?"

This time when he doesn't answer, she wrinkles her forehead. "Do you?"

As if she expected him to willingly play along with what can only be a lead-up to an elaborate insult. "I assumed it was a rhetorical question," he says.

"It lays its eggs in the nest of another bird. And then that bird unwittingly takes care of it, raises it as its own, neglecting its own offspring. This ugly bird that's nothing like its parents."

Who have you been talking to? he wants to ask. Or she could just be referring to him in this outfit, having finished his dance as a Mortemian taking on the rituals of Korean shamans from centuries past.

"In the last century, they became an invasive species. They were endangering Korean birds." Jang shades her face as she raises it to the sky. "It's a relief not to have to worry about those disgusting creatures here."

He's relieved to see Farah approaching them. He bows his head at Jang. "Excuse me."

"You will tell the *Pandia*, won't you?"

About the birds? But even if Haven would have verbalized the retort, he doesn't have a chance to because Jang has left by the time he raises his head again. He picks up another water bottle and presents it to Farah.

"You did well," Farah says. "Your father was right; you're a beautiful dancer."

"Thank you for allowing me to join you," he says. As he sips from his bottle, he squints at the sidelines. He can't see where Jang went, but he spots Diplomat Park again.

"Have you been at Artemis long?" he asks her.

"Almost eight years now."

Haven inspects the path they came down, the flicker of movement onstage. "A Korean just asked what the point of our ritual was; she called it performance art." As soon as he says it, his rudeness becomes clear. "I didn't mean to imply I agreed with her."

"I can see why an outsider would think that."

Haven's not sure if she's talking about him or Jang.

"I admit it can be constricting here. More so than anywhere else I've served," Farah says. "We remain mostly among our small community even if we are technically free to go in and out. People see us as shrouded in death wherever we are. Those who call on us aren't able to separate us from their grief. They associate us with their loved ones' deaths."

"Why do you stay?" Haven asks carefully.

"Because as you know, what we do has value," Farah says, sipping her water. "And I do not determine my worth on how outsiders view us. In the Bible, whenever angels descended from the heavens, they always said, 'Fear not.' People fear what they do not comprehend, and they deride anything different, even if it is set above them."

"I always thought it meant angels were surpassingly ugly to the human eye," Haven says.

"My point," Farah replies. "What do humans know? It is not so different anywhere else in the solar. Some people merely hide their disdain better. But we are meant to be set apart from them." She leans back on the counter and taps the base of her throat. "One look and they know who I am, Haven. But what about you? Why do you hide your feathers?"

"I'm not *hiding* them," Haven says.

"Are you so ashamed to be one of us? Is this existence too poor for you?"

"I would never turn my back on what has been given to me, on who I am." To his shame, his words shake.

Even though it was years ago now, he can clearly hear his mother saying *"This isn't the life I wanted."* He can barely picture her face, but the despair mixed with the repugnance in her tone will never fade from his memory. And is that how others see him now? His father had pushed and pushed him to go to the Alliance, and Haven had only joined to prove that he'd return, that nothing could change his mind about the future.

"I thought you were different from your father, Haven," Farah says.

He has, countless times, thought while talking to his father, *I'm not like you.* Haven would never go to the Alliance, fall hopelessly in love, be so foolish as to think she could accept him as he was.

But all his life, if he's being honest, he has wanted to prove *I'm not like* her.

"I'm Mortemian," he says sharply, and he's about to continue, but the softness in her eyes surprises him.

"We're Mortemian," she says. "It's a good life, Haven."

"I know that," he says. "This is the life I want."

"Then why do you seem so dissatisfied?"

You're reading me wrong, he wants to say, but the words get stuck in his throat.

"We serve Koreans here, as we have learned to serve the rest of the solar, despite their disgust of us. You shouldn't waste your energy or your heart seeking acceptance from them."

But Haven knows that's not true, because he's tasted the tea that Kent made for him. He's sat with—been trapped by—Thierry while she went on a tangent about some obscure symphony as she cooked. And he's shared a drink with Yoon, passing a lychee soda can back and forth with her while, for reasons other than disgust, they were both painfully aware of the surface that their lips shared.

"I'm grateful for your help, but perhaps you've done enough for today," Farah says.

"But I have work to do," he protests. The music, the dancing, and the eating together for a ssitkimkut usually goes for hours and hours. They're far from done.

"It might be good for you to return to Dunian. Step back from this and use that time to reflect." She opens a receptacle by the path with the press of a button and deposits her water bottle. "You should never be with people who treat you as lesser."

They agree on that at least, but Farah probably doesn't think they do.

NINE

WHAT DO WE *owe our parents?*
  The thought crosses Dae's mind almost every time she talks with her moms, and certainly came when she was on the call with Ocean's umma crying about how Ocean didn't even turn on video, how Ocean had hung up on her, how she just wanted Ocean to be safe after what happened with Hajoon.

  It was still a much easier call than the first one she made to her ummas. She had tried to tell them that the ship was *gone*. All the money they had put into the *Ohneul*, into *her*, blown into pieces. But one mother babbled "Thank God, Hananeem gamsahaeyo" as if God had anything to do with them still being alive. Her other mother was already talking about Dae's next steps, how to get back on her feet.

  Not for the first time, Dae had thought *What if I had just stayed dead?* as that yoke of responsibility weighed down on her. What if she had just pretended she had blown up with the ship? And then she had hated herself all over again.

That morning, Dae contacted the Alliance for the first time since the *Ohneul* exploded. The talk was brief, but Dae will be expected to give a full debrief on return. She's good at peppering a mostly true report with multiple omissions to work in her favor. The Alliance is recognizing her for outstanding leadership in the face of unforeseen and extraordinary events. She kept her crew alive and they're going to be delivered home. She almost laughed when they told her.

They're planning on a medal ceremony when she comes back. She hasn't called her moms to tell them that bit, but they might have been informed by the Alliance already. They're going to award her for a lie, for captaining a crew that never wanted her in the first place.

Dae hesitates at the doors to the back patio, next to the bustling kitchen. The architecture, like most of what's found in Artemis, is a mixture of old and new, like how the doors are traditional hanji screens that slide open electronically with a touch to the palm panels. The bedroom Dae chose has a huge walk-in closet whose doors open at her approach to convey its assembled layers of designer shoes, impressive not just in the sheer amount but because they rotate through a top display row encased in glass before a belt delivers them through a line that regularly deodorizes and dusts them, ready for whenever Yeonghui's family decide to visit this particular vacation estate. And even as Dae marveled at the UV sanitizer that ran over the shoes, she had thought about how some people are born to so much only to waste it so thoughtlessly.

Ocean's perched up on the rail outside. Dae knows already how this talk will go, but she owes it to Ocean's umma to try, doesn't she? She owes it to Hajoon oppa.

Dae walks out and leans against the railing next to Ocean, who makes as if to move away. And that's really what does it. Ocean has way too much noonchi to not get that Dae came out here to talk with her. She just doesn't care. A percolating mess is jammed inside Dae. She pulls out her trump card and plops it down between them.

The red apple has yellow freckles and rocks a little from the force of Dae's definitive placement. Ocean looks blankly at the apple, then does hop down from her seat to walk off.

Dae says quickly, "Hajoon oppa talked about you a lot, you know."

That stops Ocean in her tracks.

Dae had been a wangtta for years at Horangi, had gotten used to being a social outcast. But then at her first assignment, Hajoon oppa had been the XO of the ship. He had been the first person to include Dae, naturally folding her into his circle. And it was true; he talked about Ocean all the time. And Dae had thought how lucky this girl was to have such a kind, funny brother looking out for her. A brother who obviously cared about her so deeply.

Born close to a decade before her, Hajoon had said he'd been too much older for them to really argue. But when she was three or four years old, Ocean had been angry at him for some reason or another. Their mother said she needed to apologize, telling her "Sagwa hae."

And being the little kid she was, she brought an apple to her brother. She'd mixed sagwa with 사과, since apology and apple are spelled and sound the same in Korean. She hadn't understood why he burst out laughing, but he took it anyway, wrapping her up in a huge hug after he chomped an enormous bite out of it. For years after, he said that if either of them ever disagreed, they'd leave each other apples as peace offerings. Eating it meant you accepted the apology.

Ocean turns back. "What are you trying to do?"

Dae swallows hard. "I came to his funeral. I met you there. Do you remember that?" Ocean doesn't answer her, but Dae can picture Ocean's stiff face. Her parents had collapsed, wailing and crying, but Ocean just stood rigid. "I didn't know you joined the Alliance until after the *Hadouken* incident. And I thought I'd help Hajoon oppa's dongsaeng."

When she had taken in Ocean, she hoped she could become Ocean's unni in the way that Hajoon had become her oppa. She'd have someone to look up to her, someone she could open the way for. But Ocean was nothing like the beloved younger sister in Hajoon's stories. And somehow having Ocean around only amplified Dae's lack. How Ocean settled into the controls with an ease that Dae would never relate to. How when they were on Sinis-x, everyone rallied around Ocean instead of Dae. How when Dae stood in the *Pandia* watching the *Ohneul* blow apart before her eyes, only Von had been in the cockpit with her.

"But . . ." Dae hears the bewilderment seep into her voice. "You're nothing like him."

Ocean has gone still. "Are you done?"

Is that all this comes down to? Dae wants to ask that—after Dae hired Ocean when no one would, after all the years that Ocean has been her XO?

"Are we *done*?" Dae repeats. "Is it so easy for you to walk away?" Ocean doesn't answer that. She always goes eerily quiet whenever Dae's trying to talk to her about anything important. "Your umma called me last night."

Ask a Korean *What do we owe our parents?* and the answer is always *Everything*. Dae came into the world in debt. So what if she'd never wanted to the join the Alliance, be a captain? These were her non-options to honor her parents. Her mothers had worked so hard in the Alliance so that they could pass that legacy on to their child. And what was Dae supposed to say to them? *No, thanks, umma. I'd rather become a dentist.*

Any anger she might have felt was ungrateful, had to be swallowed down. You don't say certain things, and you especially don't say them to your parents who have raised you and given you everything you have.

But ask Ocean that same question: *What do we owe our parents?* And what would she care?

"She called *you*?" Ocean asks sharply.

"Of course she did! Because *you* told your parents you weren't going back home and you didn't even tell them why, even though you're their only child now! What were they supposed to do? Are you seriously getting involved with this Teophilus Anand madness?"

Ocean shakes her head, not in answer but to negate Dae's last sentence. "Teophilus Anand madness?"

"You're going to get yourself killed," Dae says. "We have a chance to walk away from all this. But instead of going *home* to your *family*, you're what, taking Teophilus's side and joining some raiders?"

"He's my *best friend*, Dae," Ocean says.

As if Ocean's capable of that. As if this isn't some sort of ploy—one that Dae admittedly hasn't put together, but something obviously for personal gain when it involves the last remaining Anand.

"They're your *family*, Ocean!" Dae says.

TEO'S DURUMI

"You think we should ignore what's happening here?" Ocean asks. "When we know that they're going after Teo, and next, the Alliance?"

Dae laughs. Where does Ocean get off trying to sound noble? "I don't know anything about that," she says. "You've made yourself out to be some sort of hero. But what can you possibly hope to do, Ocean? You're just one small person. But you're more than that to your parents."

Ocean hides her face with her hand. That simmering anger rising in Dae tastes so familiar. She's used to stifling it, but Ocean's just shutting her out, like she's shutting out the truth. She's always been that selfish. Dropping out of Sav-Faire after her parents saved up the money to send her there. Enrolling in flight school right after Hajoon died as a pilot. And now, this.

"You think Hajoon oppa would have made this choice?"

"I don't know," Ocean says.

There's a hitched breath in Ocean's answer, but the words are already pouring out of Dae like lava. "You have a duty, Ocean. As a decent person. As a daughter, a sister, and as an XO." What's made Ocean this way? Was it all those years at Sav-Faire? Was it the fact that Hajoon oppa died so long ago, and Ocean never got to experience that kindness in her life? Dae wants to feel bad for Ocean, but she's just overwhelmed with grief at Hajoon oppa's death. "He would be so sad," Dae says. "If he could see you right now." Dae's mediocre at everything. Including this. How could she ever have expected to take Hajoon's place in Ocean's life, to somehow fill that void? "God, I wish he had never died. I wish—"

And then Dae finally sees that Ocean's face is white as a sheet. It stems up her rush of words. A long silence stretches out between them.

"I wish it had been me too," Ocean says. "Thank you, Captain. For finally being honest with me."

Ocean turns on her heel and walks to the patio door. Before she has a chance to slap her hands to the panel, though, the hanji double doors part. Maggie stumbles out.

"Ocean!" she yells, grabbing her by the shoulders.

"What is it?"

Dae could spit out the bitter bile in her mouth. A distressed Maggie was so desperately searching for Ocean. And Ocean immediately answered her.

"It's Von," Maggie says. "He's gone."

TEN

"THE AIR SMELLS different here." Teo sinks into the seat, removing his hat and peeling off the prosthetic facial hair. He scratches all along his chin and up the sides of his face.

Diplomat Park watches from behind his desk with some amusement. "I'm surprised you didn't go for a fake nose."

"My nose is already large enough," Teo says. "Plus, I've tried the rubber ones before. My skin always breaks out."

Maggie was, unsurprisingly, talented at applying makeup and prosthetics. She had done it happily without asking for explanation, only prattling on about her stint as a grip for a low-budget serial. He had been fairly certain she wouldn't ask him questions, but he was equally certain that if given the opportunity, she wouldn't think twice about tattling on him.

"Thank you for indulging my request you come alone. But next time you should do something about your hair. To anyone with a discerning eye, that's an expensive cut."

Teo resists touching it, certain that's just Park's way of handing out a compliment and insult with one thrust. Diplomat Park could have come to the estate, but Park isn't the type of person to come at one's beck and call, now, is he? Instead, in response to Teo's query, he'd merely sent the seowon's address and an appointment time.

Teo's never had trouble slipping out undetected, but he gave himself a buffer so he could trace a roundabout route to the Artemis seowon, and he'd considered if getting in was another test of Park's. While he was contemplating whether he would be desecrating a Korean institution by scrabbling up the back stone wall, a Seonbi had merely opened the gate to lead him down the dirt path, through the perfectly manicured grounds to Park's office.

"You mentioned the air?" Park asks. "It's probably because you're smelling what Korea was like a few hundred years ago. Prior to its sanitized and filtered condition. Ironically, Artemis achieved this past stage of Korea's heritage by utilizing state-of-the-art technology. Your family's technology."

A knock comes from the door. Park kneels before it, touching a panel on the wall. A pair of hands pushes in a tray with two glasses.

Wide windows stretch to Teo's left, providing a view to a private inner courtyard with a pine tree that's probably close to a century old. Books fill the rows of shelves behind Park's desk. Physical records are a luxury that not very many afford themselves in this day and age. Teo tests the yellow flooring covertly. It must be traditional hanji floors as well.

Back at the desk, Park places one of two cups in front of Teo. The glass is already sweating. The room is a bare respite from the steadily rising temperature outside. Ice cubes cluster in the drink, along with slices of a green plum. Teo wants to press the glass to his face, but settles for taking a sip of the maeshilcha.

"You're not going to ask me to test your drink for you?" Park asks.

"The thought occurred to me," Teo says. "But what use would you have in poisoning me or in putting me to sleep? You had a chance to detain me before. Plus, what guarantee would I have that because you tested it, it's jake? You could have an immunity to what's in there or you could slip something in from your tongue while you test it."

"You've already considered all that?" Park smiles over the rim of his glass.

A drink is never just a drink when you're talking with a Diplomat. Just like a talk about wine vintage is rarely just about wine vintage.

"I told you I had a few threads to follow here on Artemis," Teo says.

"And I'm one of them? How flattering."

Round two. But it was easiest for Teo to start here.

"My father said the Seonbi helped him at an important juncture in his life," Teo says. "He didn't say how or why, but he always spoke highly of your people."

"He would have," Park says. "After I met with you, I inquired around. His involvement with the Seonbi and their influence on him is well known here, even if it's kept quiet elsewhere."

Park places his cup down. He picks up a fan and waves it languorously, the gusts causing the string of beads hanging down from his hat to sway. Teo has to keep from leaning forward to catch a whisp of the breeze.

"Why would it be kept quiet?" Teo asks slowly.

Park closes his fan with a snap, making Teo all the more aware of how the air smothers him. "You're familiar with the Penelope Mine incident?"

"Apparently not as much as I should be," Teo says.

"Tell me what you know."

Park's patronizing manner scrapes at Teo like a pumice stone against a heel.

"My father pushed Mercury's mines to produce so he could win the Alliance contract. The mine collapse at Penelope happened because he pushed them too far."

"People died," Park says. "It was passed off as a horrible accident, but Mercurians knew who was at fault. I think it'd be reason enough for any of them to hate him." Park sips his drink. "To hate you, by extension."

All Mercurians *should* hate him. Except Phoenix took a knife for him yesterday.

"The guilt killed your father. He came here as a retreat. For counsel. It's one of the few places in the solar where you can get away from the constant barrage of the outside world."

"He came for counsel?" His father had been away for business so often when Teo was young, he doesn't think it would have registered if he had fled to Artemis.

"You're not the first Anand to come to Artemis seeking atonement," Park says. "The Penelope Mines opened your father's eyes to how terraforming could be used for the worst. It wasn't about humanity traveling among the stars and furthering civilization. It was about how a group of people could be transplanted to a planet and worked to death to exploit its resources."

Teo's sweating so much, he can't even remember ever feeling dry. Park, on the other hand, is as cool as if ice water runs through his veins, even underneath the layers of his hanbok and vest.

"I don't follow," Teo says.

"What would you say your father's most important ethos was?"

"Sustainable space. Anand Tech got its start in terraforming, but . . ." Teo pauses when Park nods. "He shifted gears after Penelope."

"It became very important to him that terraforming wasn't the future of space travel. But to ensure that he needed political power. And to attain that he needed capital. And for that . . ."

"So he kept mining in Mercury for that capital?" Teo asks, a sour taste in his mouth. "Even after Penelope?"

"Speaking now as a Diplomat rather than a Seonbi, I believe he thought the smaller sacrifice was necessary for a larger goal."

"Smaller sacrifice? Is that how he saw Mercury?"

"Trees are all the same to someone considering the larger forest."

"Maybe I really am lacking, because this . . . I don't understand this," Teo says. "This is the conclusion he came to here? This is how the Seonbi thought he should atone?"

"Well . . ." Park smooths his eyebrow with the crook of his thumb. "Seonbi have many tenets, and one of them is the disavowal of power. From what I hear, they tried to lead him down a different path, but your father . . . His guilt was a siren call. Like so many powerful people who come to the Seonbi for guidance, he selectively picked what he wanted to hear. Above all, I think he wanted to absolve himself."

"But atonement shouldn't be about our own guilt," Teo says bitterly. "It should be about those we've wronged, shouldn't it?"

"Ah, well . . . he wouldn't be the first powerful person who convinced himself he had altruistic aims even when he was serving selfish desires. I can see how he might have twisted himself into believing this was the path of integrity."

"How?" Teo bites out the word.

"He was well aware of what he was doing to Mercury. How could he not be, when Penelope affected him so much? Perhaps he thought he was taking on those sins to create a better future. He believed terraforming should be stopped, at all costs."

"At all costs." That's never a good thing to say, even when it comes from someone with a concrete grasp of value like his father had.

"Or perhaps not. I'm not here to make excuses for your father. That's more your duty, as his son."

"What if I don't want to make excuses for him?" Teo asks. "What if I want to blame him?"

"Then that's your right as well, as his son." Park unties his black heungnip, removing it from his head to place on the desk.

How much of Teo wants to let this go, to let his father's sins die with him, to run off somewhere where no one will recognize him?

"You've been helpful," Teo tells Park. He'll have to sort out exactly how helpful later.

Park swirls his cup so the partially melted ice cubes clink together. "I so like to be helpful," he says sardonically.

Teo pulls out a roll of glue from his pocket. "Do you have a mirror on hand?"

"What do you take me for?" Park rises from his seat to go to a closet on the side of the room. The door swings open to a floor-length mirror. "Have at it."

"With pleasure," Teo says. As he reapplies his beard, he comments offhandedly, "You know, now that I've met you, Ocean's steadies at the Alliance make a lot more sense."

"How's that?" Park asks, amused. "Were they very different from me?"

"They were a lot simpler," Teo says. He wouldn't say that Ocean has *chosen* her steadies, but more that she's let them happen. "Do you know a good seamstress?" he asks casually. "Preferably someone who works fast. And is discreet."

"All my contacts are discreet."

"Of course they are."

Park's comm rings on the desk and he frowns as he picks it up. "Speak of the devil," he says before putting in his earbud. "How'd you get this number?"

Something in his face shifts, though not in a way Teo can pinpoint. Park glances at Teo before he waves his hand over a device on his desk. In the next moment, Ocean's voice comes through.

"Joonho, I need a favor."

• • • • •

"Did you know it was me? On the video comm, when you were flying into Artemis?"

Joonho isn't looking at Ocean when he asks. The air outside is sweltering, but he looks as cool as a persimmon slice. The wide brim of his heungnip shades his face.

Ocean kneels as she squints off to where he's scanning. "I was a little preoccupied," she says. "So, no."

Joonho motions to her. They flatten against the building as he signals with a fist. Across the street from them, guards scurry down the alleyway. "Did you know I was stationed here?" he asks. "At Artemis."

They're waiting in the shade, but even this late in the day, the air wavers as if they're positioned over the coils of an oven. That's bad enough, but Ocean feels a suffocating, clawing in her chest. She doesn't want to make small talk when she has no idea where Von might be. Maybe he's just lost, or maybe he's seriously hurt, or . . .

"No," Ocean says. "I didn't keep in touch with anyone from school."

Joonho narrows his eyes at her. He reaches into one of his sleeves and pulls out a water bottle. "Here."

She turns it down, keeping her ears and eyes perked. "I'm good."

"You should stay hydrated. You're not used to how hot it gets in the summer here. It's just like Korea."

This does bring Ocean's attention back to Joonho; he's studying her. She shakes her head. "I don't share a drink with just anyone."

Joonho's comm beeps. Ocean tenses, but the message just comes through: "All clear."

"Let's move on to the next quadrant," Joonho says.

They've split up to comb Artemis. Teo, under stringent protest, is back at Yeonghui's mansion with Maggie and Lupus, searching the grounds there in case. Lupus had offered to tap into any CCTV feeds, but Artemis is one of the few cities in the solar that has a noticeable lack of public surveillance, all in line with its desire to maintain an ascetic, traditional environment. Phoenix and Cass are with another retinue of Joonho's guards, and Hurakan, Aries, and Dae are with yet another set.

Joonho moves on swiftly, murmuring directions into his comm. He beckons Ocean onward.

"I wouldn't expect you to put yourself on the line for someone else," Joonho says as he leads her. "Who is he?"

"Von Kent. Xenobotanist on contract for the Alliance," Ocean says, although she's sure Joonho's seen the file. He probably knows more details about Von's life than Ocean does.

Joonho's shoulders tighten. For a few moments, the stones crunch beneath their shoes.

"But . . . he's engaged?" he finally ventures.

"Yes."

They're not in Sav-Faire anymore. If he wants an actual answer, he can ask an actual question. But even as Ocean thinks that, guilt creeps into her. When she called Joonho, he hadn't said *Are you sure?* or *He's probably fine*, but had reacted swiftly and methodically.

Ocean shields her eyes as she checks the sun's position in the sky. It's already lowered itself in preparation to kiss the horizon. They don't know how long Von's been missing. But no one remembers seeing him after last night's movie. Ocean could rack her brain with *I should have checked on him earlier* or *This is my fault* and each insistence could be as true as it is useless. But a tide is rising against her every time she pushes those thoughts down.

"This . . . Von. He followed you from the *Hadouken*?"

"I told him not to," Ocean says to Joonho's back. "He could have done his research anywhere. But he said that he'd already told Sumi she didn't have to worry about him. Because he was safe with me."

When she lowers her hand, her eyes gather tears. She angrily swipes away at them. This damn *sun*. Another beep sounds, this time from her own comm. She jabs her wrist and a video of Phoenix pops up.

"Any luck?" he asks.

"Nothing yet." Her chest hitches when she says it.

"Don't worry," he says. "We'll find him."

The video closes up and they keep trudging in silence. The process is laborious. They are canvassing every building whether it is inhabited or empty.

"He's different from what I'd imagined," Joonho remarks. "This Phoenix."

"I think he'd be rather gratified to hear that," Ocean says.

Joonho halts them when they get to another street, this one lined with shops and restaurants. He gestures to a row of hangari lined up next to the wall, and Ocean perches on one of the black earthenware jars with a silent apology for whatever might be held in there. The fatigue practically clobbers her, and she lets her eyes slide closed for a moment as she pictures what the cool dark interiors might hold, a paste dense with flavor like gochujang or a makgeolli that has sediment settled on the bottom. Von loves the sweet effervescence of makgeolli.

"Thank you," she says.

"I haven't done anything yet," Joonho says tiredly. "And really, it's becoming more trouble than it's worth to keep a lid on all of you."

"That's not true. Not the first part at least," she says. "And thank you for letting my crew help."

"Your crew," Joonho muses.

Ocean keeps her eyes closed. A drop of sweat slides down her back. Another one trickles down her temple. She should gather her strength so she can call upon it if she needs it. When she needs it.

"Well," Joonho says, an odd tone in his voice. "I never thought you'd ask me for help."

ELEVEN

THE DRIPPING SOUND is what wakes Von. He rolls over on his side and inhales the smell of moist dirt. His body aches all over. Did he fall asleep on the greenhouse cot again? It's *far* too cold for the plants. His eyes fly open.

It's too dark to be the greenhouse. He sits up and rubs his arms. He can't identify where the dripping is coming from, but the gristly floor is damp. He scans the room and nearly jumps out of his skin when he spots a woman sitting against the door.

"Oh hello," he says brightly. "I'm sorry, you startled me."

The woman is bent over something in her lap. She has black hair, or at least it appears so. It's difficult to see in the dim lighting.

Von clears his throat. He doesn't want to be rude, but . . . "Can you tell me where we are? I . . . don't remember how I got here."

Or much else, really. He puts a hand to his head. *Ow.* No windows, and no other door except the one that the woman is in front of. A single, ominous light bulb hangs from the ceiling.

"I say," he ventures. "This is . . . rather sinister." Then he bites his tongue. What if this is this woman's *home*?

The woman raises her chin, and he freezes. But she only smiles at him. Von relaxes and manages to smile back, while trying to tell himself that the woman's expression only seems menacing because they're in a dank *but otherwise perfectly fine* room.

"I don't think I got your name," he says.

Then the woman shows off the object she was rotating in her lap. The single light bulb throws enough light that it gleams on the reflection of her sharp knife.

"My name's Alessa," she says pleasantly. "And . . . you're Von Kent, aren't you?"

Von wants to scramble backward from her, but he clamps down on that instinct. You don't make sudden movements around unknown animals or people. He opens his mouth to speak, but only a squeak comes out. Alessa's smile spreads.

"I—" Still only a scrape of noise. He swallows and tries again. "Have we met? I'm sorry if I've forgotten."

Alessa laughs. "Marv. You're *terrified*."

Von wants to assure her that he's not, that he's reasonable and he doesn't want to judge the situation until he has all the facts, which he would if only he could remember exactly how . . . Von strains his memory. *Oh*, he had heard rumor of a patch of *Cypripedium japonicum*, which went extinct a century ago and can be found only on the Moon because they repropagated it here. The garden wasn't too far from where they were staying, and when else was he going to get a chance to study it? It had been so beautiful and he'd immediately sat down to take a sketch of it to bring to Sumi, and . . . and . . . then what?

His hand goes to his head again. "Ow." This time he says it aloud.

"Yeah, sorry about that," Alessa says. "You were conked out for longer than I expected. But I wanted you to be awake for this next part."

"Oh . . . oh no," Von whispers.

Alessa laughs again, and Von finally allows himself to hear how awful her utter glee is. Alessa brings the knife to her mouth and licks it. Von shudders.

"You're friends with Teophilus Anand, aren't you?"

It strikes him that he could deny it in this moment. Denounce Teo. Say that Alessa's mistaken somehow.

"Yes," Von manages. His throat is closing up and his breaths are short puffs.

"Well I'm a particularly good friend of Corvus's. Do you happen to know him?" Alessa asks.

This time Von can only nod. Tears gather in his eyes. *Oh no oh no oh no.* He clasps his hands together as if in prayer, but mostly so his ring bites into him. The special leaf edge that Sumi designed for him.

"What are you going to do to me?" he whispers.

"That's a good question," Alessa says. "I'm going to kill you."

Von whimpers. He's never been brave. He's never *had* to be brave.

"But I'm deciding *how* I'm going to do it." She twirls her knife in her hand and it glitters in the light. "I like to draw these encounters out. But this house isn't particularly well insulated, so I can't have you screaming. Are you good at screaming?"

Von sucks in all the air he can into his lungs, ready to show her exactly how good he is at it. But then he's flat on his back, gaping at the light bulb above him. He coughs, and spittle flies from his mouth. Alessa's face gloats over him. He didn't even see her moving.

"Not so fast, Von," Alessa says. "Now—"

A shrill ringing interrupts her. Alessa clicks her tongue and swipes a holographic display over her eyes. She scowls as she steps away from Von. He hurriedly rolls away, but Alessa's hand darts out to grab him by the collar of his shirt, holding him effortlessly.

"Emory, *what*—" Alessa barks into her earpiece and then cuts herself off. She drops Von's collar with a shove. He hits the ground hard. "Corvus."

Her voice is reverent and she paces quickly to the room's door again, her movements as hushed as her voice.

"Yes, Corvus . . ." She gasps and drops to her knees. "You mean it *worked*."

But Von can't afford to concentrate on the bits and pieces of the conversation. He scrambles to the opposite wall from her. His body aches and his head hurts, but he can't stop the skitter of thoughts. His dads his sister and *Sumi*. He just called them to tell them he was alive. What's going to happen to him, what's going to happen to them? He can't put them through this again.

"Help me," he whispers. And then he bangs his fists against the wall. "Help! Ocean!"

It's cement and he can't say whether it will do any good, but he beats his fists bloody. Then his hands are grabbed and jerked roughly behind him.

"Shut up! Shut up, you—No, not you, Corvus. It's—he's one of Anand's. I found him wandering around . . . No, he's not *important*. I was just going to have a little . . ."

Then Von's arms are dropped. He falls.

"Let him go? But, Corvus," Alessa whines. "He even said he's *friends* with Anand! Isn't that enough? You . . ." But then her hand goes up to her ear. "Corvus. Hold on."

Von rotates his head against the floor too. Alessa shoves her foot against his back. "Stop," she hisses.

His chest heaves and he would scream if he could. But Alessa's foot digs into him and he doesn't think he can inhale enough air without her noticing. He wants to, but he keeps seeing the flash of her knife, the flash of her leer. He can't lift his head and his cheek is smashed against the dirt.

Alessa says, "No, I thought I heard—"

Then the door flies open and a body rolls in. Alessa kicks Von back as she leaps forward. Her knife arm is in the air. She hits the bulb overhead and light goes skeetering around.

There's screaming, and yells to "Get down!" Gunshots blaze out and Von curls up into a ball, covering his ears. His dry sobs shake him, and for a moment they fill the chamber he's created with his hands and his head.

Then another voice cuts through the noise.

"Von!"

Von opens his eyes. The swaying light bulb marks a pendulum of shadows. Dust is settling and he blinks as he sits up. Crouched in front of him is Ocean, her face as white as a calla lily petal. She holds up her hands and her gun dangles from her fingers.

Behind her, a passel of guards have crammed into the room. Two of them are down, nursing wounds. Von gags at the sight of blood smeared on their skin. Alessa's nowhere to be found.

"Von, are you jake?"

Von hears Ocean through the ringing in his ears. He blinks at her again and then throws himself at her, bursting into tears. Ocean's arms are around him, her hand is smoothing his back.

"I knew you'd come," he says.

TWELVE

"**You never said** what you were doing here on the Moon," Farah says from the darkness behind Haven.

Farah's coming out the back door of her home, with two ale bottles in hand. She holds one out to Haven and he takes it as she joins him on the low, flat table under the pergola. She left the door open, so that it slants a yellow slice against the grass. It's only been . . . what? A few days, but he's already nestled into this routine. He had just finished mopping and scrubbing down the kitchen before escaping to the backyard. He sits cross-legged on the table. The trellis is overgrown with grape leaves and lights wind through them, dimly illuminating the yard.

Haven thanks Farah as he wipes the sweat from his brow. "I'm visiting, in a manner of speaking." He hasn't been instructed on what exactly to say or not say, he realizes, so he finishes vaguely, "I'm here on Alliance business."

"Oh *Alliance* business," Farah says with a scoff. She dispels any worries Haven had that she might ask for details. "Did your father get you caught up in that?" Distaste distorts her face. "I never understood why he glorified his time with the Koreans so much."

It somehow rubs Haven the wrong way, hearing his own sentiments from Farah. "It was important to him that I see a little of the solar," he says politely. "But I'm eager to go back."

He still hasn't heard from the others about arranged flights, and it wouldn't surprise him if Diplomat Park chose to conveniently forget him. He's reluctant to follow up, but he's caught himself thinking about what snacks Thierry might be preparing. What music Kent is playing as he waters his plants. A yearning flits in his chest and he lets the ache settle there, along with the comforting weight of his assurance to Farah.

"I wanted to apologize," Farah says. "My words to you yesterday were harsher than they needed to be."

"No, I don't think I presented myself well," he says. "I'm sorry to have been a hindrance to your work here rather than an aid."

"Not at all," she says. She glances back at her house. "Thank you for cleaning the kitchen. It was . . . quite thorough."

Haven's always garnered satisfaction in the ritual of cleaning. "My father always said you should never dust half the stairs."

"Yes, that sounds like Masoud." Farah laughs. "Well, to reward you, we'll have an actual home-cooked meal tonight. The last few nights were a little haphazard, but Basim has apparently been preparing a sumptuous meal."

It's been so long since he's had any food that reminded him of home. The thought should warm him, but he thinks instead of that meal with everyone crammed into the *Pandia*'s kitchen, all of them blessing the food in their own ways, all of them sharing space and gratitude. And despite everything, he can't stop from thinking about Yoon perched on the counter next to him, her head bent as she took naan from the plate he was holding, her open, happy face near his.

"Haven?" Farah asks. "Will you eat with us?"

Haven turns the memory away. "Yes. I'd be honored."

The light from her house flickers. Haven follows Farah's gaze back to the house. The hand holding his bottle drops, and he vaguely hears the clunk, barely feels the splash of liquid on his arm.

Yoon's there, leaning against the doorway as if he summoned her with his memory. And there's something unfair about this, that she's such a solid figure, when he knows it's not possible for her to be here. As she walks closer, she should evanesce. But instead, he realizes that she was never gone, not really. Because even though she's back-lit, he knows the fullness of her upper lip that curves over her bottom one. That slight slope to her right shoulder that evinces an old injury. And then she's close enough for him to see her face.

Does she look at everyone like that, as if she's memorizing the curvature of their face, as if she's trying to remember them while they're standing there? It can't be just him, but he wishes it were. When he goes back home, he wants to take that one piece with him, and that's all right, isn't it?

He's standing but he doesn't remember rising. It's just like that first time in the subway, just like that time he saw her in the Coex ballroom. His feet carry him toward her. When she's before him, he reaches for that skin in the way he's imagined so many times: his fingers cupping her face, the thumb brushing over her cheek.

The moment he touches her, though, her lips part in an inhale and he realizes his mistake. He jerks his hand back. His fingertips are burning, but in a completely different way than the hotness racing up the back of his neck.

"XO Yoon," he chokes out as he steps back. He wants to clutch his hand to himself. Farah's stood as well, and she regards him with obvious surprise.

"I'm sorry to interrupt," Yoon says smoothly to Farah. "I was hoping to talk to Sasani?"

"I—I mean, if he . . ." Farah coughs.

"I'm sorry, I didn't introduce myself properly," Yoon says. "My name's Ocean Yoon. I'm a colleague of his."

How ironic that she uses the exact same word he did when he was talking to Jang.

"Farah Oshnavi," Farah says. Something in her face hardened with Yoon's words. "I grew up with Haven's father on Prometheus. Although I lead the Dunian commune now."

"That must be challenging," Yoon says.

"Well, Koreans—" Farah stops herself.

"Yes," Yoon says calmly. "I agree. I apologize on our behalf. But also . . ." She bows her head. "Thank you for what you do."

"Do you understand what we do?" Farah asks warily.

Yoon straightens to meet Farah's gaze. "My brother died a number of years ago," she says. "Mortemians performed the ssitkimkut for us on Marado, off Jeju. I don't . . . I don't remember a lot of that day." She pauses. "But I'm grateful for what I do remember. For what you did for him and my family. For . . ." Yoon trails off and her hand comes up to her face.

"Yes," Farah says.

Haven's chest is tight and he swallows against the hurt in his throat.

Yoon drops her hand from her once-again composed face. "And thank you for taking care of Sasani for us too."

A glow spreads in Haven, although he tucks his chin when Farah glances at him. "We've put him to work. We had him dance the ssitkimkut yesterday."

"I'm sure it was beautiful," Yoon says.

Farah pauses, then asks, "Have you seen him?"

"Not exactly, no," Yoon says. She gives a small smile, more to herself as if in a private joke, and Haven bites his lip. She meets his gaze then. "But I've always thought that Sasani moves like a dancer . . . Or like a bird in flight." She stretches out one arm, and Haven sees an echo of himself in that movement. "It's why your tattoos are on your back, right? Like wings."

Haven rubs the back of his neck. "Yes," he says quietly.

Farah looks back at Haven. "Well," she says. The word has a note of understanding, tinged with something like regret. She nods at him. "I'll leave you to it." She squeezes his shoulder and leaves them.

Haven has to swallow a few times. He's not sure where to look. Tea, he should offer Yoon tea, shouldn't he? But this isn't his house, and he isn't Kent. He still has his bottle in his hand, but it's half finished. And the last time he and Yoon shared a drink . . . His skin prickles at the memory.

"I'm sorry I don't have—" he starts as Yoon speaks too.

"I'm sorry I interrupt—"

They both stop. Haven gestures at the table. "Would you like to take a seat?"

Yoon does so, and Haven sits next to her, making sure to leave a reasonable space between them. He worries the label of his bottle.

"How is everyone?" he asks. "Is Anand holding up?"

"Teo's . . . as well as can be expected," Yoon says. "And as for everyone . . ." She hesitates. "Well, that's why I'm here. Von was kidnapped this morning." Haven jumps to his feet and she puts her hands up. "He's jake! We got him back."

"You mean . . ." And something tells him that this is true. ". . . *you* got him back," Haven says as he takes his seat again.

"Well . . . yes, with some help," she says. "It . . . sounds like the kidnapper is connected to Corvus."

Corvus again. That reminds Haven. "The ssitkimkut I performed," he says, "was for the Seonbi guard who tried to kill Anand."

Yoon's eyes narrow. "He died?"

"I don't know the specifics," Haven says. "But . . . I did hear that he was being interrogated by Diplomat Park."

Yoon frowns. "That's troubling."

As she mulls that over, Haven also turns this new information over in his head. "Was Kent hurt at all?" Haven asks, and a shadow passes over Yoon's face. "What is it?"

Yoon pauses, and then says briskly, "Well, I'm sure he wouldn't mind having you look him over."

Haven goes warm. "Are you . . . You're asking me—"

"I was worried about you."

Haven's stomach jumps and Yoon looks away from him.

"We're worried, I mean. About your safety."

His stomach settles immediately. No, not just settles. It forms a pit.

"Ah," he manages to say.

"I thought it would be better for you to be at the estate with us," Yoon says as she scans the backyard. "Although I'd rather not draw you back into our mess again."

Haven takes a deep breath. This is exactly what he didn't want. He didn't want to get involved in all this. He wanted to return to his father. He didn't want to see Yoon again, and he didn't need to learn how this light curves around her face.

He hears himself say, "Well, if it's dangerous to be out, I should probably go back with you."

"That might be for the best," Yoon says. "At least until we get you on a flight to Saturn." That sobers him as Yoon continues, "I imagine this whole Alliance experience wasn't exactly what you and your father had in mind."

"You could say that," he says with a trace of amusement.

Yoon's staring at his mouth before her eyes flit up to meet his. "I'm sorry to take you away from here," she says. "How has it been for you?"

Confusing, Haven wants to say. But he tilts his face to the sky and thinks of the sweat sliding down his neck the day before. Of the peace that came with his movements. A smile touches his lips. "Some of it has been good." When he lowers his head, he finds Yoon watching him. "What is it?"

"I know you have your challenges," she says. "But you're . . . You're a good person. And you have so much certainty. I don't know what that's like."

"You don't think you're a good person?" he asks.

"Do you?"

Those two words jar him, pain him more than he can say. They look away from each other, and that movement is as familiar as the tightness in his chest. He forces lightness to his next words. "How are we getting back?"

She doesn't answer him right away and when he turns to her, he's surprised to see her grin.

"Sasani, want to go for a ride?"

THIRTEEN

WHAT OCEAN REMEMBERS from her first driving lesson with Hajoon is her sweat-slicked palms. The strain of her tense calf muscles. The catch as her feet shifted on the pedals, one coming down while the other relaxed, as she tried to feel out the right transition moment. And then the sound of the car sputtering and going dead when she got it wrong.

But when she whipped her head to the passenger seat where Hajoon was, he had his elbow up on the ledge of the open window, his fist propping his chin as he considered some far-off object.

"It happens to everyone," he said without looking back at her. "Don't worry about it."

Now, she's more comfortable behind the wheel than anywhere else in the solar, and she has a different passenger altogether, but her hands are sweat-slicked again.

Sasani has the window down as Ocean drives them on the long road from Dunian. He trails a hand out, his fingers fanned. She's thought about those fingers more than she wants to admit: the spread of them when he's speaking, the motion of them in the air when he describes how he dances, how he carefully unwound the entangled wires of his earbuds as he smoothed away her snarl of thoughts. And now, the feel of those fingers brushing her face.

He's always moved with a controlled grace, but he had jerked his hand back when he touched her.

"It's been a while since I've driven manual," she says.

Sasani pulls in and rolls up the window, enclosing them in their own space. When he first got into the car and shut the door, Ocean had thought, irrationally, *No escape.* He's tall; he had to adjust the seat. She's aware of the sprawl of his legs, the way he rests his arms. The sinew of his wrist. How his presence fills the car like a spread of wings. How the smell of sweat mixes with his scent.

Ocean scans the rearview mirror, but there's nothing to see there. Dunian's already long gone, and the edge of Artemis is approaching. The night is pitch black, with the road lights briefly illuminating Sasani's skin as they pass under them, revealing his temple, the hollow of his throat.

"When I went to Sav-Faire, I would come home only once a year. But I'd always go driving with my brother then. First, he used to drive me around. Then, he taught me, and then he let me drive."

Long before she was of legal driving age, and usually late at night when there was less chance of anyone else on the roads. Most places in the solar have automatic cars now, or vehicles where you just punch in your destination and are taken where you need to go on tracks. Teo has clearance that allows him priority in lanes and routes, regardless of heavy traffic.

"And then . . ." Ocean flicks on the turn signal to change lanes even though no one else is on the road with them. The clicking is enlarged here, the blinking light augmented in the darkness. But when she's with Sasani, everything already looms larger, closer. Close enough to understand just how impossible it is to attain.

The dirt road switches onto a smoothly paved one now that they're approaching Artemis. She hears the road beneath the tires change, but she feels the shift in her chest too.

"But there's no use thinking about what if, how life would be different if he were still here," Ocean says.

"We disagree there," Sasani says, but it's gentle. "I don't think it's wrong to think of what could have been. As long as you don't drown in it."

"You don't have any regrets you'd rather sweep under a rug?"

Sasani smooths back his wind-ruffled hair, and from the corner of her eye, Ocean can see the long line of his arm muscles. His black shirt covers his arms up to his elbows, hiding his tattoo. She's seen the extension of his etched feathers before, but she doesn't know where they end, how far they spread across his back. Sometime along the line, she started to hunt for where it might peek out, whether from his sleeve or from the curve of his shirt collar.

"My mother left my father and me when I was quite young," he says. "I look like her, you know. In case you were ever wondering why I don't look like the typical Mortemian from Prometheus."

"The thought crossed my mind," Ocean says.

She hears the slight smile in his voice as he continues, "Well . . . yes, I suppose it did." He lets out a breath. "Sometimes . . . I think I should have tried harder to make her stay. Or at least told her that I wanted her to."

Ocean opens her mouth, then closes it.

"What were you going to say?" Sasani asks.

Ocean winces. "I was going to ask," she says slowly, "whether you did want it. But . . . that can be hard to know."

"Yes," Sasani says. "I . . . don't know if I did or not. It's not just whether a person stays or not. It's how and why they stay too. But even though she left, she remained in other ways. I resented the way my father would look at me and see her. The way other Mortemians would look at me, and see someone other than one of them." Sasani shrugs.

She's missed the stretch of his shrug. Sasani's shrug is a languid gesture like a cat preening in a warm patch of sun. It has more variation, much more meaning than a noncommittal deflection. But then again, Ocean doesn't think Sasani's ever performed a meaningless motion.

"I know a little of what it's like to be looked at as someone else in the wake of an absence." She feels Sasani's sideways glance. "As for the second . . . appearances are overrated." Words were never so easy to express before. They'd done this in Sasani's infirmary on the *Ohneul* and in the *Pandia*'s common room, but she never thought she'd miss it this much. "I don't think I've ever seen you as anyone other than a Mortemian." She slides him a smile only to find him staring at her. Their shared glance is a hot coal inside her. He swiftly looks away.

"In any case," he says, clearing his throat, "it's possible that it was good she left. After all, endings aren't necessarily bad. Maybe she and my father would have only made each other unhappy. And"—Ocean hears the smile in his voice again—"speaking as a Mortemian, well, I don't feel that endings are the end." He hesitates, then says, "You're so happy behind a wheel. I think . . . your brother would have liked that."

"I think so too," she replies.

Ocean meets his dark, fathomless eyes again. He's always regarded her so openly. Even the way he diverts his gaze from her reveals much. Often his expression is too serious, with the downturned corner of his lips, the indent between his brows when he frowns. But now he has that smile that's always just hinted at around his mouth. She follows the line of his jaw up to his ears. Ocean wonders what it would mean to trace the outline of that ear, not just with her hands but with the words remained unspoken until now. Her lips part against her will. Sasani's eyes go to her mouth.

But she closes her throat around the thought and faces forward. She drew the line in the infirmary. Sasani has a fiancée, he has a father to honor, a home to return to, and a future that doesn't involve the kind of death she's wrapped in.

"Yoon?"

One of Ocean's hands is on the wheel, and the other rests on the gearshift, but she's thinking instead of her hands hovering over his skin, of the solid warmth of his shirt if she were to press a palm to his back. But it's fine because Sasani never has to know how she's too aware of his breathing. Of the skim of his gaze on her skin, and the two of them alone in this car.

"You know it's been a few days since we last saw each other?" she says.

Ocean keeps her eyes on the road before them. The car's headlights guide them. Sasani acknowledges her question with a bare scratch of sound.

"It feels like it's been much longer," she says.

• • • • •

"Does this mean we can finally watch the next episode of *Cemetery Venus*?" Maggie asks. "We've been saving it."

Sasani hasn't even stepped over the doorway and he freezes. Despite everything, a grin spreads on Teo's face. Sasani's *back*.

"Oh no," Maggie says dismally. "Did you already watch it with your new friends?"

"New . . . what?" Sasani still has one foot in midair. He's got fantastic balance. "No, no, I'm only surprised you saved it."

"It didn't seem right to go on without you, now did it? Bon, Kim Minwoo says it has one of his favorite scenes he's ever acted, and I'm dying to see! Aren't you curious?"

"I am," Sasani manages, but he's distracted by Gemini, who happens to be walking by.

"All right, Sasani?" he says without turning his head, as if Sasani's come home after a long day at work.

Teo slips in next to him. "Welcome back," he says.

A mess of emotions flickers across Sasani's face, all too quickly for Teo to interpret. "Anand," he says, "I hope you haven't done any crying without me." Teo's grin slips a little, and Sasani's eyes soften. "How's Kent?"

"Sleeping right now," Teo says. "It was . . . it was a lot." Nearly everyone had leaped into action when they realized that Von was missing. Meanwhile, Teo had just been dropped off at Yeonghui's mansion, like a child being brought back home after a playdate. Teo says, "He'll be happy to hear that you're back."

"Have we found out anything more?" Ocean asks as she walks past Sasani into the room, and even if they came in together, Teo notes with interest how Sasani's attention follows her.

"Lupus is on it," Teo says.

"Sasani! You're back!" Cass walks in as she tosses a tangerine up into the air. "You can join our PT tomorrow morning!"

"PT?"

"Gemini says Ocean sucks at throwing and taking punches." Cass jabs a thumb at Ocean.

"Yes, well. He would know," Ocean says mildly.

"He asked me to whip her into shape, but I think everyone should join in."

"She means she wants to show off in front of everyone," Aries says from the couch, and ducks before he's finished speaking, neatly dodging a cuff from Cass.

"It's for your protection!" Cass protests. But then she concedes, "But also, yes."

"Gather round, team." Phoenix strides into the room, ushering in Lupus.

"Team? Are we a team?" Cass scoffs.

"Crew? Comrades? Fam?" Phoenix asks. At that, he notices Sasani. "Sasani! Welcome back to the . . . coalition?" He takes a chair and gestures to Lupus, who as usual is toting their tabula. "Lupus has information for us, but uh . . ." He scrutinizes the group. "Anyone who gets squeamish or would prefer not to get involved should leave the room now."

"Yikes." Maggie's already halfway across the room by the end of Phoenix's sentence.

Sasani hesitates before he says apologetically, "I'll check in on Kent."

Other than the *Pandia* crew, that leaves Ocean and Teo. Teo could have sworn Dae was in the room with them, but she must have slipped out sometime after Ocean came back. The two seem to be more at odds than usual.

"Teophilus . . ." Phoenix bites his thumb. "This might be difficult for you."

"I should see this," Teo says firmly. "It involves me . . . and . . ." The side hallway is dark; its shadows have already swallowed up Sasani. "It's the least I can do now that I've involved everyone else."

That sobers them all, and Gemini speaks up from the other side of the room. "So what do we got, Lupus?"

"I used a program to compose a portrait of Alessa from Von's description. Then I matched that to databases across the net. News reports, arrest records, anything that might garner a hit." They tap their screen and project the display for the room. "No CCTV here on Artemis, as you know."

Teo reads the report aloud. "Alessa Papanikolau. Greek?"

Lupus nods, throwing more displays around the first. A news article. A profile. "Once Von wakes up, we can confirm that this was indeed her. But I'd say it's likely."

"How's that? Does she have a criminal record?" Teo scans all the windows Lupus has populated.

Lupus throws up another screen and hits play.

"—a tragedy here at the Papanikolau household . . ."

The footage goes over to three bodies. Blood, so much blood. And their insides. Teo turns and retches.

"Phoenix warned you," Lupus says placidly.

"*Lupus*," Cass says.

"Sorry. I'm told I need to work on bedside manner," Lupus says. "Anyway, she doesn't have a criminal record. But her family was murdered and no one ever found the culprit. She was the surviving member. Ended up inheriting all the money. It was a lot."

"Wait, I've heard this story before," Cass says.

"You think there's a connection?" Aries asks. "It's . . . I mean . . . that's a gruesome way to inherit . . ."

Teo knows that all too well.

"That's distinctive knifework," Gemini says flatly. "I recognize it."

Ocean's hand is on Teo's back, smoothing it down. But he has to see this. He straightens and stares at the screen Lupus has paused on. He examines it clinically, but a blackness encroaches his vision.

"Is that . . . is that what my family looked like?" he asks faintly.

He's avoided all the footage so far. He doesn't care if it makes him a coward.

"This morning, she did have a knife on her," Ocean says. "She sliced up a couple of Joonho's guards, but I think she was too concerned about escaping to do much damage." She pauses. "That's how we found Portos in Penelope."

Not just stabbed or sliced. Gutted, split open. Teo slams his fist up to his mouth. Someone had been disguised as Teo as they did this to his parents. No, not just someone anymore. Alessa Papanikolau.

"It's Corvus's preferred method," Phoenix says quietly. "He probably taught it to her."

"I need to—I can't—" Teo pushes off Ocean's hands.

A raging ball of misery and fury roils in him. He wants to hurt everyone. He wants to kill Corvus. He wants to make them all suffer. He's stumbling, not sure of where he's going, just that he needs to leave.

Strong arms wrap around him.

"I have you."

No no no. He doesn't want this. Teo beats his fists at Phoenix's arms. He doesn't want this, not from him. Phoenix was *with* Corvus, he loved him, maybe loves him still, but Teo—*Teo's family*—is responsible for Phoenix's parents dying, for Corvus's parents dying. But his amma and his baba. His brother.

Teo's dropped to his knees, but through it all, Phoenix's arms are tight around him.

"I have you, Teophilus."

· · · · ·

Haven doesn't know if he should have stayed in that room. He didn't want to be callous, but at the same time, he wasn't sure he should get any more involved. He flexes his fingers against his knees. Kent stirs in the bed next to his chair. The enormous mansion has ample rooms for everyone, and the one Kent chose has large windows and a skylight as well. Haven recognizes many of Kent's plants clustering the room.

Kent opens his eyes and bolts upright. "Sasani!" he says joyfully. His arms spread wide before he remembers himself and sits on his hands. "Oh good. We've missed you! I have a cutting of a plant I wanted to give you before you went back to Prometheus."

"A plant?" Haven asks.

"Yes!" Kent says. "A lotus flower! I thought it might be meaningful for you as a Mortemian, since they often symbolize rebirth and purity and transformation and well . . ." He trails off. "I wanted you to remember us."

Haven blinks and rubs his neck as he studies one of Kent's ferns to the side. Thierry's bright greeting, Kent's kindness, and even Gemini's manner, acting as if he expected Haven all along. If Yoon hadn't come to get him, he might not have ever seen them again.

"Thank you," he says. "It's very thoughtful of you." Haven takes in Kent's puffy eyes, the perspiration on his forehead, and his restless hands. He asks, "How are you feeling?"

Kent's beaming face abruptly falls. "Oh," he says. Then, again. "Oh, I . . ."

"Can I get you anything?" Haven asks. "Tea, perhaps?"

Kent subsides. "I don't want to be a bother, Sasani," he says. "I'm fine without tea, but maybe . . ." His voice trails off.

"Maybe I could sit with you, then," Haven says. "If you don't mind."

"No!" Kent blurts out. "I would love that."

Haven nods. "Of course."

Kent sits still for a few minutes, but then he starts fidgeting. He brushes his fingers against the leaves of the plant at his bedside table.

"Sasani, I was scared. So so scared," he says in a small voice.

"I would have been scared too," Haven says.

"It's not that, it's . . ." Kent trembles. Fiddles. Then the words pour out. "Everyone thought I followed Ocean to support her. Even Sumi told me I shouldn't try to rescue everyone. I'm always bringing home strays, burying broken birds out in the yard, or recovering plants from stores where they're obviously withering away. I have since I was a little kid. But I never thought about it as rescuing everyone. I was always trying to save the one in front of me."

"The one in front of you . . ." Haven asks, "Is that why you joined the *Ohneul* with Yoon?"

"I didn't even really know her back then. But after I heard about her expulsion from the *Hadouken*, I went to visit her, and she was so . . ." Kent's head droops as he hugs himself. "Well, that's what I told myself. And it made me feel good."

"Kent . . ." Haven starts but then clamps his mouth shut. He recognizes when someone needs to work something out.

"Maybe I only did that, have only ever done anything, to feel good. To look like a hero. To make people think I'm nice. When really I was just hiding."

"Hiding from what?" Haven asks gently.

"The algae research has been ready for almost a year," he says.

Haven feels his eyes widen. "Why . . ."

"I was scared," Kent says. "So I've been using Ocean to hide. And all this time I told myself I was helping her, supporting her, saving her. When really I was saving myself. While I put my family and Sumi through—" Kent breaks off. "And today, I made *Ocean* save *me*. But that's not new. I've always stood by while Dae bullied her. I always run to her for help."

Kent's facial muscles jerk in a way that tells Haven his stiffness is holding back tears. Haven studies his hands to give Kent some space. He directs his next words down to his lap.

"There's more than one way to save someone, Kent," he says. "I've always been grateful for your kindness. It manifests in countless ways." He raises his head. "It's a genuine kindness. Not a self-serving one."

Kent blinks owlishly at him. His eyes water and one of his hands goes toward Haven before he, again, remembers himself. Haven hesitates and then reaches forward. He does it slowly, giving Kent every opportunity to repel him. But when Haven sandwiches Kent's palm between his own, Kent doesn't rebuff him. Instead, his watering eyes finally overflow. His other arm comes up to cover his eyes as the tears track down his face.

• • • •

When Corvus first came to Alessa, she assumed he had made a mistake. She showed up at the restaurant for the rendezvous fully prepared to tell him that he had asked after the wrong twin. It didn't happen often; it had always been clear where the line of succession would fall.

The host led her to a back hallway, slid open the door for her, and there was a sliver of a man sitting poised in that room. A vapor of a human. He was the type of person who fades from memory the moment you turn your head.

Until he looked at her with his pale, pale eyes and smiled. As if she was exactly what he had expected, exactly whom he had wanted at the door. Any words Alessa would have said fell completely by the wayside as she stepped in, barely registering the door closing behind her.

"Alessa Papanikolau," he said, pronouncing her name precisely and with such care, as if he had practiced it several times. He folded one leg up like this wasn't a high-end establishment, the ceramic teacup held delicately in the air with his long, elegant fingers.

No wonder she sat as if under a spell. Who in the last several years had even bothered to address her? Corvus has a habit, and she hadn't learned yet that that's what it was, of not directly meeting her eyes when he's in conversation with her. He tends to rest his gaze on her shoulders, on her forehead, sometimes drifting to her ears. But still, from the beginning, he somehow made her feel seen.

It wasn't even until they were done eating that she thought to ask his name. If he hadn't already known how inexperienced she was, he would have by then. She cringes at the thought of it now. To this day, she can't recall what they ate, what dishes he ordered because she had been so nervous.

"About your proposal . . ." she began.

"Oh, we don't need to talk about that," Corvus said. "I prefer first meetings to be all about pleasure. Once we're more relaxed with each other, we can talk business. Let's save it for the next dinner we share."

The prospect of another dinner silenced her at first. Another opportunity to dine with Corvus, to be led to some cloistered space as if she was worthy of being courted. She couldn't remember the number of times she had eaten at this specific restaurant with her family as they wooed or were wooed by other powerful companies. But she had always been shoved into a corner. She had learned to carefully portion out her tea to last the night because no one would remember to refill her cup.

"You have the wrong person," she blurted. "I'm sorry you've wasted your time and your money on me."

Corvus took a long sip of his tea. "I assure you, I have done neither. As to the first, sharing a meal was far from a waste of time. As for the second, I don't intend on paying for this meal; you're going to do that."

"What?"

"It has long frustrated me how money dictates what we're able to do," he said. "It keeps people to the lowest standard. It directs how people treat you. And it would normally keep me from eating at such an establishment, enjoying the company of someone of your social strata. But I did not want that to be the obstacle preventing us from meeting."

Alessa was still stuck on his previous statement. Was this a con? Had he asked her here to get a free dinner at an expensive restaurant? How naive had she been?

"You can pay for your own meal," she spat out and stood. The chair rasped against the floor and her raw feelings.

"I could," he said. "But I'd rather that you did."

"How dare you!" She slammed her palms down on the table.

"Yes, how dare I?" He pressed a cloth napkin against his lips. "How dare I deign to request an audience with you when I don't intend on paying for it? How dare I ask for a moment of your time when I'm a person who would have to scrape for a year to pay for one meal here? I'm not even worthy of washing your feet, am I?"

"That's not what I meant," she said, flustered. Something in her was telling her to leave right away. But that something was stemmed when he met her gaze squarely.

"Could you try and see it my way?" he asked. "I merely want a chance to prove myself. Isn't that something you can appreciate?"

Those words stopped her breath.

"I asked you here today because of your money, but also because of your potential," he said.

He lifted the ceramic kettle to pour some more tea into her cup, as if her gaping mouth was permission, as if he took it as given that she would sit and listen to him more after what was supposed to be an insulting supposition.

"I believe in being upfront as a rule," he said. "You haven't had much of that in your life, though, have you?"

"What do you know about my life?" she asked, even as she sat.

"Perhaps no one has told you in so many words that your favored brother will carry on your line and inherit most of the assets and money of your family. Why do you think you failed? Or maybe they've twisted it around somehow, told you how lucky you are that you don't have to handle the business. Now you don't have to concern your pretty little head about such ugly affairs. You're set to inherit quite a sum of money, you have an ample allowance as it is, and you'll marry well. Probably someone vapid, but equally rich."

As he emotionlessly laid out her future, his eyes seemed to be completely washed of color.

"But perhaps you're meant for something more?" he asked. "Just like me. We can each be a part of something greater, something monumental."

Alessa closed her hand around the cup. Not too much later, Alessa would find out how Corvus studied her. It was how he handled everyone, by getting into their skin. He had even chosen that specific restaurant because he knew it was her family's favored meeting place. But even that knowledge didn't repel her; he had put in the effort to discern her potential. No one had bothered to do that with her before.

"I'm listening."

It was the first of many meetings between them, many dinners where she paid the check. He was the man with the ideas, and his vision included her. It was true he needed money to fulfill his ideas, but he could have gone to her brother, her father, or her mother.

Corvus had opened her eyes to how she was stultified and smothered in her present state. And he had shown her exactly what she needed to do to break her chains, to free herself of the gilded cage of people who had never bothered to believe in her.

Alessa has grown since that first date with Corvus, when his mere regard lit a fire inside her. He molded her, taught her, has made her the best person she could be.

But now Amell is a part of Corvus, resides in him. That's closer than she's ever been. When will she become a part of Corvus too?

"*Not yet,*" he said over the comm.

Just having his voice in her ear makes her insides flutter.

"*I need you for other things for now. But soon.*"

Emory sent Alessa a recording of that joining of him and Amell. Amell's head tilted back, his mouth open in a wordless cry. Corvus convulsing with him, his neck muscles rigid. What did he see? What did Amell see?

There's so much she still wants to learn. She recognizes now why taking the scrawny scientist was wrong. As Corvus explained to her, they should focus on punishing those who deserve it, on meting out justice, on evening the scoreboard. Von Kent's not one of those, nor would his death have aided their cause. He's not Korean and has perhaps only been led astray. They'd be the villains if they indiscriminately hurt others.

She hasn't pinpointed where they're staying yet, but she's not concerned. She can survey the area where she found Von, and she's sure that sooner or later, she'll track down someone who does deserve punishment.

Sometimes she gets carried away, but that's why she has Corvus to rein her in.

Alessa wants to peer into Corvus's soul, into his mind, and she can't wait until the day he takes her too.

FOURTEEN

TEO ISN'T MUCH for odes, but when he opens the door to Phoenix's room, he has to give that moment its due. Phoenix's hair glows in the morning light. He's apparently a stomach sleeper and he has one bare arm flung over the sheets while the other cradles his head to reveal the peak of an ear, the flat expanse of his cheek.

"*But soft! What light through yonder window breaks?*"

Teo sits at the edge of the bed, and Phoenix opens his ever-startling blue eyes, focusing on Teo over his arm.

"I would think you'd be a lighter sleeper," Teo says. "What if I were here to slit your throat?"

In answer, Phoenix's hand comes out from underneath his pillow, and a gun points at Teo.

Teo holds up a spoon. "It's good I'm here to bring you breakfast then."

Immediately the gun disappears. Phoenix rolls over and sits up, the sheet sliding from his body, revealing corded muscle and golden skin. His cheek has a crease from his pillow. Teo hands over the spoon and bowl and sits back to observe, because Phoenix won't even notice. He digs into the bowl, his spoon dripping milk as he chases fat banana slices. He says his throat clogs up at the idea of Teo's favorite sugary cereals with marshmallows or unnatural colors, but he does like his granola.

Teo wonders who's going to witness all these mornings of Phoenix in the future. He envies them this—the edge of Phoenix's body, the curl of his hair. He hopes they don't take it for granted. But at the same time, he doesn't envy them; it's a lot to measure up to. He pulls himself from tracing the light on Phoenix's skin to find Phoenix observing him.

"My eyes are up here, Teophilus," he says. But he's solemn, and his eyes have a luminous quality, something like hope limning them.

Their wristbands light up at the same time and Teo palms the message forward to see it's from Lupus. His stomach rises in his throat—what could this be after last night's horror show? But he pushes down his fear. Phoenix moves over on the bed to make room for Teo, depositing his already-empty bowl to the side as he grabs his tabula. The ease with which he makes the Teo-sized space is too casual, as if Phoenix's body doesn't contain the memory of holding Teo's the night before. Teo can't move until Phoenix shoots a quizzical look at him. Right. This is nothing. This means nothing. Teo scootches next to him.

Phoenix casts around confusedly before Teo realizes what he's looking for and nabs his gold spectacles for him from the bedside table. And then he has to tear his stare away from the still unfamiliar sight of Phoenix in glasses. Phoenix opens up his screen for the two of them, the video panning a dark, spare room.

A knock comes from the door before Lupus pokes their head in.

"Mornin', dear," Teo says and Lupus ducks their head at the greeting. Their eyes are half lidded, but Teo suspects they're on their way to sleep, not the other way around.

"Two things," Lupus says as they close the door behind them and perch on the edge of the bed. "First, I've confirmed with Von that the person who kidnapped him was Alessa."

Teo's stomach drops. "How is he?" he asks quickly.

"Better, I think?" Lupus says. They point to their screen. "Second, I've been poking here and there, starting from when you said you parted with Corvus. I had your friend Omi check into one of his more recent hideouts. This is it."

The camera shows steel tables with old splatters smeared on them and then a large furnace in the corner. A light flickers on and a hand comes forward to open the furnace door. Omi, presumably, sifts through the ashes inside. Teo half suspects, half dreads what's coming next and he squashes back the inappropriate comment about kitty litter before a hand comes up and particles of bone emerge.

"What does it mean?"

"Omi suspects some experiments were going on down there. It's hard to tell exactly, but at least a dozen bodies were burned. Maybe more, if they disposed of other ashes and bone elsewhere." Phoenix draws in a sharp breath, but Lupus continues, "Omi is going to ask around, see if there's been a rash of missing people or if anyone involved with Corvus might talk."

"Tell him to be careful," Phoenix says.

"You think he won't be, if I don't?" Lupus asks.

Phoenix gently cuffs them over the head. "You dolt, I want him to know I'm worrying about him. It's dangerous territory."

"I'll tell him that instead."

When Lupus leaves, Teo rewinds the video. "Where is this?"

Phoenix opens the other attachment from Lupus on the side. "Mercury. Circe or Base 2."

"Did Corvus do a lot of experimenting while you were with him?"

Phoenix's mien adopts a far-off quality. "Yeah. Ever since we were kids. His parents were scientists, and I think it was one of the ways he was trying to hold on to them." Phoenix snaps out of that and his focus sharpens on Teo. He bites his thumb.

"What is it?" Teo asks. He looks, suddenly, so guilty.

"It feels . . . wrong to talk to you about this, somehow."

Teo flinches. "Like a betrayal?"

Phoenix doesn't answer that directly. "He was always tinkering and always wanting to know *more*. He told me once that someone took him in after his parents died and taught him a lot, but . . . he died in the mines. I never got the whole story."

"The Penelope Collapse," Teo says flatly. The same one that had taken Phoenix's parents.

"Yes," Phoenix says. He holds Teo's gaze. "But he never did this type of experimenting when we were together. Not on animals, not on humans."

"But you've seen him kill someone before."

"Once. And then I left." Phoenix throws back the covers to leave the bed. He grabs the shirt draped over a nearby chair to pull it on. "It wasn't just that he killed a man . . . It was the way he did it." When his head pops through the neck of his shirt, it leaves his glasses askew and hair mussed, throwing Teo's heart into a confused disarray at the dissonance of Phoenix's words and the endearing sight. Phoenix drops his glasses on a side table and pulls on his pants. "He gutted him. Sliced his stomach open and then the way he looked while he did it . . . Like he was . . . compiling every single detail he could about it."

Gutted. Sliced open. Like their LP on Mercury, like Alessa's family, like Teo's. And others too. The realization stops cold all of the fuzzy feelings that had been crowding Teo.

"The Mercury Murders," Teo says. "That was him, wasn't it? He framed you?"

"It was easier for him to pin the job on someone else than to drum up attention for himself." Phoenix shrugs a shoulder. "He had plenty of my DNA to work with."

"He . . . he didn't have to use *your* DNA."

"He was upset that I left." Phoenix combs a hand through his hair.

Teo waits, but when Phoenix doesn't continue, he says, "Wait, that's it?" Phoenix turns to him, and Teo asks, "How can you be so forgiving?" The words bite out and something jabs into his heart.

Phoenix frowns and lifts his arm toward Teo, and Teo doesn't know what he's intending—maybe he wants to fix Teo's shirt, maybe Teo has something on his face—but Teo's hands snap up to ward it off. He stumbles back. Phoenix flinches and steps backward too. But he's not far enough.

"Phoenix, he—" Teo clasps his hands behind his back. "You shouldn't forgive him that."

"I can choose to live how I like," Phoenix says.

His blue eyes lock on Teo's. Teo swallows. "You may be forgiving, but I want to hold on to my hate, Phoenix." He thinks back to the day before, to his conversation with Park. "And because of that, I know I can't ask people to forgive my father. How could I? They have every right to hate him. To hate . . ." He breaks off. "Don't you?"

"Do I?" Phoenix asks. His voice dips low, while the corners of his mouth tighten. "Should I? I ask myself that all the time, Teophilus."

Please don't Teo wants to say. Instead, he steps forward and detests himself for it. He detests how his whole body vibrates when he's closer to Phoenix's skin, detests what he's going to do next. He places his palm against Phoenix's chest, spreads his fingers.

"Are you tempted to let go of your hate because I've made you feel things for me?" Teo asks.

Phoenix's heart hammers against Teo's hand. His body is so solid beneath Teo's touch, but Teo thinks if he were to push him, Phoenix would yield to him, would fall back on the bed.

"Because I'm complicit in this, Phoenix," Teo says. "In what my father did. I was ignorant to it, but willfully so. And even though I need to do right by my family, I need to make things right too. And you . . ."

"What about me?" Phoenix pulls Teo's hand down.

Close to the beginning of their relationship, Phoenix had crouched before Teo in his ship's common room. *"What do you need?"* And another time he'd pressed his hand to Teo's chest. *"Teophilus, what do you need?"*

"You should think about what you need," Teo says, "instead of letting other people take advantage of your easy forgiveness."

Phoenix's hand tightens around Teo's as he goes pale. Teo's heartbeat staggers.

Phoenix says quietly, "Your hands are shaking."

He releases Teo and pushes past him. Teo doesn't move until he hears the door click and knows he's been left alone.

FIFTEEN

OCEAN SWATS AT Hurakan's lazy swing. As if the movement is connected, his leg comes around and sweeps hers so she lands flat on her back. Again. As she lies there, the *maem maem maem* of the cicadas rises in her awareness, clamoring for her attention. The morning is already sticky hot.

"Come *on*," she says in exasperation to the sky.

"Pay attention, Ocean." Hurakan holds out a hand and she grasps it.

All the training at the Alliance is done via simulation, and she could add in handicaps like her shoulder or how her leg's still sore from their Mercury run. But even if Yeonghui's home was tricked out with the equipment, which wouldn't surprise Ocean, she's sure Hurakan and Cass would still choose to spar hand to hand.

"Good lord *no*."

The last word extends to a wail as Maggie goes flying by her. Maggie belly flops onto the grass and remains unmoving. Either because she's been conked out, or because she's prey playing dead. Ocean twists her head back to Cass, who's crossing her arms.

"Cass," Aries intones from the side, where he's sitting under a tree.

Despite the admonishment, his attention is fastened on his tabula. Lupus is tucked in next to him, their eyes hooded but focused on their own screen. They yawn. Ocean's surprised to even see them awake; she's been under the impression that they keep to a completely different cycle than the rest of the team.

"You said this would be *fun*," Maggie accuses Cass as she lifts her head.

"Aren't we having fun?"

"I thought we were going to be stretching. Jjimjil yoga. Anti-grav Pilates." Maggie slaps away Cass's hand, which is encased in a large boxing glove. "*No*. I'm *not* doing this." She huffs and gets up, brushing herself off before she stalks back toward the main building.

"I haven't even brought out my power gloves! I was going *easy* on you, I swear!" Cass yells after Maggie. She turns back to the others. "We need more victims."

"Victims," Aries says. "Said with no irony."

Hurakan strikes at Ocean and she blocks it. It's a harder hit than before, more concentrated. When he moves with liquid grace closer to her, she's ready for it. Or, at least, she thinks she is, before he slips to the side, grabbing her by the wrist and using her forward momentum to spin her around until he's got her arm pinned behind her and her body slammed against his.

"How are you getting out of this one?" he asks into her ear. Ocean attempts to pivot, but Hurakan holds her fast, moving with her to tighten their bodies into an even closer lock. "Your reflexes are really only good with a gun, huh."

"Here to join us, Sasani?" Cass shouts out.

Sasani is walking toward them, smoothing down his hair. He matches eyes with Ocean before skimming his gaze away. Hurakan drops his hold on her.

"Um, no," Sasani says. "Phoenix asked me to come find you, Aries. He wants to talk to you."

Aries stands with a groan. He pats Lupus on the head. "Keep an eye on Cass for me, will you?"

"Yes, sir," Lupus says as Cass squawks indignantly.

"What is that supposed to mean?" Cass shoots at Aries's departing back. She whirls on Sasani with an evil glint in her eyes. "Well, now that you're here . . ."

"Oh." Sasani steps back, his hands up. "I don't plan on fighting ever. And I'm not going to touch a gun."

Ocean's shoulders hunch up to her ears before she forces them down again.

"Then do it for your health." Cass flicks off his protest. "Let's go over the basics, yeah?" She waves Hurakan over. "Gemini, show them a good punch." When Hurakan aims a punch into her outstretched glove, Cass shrugs. "Adequate." She beckons Ocean. "You next." Ocean forms a fist and strikes Cass's glove, putting her shoulder behind the movement. Cass *hmms* an assessing noise. "They teach you shit about fighting at Alliance, don't they?"

Ocean can't argue with that. "I didn't have much reason to learn beyond the basics. I'm a pilot. Was a pilot."

"Still are, as far as I can tell," Cass says. "That's the Alliance for you though. Everyone's placed in their little boxes." Cass grasps Ocean's arm to move it in slow motion, showing her exactly where to extend her elbow to, where to direct her fist. "You're aiming for my hand. You need to aim *past* my hand. You know your punch hurts you even while it hurts your target, yeah? Einstein said it best. Action, reaction. That's why *where* you hit is as important as your recoil: recovering quickly enough to strike again. People say landing a good hit is like bowling a strike—it's all in the follow-through—but that's wrong."

Cass gestures to Ocean, who punches forward again, but Cass has already danced to her side and then behind her.

"Leaves you open here." Cass taps her shoulder. "Here." Cass thwacks her back with her glove. "And here." This last is a light chop to her rib. "Following through is only smart if you're absolutely certain it's your finishing move. As for me, I never fight like I'm damn sure of anything. Now you, Sasani," Cass commands.

Sasani warily brings up his hands. "I don't see the point."

"But that's the kicker, isn't it? You never know what to expect," Cass says, unperturbed, before she jabs lightning quick at his head.

Sasani balks, but Cass pulls her punch and instead spins. Her leg slams into his torso, hurling him to the ground.

"Cass!" Lupus calls out.

"Don't tell Aries," she protests, and she helps Sasani, who takes her outstretched glove begrudgingly. "You're green, aren't you? Gemini said you might be. I guess all your muscle doesn't translate to reflex."

Sasani casts a glance at Hurakan, but Hurakan's holding up a flat palm to Ocean, presumably a landing pad for another practice punch. She raises her eyebrow at him and he winks.

"It's not that different from learning a dance move," Cass assures Sasani. She whips by Ocean with a combination of two punches and then a kick, distracting her. "It's not isolated movements, but you have to connect them, see? Here, try it!" Sasani's jaw clenches

TEO'S DURUMI

and when he doesn't move, Cass repeats, with a slight edge to her voice, "Try it!"

"Cass?"

"Try it, *please*," Cass amends before she sticks out her tongue at Lupus. "Happy?"

"Very."

Sasani shrugs, but his body loosens as he does so. He sketches out an approximation of Cass's movements. Clearly, compliance is the least troublesome option.

Cass stands back. "Good, at least you breathe properly. Now let's talk about how you're making your fist and how to extend your leg."

"Eyes here, Ocean," Hurakan says, drawing Ocean's attention back. "It's only fair." He holds up his palm but when she focuses on it, he suddenly draws close enough that she sees the green flecks of his irises, the sweat streaking down his face. "When you're fighting with someone who's better than you are, you owe them your full attention."

She feels his heel on her calf before she's flipped back. Hurakan, the tree line, sky. Ocean's on the ground before she can make sense of it. But instead of offering her a hand, she hears Hurakan heave a breath in and out.

"—or that happens," he says. When a hand crosses her line of vision, she grabs it. "You're not using your center of gravity properly," Hurakan says as he helps her up yet again. "Coming from someone who constantly gets in scraps with much larger people, it's your only advantage."

"Teo did mention something about your shoes having heels."

"That snitch," Hurakan says lightly. "He had no right."

Hurakan's focus drops to her right shoulder and he skims a hand over where she knows a splotch of scar tissue is. "This where you were shot?"

"It's still a little stiff," she manages.

Hurakan steps back and lifts up his shirt to point to his ribs. "This is from a knife." He drops his shirt and rolls up a sleeve to show a patchwork of white lines. "Broken bottle here." He grins. "There's more too. But no bullet holes yet."

"It must be your winning personality."

He laughs. "A little charm goes a long way, Ocean. I'd tell you to try it, but I kind of like how you are." He puts up his fists.

"You might be the only person who thinks that." Ocean imitates him.

"I think you'd be surprised."

"Sasani, *where* are you *looking*!" Cass barks.

Hurakan throws a tap at Ocean's shoulder then and she moves to block him.

"Good," Hurakan says.

• • • •

"What did he say?" Phoenix asks.

Dae keeps herself from replying that he could just ask. After the morning training session that she had made sure to stay far away from, Phoenix had requested that she accompany him, Cass, and Maggie to the Artemis repair shop to check on the *Pandia*. He claimed blithely that it couldn't hurt to have a Korean along, just in case the technicians didn't speak Common. Dae would have refused, but she didn't mind an opportunity to get out of that house. Besides, unusual for most Alliance ships, she was probably the only crew member who could understand and speak Korean fluently.

But as she could have guessed, the repair shop had plenty of mechanics that spoke Common just fine.

"They appreciated the extra marks from Teophilus," she says. "They should be done within a day or so." Phoenix nods, although she can trace the quick flex of his jaw at her answer. "So, you decided to take him up on his offer?"

"We can't do anything while we're stranded here. It's better to have our ship up and running as soon as possible than to salvage my pride," Phoenix says. He slides her a look-over. "I heard he made you an offer too."

Dae's hands tighten into fists. Of course the Anand prince would brag that she was his charity case, that he offered to buy Dae a ship, for all his words about how it was his plan all along or that it was his fault in the first place it got blown up.

"He told you?" she asks.

"No, I overheard him talking to Ocean about it. He wanted some advice on what would be a good ship to procure."

Dae's fists ball up even more painfully. "He told *Ocean*?" Her teeth grit. But when she notices Phoenix's eyes on her, she tries to unclench everything. "I'm still thinking about it."

"It's hard, isn't it?" Phoenix asks. "He offered it to us as if it was nothing to him. Because it is nothing to him."

Her hands want to claw this time, but she's stopped by Phoenix's smile. It's rueful, commiserating. She lets out a short huff as she touches her tightly braided hair, checking to make sure every strand is in place. At the other end of the garage, Maggie's telling a story to a mechanic, her arms gesticulating wildly.

"I hope she's not saying something she shouldn't," Dae mutters.

"Why do you think I had Cass stick to her?" Phoenix asks mildly.

Sure enough, Cass stands right beside Maggie, one hip jutted out, her arms folded over. The garage mechanic nervously shifts every time Cass does, paying more attention to her than to Maggie.

"You have an interesting team," Dae says.

It's what she used to say of the *Ohneul*. An interesting crew that would hopefully be attractive to anyone wanting to hire them: an in-house mechanic; a xenobotanist whose energy recycling kept their expenditure at the minimum. They were a Class 4, so the fact that their older medic had been more interested in hwatu than anything else hadn't been a problem, and Dae had taken care of that anyway by hiring a Vulture, which added to her savings. And . . . she had Ocean.

But her crew doesn't rally around her like Phoenix's does to him.

"Cass was a bit rough around the edges when we first took her on," Phoenix says. "She's actually one of the only people we've brought onto the *Pandia* without Gemini's approval. They butted heads constantly in the beginning."

"What made you decide to keep her?"

"Because I found out she was sending all her money to her family back on Mercury."

Dae nods. "You felt bad for her."

"It spoke to her loyalty. I wanted to earn that." Phoenix glances at Dae. "I think she eventually recognized that in Ocean, even if Ocean shot her through the heart not so long ago." Dae clicks her tongue, and Phoenix asks, "You disagree?"

"Ocean's not the type to stay," she says.

"But she was with you for a long time. That's significant, isn't it?"

She stops. "She had nowhere else to go." She taps her own shoulder. "She's going with you now, anyway."

"Is she?" Phoenix says. "It seems to me she's still thinking it over."

"Good luck with her," Dae says. "With the famous *Crane*." She mutters the moniker sourly.

The irony of *Ocean* being called Crane, one of the beloved symbols of the unified Korea, has never been lost on Dae. The birds have long represented peace and longevity, and it's a name of honor that Ocean probably doesn't even fully comprehend.

"Ah," Phoenix says. "Gemini told me about that call sign. So you're jealous of her talent?" Dae's about to snap back when Phoenix smiles that commiserating smile again. "Me too. I've always been supremely untalented."

"What are you talking about?" Dae says tiredly. "You're Phoenix. You're the most famous living raider captain."

"Exactly," Phoenix says. "All that pomp, all that flair. You've seen the videos, haven't you?"

Dae doesn't know an Alliance kid that hasn't. They've racked up millions of views on AV.

"But captain to captain," Phoenix says, and Dae warms at that despite herself, "I've never seen myself as more than the red cape that distracts the bull. The flashier I am, the more it distracts from my crew. And it keeps them safer." He raises his eyebrows at her. "What does being a captain mean to you?"

The question floors her, even if she's taken all the classes, studied all the texts. The Alliance answer is there for her immediately. *Honor in service.* But what does that even mean?

"The Alliance only works if those on top remain strong."

"But how do you quantify strength?" Phoenix asks. "Unyielding authority? The ability to withstand opposition? A sword has to be forged in fire, but not every metal is meant to be shaped into a weapon."

Maybe the Alliance didn't shape everyone into a weapon, but they did shape people into tools. And if they couldn't find a use for you, they'd ask you to captain a Class 4.

Phoenix says, "It's a mistake to measure yourself against anyone else."

"You're assuming a lot about me," Dae says stiffly.

"Maybe," Phoenix says. "But I asked you what it means to be a captain, and what it means to be strong. I don't think those answers are the same for everyone. It might be worth thinking about why you even joined the Alliance in the first place."

"Being a part of the Alliance is every Korean's dream."

"So maybe that's why Ocean stayed with you so long?" Phoenix asks.

The automatic denial is on her lips, but the words get caught there. All she can think about now is Ocean's white face from the other day, the way she must have taken Dae's words.

"Did you just bring me along to lecture me?" Dae asks.

Phoenix raises his eyebrows when she says *lecture*. "You and Maggie seemed to be the antsiest in the house, actually," Phoenix says. "Maggie was like a pent-up molecule about to combust, and you've been unhappy since a few days ago."

"Then you didn't need my help after all."

"Yes and no," Phoenix says. "I've found that when I'm eating at a Korean BBQ, I'm never ignored if I have a native sitting with me. This was the same principle." The comm at his ear beeps, interrupting them, and he nods at Dae. "Excuse me." He walks a few paces away, but Dae hears his exclamation anyway. "He *what*? Where are you?" Phoenix scowls, and even when he speaks to Dae, he can't control his frown. "Can you wrap up here with Cass and Maggie? I'll meet you two back at the house."

Then he's quickly off before she can ask anything.

• • • •

Teo's being followed.

He had been walking in too much of a fog to notice at first, his thoughts consumed with the meeting he just had, so he doesn't know when it started. He's used to the feeling, but this has a different quality to it. It's not like someone wanting to snag a picture of him, and it's not the slinking way Gemini trailed him when he left Yeonghui's manor that morning. Teo may have given him the slip when he went to visit Diplomat Park, but when he'd tried to do the same today, Gemini was doggedly on his tail. But Teo no longer senses his friendly shadow.

Teo sidles down a side street, and then quickly ducks around the bricked corner of a building. He adjusts his cap and uses the movement to covertly cast an eye back through the crowded street behind him. He can't spot anything out of the ordinary. He shoves his hands in his pockets, resuming his casual stroll.

He passes by a storefront that has mannequins adorned with hanboks. The whole row of them are brightly colored except the black one at the end. He kneads his forehead, trying to stem the whirling thoughts that the dark hanbok provokes.

Then the window explodes.

Glass shards fly everywhere. People are screaming, ducking for cover. Teo stumbles and the brick wall next to him hacks a powder cloud. Teo reflexively grips his arm and when the contact stings even more, he pulls his hand away to see red. He gawks at it.

He has to get away from this crowd. They're shooting at *him*. Teo's running, but everywhere he twists, he's going against the tide of people who don't know where to flee. He shoves his way through the crowd, down a dark, narrow alley. Away from people, away from the mayhem.

A hand reaches out to yank him into the shadows. Teo throws a punch into the darkness, but his knuckles only graze skin. A hand goes flat against his stomach, firmly pushing him to the wall. The person's other hand comes over his mouth.

"It's me," Phoenix says in a low voice.

Teo drops his hands, but Phoenix pushes closer as if to muffle any of his other protests. Phoenix scans their surroundings, leaving Teo painfully aware of how he's left panting against Phoenix, how Phoenix's hand burns where it rests insistently above his hips.

"Why would you come down an empty alley?" Phoenix snaps at Teo. "Are you trying to make yourself an easy target?"

Teo opens his mouth to speak and when his lips brush Phoenix's hand, Phoenix snatches it away.

"They were shooting at me," Teo says. "I didn't want them to accidentally hit someone else."

Phoenix lets out a low hiss. He puts his hand to his ear. "Yeah," he says into the comm. "I've got him." After a few moments, he taps the comm again. "Gem is marking your sniper. He thinks it's Alessa."

Alessa come to finish off the job of murdering the entire Anand family. "Gemini was marking me this morning too," Teo says. "Did you put him up to that?"

Phoenix says heatedly, "Next time it might not be bullets, Teophilus. Next time it might be a bomb, and Alessa won't care how many go down with you. Are you seriously that unaware of how much Corvus wants to kill you?"

"I won't come out again," Teo says. "I didn't mean to endanger other people. I was only trying to find answers."

Phoenix doesn't respond right away, giving Teo ample opportunity to take inventory of all the places their bodies have melded together. His face is too close for Phoenix to see, so even while the adrenaline is coursing through him, Teo lets his eyes slide closed, to feel how good this is. This is not the time or place to be doing this, but what other opportunity will he have?

"I wish you wouldn't endanger *yourself*, Teophilus." Phoenix finally releases Teo, stepping back to run his hands roughly through his hair. "Well? Did you find your answers?"

Some. But mostly more questions, more pathways to go down to confirm the suspicions he doesn't want to have about what the people around him are capable of.

"How do I change what my father did, Phoenix?" he asks. "I don't know how to make it better. He started this gargantuan machine and I think it might flatten me if I try to stop it."

Phoenix drops his hands. Meets his gaze squarely. "Are you the same as your father?"

"No," Teo says. At one point, it would have made him unbearably proud to say that he was.

"I don't think so either," Phoenix says. "How are you going to solve this?"

It's such a monumental question, it feels unfair for Phoenix to ask that of Teo, but his expectant expression holds an undeniable trust.

His father was so much smarter than he is, and his brother was so much kinder than he is. But was this the best they could come up with, this pattern of sacrificing Mercurians to prevent the same tragedy from happening elsewhere? Maybe Teo's father had some better explanation for it, maybe some other motive than his flawed principles. But how will Teo ever know that? How will he ever be able to judge his father now except by his actions? Actions, after all, speak louder than words.

Except, that's not true. Because when he's with Phoenix, he wants so much to act. He wanted to respond to Phoenix's hand against his hip, their bodies against each other. But he can't and he won't.

"The first step is to acknowledge that there is a solution," Teo says. "Even if I don't know it yet."

Phoenix nods. He touches his ear. "Yeah, Gem. We'll see you back at the house." He halfway reaches out a hand to Teo before he turns abruptly away. "Let's go, Teophilus. It's good that Sasani's back with us. We'll have him check that arm."

Phoenix leads the way down the alley, but Teo clears his throat. "Actually . . . since I'm not likely to come out again, would you come to a tailor with me?"

"Is this really the time for shopping?"

"It's not for me."

SIXTEEN

HE'S IN LOVE with her. He will be until the end of his days.

Which is why Arturo's waiting in the park to propose.

They had a huge fight the night before. She told him she was pregnant, and . . . he took it badly. He was an idiot. He was surprised, that's all. It's not exactly what they planned, but that's fine, isn't it? It's not like he planned on meeting Marija either. He dropped by that restaurant a year ago on a whim, and he never expected to leave his phone number with the waitress there and certainly never expected to hear from her again.

Their first date ended at this park, and they watched the sunset from this bench. Arturo had thought nothing was more perfect than this. It was winter then, and they were shivering, but they hadn't been willing to admit it was too cold to be outside.

Her breath on his face had been so warm. His hands had been so cold, but he'd buried them in her long raven-dark hair.

He was warned that they were moving too fast. But too fast, too slow, how does anyone judge? He wants her, wants more and more, will never have his fill. He's greedy of his time with her, swallows it in gulps. The days always too short, too fleeting. He was drunk on his happiness.

And then she told him she was pregnant.

Oh, her *face* when she saw his reaction. Guilt shrivels up his insides. He couldn't help it. It wasn't *her* and it wasn't even the pregnancy. The fear had consumed him.

My father was not a good man, he had wanted to say. *I don't know if I can do this.*

But what had come out of his mouth instead was "How could you have let this happen?"

Unforgivable. But he's going to try. He asked her to meet him here, the place of their first date. He wrapped up a bouquet of stargazers, her favorite. He'll get on his knees to first beg her forgiveness, and then to pull the ring box from his jacket pocket.

I want to be a good father, but I need your help. I don't want to live this life without you.

He checks his wristband. Still some time before she comes. She's always late to everything. He smiles at that thought.

Someone sits on the bench next to him and Arturo peeks at the stranger, surprised.

He's like a person whose saturation has been turned down, with the palest blond hair. He has on a long coat, even though it's not particularly cold. He's wearing a glove too, although only on his right hand.

"I hope you don't mind," the stranger says with a slight accent. Faint freckles sprinkle his face. "The view from this bench is quite nice."

"I agree," Arturo says. He can't deny anything to anyone today. Today is going to be a wonderful day. "The sunset in particular."

"Are you also here for the view?" Despite his words, his eyes are fixed on Arturo rather than the city.

Arturo checks his watch again. If she's too late, they'll miss the sunset. He hopes she comes, that she's not so angry she'll ignore his message. Surely she'll come.

"I'm here to propose." He's a stranger, but who cares? "You're the first person to know. I mean, other than the man at the ring shop."

"How lovely," he says. "Congratulations."

"Thank you." Arturo beams. A sudden frisson of doubt makes him falter and the stranger catches that, probably since he hasn't stopped examining Arturo.

"Nervous?"

"Isn't everyone?" Arturo says. "I mean, even if you're absolutely sure they'll say yes, it's nerve-racking."

"It's wondrous to be joined with someone."

"Are you married?" Arturo asks.

"Do you think she might refuse you?" As if the stranger didn't even hear him.

"I hope not." Arturo laughs.

"Even if she does say yes, there's no guarantee of anything, is there?"

The smile slips from Arturo's face. "Excuse me?"

"I don't mean to be rude," the stranger says. "Life is just so uncertain. Do you love her?"

The stranger emanates a strange, noxious cloud. Arturo's irrationally worried it'll cast a shroud on what he's about to do.

"That's why I'm proposing, isn't it?" He tries a chuckle even while he's weighing whether he should move on, if he should message Marija and meet with her elsewhere. But he was supposed to propose to her *here*.

"People remain together for all sorts of reasons," the man says. "I think often because they don't want to face life alone. But I apologize . . . I lost someone myself. Someone I thought would be with me for the rest of my life."

"Ah." The poor guy. A bad breakup? Or maybe his lover died? "I'm sorry to hear that."

"Does she love you?"

"Yes," Arturo answers confidently.

"And yet you keep glancing at the time," the man says. "Part of that is because I make you uneasy, but part of it is because you're not certain if she'll show up. Maybe she won't. Maybe she's already left you."

"What?" Arturo frowns. He stands. He's had enough of this. Arturo has to call Marija, tell her not to come to the park after all.

"Don't go."

That suddenly vulnerable plea arrests him. He owes nothing to the man, but he turns around. The glove the man's wearing glows blue now, casting an eerie pall into the puddled light around him. The man is doubled over, gagging. Arturo instinctively reaches out.

"Are you all right?"

Pain explodes in him. Bewildered, Arturo looks down at a knife jutting out of his side.

Then the man places his gloved hand on Arturo's forehead and the explosion of agony wipes everything else out. It's like the man's fingertips are drilling into his skull, and Arturo screams.

Hands, pale hands before him, interlacing with another's.

"You're mine."

The face on the bed below him is young and unscarred, the eyes open and clear like the water. The ache tears through him.

Arturo moans and drops to his knees, his mind overcome now with the flashes of these scenes, these memories he's never seen before.

He's soldered a new security board with wires in colorful loops. He can't wait to show him. His booted feet kick up the dust as he walks back and forth on the path. Back and forth. When will Bradford come home?

Far off, he hears an implosion. A crash reverberates the still air.

Drool dribbles from Arturo's mouth as the realization from the memory crushes him.

And then, blessedly, something that does belong to him.

Arturo's *mother sings to him, her cool hand brushing back his sweaty hair from his forehead. It's too hot to have his head on her lap, but his body is feverish, his mouth dry. He doesn't want to move.*

And then that memory crumples into dust.

What had he been thinking?

Arturo *hits the dirt. He fell off the swing because he lifted his hands, thinking he could fly. The pebbles dig into his skin. His scraped palms are red hot, but as he pushes himself up he—*

A white light spasms through his head, sucking him dry.

Gone.

Marija sits at the table. The morning light filters in, tentatively mingling with the white rising from her cup. Her hair's tousled from sleep. Her shirt is too large, baring one shoulder.

"My father left my mother when she was pregnant with me. She never heard from him again."

Why didn't he remember her confession when she told him she was pregnant? He had been so consumed with his own problems, his own thoughts.

The steam rises from her drink into the curves of her face, her trembling lashes.

"*I have not felt this, trusted this with anyone else before.*"

"This memory?" he asks.

"*No, this heart.*"

No. No, he wants to keep this.

Don't go. Don't take this from me.

Arturo cries. His hands come up to the man's arm, beating at it, but he can't break his hold. They're connected by that glove, by the points of suffering.

"Please," he begs. He barely recognizes his voice, it's so mangled. "Please." The word smears in his ears.

But then that's gone too. Leaving an emptiness in him.

Gone. Even if he can't remember what it is that left him, he's lesser without it. He's not who he was a second ago.

Please.

He's supposed to propose to her. To this woman. He is in love with her. He will be until the end of his days. He is in love with her. He is in love. He is.

Arturo grabs the man's arm and wrenches it away from him with all his strength. It's like pulling out his own ligaments, his own sinews. A shriek stretches like a gooey string from him.

Then he falls backward, suddenly freed. Liquid pulses down his face and he swipes at it dazedly. His hand is drenched in red. He lifts his head to see the other man also on the ground, convulsing.

Arturo rolls over onto his knees. He has to . . . he has to . . . what? The urgency of what he has to do clashes with the anxiety of not knowing what it is. He crawls forward. He grabs at the bench next to him, pulling himself to his feet. He lurches forward. He has to . . .

He puts a hand to his side and his fingers scrape across a knife handle. That. When did that happen? Some vague idea tells him he should leave it in for now, that if he pulls it out, he'll unravel. He stumbles forward, vision blurred from the blood in his eyes. He needs to keep going, right? One step in front of the other. There's a reason he's doing this, right?

Call. I have to call her. I have to tell her.

Tell her what? Call whom? His fingers fumble at his wristband, leaving a smudge of blood.

A blare of noise cuts through the confusion in his head. A flare of lights to the front of him, surrounding him, but the sky above it is orange, red, the last of it fading because the sun's finally setting and he's missing it because he isn't up where that nice view is, where he's supposed to be sharing that view.

It's the last thing he sees.

• • • • •

Corvus rolls over on the pavement, coughing up fluid. When he's able to sit up, he tracks the splotches of blood leading away from him. While he was writhing on the ground, Arturo got away, not even checking to see if Corvus was all right. How thoughtless.

"Corvus! What's happening?"

The voice reverberates in his head and Corvus spits out more blood before he replies into his mouth mic.

"Fine. I'm fine. But he got away."

"How?"

Corvus hadn't even planned on absorbing the other man when he sat next to him. True to his first words, he had wanted to enjoy the view. Amell was the careful first choice, and Corvus has been monitoring himself since then to check for any adverse side effects. But witnessing Arturo's grievous doubt had made him activate his glove. Anything to ease that anxiety. Arturo hadn't wanted to propose. Not really. Some other drive pushed Corvus too, the him that he now was. A new aggression grated in him, a new strength that hadn't been there before.

Corvus tried to be gentle, and the drawing out of Arturo's self had been too slow. He'd been too indulgent of the other man.

But it shouldn't have been possible for Arturo to pull away. Corvus had already siphoned a chunk of him. He can see the woman in front of him. *Marija*. She abides in him now too, or at least the version of her that existed within Arturo.

"Do you want me to come get you?"

If Alessa were here, she probably would have already killed Arturo in a rage. But she's still in Artemis, hopefully laying low for now, and thankfully it's only Emory on backup. He needs to complete his union with Arturo.

"No," Corvus says. "Hold your position."

"Yes, Corvus."

Corvus totters to a stand. He follows the path the blood has laid out for him. The sun hasn't quite set yet, but the streetlamps are already glowing. He walks down the hill from the viewpoint. He's so intent on the splatters that he almost bumps into her.

"Pardon me," he says automatically as he dips his head in apology. Freezes.

It's her. The same dark hair and dark brows from Arturo's memory, now Corvus's memory. She frowns at him, at the tenderness that's blossomed in him.

"Do I know you?" she asks.

His hand twitches. He could take her now, join her with the Arturo in him . . . but no, Arturo's getting farther away by the minute.

"My mistake," he says to her, even if it isn't. But he doesn't move on yet. He clasps her hand in between his. Like seeing her face, it's a double-image locking into place, her fingers filling in the spaces between his. He says, "You should keep it."

"Excuse me?"

Corvus is already past her, beyond her face gone pale, taking long strides away from the park. The blood on the ground is barely discernible unless you're checking for it. He follows it down the hill and then to the sidewalk. A long line of idling cars locked in a standstill, windows rolled down, people hanging out of them in curiosity or irritation.

"What's happened?" he asks the first man draped over his window.

"Some crazy person." He scowls. "Ran out into the street and got himself killed."

"Ah," says Corvus.

"Why'd he have to do it in rush hour?"

"If he had a death wish, he should have done it somewhere he wouldn't inconvenience others," the man in the car to the right of him agrees.

Corvus recognizes that before he might have pitied the man. Or felt some sort of sorrow at how callous he was. But now, an aggression rises in him. How *dare* he. What right did he have to live when Arturo had died in front of him?

Corvus has to show him how wrong he is. The man has to see who Arturo, beautiful decent Arturo, was. Then he'll understand.

Corvus yanks the glove back, tight against his skin, to activate it. He grunts as those blue lines sink into his nerves. He's getting used to the hurt, now that he anticipates it. The glove glows when it connects.

He swivels and slams his hand on the driver's face, instantly sinking into it. The man screams, but Corvus ignores that. He'd thought he was being considerate by taking Arturo slowly, but it had only allowed Arturo to pull away before they were finished communing. He won't make that blunder again. He snatches the man's life with a violent jounce and the man's self crashes into him like a wave.

The crisp ruffle of old money on his fingers; ah the rush of pleasure at the first hill he crests on his hoverboard—

"Corvus!"

Corvus hears the yell through his comm and snatches his hand back. The man slumps over the window. Depleted.

He swivels drunkenly toward the sound of terrified shouting. Corvus steps around to the first man he talked to. The man at the car jabs at a button, but his window rises too slowly. Corvus shoves his gloved hand on that forehead too.

Chlorine smell of a pool, the slap of hands on wet shoulders before diving in the water, down down cutting through.

"Corvus, please!"

Gone. *Mine.* It's all Corvus's now.

He laughs. That emptiness in him, he can banish it, can't he? He *feels*.

He hears sobbing in his ears as Emory pleads with him. "Stop, Corvus, please." Her words mingle with screaming. He moves down the line of cars, all waiting for him to take his fill. He smashes his fist through the next window. Car doors open as people flee, but he lets them go, moving onto those who are unaware.

Bradford folds Corvus in. "It's all right to cry, Corvus. It's all right to miss them. I know . . . I know I'm a poor substitute. But I'm going to try."

Corvus never had a chance to tell Bradford what he meant to him.

The memories clash and absorb one another. They mingle and buoy him. He's so much more complete now. Now no one can reject him or renounce him. It all belongs to him, but he belongs to it all.

He is the vessel, he gives of himself, he is truly a self without self.

SEVENTEEN

OCEAN HEARS THE machine whirring even through the song playing on her nimbus. As she walks toward the dining annex, she pulls the device down around her neck and pushes aside the cloth flaps in the doorway. Yeonghui's chef, Yao, is at a counter behind a glass divider. Long noodle strands wind down from the silver mechanism over a steaming bath. He cuts them at intervals. His assistant, Boyeong, stirs them with a pair of long chopsticks in one hand, while she smokes a cigarette with the other. Sun streams into the large kitchen, catching the white whisps before they're sucked into the exhaust fan. Ocean can't remember the last time she saw cigarettes outside of a film, although she suspects these are medicated.

Yao gestures Ocean toward the table at the end of the room, but when she sees who's sitting there, she almost reverses course. Sasani raises his head then, and she's trapped. He hunches his shoulders like a bird about to take flight.

"Joining the show, Miss Yoon?" Yao prompts when Ocean doesn't move. "Shall I have Boyeong steep some tea for you?"

"Oh, no," Ocean says. "I'm just—"

She's distracted when Sasani goes over to the side cooler that takes up almost the entire left wall. He opens it and pulls out something to toss to her. Ocean automatically puts up a hand to catch it in midair and the weight of it landing is cold and reassuring against her palm. She rotates the can as she considers the design of the lychee soda. It's some testament to Yeonghui's stock that this exists here. It's been a running joke between her and Teo that it can't be found anywhere in the solar. Well, Teo has some secret supplier for it, but he's never divulged that information. He claims he'll take it to his grave.

Ocean wants to ask Sasani how he knew, but she catches him staring at the can, red creeping up his neck. He sits hurriedly at his seat.

"Miss Yoon?" Yao prompts again.

At his table, Sasani rests his cheek on the heel of his hand, his attention rapt on the old man's motions.

"Sure, I'll stay," she says to Yao, holding up the soda. "But no need for tea."

Sasani's eyes snap to her, startled. Ocean takes the seat next to him, but keeps her own gaze on Yao and Boyeong's noodle sorcery. Boyeong relinquishes her chopsticks to grab a mesh net, drawing the noodles out to take them to the sink, where she runs them under cold water. She keeps a lock on the cigarette in her lips.

Ocean cracks the tab on her drink to take a long pull. "Naengmyeon from scratch?" The chewy noodles will be perfect for this weather in a savory broth chilled with ice.

Yao grunts. "Miss Jang prefers her dishes to be as authentic as possible. We had this machine ordered from Shinjeong Co. It has several different noodle settings."

"Seems like a lot of effort for little payoff," says a voice from their right.

Joonho stands in the doorway that leads to the walkway, his hands in his sleeves. Behind him, Teo grimaces at Ocean apologetically. They're leading Maggie, Dae, and Hurakan.

"Hi, Joonho," Ocean says. At this point, she's no longer surprised at wherever or whenever Joonho might appear. "What brings you to our neck of the woods?"

Joonho glides into the kitchen area. He places his bag on the counter in front of Yao. "If you would please," he says. "Directions are inside." He turns back to the others. "I'm here to retrieve my car. The one you borrowed." His eyes flick to Sasani. "I see that the pickup went smoothly."

Ocean remembers the ride from Dunian. Driving through the haloes of street lights and Sasani's quiet, steady voice. The way that closing the window had encased them in their own world.

She says, "Your car handled very well."

There's a faint line between Joonho's eyebrows. "You're welcome," he says. "I thought I'd take the opportunity to check out your . . . lodgings while I was here. And I brought some tea for everyone." He scans the room. "Although, I believe this isn't everyone?"

"Oh . . . I'm sure they're around," Teo says vaguely. He rubs his arm and Ocean's focus zeros in on it. Despite the fact that the mansion is rigidly air-conditioned, she hasn't seen him wear long sleeves before now. He shakes his head just the tiniest bit.

"It seems I caught you coming back from 'around' when I entered," Joonho says. "Which, if true, is ill-advised, considering what happened to your other compatriot." Teo opens his mouth to reply, but Joonho asks Ocean, "How is he? Your xenobotanist?"

"Better," Ocean says. "Thank you."

"Good," he says.

His soft tone surprises Ocean. She'd remark on it, but she recognizes then the cups that Yao and Boyeong are bringing out of Joonho's bag. They're standard Sav-Faire design, which are purposely shaped so they don't fit neatly into their saucers. They betray even the most inconsequential discomfort in someone's hands, the nerves shivering through their fingers.

"Joonho," she says dryly. "You really didn't have to."

Joonho helps distribute the saucers on the tray. "I wanted to talk to Von more about his kidnapper," he says. "Did we confirm who it was? Or what they wanted?"

Dae drifts over to the window seat far from them, while Maggie naturally gravitates toward the kitchen. Teo and Hurakan sit across from Ocean and Sasani.

"She's connected to Corvus," Teo says casually.

"Come now, Teophilus." Joonho smiles. "I thought we were allies. Ocean certainly seemed to think so when she asked me for help in tracking down Von."

Maggie touches her finger to the teakettle and *tsks*. "This is way too hot for green tea! You have to brew it at around 160 degrees or it'll be too bitter!"

Joonho placidly pinches Maggie's hand from the kettle as he continues, "If she works for Corvus, it's curious that Von came through without a scratch. And without a demand. I'd have expected him to either be killed outright or to be used as a hostage to bring out Teophilus."

"Yikes," Maggie says.

Joonho directs his smile at her. "It's curious and fortunate, of course. That goes without saying."

Von *did* say that Alessa had been about to torture him or worse, but Corvus had stopped her. He had been sure of that point. Ocean frowns.

"*I'm* curious, Diplomat," Hurakan says. "You didn't find out more information from the guard who tried to kill Teo?"

Joonho shakes his head. "I'm afraid not. As I was telling Teophilus, I haven't found any leads."

Sasani tenses next to her. Joonho picks up two saucers with their cups and walks over to the table. He places one set in front of Ocean and then waits behind Sasani's seat, holding his own.

"Diplomat—" Teo starts to say and Ocean's not sure how he manages such an even tone when it sounds like his teeth are clenched together.

But Sasani's face is expressionless as he leaves his chair to allow Joonho to take it. He leans against the back wall near them as Yao and Boyeong pass out tea to the others. Ocean makes to rise from her seat as well, but Joonho's hand shoots out to grab her lychee soda at the same time she does.

"I prepared yours correctly, didn't I?" Joonho asks. "Two sugars, no milk."

"Oh, that's right!" Maggie says excitedly. "You and Ocean *dated*. What was that like?"

Joonho smirks as Ocean sits back down. But when Joonho nudges her cup and saucer closer, Ocean sips from her soda instead. Judging from the heat radiating from the tea, Maggie's correct; it's too hot.

TEO'S DURUMI 173

"We had been going out for a couple of years," he says, "but she took a leave from Sav-Faire and then never came back. She sent an email to break up with me."

"Ouch," Maggie says.

"It was all very cordial." Joonho smiles up at Ocean.

And she doesn't know what's coming, but she recognizes the tenor of that smile. Everything in her goes taut.

"She was only going out with me to feel more Korean, anyway," he says.

Near the window, Dae bolts to her feet, then stops short at Ocean's raised eyebrows. Her cheeks flame red and she drops her head. Ocean waits for her own answering hurt to Joonho's jab, the one that matches Dae's outrage. But her surprise at Dae's action suffuses a strange relief in the wake of Joonho's expectant, triumphant smile.

She says calmly, "If you went out with someone at Sav-Faire because of how you felt about them, it was a weakness."

Joonho's face wipes clean. His cup rattles as he puts it down. "That's cold, Ocean." He pauses, and his next words bite out. "But maybe that's to be expected of someone who's taken lives."

Ocean's hand comes up reflexively and she knocks her cup. Scalding tea flies up. Then, as if in slow motion, Sasani's arm comes down in front of her to block it. He somehow, impossibly, catches the cup before it tumbles to the ground. Joonho has leaped to his feet and he moves to steady Ocean.

"Ocean, are you—"

But before he can touch Ocean, Sasani's snatched his wrist. Joonho's face snarls into one of disgust. He rips his hand away.

"How dare you," he spits.

The words immediately bring the room to a standstill, but Ocean's suddenly hot, prickling with energy. Joonho stands before her, but she can barely see him through her sparking vision. Sasani places Ocean's cup down. Not a single shiver of porcelain as it meets the saucer. He turns to Ocean, and there it is, that calmness that has always steadied her.

"Did you get any on you?" he asks.

He's scanning her, and already that motion is an echo of the times she's been in the infirmary with him, the time Hurakan carried her in from Penelope and she heard Sasani's desperate *"What happened to her?"* But that's wrong; he shouldn't be worrying about *her*.

Ocean's reaching for him until she catches herself. She turns the motion into a rotation of both her arms, as if to prove no damage has been done.

"You're the one . . ." The words get caught. She clears her throat. "You're the one who got hurt. Come on."

She exchanges a glance with Teo as they leave, and he nods. As she holds the cloth flaps open for Sasani to pass through, she hears him say, "Diplomat Park, I believe you've overstayed your welcome. But before you go, I do have a question, as well as a piece of information which may be of interest to you."

· · · · ·

Yoon runs her hand under the cold water. "I guess this kind of thing is what Adama wanted."

"Pardon?" Haven asks. He already put his arm under the rush of water at her behest. He leans against the bathroom counter, holding a wet towel to his burns, although to be honest, he had hurried here to take care of *her* even if she claimed she was fine. Yoon always says she's fine.

"Nothing," she says. "I'm thinking about what I maybe should have done."

"I'm sorry if it wasn't my place to interfere," Haven says. Ever since they landed in Artemis, all the conversations have taken on layers, like how the humidity here adds a sheen of sweat, as if the mist of perspiration is an extra application of facial powder.

"Sasani." Yoon turns off the faucet and somehow the silence is louder than the rush of water was. He waits for her to continue, and they meet eyes in the mirror's reflection. She says, "I wouldn't say this to most people, but you don't have to ask my permission to help me."

Haven's indrawn breath is too loud in the close quarters of the bathroom. In the kitchen, had he imagined her reaching for him? A while ago—it seems like another lifetime—he had played hwatu with her on the *Ohneul* and told her that she didn't have to ask permission to lay hands on him, if it was to save his life. A familiar flush heats his skin.

Someone knocks at the door.

"Sasani, could I have a word?" It's Park's voice.

It snips the thread of their conversation. Yoon busies herself, toweling off her arm. "It's up to you." Haven wonders if Park can hear them.

Haven opens the door to Park, who has his hands hidden in the folds of his robes. "Yes?"

"I would like to apologize to you. Privately."

Some childish, perverse part of Haven wants to tell Diplomat Park that he's free to do it here or not at all. "You don't need to apologize to me," Haven says.

"Nevertheless."

Haven thinks of how Jang talked about performance art. He despises ritual without meaning, or rather, ritual for appearance's sake. Anyway, he has the distinct impression the apology's not for Haven, who sincerely desires nothing of the sort from Park.

"I'd flush your hand under cold water one more time," he tells Yoon. Then he bends his head to Park. "Lead the way."

Park's expression flickers, but he sweeps back toward the patio doors. Right before Haven follows him through, he hears a *psst*. Thierry pokes her head into the hallway.

"If you need anything, give a shout," she whispers, as if Haven's going into some back alley and Park might knife him, as if the Diplomat isn't a mere three steps ahead of him.

She ducks back and Haven joins Park out on the patio. Park presses the panel and the doors glide shut behind them. He doesn't say anything at first, and Haven listens instead to the trill of the bird above them. The enclosed back garden is cool, and a slight breeze whispers through the plants and caresses a shiver across the surface of the pond before everything goes still again.

Park affects a completely uncontrite demeanor. Perhaps he won't apologize at all; he'll stand here in silence for the appropriate amount of time before striding back into the room with his perfect topknot.

Even with said topknot, he isn't quite as tall as Haven. His hands remain in the deep folds of his tunic and maybe he actually is hiding a knife. But when he does remove a hand, he extends it toward a nearby tree blooming with pink flowers.

"Crepe myrtle. Do you know the significance?"

Haven shakes his head. Kent probably would, with his earnest offering of the lotus flower that had touched Haven more than he could say.

"They were planted specifically around Artemis and we have several at the seowon. They represent the Seonbi's resolve to live a transparent and virtuous life," Park says.

Haven's not really in the mood to sit through another Artemian nature lecture from a Korean. "Why did you lie about Lee Taekwan?" Haven asks. "I saw you at his funeral."

Park doesn't bat an eye. "I don't believe in giving up information if it doesn't benefit me."

"Jang said he was under your authority when he died."

"That's technically true." He plucks a pink flower from the crepe myrtle tree. "He was murdered in his cell." He peels off a petal and lets it float to the ground. "I had no leads as to what happened. Until today, thanks to Anand."

Haven has no idea what he's talking about, but he's certain that's what the Diplomat intends.

Park shreds the flower to pieces in his hands. "Not that *you* need to worry about that. Your family name is Mortemian, but you must not take after your father."

The last sentence is such a non sequitur, it draws the next uncensored words from Haven. "Reason would follow, then, that I favor my mother."

"You *are* rather pretty."

"You are not my type, Diplomat Park," Haven says, half amazed at what's coming out of his mouth. Anand must also be rubbing off on him.

"No, that feeling is mutual." Park's mouth twists. "As are others, I suspect."

"This is a strange way of apologizing," Haven says.

"I do want to say I'm sorry," Park says. "I should not have reacted that way."

Haven's disinclined to respond to that, nor does he feel that the truth of that statement is an apology at all.

"We do not have much reason to mingle with the Mortemians on Artemis."

"I suppose not," Haven says. "But in the centuries since Mortemians came into practice, people have distanced themselves from death even more. It's a shame, I think. It is a poor life that denies death's existence."

Park flinches. "And you would suggest, what? That we welcome death?"

"I would never suggest you integrate it into your city or your seowon. Much better to keep it separate, in a small, shunned commune." Haven says dryly, "It's how the rest of the solar deals with us."

"Isn't that easier for everyone involved though?"

"To do something the right way doesn't always equate to the easier route," Haven says firmly. "To scapegoat a group unites the remaining people, but perhaps there's a way forward without instilling fear. Without separating out others."

"Thank you for bringing it to my consideration," Park says. "We can't always know what people want or need if they don't speak up."

Condescension aside, Haven thinks that maybe this is what Park never understood about Yoon. It isn't only what Yoon says that matters. It's what she does that matters—even the words she chooses not to say. But even if Haven wanted to, he wouldn't share that with Park.

"May I offer you some advice?" Park asks.

Haven hopes his eyes are transmitting exactly how little he cares for Park's advice, but Park only smiles.

"You have feelings for Ocean, don't you?"

Such a trite way to put it, but all too accurate all the same. How else could he explain this turmoil, this clash of want and fear? Of despair at times, while at others, he thinks nothing could be headier than her laughter. He's spent his life being aware of how people keep their hands off him, but he's never felt how insurmountable a few centimeters were before he met her.

Whatever flashes across Haven's face turns Park's smile smug. "But Ocean must not feel the same."

Haven drops his eyes from Park, concentrating on the smooth bark of the crepe myrtle tree behind the Diplomat, with its varying patterns of brown and white. He doesn't want to admit how much he loathes her name being dropped so carelessly from Park's lips.

"You're careful to not look at her," Park says. "We learned at Sav-Faire that it's not about what draws a person's attention but about what they avoid looking at." Park steps directly into Haven's view again. "If it had been you in the underworld instead of Orpheus, Eurydice might have made it out alive. I might have been fooled myself, but you were right there when her tea spilled."

Haven lets Park lock eyes with him. "I don't know what you're talking about."

Park laughs. "The avoidance tactic straight into denial. So textbook." But Park's next words are gentler, and the kindness of them pierces Haven. "I've been there, Sasani, and I'm only telling you this so you don't suffer the same mistakes I did. It's painful to witness." Park drops his voice. "Has she let you touch her? With those hands? Have you seen her naked?"

"Excuse me?" Haven chokes out.

"She has a small mole high on her inner thigh. I kissed it many times." Park tilts his head. "She liked that."

Haven closes his eyes. "I think you are misunderstanding our relationship."

"Is that so? Maybe she's never let you in as close as . . . that."

And Haven thinks, *Has she looked at you the way she looks at me?*

"She used to tell me she'd be with me for as long as I wanted," Park says. "But what kind of promise is that—as if a relationship is based on one person's feelings? And she *knew*—had to have known—she was handing me an empty promise. She left me in the end anyway."

"Why are you telling me this?" To search Park's face now would mean Haven's seeking some sort of answer. He won't give Park that satisfaction.

"I told you. I'm giving you some advice. As someone who's been there. But maybe I don't need to tell you. I saw your face in the hangar when she pulled out her gun."

In that moment, her face had gone all cold and calm, and the problem wasn't that he had thought she was going to kill someone again, but that he hadn't known what she was going to do at all.

"Don't expect her to stay."

"I don't expect anything," Haven says.

"Hmm," Park says, but before he can continue, the patio doors slide open.

Yoon stands there unconcernedly, as if she just happened upon them.

"Speak of the devil," Park mutters.

Yoon has a packet in her hand and she tears it open with her teeth, pulling out a twin ice cream bar. She holds it up.

"Want to split a Ssang-Ssang Bar with me, Sasani?"

The casual question, coupled with the way she pays attention to him and completely disregards Park, breaks down his defense in one go. He's not like her, and he's not like Diplomat Park.

"Yes," he says automatically.

"Hmm," Diplomat Park says again, radiating that same smugness, and Haven wants to shrivel up at how weak he is.

"I'm not interrupting, am I?" Yoon asks. "How long does it take to say, *I'm sorry, I was an asshole?*"

Park walks forward and pauses next to Yoon as she carefully pulls apart the two sticks of the double ice cream bar. "Ocean," he says.

Only then does she look at him. "Joonho."

Park frowns. "I almost forgot to tell Teophilus something important," he says as if it just occurred to him, but Haven has long stopped believing every word that comes out of the Diplomat's mouth. "He should keep up with the news, if he doesn't already."

He takes his leave without another word. Yoon holds out Haven's half of the dessert, and after he accepts it, she leans back against the railing next to him. Haven's acutely aware of the proximity of her arm to his, and for the first time, he despises how aware of it he is, when she isn't at all. Now after his conversation with Park, he's thinking about looking or not looking at her, and what's better or what will reveal too much.

"Aren't Diplomats generally civilized?" he asks.

"Extremely," she says. "It's why I left Sav-Faire in the end."

Park had been so clearly evaluating Haven as he talked about opening Yoon's legs to kiss her in an intimate spot.

"Why would you . . ." He clamps his mouth shut around that question. As if it's his business. He fixes his attention on his bar instead; it's chocolate flavored.

"You can ask me," she says. "If you want to know."

There's no end to what he wants to know about her. But a person's made up of more than what they're able to say about themselves.

"Do you have good memories with him?" he asks.

Her eyes widen and she turns her head away. Not to avoid it, but to think it over, as she always does when he asks her anything.

"I don't know," she says finally. "I'm not good at keeping memories. When I break up with someone, I tend to focus on the bad. It helps me move on more quickly."

He puts aside his finished ice cream stick. "But it's not a very complete picture," he says gently.

"No, I suppose not."

How will she remember Haven, if she bothers to remember him at all? It makes him, surprisingly, pity Park. It's a sort of death to be obliterated from memory like that.

"When I was a kid," Haven says, "I used to love watching my father cook. Like his qottab." He makes a folding over motion with his hands.

If Yoon's surprised by the turn in topic, she doesn't show it. "My mother makes dumplings by hand too. Every new year, we would make them together for rice cake soup. She always said if you made beautiful dumplings, you'd have beautiful daughters."

"How did yours turn out?"

"My daughters were doomed."

Yoon smiles wryly, and it's such a good smile. He's been learning all her smiles. As she bends her neck, the sun warms her hair, bringing out the red tones. A sheaf falls forward, hiding her face from sight. So, that's why Anand calls her Red.

He says to that fall of hair, "Sometimes when you're in a moment, you already know you're going to miss it later. But when you're a kid, you don't have that self-awareness. And it's not like I won't ever see my dad baking again. But I miss sitting at that table with him then, the flour on my hands. That self-absorption. The kitchen will never be that big to me again." He hesitates, then says, "It's good to have memories to miss, though, isn't it?"

She tucks her hair behind her ear. Her light brown eyes can see right into him, and oh, he wishes he could tell her everything.

"Yes," she says. "It is."

And he already knows; even as it's happening, he's missing this moment. Gods help him. He's just sparred with her ex-steady and maybe he didn't lose, but he certainly didn't come out victorious. His insides are as twisted as ever, and for the rest of his life, he's going to yearn for this moment, splitting an ice cream bar with her.

"Will you stay?" he asks her, his voice breaking above a whisper.

It's only when Yoon's hand comes up to cover her face that he realizes he's said the words aloud. He wishes he knew what his expression revealed, wishes he wasn't always laid so bare before her.

"I'm not going anywhere," she says. She drops the hand but she's facing forward again. Not that it matters because even if Haven closed his eyes, he'd be able to mark the exact hue of hers and precisely where her eyebrow splits. "We can stay here as long as you want."

His chest constricts. "As long as I want," he says dully.

She licks her slowly diminishing ice cream bar. "I imagine your fiancée is excited to see you again."

She's never been as blatant as this, and he detests it. How can she come in here, offering to share food with him, taking a seat next to him, trying to ease him, only to push him away? This carefully measured distance always, as if the handspan is happenstance and not an acknowledgment of how he keeps agonizing track of the space between them.

"We're not engaged anymore," he hears himself say. Distantly, he's surprised that Anand didn't tell her already.

"What does that mean?"

Haven lifts his head at the unexpected sharpness of Yoon's tone. She's staring at him. "I let her go," he says.

Yoon's mouth opens, and he can hear the question on the tip of her tongue. *Ask me* he wants to say. *Ask me why*. But the words seem to be stuck in her throat, and he notices her melting ice cream. A thread of chocolate slips down the stick, running down her hand and—

Haven grabs her by the arm, stopping the ice cream's path before it drips down to her elbow. Without thinking, he swipes the chocolate up the line of her arm with his thumb. He bends down, opening his mouth as he leans toward her wrist before he stops completely. His muscles have locked and he wishes he could say his mind has gone blank, but he's hyperaware of the pearl of sweat on her skin, her pulse thrumming against his fingers, and how hot his body is.

"Sasani?" Yoon says from above him. Her voice is cautious. Quiet. "What are you doing?"

Haven abruptly straightens. He drops her hand and her ice cream falls. Panic and embarrassment are twin birds flapping in his chest. He looks down at his offending, chocolate-smudged hand. "I'm sorry," he says. "I—" *I* what? What possible explanation can he give when his tongue was just a centimeter away from tasting her? He needs to apologize, and he's about to throw himself down on his knees, *something*, when Yoon's posture stops him.

She's holding her arm to her chest, as if it's an injured animal. The ear facing his is red.

"Yoon." The name rushes out of him, but when she looks at him with her wide eyes, it's not what he wants to say.

Ocean he wants to say. Her name is threatening to spill from him. *Ocean Ocean Ocean.*

But then another voice cuts through everything.

"You have feelings for Ocean, don't you?"

Park's snide question.

"But Ocean must not feel the same."

The words slice into him and Haven's hand goes to his chest.

"I'd do it again. They used to call me Headshot. It's because I don't miss."

And this last one is Yoon herself—and wasn't that Yoon's way of looking at him and saying *You aren't the life that I want*?

Again, he doesn't know what's on his face. But he stumbles back. Yoon stands before him, and he can't read her.

"Yoon," he says. "I . . ." His throat clicks as it stops up on his apology.

Yoon half smiles at him before looking away. This smile he hates and loves in equal measure. The curve of it carves into him like shame. "It's fine, Sasani," she says.

Haven tears his eyes away from her. On the ground between them her dropped ice cream bar has melted into a puddle. "I—" He grabs at his chest, bunching up his shirt. His heart is still racing. He doesn't know what he's saying. "I'll go get something to clean that up."

Haven leaves before Yoon can respond. By the time he returns, she's gone.

EIGHTEEN

TEO HEARS THE chattering voices from the dining area. One of them he identifies as Von, but the other is more demure. He peeks in to spy Von sitting at the table with Yeonghui. Marv. It's apparently a two-for-one combo today. The timing's so impeccable, she might as well be sharing calendars with Park, which would make the information that Teo shared with the Diplomat earlier today rather dangerous. He swallows down his discomfort and plasters on a smile.

"Yeonghui, what a pleasant surprise!"

"Oh, Teo!" Yeonghui embraces him in a cloud of perfume and rustling silk. "I heard that Diplomat Park made a visit." She nods to the tea set. "And left some tea."

Teo's not certain whether she means she heard just now from Von, or the servants had alerted her. "I'm sorry you missed him."

"He's very kind," Von says. Teo wants to know if they're possibly talking about the same person, but Von continues, "He came to check on me before he left! And I was chatting with him about my algae project. He's an astonishingly good listener! Anyway, I told him I wanted to present my findings somewhere, and he said he could get me into the Alliance Con next week."

Teo blinks. "Von, that's . . . amazing. You're going to present?"

Von ducks his head, twisting his hands in his lap. "It's about time I did something with my research. Next week feels . . . soon, but . . ." He musses his hair. "I guess I've had everything ready for a while. And Diplomat Park! So helpful!" He beams at Teo.

Diplomat Park is a snake, but Teo will never tell that to Von's face even under torture. Besides, if anyone were to change Park, it would be Von. Teo pats Von's shoulder. "Good for you," he says warmly.

Yeonghui clears her throat. "Although, this tea he brought is somewhat bitter," she says. "Maybe it could use some sugar."

Ah, this again.

"Oh! I probably left it to strain for too long," Von says apologetically.

Teo tries for a smile that he hopes isn't as grating as it feels. He's losing his touch. "Vonderbar, do you mind if I have a few minutes with Yeonghui?"

"Oh! Of course not! Old friends should have the chance to catch up." Von says sunnily to Yeonghui, "A pleasure, even with the poor tea. You should come by some other time so I can brew you a proper cup."

"I'd love that," Yeonghui says.

Teo watches Von go, and remarks, "One of my nicknames for him is Hoddeok."

"I can see why," Yeonghui says. "He's very sweet." She turns to him. "Although I understand he had quite a scare recently."

It would have been impossible to keep a secret from the servants, but it begs the question of whether she also knows what happened to him this morning. His arm twinges.

"But perhaps that's what happens when people wander outside of their boundaries," Yeonghui says.

That's callous, and Yeonghui's attempt to maneuver him into another one of her puzzle box conversations wearies him. He thought he had already foisted off her political maneuverings with his latest foppish affectation, but apparently not.

"I love toeing the line," he says.

Yeonghui takes a sip from her tea, although she doesn't react to the so-called bitterness. "Teo, what are you going to do once you've cleared your name?"

"Try to fix some of what my old man messed up," he says.

Yeonghui frowns. "Mess? What are you talking about?"

"You talk about boundaries and lines. But there might be such a thing as too much power or money," he says. Maybe Yeonghui will understand. She's the child of a dominant force as well.

"There's no such thing," she says.

Well, maybe not.

"Your father worked so hard to build his company. Are you not going to build on his legacy?" she asks. "We could do so much together, Teo."

"What do you think his legacy is, Yeonghui?" Teo asks. "If you had asked me a year ago, a month ago, I would have said it was to serve the solar, to do good for people." He had so confidently said so to Phoenix when they first met. "But you already knew that wasn't true, didn't you?"

Yeonghui's eyebrows scrunch together. "Surely you were never that naive."

But Teo's not only that naive; he also still believes that it's what his father intended, at least initially. He replies, "Why would I want to build on a legacy formed on blood and exploitation?" He watches her carefully, but Yeonghui's eyes only narrow in response.

"You know what it takes to run a business like our fathers did," she says. "And you know that we only survive because we can never be satisfied. Didn't you learn anything?"

Teo learned how to read disappointment on his father's face. He learned how to use himself to try and win his approval.

"I learned very little from my father," he responds to Yeonghui. "Maybe that's good." But the truth of that creates a deep fissure inside of him that he doesn't know what to do with yet.

Yeonghui's nostrils flare. She leans back in her chair, away from Teo. "I see."

The mood between them has the flatness of day-old soda.

Teo scratches his temple. "We'll be out of your hair soon. Again, I can't tell you how grateful we are for your hospitality."

"Yes, I'm sure," Yeonghui says. She rises from her seat, but doesn't bother to try and embrace Teo again. "Good night, Teo."

Teo gives her a head start, to make sure he won't overtake her path out of her family's property. Then he goes through the doorway into the kitchen they were all in earlier, depositing the used teacups in the sink on the way. He leaves through the cloth flaps, outside into the long covered walkway that leads eventually back to the main mansion. Once there, he passes the front living room but stops short without knowing why.

Then he hears his brother's voice. He backtracks to the doorway. He recently asked Lupus to set up the room's multiple screens to be on a constant newsfeed. One displays the trending news from

AllianceVision. Lupus has engineered the others to draw from the keyword net that they've cast.

" . . . Despite everything, yes." Declan—No, not Declan, not anymore and not ever again. It's Hadrian who squares himself in front of the camera. "I worry for him. He's my *brother*."

Teo wonders wearily how many times Hadrian can assert something until he starts believing it himself, if any of that feeling has the possibility of seeping into the man's body. His nails dig into his palms. But he braces himself, leaning against the doorway to keep watching.

"I can't help but think about him out there, all alone. On the run. And I've said this many, many times before: If you see him, *don't* try to engage. He's a danger to others and to himself."

From the beginning, Hadrian basically cast Teo as a madman who can't be trusted. Imagine now if Teo were to drop down and start raving about deepfake suits and someone impersonating his brother.

The time stamp on the conference is today. Hadrian's wearing one of Declan's favorite ensembles. Teo tries not to think of Hadrian shoving his hands through the pristine clothes lined up in his brother's closet.

"Let the Alliance handle it," Hadrian says into the camera. "This is for your safety, but also for my brother's. I don't want a situation where some vigilante takes him down in a crowded street."

Teo's arm twinges from where he was hit, and he has to keep from clutching at it. He misses what Hadrian says next, but then the man pauses as he takes a question from off-camera.

"Do I think he's hiding out in Korea?" Hadrian blinks at the person asking. "Well, that would certainly make it easier. He'd be spotted and arrested immediately." He faces the camera. "If I were him... and I know I shouldn't say this on a live stream..."

If it shouldn't be said, Declan would have never said it. But Teo stares at his brother's image through the screen, as he has hundreds of times before. Declan, always so self-assured and confident in front of the camera and always aware of how he came off. Even in delicate or high-pressure moments, his brother would say the right thing, perform the mental checkmate. Teo, on the other hand, only became too aware of the camera when he started turning to hide his cheek.

"Babu, don't come home. Hide away and live out your life without harming anyone else," Hadrian says. "If you come back, I don't know if I can protect you. From the Alliance, from the media, from anyone who might want to take revenge for all the harm you've caused, for all the people you've hurt."

Hadrian rubs at his forehead with two fingers from his left hand.

Checkmate.

Teo leaves. He walks away from the flashing cameras on-screen, each spark a jolt to his retinas, away from the shouted hubbub rising. He grips the banister of the staircase, then lifts his foot for one step. Then the next. And then the next and the next. At the second floor, he goes down to the end of the hallway and knocks at the door. The paper screen shows a trace of the light, but it doesn't necessarily mean Sasani's awake or even there.

"Come in."

Inside, Sasani is sitting on the bed, elbows resting on his quads. Teo closes the door behind him and sits in the chair next to the bed. Sasani has the demeanor of a sad little sock at the end of the day, and he rubs at his eyes. When he sees Teo's face, though, he straightens.

"Anand, are you . . ." He hesitates, then asks, "How's your arm doing?"

Teo is startled into holding it out. "How'd you know?"

"You've been carrying it differently, although I didn't want to bring it up while Diplomat Park was around."

"That's judicious of you," Teo says with a faint smile.

"What happened?"

Teo unbuttons his shirt and pulls his arm out to show Sasani the wrap. "I was shot."

"What?" Sasani asks sharply.

It actually feels a bit far off now. "It only grazed me," Teo explains. "It was a lot of blood, but Phoenix cleaned and wrapped it up. I would have asked you to check it sooner, but by the time I came home, Diplomat Park was here."

Sasani's already pulling on gloves. "Only 'grazed' you," he murmurs. "What is it with all of you? Kent's kidnapped. And Yoon—" He snaps his mouth shut as he carefully unwinds the gauze around Teo's arm.

"How's her leg looking?" Teo asks.

"I haven't seen it lately," Sasani says a little too quickly, but his next words are collected. "But judging from our early morning PT, she's moving just fine on it. And luckily, your bullet wound is cleaner than hers. Doesn't even need stitches. Phoenix did a good job."

It'll likely just leave a white scar to match the one on his cheek. "I don't think it's his first bullet hole," Teo says absently.

Sasani tests the arm's range of movement, his grip on Teo firm but delicate.

"Was this Corvus's doing again?" he asks.

"Yes," Teo says, shaking himself. Gemini hadn't been able to capture the sniper, so he can't say definitively whether it was Alessa or someone else working for Corvus. He hesitates as he remembers how Sasani left the room when they were talking about it before. "I'm sorry to bring you back into all this."

"Yoon said the same thing," Sasani says briskly.

"Did she go pick you up at Dunian?" Teo asks.

Sasani sits back on the bed, but his eyes are considering something else beyond Teo. "You asked me once if I'd seen her fly. And watching her at the controls when she was flying into Artemis..." He trails off. "But it's something else entirely sitting next to her while she's behind the wheel of a car."

Teo knows something of that. But he's stilled more by the slight curve to Sasani's mouth, which hooks into Teo to drag him out of the newscast he just saw.

"You're in love with her, aren't you," Teo says.

Sasani's head jerks up. "What?"

"I've known it for a while. But... the way you were looking at her today. That was a dead giveaway."

He's known it for a while, but today was also the first time he saw Ocean and thought, *oh. When did that happen?*

"I'm not... I don't..."

"You think you can avoid the truth by refusing to speak it into existence," Teo says slowly. "But your whole being trembles with it."

Sasani stares at him, the denial dead on his lips.

"Frankly, I think you'd be good for her," Teo continues. "As a friend or steady or lover or whatever."

Yeonghui asked, *"What are you going to do once you've cleared your name?"* But Teo hasn't really allowed himself to think about what's beyond failure or success. His answer shouldn't be Ocean's either. What has he left for her after bringing her into this do-or-die mission?

"What are you saying?" Sasani rubs the back of his neck.

"It did a number on her, what happened on the *Hadouken*," Teo says. "Our captain turned against her, and who is supposed to have your back if not your captain? The whole crew turned against her. I blame myself for that. I had been calling her Headshot for a while and that kind of thing sticks. It wormed into their heads, and it skewed their perception. But you know what it's like to be ostracized by Alliance kids, don't you? And from the moment you found out I named her that, you were ready to tell me I was wrong. She could use some of that in her life. Would you be there for her until the end?"

"I can't," Sasani says.

"Why not? Because of your father? You can't be *friends* with her, even?"

"Friends." Sasani laughs shortly. "I thought I could—I tried—" He breaks off. "She doesn't *want* me. Don't push me on her."

Now they're getting somewhere. "What makes you say that?"

"She told me about what happened on the *Hadouken*. She said she didn't want me to get the wrong idea about her."

"She told you she killed all those people. And you had a hard time with that."

"Of course I did! She said if she had to do it again, she would."

"Of course she would. She saved my life that day, Sasani."

Sasani flushes. "I didn't mean—"

"I know you didn't." Teo waves that away. "She killed people for me. I'm living a life that came at the cost of others. We put each other in those positions. I don't know how we didn't end up hating each other after that."

"You don't hate each other," Sasani says brusquely. "Not even a little."

"Oh, I don't know about that." Teo doesn't need to explore that idea though. "You think she told you all that to push you away. She probably thought so too—god, she probably thought she *wanted* that."

Sasani draws in a breath, a pained punctuation. "Why are you asking me for this? She has you."

"She's always going to think it's out of obligation. No matter how our friendship started, that's how it is."

Sasani flexes his fingers. He says, more to his hands than to Teo, "You don't understand. I have to go back home. It's a promise I made to my father, and to myself."

Even if Teo did understand, it doesn't change anything. "And this promise," Teo says. "Does it honor your father? Yourself? Are you living generously?"

"I can't break it," Sasani says.

Teo becomes aware of the hum of the aircon in the room. It's been on this whole time, fighting the humidity of Artemis's summer. But only now is the noise growing somehow, as if its nothingness is trying to take over the space in the room while they're talking about the most important person in Teo's life.

"I'd be giving up on who I am if I did," Sasani says.

"So, you're giving up on her instead," Teo says. "If it's that easy for you, then maybe you don't deserve her."

Sasani grimaces and that small movement wounds Teo. Sasani has never seen Ocean with anyone else, will never comprehend the gift of how *this* is closer than she lets herself be. Ocean, who doesn't say *I care about you* but says *Have you eaten?* Ocean, who doesn't ask *Do you trust me?* but says *Want to go for a ride?*

Teo takes in the firm set of Sasani's mouth, the hunch of his shoulders. "Then that's your decision," he says. He pulls out a folded piece of paper from his pocket. "This is for you."

"What is it?" Sasani asks as he unfolds the delicate hanji paper, revealing the calligraphy scrawled across it.

The stark beauty of the letters that Park has painted is such a dramatic presentation, paired with the fact that it's on hanji, which is a rare commodity these days. Teo presumes that part of it was so that he wouldn't leave a trail by transmitting the data otherwise, and part of it was just to show off.

"It's your flight information to Saturn. Park gave this to me before he left. You're headed out first, four days from now."

The paper crumples in Sasani's hands. "I see," he says.

Teo swallows. "But we're heading out soon after that too. Ocean and I will go with the *Pandia* since that's nearly fixed. Dae and Von are headed back to Earth, but Maggie's going back to Venus; she says she's done with all this nonsense, which . . . I can't blame her."

"Where will . . . where will the *Pandia* go next?"

"*Babu, don't come home.*"

A trap? Or is it a threat? "I have some ideas," Teo says. "But I'm not entirely sure yet." He sighs, kneading his forehead.

Sasani smooths out the paper again, methodically flattening the wrinkles as if he can undo his actions. As he folds the paper up, he says, "I'm sorry."

"For what?" Teo asks, startled.

"This must . . . this . . ." Sasani's fingers spread, brushing against his chest, and that gesture pains Teo. ". . . must all seem so trivial to you."

Yes, and no. "Sasani . . . I just don't want either of you to get hurt."

"Me?" Sasani asks hollowly, and Teo wishes he could hug him.

"You're going back home and you're following your father's footsteps." Teo hesitates. "If I had that choice open to me, I . . . might have taken it too." He holds out his arm. "Would you wrap me up again?"

Sasani does so, his movements assured. "I'd like to check on it tomorrow. Keep an eye on it."

"I'll take off my shirt for you anytime," Teo says blithely. He expects Sasani to turn away, for his neck to turn bright red like it always does.

But Sasani merely pulls off his gloves to throw them in a nearby receptacle. It beeps and whirs as it identifies and sorts the item. "I don't know that Phoenix would like that very much," he says neutrally.

"*Sasani*," Teo says, half in shock and half in delight.

For the first time, Sasani smiles. "You might be a bad influence." Then he says thoughtfully, "Although I'm grateful for it."

"Well, I'm relieved if you think that." Teo pulls on his shirt and buttons it up. "Anyway, if I ever see the other end of this Corvus business, I'd like to visit you from time to time. If that's all right with you."

Sasani's eyes flick to his. "You'd want to?"

"Would I ask you if I didn't want to?"

Sasani mulls that over. He nods. "I'd like that."

Teo grins. "Consider it done, then. Don't say I didn't warn you when I show up on your doorstep." He stands. "Now get some sleep. You look like you need it."

Sasani nods again, but even if he does sleep, Teo doubts it will be restful.

NINETEEN

AMELL'S VOICE IS a quiet patter in Corvus's head. Or should he say the essence of who Amell was? Or is it that Corvus shares his body with Amell now? Corvus had always considered Amell necessary, but perhaps . . . abrasive. That was before they joined. Now Corvus appreciates Amell's rage, his hunger, better than before.

The more he eats, the more ravenous he becomes. He tried explaining that to Emory. Poor little Emory, kneeling before him as she rubbed her palms to plead with him. *Corvus no, we should stay in, haven't you had enough, don't you think—*

Corvus's lip curls as he thinks of it. When she had fallen asleep finally, it was with morning light creeping over a face tracked with the pitiful trail of tears. He had slipped out on his own.

They wasted no time fleeing from Brazil. Not that Corvus really made much sense of where they were going next; he'd been somewhat . . . preoccupied with sorting through it all. He doesn't even remember how it ended on that road, only that he came to in the back of their ship. It could have been years that he was asleep, but it somehow didn't surprise him that it had been only days. New country, new time zone, new memories swirling in his body.

Corvus muses to himself as he stalks the busy walkways of the neighborhood marketplace. So many people mill the streets, it's like ants pulsing over a sidewalk crack. They're kissed in shadows and it's so crowded no one notices when he takes the first man.

He touches his gloved hand to a forehead as someone squeezes past him, brushing aside their dark hair while his other hand cups the back of their neck. It could be an amorous gesture, until their legs give and their mouth opens in a distressed cry. Corvus also convulses, his muscles rigid as the glove connects his nerves to that person's.

There is no way forward without pain. It's like Corvus has been lit on fire, burned to a black crisp, and then formed all over to burn again. That man's consciousness slams into Corvus.

Unfamiliar smells assault him, not from the market around him, but from this person's memories. *Leftovers in the fridge and the putrid wet slick smell coats his tongue, the inside of his mouth—*

Corvus retches before he drops the man to the ground and moves on. He doesn't bother to suck everything from him. A little taste here and there will allow him to sample more. He learned in Brazil how to latch and unlatch.

What Garrett never understood was that pain's never been Corvus's end goal. He wants to break down what separates people. You can't force another person to feel, but the desire to hurt someone who has hurt him . . . that's a form of empathy, isn't it? It's drawing someone in to feel your pain. No matter how close two people get, they'll never truly know each other. It's the tragedy of existence. Garrett never saw it as a tragedy, but then again, he was the one who left.

Corvus grabs the next person, a woman with olive skin like Alessa's, and slaps his hand to her forehead.

This time it's his own memory that floats to the surface, of *a man with bushy eyebrows ruffling his hair.*

"Stick with me, kid. You'll be just fine."

In his mind, he sees *his hands are so small next to Bradford's, but they deftly arrange the wires and—*

"Hey. Not bad, kid. Not bad."

Corvus's heart swells at the memory. But when he drops the woman, the glow in his heart is replaced by a terrible ache when he remembers that Bradford is gone.

"Corvus!" Emory's voice cuts into his ears, ringing out clearly even with all the excess noise. "Where are you?"

Disgust glances through him, and there's enough of him that recognizes the feeling as not *his*. It's Amell, who always thought Emory was so pathetic. Corvus *understands* though. He remembers that first day he showed up at her home, where she had whiled away her existence, waiting for each day to pass. She'd barely been past childhood when the Penelope Mine Collapse had taken away her right arm, her legs.

Corvus had created legs for her to run with again. Had fashioned an arm for her to grasp things with. She'd had no guarantees, just a stranger's pledge, his hope, when she submitted to suffering. He regretted the agony he put her through, but there had been no way to gauge how painful it would be to wire the machines to her nerves. That misery had fused them together too, their dripping sweat mingling as she keened and he yelled *I'm sorry I'm sorry I'm sorry.* She could have hated him for that. The fact she was standing now was due as much to her tenacity and her efforts as to his technology.

But it had been a baptism of sorts: for her to learn to walk again, one step in front of the other, to arrive at Corvus's waiting arms. She would have done anything for Corvus, even if he hadn't promised that they would pay Anand Tech back, that they would dismantle the Alliance. She had understood from the beginning that Corvus meant to heal what was truly wrong with the solar, that pain was a necessary catalyst.

"You can't affect change unless you compel the other person to understand what they're doing wrong. What we need in this solar is compassion."

Emory understood it. He could tell by the burning conviction in her eyes as he spoke to her.

"War, anger, blight, it's all a result of our unwillingness to see another's perspective."

"Emory," he says now. "This is for us." He's not sure if his mouth mic is picking up the screams around them. No matter.

He's already sweat through his shirt. The next breath he drags in, he holds in his chest. *Calme.* Even now, whiteness spreads at the edge of his vision. He stumbles.

"Corvus." Worry vibrates over the line. "I'm coming to get you."

Why won't she *listen* to him?

"You don't get to say when I'm done," he snarls. "Only I get to say it, you *robot.*"

He punctuates the last word with a snatch of the next person's ponytail. He siphons her.

And then another.

And another.

He has, no he *is* Amell now. He's Gene. He's Saul, he's Anita, and when he reaches into another mind, he's Weiliang.

But then what is this emptiness still yawning inside of him?

He jerks the next head back and slaps his hand down. The memories flick by too quickly for him to track, as well as the pure, undiluted emotions. *A ball juggled between her feet, her overwhelming love for her mother.* Wrapped up in *colors, warmth, sadness, joy*—

"Corvus!" The scream somehow breaks through. "She's a child—"

He hears himself wail as something latches on to his arm, wrenching him away. He stretches his gloved hand upward as he collapses to the ground. Lightning lacerates his body. He's grasping, grappling. His left hand grabs a neck, and he shoves his right hand down onto the next forehead.

"Corvus!"

Corvus's eyes fly open to find Emory kneeling before him. Her hands are on his wrist. Feet stampede around them, but he's homed in on one person only.

"Do you—do you want to take me now?" Emory asks.

But he's never seen her direct such an expression at him before. She quivers and tears trickle from her eyes, but she doesn't move his hand from her forehead.

"Corvus?" she asks.

The aftershock of another blistering bolt shatters him. He doubles over and vomits. Emory gathers him up before she crouches and with a creak of gears, launches into the air. Corvus can't stop gagging. But he hears his own voice heave out feebly.

"Don't leave me."

"I've got you, Corvus," Emory keeps saying.

People, objects fly by, but Corvus can't tell if he's really seeing them while Emory sprints, or if they're memories. Tears stream down Corvus's face. He wheezes through the misery, can barely keep from telling Emory he doesn't want *her*.

"Garrett," he whispers.

"Don't talk, Corvus," Emory begs. "Save your strength."

His canned breath takes over every other sense. And the next memory that slams into him is his own. That first time he remembered how terror could blot out everything until his existence narrowed down to the funnel of air he sucked in and out. He had been a small child hiding under a desk, while his parents were murdered.

But it wasn't until years and years later, when he stabbed his first person, that he understood exactly what had been done to his parents.

What would it be like if he plunged this knife into the man's stomach and dragged it all the way . . .

And that was when he lost Garrett. Blood splattered, he had held out his hands to Garrett. He'd been ecstatic because he *finally* figured it out. Ecstatic and wrecked all the same because he knew how much pressure one needed to apply to rip another human open. He'd never forget the excruciating anguish that imprinted someone's face as it was done to them. This was what his parents had experienced to protect him.

He wanted to share this with Garrett, for Garrett to unlock another mystery within Corvus. But Garrett hadn't met that grievous joy and conflicted agony. He'd only frozen in horror. It was the last time they had seen each other in person, with Garrett walking away from Corvus's pain, Corvus's joy, who Corvus was.

TWENTY

When Teo opens the door, he makes out the shape of someone sitting in the dark room and his heart seizes. He reels backs before the person speaks up.

"It's me."

It's Phoenix's voice. Teo turns on the light and Phoenix squints. He blinks a few times as Teo closes the door behind him.

"What is it?"

"Lupus picked up on some news. I think you should see this." He pulls out his tabula and hands it to Teo. Phoenix puts on his spectacles before reaching over to hit Play. The footage is from a traffic camera. Instinctively, Teo searches for Declan, but then he identifies another distinctive head of hair.

"Corvus."

"It's from Earth. Brazil, actually, a week or so ago. And then Lupus used that to track a similar incident in Singapore just yesterday. But this one has a clearer view from traffic cams."

The whole road of cars is stopped for some reason, and as they watch, Corvus thrusts his hand on someone's head, the movement accented by the arc of a blue light. There's no sound, but the man's mouth opens as if he's screaming, his face screwed up. When Corvus pulls away, the man collapses over the side of the car. Then Corvus is on to the next. And the next. If a door is closed, the window up, he crashes his fist through the window. Soon people are escaping out of their vehicles, running from him. Some of them he pursues, jumping onto the hoods of cars, darting into the crowds and nabbing people before having them cowering before him. At one point, Corvus clutches the side of a car as he bends over, his face contorted.

"What is he doing?" Teo asks.

"No one knows," Phoenix says. "But the reports say all those people died. But not right away. When they were found, they were physically still alive but there was no brain activity. They were basically all in comas."

"Did they catch him?" Teo asks, even if he knows the answer.

Phoenix shakes his head. "No. And that's not all. All of them had strange lacerations on their foreheads, as if holes had been punctured through their skulls." He says, "We'll get Lupus to pull more detailed medical records. I'd like to get Sasani's opinion; he might have some insight."

Teo rubs his face. Drained bodies. Corvus in a rampage in Brazil. Next in Singapore. Hadrian warning him away from Korea.

"We need to get back to Earth," he says. "How's your ship looking?"

"Almost ready to go," Phoenix says, then seems to deliberate. "Back when you said you'd pay for the repairs on your own, you offered to pay extra for them to be done quickly. Do you remember?"

Teo remembers that stilted conversation, and the way Phoenix had become flat and cutting. "Yes."

"I thought . . . assumed, back then, that meant you wanted me gone more quickly."

"What? Why?"

"You didn't?" Phoenix asks, his eyes intent on him.

Teo looks away. Instead of answering, he asks, "Why were you here in the dark?"

Phoenix looks out the window. "I've been thinking . . ." His mouth turns down. "I was watching and rewatching that clip. I never thought he could . . ." He trails off. "I can't help but think, is there something I could have done?"

Anger blazes through him. Not just at the horror of what Corvus has wrought, which Teo is sure he doesn't even fully comprehend, but at the dark grief in Phoenix's eyes.

"This isn't on you, Phoenix."

"No?"

Phoenix's blue eyes are so muted. Teo's reaching for Phoenix before he can stop himself, wrapping his arms around him, cradling Phoenix's head against his chest. "No," he says, and then again more fiercely. "No."

Phoenix's hands grip Teo's shirt. Teo hears his breathing slow as they're pressed up against each other.

Phoenix says softly, "What can you tell me about assuming other people's guilt?"

"That's different," Teo says swiftly.

Phoenix relaxes his hold on Teo's shirt, only to spread his fingers, pressing the palms against Teo. The contact sparks through

Teo's body. He tries to keep from trembling but Phoenix can probably acutely hear how his heart thunders through his chest. Teo makes to pull away, but Phoenix firmly holds his position.

"Don't do that," Phoenix says.

"Do what?"

"Don't avoid this, don't pretend this isn't happening, don't pretend you haven't been pushing me away."

Phoenix holds a duality—no . . . a whole gradient, a multitude, a vast solar. He's raw, yet assertive. But even while he demands things of Teo, he's still giving so much to him. Giving something that Teo doesn't know if he can hold.

"I have obligations I've been running away from my whole life," Teo squeezes out against the tightness of his throat.

Phoenix straightens. "You told me I should think about what I need." He takes Teo's hand and presses it against his own chest. The beat of his heart is so erratic, so fast, that Teo doesn't recognize it for what it is at first, even though the thrum of it is strong.

Teo swallows. "What do you need, Phoenix?"

"I need my crew to be safe," Phoenix says. "I need to remember where I come from and what brought me here. And . . ." Phoenix turns his gaze on Teo.

A shudder trips up Teo's back. "And?"

Phoenix pulls Teo to him, kissing him full on the mouth. Teo's response is immediate, instinctual. His hands are around Phoenix, then in his hair. That *hair*. Phoenix's lips are hard against his and then pliant before they open to Teo's tongue. Phoenix groans and Teo devours that noise, wants it inside him, and they're kissing as he pushes Phoenix down on the bed.

He breaks from Phoenix's lips to mouth at his jawline. His hands are tilting Phoenix's head back and Phoenix willingly moves for him. He grips Teo's shoulders tight enough to bruise. His gasp cuts through Teo's mind, bringing everything into sharp clarity.

It's in the way Phoenix's skin tastes against Teo's tongue and the way his skin looks against the bedsheets. If Teo does this, if he lets Phoenix in, it will break him. And he's been broken too much recently.

He rips himself away. "I can't." His voice comes out low and guttural.

But god, the proximity is intoxicating. He wants to immediately dive back in. Teo's so much more aware of how they're panting while their faces are mere centimeters apart. He's already folding that sound into himself, ready to replay it in his ears later when he can stand the torture of it. Phoenix skims his hands down Teo's back, and Teo shuts his eyes, shivering.

Phoenix says, "Look at me."

Teo shouldn't. But he does, and they lock eyes.

"When you touch me," Phoenix says, "it undoes me."

Teo's breath stops in his throat. His hands clench the sheets, as if to stop Phoenix's words, but he wants so desperately for Phoenix to keep going too.

"But my hope hurts so much," Phoenix says. "You said you wanted me to hate you. And I should, I know I should. But I *don't*. And when I try to put what I actually feel to words, it's like I'm lying because I can't even capture what I feel when I look at you."

Teo's the one over him, the one who's made Phoenix's hair wild, who's caused the mark already swelling on Phoenix's skin. Teo has penned Phoenix in with his arms, but he's the one who's caught.

"Tell me you don't feel anything when I touch you," Phoenix says. "Tell me this isn't serious for you. I'll believe you."

What Phoenix is offering him is as tangible as a butterfly in his hands, and he senses how easily he could crush it. The right thing would be to annihilate it.

"I can't figure out what you see in me," Teo says.

Phoenix traces a finger on Teo's face, where Teo knows his scar is. "Sometimes I think I'm the only one who sees you truly."

How can Teo respond other than to kiss Phoenix? To kiss him over and over, to put his tongue on that beauty mark under Phoenix's mouth. He presses Phoenix back into the bed, entangling their limbs. He slides his hands under Phoenix's shirt and comes undone at the noise Phoenix makes.

Phoenix opens every one of Teo's buttons deliberately, his confidence belied by how eagerly he seeks each new strip of skin revealed. Phoenix's hand smooths over every divot, flattens against Teo's shoulder blades. When his mouth closes around Teo's nipple, Teo hisses out a curse. He gives as good as he gets, scraping his teeth on hot, feverish skin. He laughs when he finds a sensitive spot on Phoenix's neck.

It's a heady push and pull, spurred on by Phoenix's moans, that quickly devolves as Teo rocks against Phoenix. Harder, rougher, messier. But when Teo slips his hand under Phoenix's waistband, Phoenix freezes suddenly. The room's filled with the sound of their panting.

"No?" Teo asks quietly.

Phoenix's chest is heaving against Teo's. "No, I mean, god *yes*—"

But when Teo moves again, Phoenix's hand clamps around Teo's wrist. Teo straightens, removing his hand. Phoenix's hair is in complete disarray and his face is flushed.

"I'm sorry," he blurts out.

"Phoenix," Teo says gently, stopping him. "We're ready when we're ready." He leans down and kisses Phoenix's hands.

"I just . . ." Phoenix falters. "It's been a while for me."

"It's been a while for me too," Teo says. At Phoenix's expression, he laughs. "Why won't anyone believe me?"

Phoenix dips his head. "I want this. I really do," he says. "You have to believe me."

Teo can't help but laugh. When Phoenix's head snaps up, he says gently, "Oh, I do." He reaches forward to kiss Phoenix under his mouth again, then moves slowly next to him and puts his arms around him. "Is this all right?"

Phoenix's assent is a bare rasp. His pulse is still a rapid staccato under Teo's hands. Teo pulls Phoenix against him and lies down on the bed with him.

"Is this all right?" he asks again, speaking to the back of Phoenix's head.

"Yes."

He kisses the nape of Phoenix's neck. Listens as Phoenix's breathing slows.

"Phoenix?" he asks in the darkness after Phoenix's pulse steadies.

"Hmm?" The reply is sleepy, relaxed now.

"I'm scared too."

Phoenix doesn't say anything in response, but his hand tightens around Teo's as they lie in the darkness together. And soon, Teo drops off into the deepest sleep he's had for as long as he can remember.

TWENTY-ONE

WHEN OCEAN COMES back down from hanging out on the roof, it's to music from the front entrance, Korean words wailing out over some tinny brass and saxophones. She pokes her head in to catch Maggie swaying, waving a whisk.

"Trot?" she asks.

Maggie spins around. "Oh hey, Ocean. Yeah." She steps to the right and back again. "What's this one about?"

Ocean listens to a few lines. Trot songs are generally about one of two topics. "This one's about longing for home."

"Hmm," Maggie says. "Is that why you're always listening to these songs?"

Maggie waits so expectantly for Ocean's answer. As always, she has that earnest demeanor of a student in class who just needs the correct formula.

"All the ajumma on Marado listen to trot," Ocean tries to explain, but can't go on.

To most people, listening to Speciation or Phantom Desires transports them straight back to high school dances, the rock cafés. You can go to practically any country, any planet in the solar, and if you play that five-note motif from *Cosmic Kill*, the whole room will burst out singing the opening line with you. But for Ocean, the sound of trot comes with the smell of the sea, the hum of mopeds while halmoni with their visors placed in their permed hair whiz by, the burble of jjigae on the stove while her umma sings along off-key.

"Your mom too?" Maggie asks. "My mom sang a lullaby to me when I was a kid that's part and parcel to every Venus childhood. It always reminds me of her."

"I always figured that would be me someday," Ocean confesses. "Listening to trot while I grew older on Marado." On her way to dive in the waters with the other haenyeo in her mother's clan.

"You make it sound like it won't be." Maggie crinkles her nose. "That can still be you, right?" Then she slaps her fist down into her palm. "Oh. Is it the no swimming thing? But can't you live on Marado without having to swim?"

She hasn't been back to swim in Marado since her failed haenyeo trial. But she could live there without having to swim. Or she could find another haenyeo clan on another island off Jeju. They'd probably be happy to have her. But Ocean doesn't know if that's a victory, or whether she wants this, her choice, to be about winning at all.

"Ah, Yao! You're *finally* here. I was thinking, for lunch today—"

Yao's arrived at the door, and his shoulders slump at seeing Maggie before he quickly straightens them with a clearing of his throat.

"Go easy on him, will you?" Ocean pats Maggie on the head.

Maggie trails after Yao. Ocean's already down the hallway when she hears Maggie's exuberant "Oh, good morning, Sasani!"

Ocean ducks into the next doorway. She's pressed her back against the wall before she even knows what she's doing. Her heart rate has cranked up far too much too fast. Sasani's answer is a low murmur. She peeks her head around the doorway. He's standing with his back to her. It's become a very familiar landscape: the slope of his shoulders, the angles of his shoulder blades, and the way he holds himself.

He puts his hands up at something Maggie's said. Just the night before, his hand had wrapped around her arm, the touch like lightning. She'd always thought of him as cool, composed, but his breath on her wrist had been wet. It had condensed against her skin, and her body had been poised, taut while everything inside her combusted.

The shave of his undercut is clean, and he must have touched it up since their PT session that morning. Ocean thinks Cass was just as surprised as the rest of them when Sasani came back after that first time, but no one remarked on it, and they've all continued since. A soft beam of light touches the sweep of his graceful neck, and she wants to follow that parabola.

He's turning as if his attention has been drawn by hers, and she whips her head back. Her hand goes to her chest to command it to slow down and it's only then that she sees Phoenix in the room too.

Phoenix is gazing out the window with an inward expression, someone who's not seeing where his eyes are directed. He has a bowl of uneaten granola in his hand, which is unusual in itself because Ocean can't recall a time he's been content eating alone. He'll often go from room to room, hunting around for someone to dine with while his food goes cold. It's possible he hasn't figured out he's always hunting around for one specific person.

"Good morning," she says.

Phoenix starts at her greeting. As he does, the lapel of his shirt flaps to the side to reveal a distinctive red mark below his collarbone. Well. That might have to do with why he's distracted this morning.

"Did you come from the rooftop?" he asks.

"Yes. Hurakan showed me the footage of Corvus." The thief is up there more often than not, keeping his vantage point even though Yeonghui assured them she has her own guards. "He said he'll be down soon."

Phoenix nods thoughtfully as he shoves in a bite of his granola, which by now is so soggy it doesn't even crunch in his mouth. "You call him Hurakan. Why is that?"

Ocean's surprised by the question. "Because he likes it. Doesn't he?"

"He prefers it, actually," Phoenix says. "But that doesn't mean he lets anyone call him that."

"Would he stop someone from doing it?"

"Probably," Phoenix says. "Much like Sasani tends to correct anyone who gets too familiar with him."

Ocean ignores the odd thump in her chest, and concentrates on Phoenix's next words.

"But I'm glad at least one person around names Hurakan properly. Speaking of, I've asked Teophilus about some of his nicknames for you. Do you know why he calls you Hummingbird?"

"I've always assumed it was a flying thing."

"Hummingbirds are the only birds that can fly backward. They're probably the most agile birds," Phoenix says. "Teophilus is

TEO'S DURUMI 215

brimming over with hummingbird facts. I think he's been saving them up for you."

Ocean's never asked Teo about any of her nicknames, not after that first one.

Phoenix continues in a conversational tone. "Did you know hummingbird hearts can beat up to 1,200 times per minute? And hummingbirds have the largest heart-to-body ratio of any animal; they're practically all heart." He takes another bite of his granola. "Teo told me they're so delicately formed, though, they normally can't stand to be touched."

"You must talk a lot about hummingbirds."

"No, not really. But Teo loves to talk about you," Phoenix says. "He told me Aztecs used to believe fallen warriors were reborn as hummingbirds. And that's how Teophilus sees you. A fierce warrior."

A fallen warrior, more like. But Ocean can't find it in herself to correct Phoenix.

He places the bowl to the side, giving up on the soft mess of it for now. "I've always thought names have a strength. I've been curious about yours though. Who gave it to you?"

"Ocean?" Ocean says. "My mom did."

"What do you think it means?"

Traditionally, Ocean would have had a Korean name connected to her brother's, one that started with the same syllable like Haneul or Hana. But instead, her mother gave her a name in Common.

"It's not a Korean name," she says. "I think she wanted me to be different."

"But it's a name of great significance for your mother, isn't it? That's what I'd imagine, given her profession."

"That's what you'd imagine," she repeats.

Phoenix smiles, as if he heard her implied *Fuck off*. "Sure, but I shouldn't presume. Just like I wouldn't make you call me oppa." Ocean winces, and Phoenix's expression softens. "Sorry. That was thoughtless of me."

"It's all right," she says. "You're not a thoughtless person."

That surprises a laugh from Phoenix. "I hope not."

"You're not what I imagined, though," she says. "From back when Hurakan first tried to recruit me."

"I like to defy expectations." Phoenix grins. "You're not the usual brand of whom Gemini brings in either, but I can see why he liked you."

"I seem to recall him saying *you'd* like me."

"Oh, I'm not so hard to please. Gem is the one who stresses about team chemistry. He's found all sorts of characters from all sorts of situations. But he's never gone so out of his way to bring someone in. Now we're mixed up in interplanetary conspiracies and space battles. Not that I'm complaining."

"No," Ocean says. "It's brought you to Teo, in any case."

"Yes, for that alone, I'm in your debt," Phoenix says, not missing a beat. "But I'm also eternally grateful you've kept him safe all these years."

He's so open and transparent. His trust in Hurakan has been so absolute all this time, and his obvious tenderness toward Teo is a balm on Ocean's own feelings.

"I could work for someone like you," she says. It wouldn't be a bad way to live. "If you'd have me."

"If *I'd* have *you*?" Phoenix laughs again. "Is that what we've been dancing around? You know you don't have to prove anything, right? You've already done enough."

TEO'S DURUMI

Ocean drops her chin. "We'll have to get through this alive though."

"Oh, I hope so," Phoenix says. "And having you would also be a strong incentive for someone else to join."

Ocean's sure Phoenix and Teo have considered their future, whether separately or together, and she's been curious how likely it would be that Teo would join them. But that, too, is probably contingent on what happens after they leave the Moon.

"I don't think I'd be the strongest incentive," she says. "Have you asked Teo directly?"

Phoenix peers over at her with a mild curiosity. The quality to the air between them tells her she's misstepped somewhere, somehow missed the mark.

"Good morning."

The sleepy greeting brings their attention to the door. Teo stumbles in, his hair flat on one side and his shirt lifted up as he scratches his stomach.

"You were gone when I woke up," Teo complains.

He walks over to Phoenix and without preamble, squeezes onto the same seat. His head droops and he rests his forehead on Phoenix's shoulder. Phoenix turns a shade of red Ocean hasn't seen before and she smiles.

"Um," he says. "What was I saying?" He puts his arm around Teo. Phoenix can't see it, but a smile spreads on Teo's face as he burrows further in, his eyes closed.

A knock comes from the door, and Hurakan's there, his hand up to his ear. "Oh, good, you're here. Cass, can you grab Lupus and join us in the front room?"

"Is this about Brazil?" Phoenix asks.

Teo sits up, all sleep and residual related feelings gone. "Or Singapore?"

But Ocean thinks Hurakan's urgent timbre indicates something more than that, and her suspicion is confirmed by his head shake.

"We should review that footage together, but like Maggie'd say, when it rains, it pours cats and dogs," Hurakan says tersely. "It'll be better to explain once we're all together."

Lupus is ushered in by Cass, rubbing their eyes. "I just got to sleep," they complain. "What is it?"

"I think we know where Corvus is going to be next," Hurakan says. He picks up a remote and turns on the large screen that takes up one side of the room.

"—So excited about this next week. We think we'll bring positive change to the solar. Anyone who wants a say in the ecological impact should be present."

It's Declan/Hadrian standing at a podium with cameras going off. Teo's moved from Phoenix to take a seat at the table in the middle. He carefully observes the screen, tenting his fingers and resting his chin on them.

"Next week?" he repeats.

"Very big news," Hurakan says. "Declan's calling for a solar summit to carry on an envirocampaign your old man supported, and it's found a home at the Seoul Alliance Con. They gave him a slot because, well, no one can say no to him right now, can they?"

"The Alliance Con?" Ocean asks. "That's where Von's giving his presentation."

"That makes no sense," Teo says. "That . . . that campaign was the one to shut down terraforming. Corvus was working to block that." His mind races as he tries to dissect what this could mean.

"He wanted Mercury to be fully terraformed, didn't he? Didn't you?" Teo asks Phoenix, who's frowning.

"I don't think this is about the campaign," Ocean says.

"What do you mean?" Teo asks.

"It's about the people involved in the campaign. Who are those people?"

"Anand Tech members. Council members who were against terraforming. Alliance members," Teo ticks off the list, and trails off as he realizes.

"Ocean's right," Hurakan says, "If it were me, I wouldn't waste the effort hunting down everyone who supported the campaign one by one. I'd have them come to me."

"This is where he makes his move," Phoenix says. "This is where we pin him."

"He has to know that we'll know that." Teo leans back in his chair. "But we have no choice." He looks around the room. "Do we?"

"It's your call," Hurakan says. "Yours and Phoenix's."

"I'm not going to make that call for everyone," Phoenix says. "You're in or you're out. Like you said, we're likely walking into a trap." He also looks around the room, and when his intense blue eyes meet hers, she nods. "But we're the solar's best bet at stopping him. We could use all of you."

Lupus yawns. "You can't do this without me," they say bluntly.

Phoenix smiles. "True."

Cass punches her fist into her palm. "We'll take him down. What's the plan?"

Phoenix asks, "Teophilus?"

Teo spreads his hands on the table. He's pressing down hard enough that his fingertips are white. His shoulders are knotted and his brow is furled. When he looks to Ocean, she unfolds her arms, but before she can take a step, he shakes his head at her.

"We capture him. Let him be judged for his crimes. And let's be ready with the evidence. At this point . . ." He takes a deep breath and lets it out. "We're not the only ones he's hurt, and there are others who will want closure. Answers." He glances at Phoenix. "Does that work for you?"

Phoenix nods, his eyes soft. "Yes."

"It'd be way easier to slide a knife into his ribs," Hurakan says. Heads snap around, and he puts up his hands. "I'm not saying I disagree. It's just facts."

"You're right," Phoenix says. "So we're going to have to plan this out carefully."

"Very carefully." Hurakan puts the screen on mute and swooshes it to the side. He holds up his comm and throws a screen from it to the wall next to the newscast. This one's a blank canvas.

"Brainstorming, excellent." Phoenix claps his hands together. "All right, team. No idea is too foolish." He beckons Ocean over. "Anyone want to start?"

"I might have a few ideas," Teo says. "Corvus wants a show? We'll give him a show."

TWENTY-TWO

NOT FOR THE first time, Haven feels a touch of surreality. There had been some burst of activity at the Jang estate this morning. Not long after their morning PT, a good portion of their group had been huddled in the front room. When he'd walked by, he'd caught Gemini's eye. The other man had tilted his head in . . . an invitation? It was something bordering on a challenge, something not far from the mocking grin he always throws Haven's way, and yet Haven couldn't interpret the motion as anything other than a beckoning.

But just because he is learning to take a few punches doesn't mean he is ready for . . . whatever urgency was electrifying that room. Nevertheless, he'd expected to hear that their next moves would be leaving Artemis and not . . . this.

He's not quite sure how he ended up here at Sonamu, which is apparently one of the most exclusive restaurants in the solar. Anand had gone purple at the name and started raving about how they only opened reservations four times a year and were always sold out within ten minutes.

Jang has some sort of connection, and invited them for a farewell dinner. She was also able to procure them a special after-hours slot so they wouldn't have to worry about any other customers. She had, curiously, asked specifically for Yoon, claiming that she wanted to get to know Anand's friend better.

Anand, much to his sputtered disappointment, was too much of a target to leave the house. Captain Song sneered something about flavored air and Kent muttered something about algae, although that's honestly all he's been mumbling about for the past couple of days. Cass and Gemini were out moving the *Pandia* back to the base to ready it for exiting Artemis tomorrow. Lupus was dead asleep and wouldn't be woken for any amount of food bribery.

Cass claimed it was a stupid idea, and Haven was inclined to agree. One of their members was kidnapped, another shot at, and Corvus's follower is still on the loose. Thierry, on the other hand, knows Sonamu's head chef and her eyes went all misty at the recollection.

But after Anand's skin returned to a normal shade, he had gone into some sort of whispered conference with Phoenix and Yoon. Haven can't say what it was all about, except that Phoenix and Yoon seemed upset, and Anand adamant. He had whirled around and clapped his hands.

"It's decided then. The reservation's for five people. In addition to our lovely host and Ocean, it will be Phoenix, Maggie, and Sasani."

"Me? Why me?" Haven blurted out.

"Because you're Ocean's steady?" Thierry said easily.

Everyone stopped and stared at Thierry. Haven's face felt red hot.

"What?"

It was just one word from Yoon, and completely devoid of emotion, but half the people in the room, including Thierry, blanched at it.

"You . . ." Thierry pointed at the two of them and then stopped. "But . . . you're always defending each other, and . . . I thought?" Her hand dropped and she wilted. "Is this one of those no noonchi moments?"

"I . . ." Haven tried, and then completely failed.

Yoon had her hand over her face, and Anand was hunched over the table with *his* hands over his head and Haven had the distinct feeling he was holding back laughter. He was glad someone was enjoying this, at least.

"It would do me a huge boon if you took the last spot," Aries said into the strained silence. "I'd like to stay behind as well to look at finances with Teophilus and where we can allocate our money."

Haven had never before fully appreciated how the talk of statistics could diffuse a situation. As with most things, at that point it seemed easier to go along.

Sonamu is attached to a jjimjilbang, a highly exclusive bathhouse for the Seonbi Embassy. Thierry explained that the menu was an eight-course meal with an accompanying drink course, a high-dining play on the traditional jjimjilbang foods. The first course isn't flavored air, but it's close. The froth before Haven is half bubbles and half distilled arrowroot. A thin slice of a spiced slow-cooked pear perches atop a carefully arranged nest of an ice cube and maybe three noodles.

Thierry happily chats away with their server, swapping childhood stories and lifelong dreams. Everyone has by now learned that Thierry used to play viola da gamba. Their small, private room is off to the side and has only one bar in front of the counter. The head chef, Carla, hasn't dropped in yet, but she's presumably busy making other froths.

"Which spoon do I use?" Haven whispers.

"The farthest left one," Yoon says as she examines her pair of delicate handmade chopsticks, which they were told were crafted by Korean nuns from centuries ago or something along those lines.

Thierry is to Haven's left, and then to his right are Phoenix, Yoon, then Jang. The last time Haven had seen Jang was at the funeral, but she barely acknowledges him tonight. Jang's dressed in a gorgeous hanbok, emerald greens stamped with pink foil peaches. Her hair is elegantly twisted up. Haven finds it strange, actually, that she wouldn't choose to spend this last night with Anand, whom she supposedly knows the best. But Haven has gotten familiar enough with Anand to recognize a sort of stiffness to his smile when Jang was mentioned.

The server places the next course in front of them, and explains the sliver of beef brisket in a crystallized yuja cage.

"We're grateful for your hospitality, Yeonghui," Phoenix says.

"Think nothing of it," she replies. "I'll brag about it to my future children. Imagine, hosting the most famous raider, Phoenix!" She leans over as she laughs, placing a light hand on his shoulder.

It's not the first time she's touched the raider tonight. But Haven would like to tell her that Phoenix is taken. Very taken, if he were to judge from the interactions he's glimpsed of him and Anand.

The server places more dishes down that have a smear of cheese and a dollop of honey. "This isn't one of the courses, but it's compliments of Carla." He gestures to the dish with a hand. "This honey comes from our favorite beehive over at the cemetery across the way."

Phoenix gives the smallest scoff.

"You don't have your own apiary?" Jang asks.

"We do, but our bees appear to gather pollen elsewhere and the honey tastes quite different. I'll bring you a sample of it later."

On the tail end of his words, a buzzing cuts in, and for one ludicrous moment, Haven thinks this is the performance aspect of the meal, that they brought in bees for ambience while they eat, until Jang reaches into her purse. She pulls out a gold bangle and presses at the far end. A small display pops up and she frowns at the number.

"Someone you know?"

"Not that I'm aware of," she says. "Excuse me."

Jang leaves for the entrance to the hall, but she's back in hardly any time at all.

"Ocean, it's for you."

Yoon's eyebrow piques up, chopsticks poised in her right hand. "Who is it?"

"It's Diplomat Park. Do you want me to tell him you're unavailable?"

Yoon considers but then holds out her hand. After Jang hands her the bangle, she slides off her stool and goes back toward the hallway. Haven drinks leisurely from his tea. Whatever Diplomat Park wants with Yoon, it has nothing whatsoever to do with him. But he can't help what he overhears.

"Here?" she asks. "No, why should I?"

As much as he surreptitiously perks his ears, he can't hear anything else until Yoon comes back.

"Phoenix—"

"Is Park outside?"

She nods.

"Can you take care of it?" Phoenix asks.

Jang's eyes go round as she mouths *Take care of it?* The left side of Yoon's mouth lifts up, and she holds the bangle up to her mouth. "I'll be right there."

The next course comes in as Yoon leaves. It's a bowl of soup, and at least Haven knows which spoon to use for that one but he doesn't reach for it.

Phoenix says casually, "Will you go check on her?"

The raider's attention seems to be on his soup, but Haven shoves his chair back. As he's walking out the same direction Yoon went, Phoenix says from behind him,

"Attaboy."

· · · · ·

Joonho probably planned for this effect, him leaning against the brick wall, the steam rising from a nearby manhole cover. He's not in his Diplomat uniform, but in a long coat with a mandarin collar, his hands shoved into pockets. His topknot is tight, slick with the wetness from having gotten out of the bath rather than hair product. He has the fresh-scrubbed face of someone who's had the benefit of a sauna room and maybe a ddae miri. Ocean lets the side entrance door slam shut behind her. Somehow, whatever city you go to, whatever planet you're on, the streets smell the same.

"You're looking . . . clean," Ocean says.

"I have a standing weekly reservation at the Seonbi jjimjilbang," he says, patting his face. "I could have gotten you in if you were interested."

A car drives by, throwing its light briefly down the alley in a slant, lighting up Joonho and then leaving him in darkness again. A bus follows after, the hushing slick of its tires cutting as sharply as the light did.

"I heard you're leaving tomorrow," he says.

"Why are you here?" she asks.

"I always wanted to come work in Artemis, on the Moon. I don't know how many times I told you it was my dream assignment. But maybe you don't remember. Or do you mean, why am I here talking to you?" Joonho says breezily, "I wanted to get a chance to say goodbye in person. Unlike our last time. It's the decent thing to do."

"The decent thing to do," she repeats. When did everyone get together to decide what that was? "If we're talking about that, then what was the other day about?"

"Are you with him because you pity him?"

Ocean doesn't know what part of the statement surprises her more. First Maggie, and now Joonho. "I don't pity Sasani," she manages.

"You should."

Ocean doesn't want to play this game. "Is this why you're here? So you could air out your grievances?"

"I just... I don't get it," Joonho says. "I don't get what's changed. Or if you were always like this."

"I don't know what you mean," Ocean says slowly. "Like what?"

"You put yourself on the line to save your xenobotanist. You sacrificed your career to help Teophilus Anand... and you're still doing it. Were you always like this? Then why—" He breaks off.

The door behind Ocean swings open and she halfway turns, but Joonho throws out the next words, stopping her.

"Or is it that I meant so little to you?"

The words could be a challenge, except for the hurt lancing through them. It's true what she told Sasani; she focuses on the negative aspects of a relationship to move past it, to learn what not to do again. With Joonho, she remembers how cold he left her. But they had been so young, and they had been at Sav-Faire of all places. One time, his harsh judgment lacerated her, and even if she doesn't remember what the words were, it left her sobbing. Even more than that, though, she remembers him coming back to the room minutes later to find her broken down, and he had sounded bewildered as he asked, *"What's going on?"*

What's going on? What's wrong with you?

Her inability to put it all to words had sluiced into something else, the *I don't know* turning into an *I don't care I don't care*. But she remembers Sasani's words now too, his serious consideration of her as he shared his memories. The deliberate movement of his hands.

"We had a good day together," she says. "It was snowing and we skipped morning seminar. I didn't have gloves, but you gave me yours because my hands were cold."

The fat flakes of snow, what it meant to marvel in the simple exhalation of air made tangible, how she had stepped carefully into his footfalls to minimize the marks they left.

"You said your mother told you cold hands mean a cold heart." He's watching her warily, although that tightness around his eyes is gone.

She forgot she told him that. She gave that up so easily and she doesn't even remember it now.

"We bought some chestnuts from a vendor, but the first one was too hot for you—since you didn't have your gloves—and you dropped it." And it had sunk, burrowing a black tunnel into the soft white snow.

The small memory doesn't erase her loneliness when she was with him, or that they broke apart, or even all he's said here at Artemis to hurt her. But it exists, and it could only have existed dependent on other good ones, however small.

Joonho tilts his head up to the sky and blows out a long breath. "That's what you remember." He laughs ruefully. "And you sent me an email to break up with me."

"My brother . . ." Ocean starts. She tries again. "I sent you that email in the middle of his funeral rites. He was dead. And I was standing there, and I couldn't . . . I couldn't feel anything." Dae said she saw Ocean at the funeral, but Ocean doesn't really remember much of anything. "I thought, *I should have been there. It should have been me.* But also *Why can't I feel anything?* And all those years at Sav-Faire . . ." Ocean shakes her head. "I despised it. I despised shoving my emotions down. And it got to be that I couldn't trust what anyone was saying or if anything was real. I couldn't trust myself anymore."

He says slowly, "You despised what you were becoming. You mean, something like me?" She doesn't deny it, and he laughs shortly. "But you were good at it. You know that, don't you?"

No, she had left because she was bad at it.

"No," Joonho says, as if she's spoken her denial. "You were good at being there, at hiding what you were thinking, at using people. And you can't shake that off, no matter how much you might hate it." He pauses. "But that doesn't have to be a bad thing."

She can't discern how much truth to glean from his words, what purpose he might have behind them. They had always been taught to weigh words against motivations.

"I thought I could figure out who I was if I left," she says. If she joined the haenyeo, she could understand what being a Korean meant. If she joined the Alliance, she could understand what being someone like her brother meant.

"Did you?" Joonho asks.

"Yes," she says. "And no. I don't know."

It's been years, nearly a decade since they were together. She's no longer able to read his face the way she used to, if she was ever really able to. He nods once and then twice, and she can't say what that means either before his focus slides past her.

"Sasani," he says, with a completely unsurprised tone. Rather than discovering him, he's inviting him into the conversation finally.

Ocean turns, remembering belatedly the door opening. She hadn't thought to question why there weren't footsteps after. Although Joonho is the one who said Sasani's name, Sasani is gazing at her, maybe has been this whole time.

Her face goes warm. But his hands come up, his expressive hands that always shape his thoughts in the air. He holds them in front of his chest as another car drives by behind him, slashing the dark again with its headlights. He's leaving tomorrow, but she thinks she'll hold on to that piece of him, the fleeting illumination that fully revealed his ache for her.

"Sasani," Joonho says again. Finally Sasani tears his eyes from Ocean, and Joonho continues, "People have always told me I take after my mother too."

Sasani waits patiently, as he always does for people to find their words.

"She passed away last year, and we held the ceremony here on the Moon." Another halting pause. "I was not kind to the Vulture in charge back then either."

"You were grieving," Sasani says.

"Yes," Joonho says. "Do you understand my behavior toward you?"

"Yes." Sasani's dark eyes are fierce. "But my understanding won't absolve you."

"You're very honest." Then, in an offhand tone, he says, "Remember what I told you about the mole?"

The mole? Joonho had talked to Sasani about a spy? Sasani's shoulders creep up.

"It wasn't true," Joonho says. "I was testing your reaction to see if you had . . . you know. If you knew I was lying, I was fairly certain you would say so. I wanted to see if you had ah . . . gotten that far. You didn't seem like the type of person who would be able to hide it."

Even in the dim light of the side alley, Ocean sees that the tips of Sasani's ears are dark red.

"That was not very polite," he manages.

"No," Joonho says. "But I was not trying to be."

Sasani narrows his eyes. "Why bother telling me the truth now?"

Joonho shrugs one shoulder. "Speaking honestly? I don't care for the idea of you visualizing it."

"Why would you think I had . . . that we were . . ." Sasani's eyes flick over at Ocean before he presses his lips together.

"Well," Joonho says. "You two have a very particular way of looking or not looking at each other." He sighs. "I suppose I'm glad after all that Yeonghui pulled me from the jjimjilbang."

"Yeonghui called you?" Ocean asks. "That's not what she said."

Joonho frowns. "She said you were leaving tomorrow and that if I wanted to say goodbye, I could talk to you out here."

A car drives by, the light again angling into the alleyway. It stays on Joonho's face for longer this time, as if allowing Ocean to trace the thoughts connecting in his head.

But even if it doesn't consciously click, her body is moving, her hand going into her jacket. It isn't her imagination that the light is remaining too long; it's because the car going by is moving much more slowly. She hears it stop and back up and she shoves Joonho down as she moves in front of Sasani. A spray of bullets hits the street and the wall. Sasani has his hands around her as they hit the ground.

TWENTY-THREE

"**WHAT DO YOU** think they're eating right now?" Teo muses up to the ceiling. He's lounging on the couch.

Next to him, Aries hunches over his tabula with its glowing keyboard inlay. "Steak?" he offers distractedly.

On the other side of the room, Dae and Von talk in low murmurs. Teo can't hear what they're saying, but the cadence is easy, reassuring. Aries explained earlier he doesn't want a direct line to be traced from Teo's offplanet accounts into Phoenix's account. Furthermore, he's funneling Teo's money, or rather now the *Pandia*'s money, into several other projects. Teo assumed stocks were involved, but apparently Aries has other plans for it.

Teo wrests himself from thoughts of steak, filet mignon, tartare, dry-aged, grass-fed, even if he doesn't think it'll be anything that pedantic at Sonamu. His stomach is uneasy for another reason though.

They could have turned Yeonghui down, but it's not like she doesn't know where to find them. He'd been curious as to what she might be intending, what they could find out from her, so he'd done the best thing he could by sending Phoenix so he and Ocean could look after each other. It still doesn't feel good.

Teo sits up abruptly. "Where are you sending the money?"

"Right now?" Aries says. "Lucian Orphanage in Penelope."

"You send money to orphanages?" The screen in front of his face is set to transparent so Teo can see what he's doing, but Aries is the type of person whose jokes are as dry as his expressions. "You're making this up, right?"

"It's where Phoenix was sent when his parents died in the mines," Aries says.

Teo mulls over that. "Where else? You're not using the money on ship upgrades?"

"Some of it. And some of it goes to our own personal accounts. But the bulk of it goes to different funds Phoenix has set up. For example, one of his projects on Mercury provides seed money for businesses that need a little help. He also has an emergency fund for health expenses."

Unbelievable. Phoenix might be a saint.

"Do you have your gun?"

Teo nearly jumps out of his skin. Gemini has materialized in the doorway as if the shadows converged on one spot to form him.

"Aish," he says. "Yes, Phoenix gave me one." He cranes his neck around. "Did you pick up what I asked you to? How's the *Pandia* looking?"

"*Yes*, but we have more important things at hand than your dry cleaning errands," Gemini says shortly. "And bad news—the *Pandia*'s not quite ready. They're working on it from the hangar. But we might be out of time."

"Out of time?" Teo repeats.

Aries presses a button and the screen disappears. He pockets the tabula. "Trouble?"

"Maybe. I'm not sure," Gemini says.

The lights suddenly cut. Von cries out from his corner. Teo pulls out his gun from the holster. His mouth is dry and he blinks rapidly to adjust his vision.

"Marv," Aries says.

"Well, now I'm sure," Gemini says.

A bright light blinks from Teo's right and he sees Dae holding up her comm's beam.

"Shut that off," Gemini hisses at her.

She does quickly, throwing them all into black again.

"Dae and Von, get over here. All of you, follow me." Teo feels Gemini's hand on his shoulder, guiding him. "When Cass and I came back, the guards were gone." Gemini's leading them all by voice as they walk toward the back. "It honestly could have meant nothing, but . . ."

"Now we have no power," Teo says.

"Exactly."

"Is it . . . is it Corvus?" Von squeaks.

Gemini kneels at the side patio door leading out to the fountain and garden. Teo grasps at shadows, trying to separate out actual forms, but it's impossible for him. Suddenly, Gemini curses. He tackles Teo to the floor as the glass above them breaks and something comes flying through.

"Get away!"

Gemini pulls him up and shoves him down the hall. An explosion slams Teo's senses. Glass shatters everywhere. Fire climbs up the walls, devouring the curtains. Aries immediately rips them from the wall and balls them up, smothering them.

"Stay here!" Gemini shouts at them.

I can fight too Teo wants to say, but his hands are frozen. Gemini pulls up a mask and then a black hood. He's got knives in his hands and then he's disappeared into the black.

"It's hotter than the hair of Hades in here, isn't it?" Cass materializes out of the gloom and smoke and punches her fists together. They immediately light up green, showing off her oversize power gloves and the slouching figure of Lupus behind her. She quickly scans them. "Alliance. You got your sword?"

"I always have it on me. It's regulation," Dae says as she stands.

Cass rolls her eyes. "You're with me, then." She runs straight through the flames to get outside. Teo hears her yelling, "Come and get me!" and gunshots immediately answer the challenge.

"I—" He tries again.

"Take care of Von, will you?" Dae says to him before she pulls out her bonguk geom. She passes through the flames too, and Teo hears her yell, "Yeolyeora!"

Von's on the floor, hugging his knees to his chest. "How we doing, Von?" Teo asks as he crouches near him.

"Good, good, jake, great." Von's voice creeps up higher with each word. Teo can relate.

"I guess I'm the getaway driver again?" Aries sighs.

"We have options," Lupus says. "Garage is this way."

Teo helps Von up so they can hurry after Lupus. He'd insist he's Alliance corps, he's trained for this, but he's not entirely certain he's not made of porcelain either.

"You excited about your algae presentation?" he asks Von conversationally.

"I'm not ready," Von says suddenly. "I'm not ready for any of this!"

They've arrived at the garage. Lupus slinks around the dark space while Aries tuts at the options, including some very pretty sports cars Ocean would probably drool over. *Ocean.* He needs to call her. He wrests his attention back to Von, who's twisting his hands together.

"What are you talking about, Von?" Teo says.

Von shakes his head emphatically. "Do you think it's her? Is she back? Is it Alessa?" The words come out in a stream, and Teo's heart could break.

"Goddamn Artemis. Finally found an automatic," Aries intones as he pats a larger SUV. "Electric start. Can you work it, Lupus?"

Aries opens the door and Lupus pushes back their hood as they scramble in. They jimmy the panel and plug into it. A flick of fingers and a screen opens up from the small pocketpad they have.

"Got 'em," Lupus mutters. "Should I ping Gemini and Cass?"

"They'll hear me coming." Aries yells over at Teo and Von, "Get in!"

Teo climbs into the middle of the three rows of seats, while Von scrabbles to the back row. Teo dials Ocean's number on his comm. The call's ringing and ringing and Teo's anxiety claws at him. She has to pick up, has to pick up, has to—The line clicks.

"Stay calm," Teo says immediately, which is probably the worst way to start a call, like saying *First of all, no one is hurt.* "Are you jake?"

"They've served the fifth course." It's Phoenix, and his voice is smooth, as requested. "I'm enjoying it with Yeonghui and Maggie. Ocean's missing it though. She's outside."

"Outside?" The garage door is opening before them.

"With Diplomat Park. And Sasani."

"Diplomat *Park?*" Teo spits.

Bullets ricochet into the garage and off the car. Teo and Von duck down into their seats. In contrast, against the grain of common sense, Lúpus punches the panel to slide their window down. They have their gun out and open fire as the car roars forward. They give a little whoop.

"Hopefully everything's all right," Phoenix says.

Even as Teo tumbles around in the car, his dance punctuated by the jeep's squealing tires, he fights the urge to laugh at Phoenix's mild tone. Is Yeonghui a part of this? Is Diplomat Park? If Yeonghui is, then Phoenix can't let on that Teo's on the other end.

"'Something is rotten in the state of Denmark,'" Teo quotes.

"Ah," Phoenix says.

"Teo, right door!" Aries yells.

Teo flings open the right door as Aries careens the car around and skids to a stop. Dae and Cass jump in and the vehicle lurches forward again. Dae tumbles into the back with Von, while Cass stretches over Teo to open the other door but then lets out a string of highly colorful epithets.

"What's wrong?" he asks before he sees the dark patch on her sleeve, black in the darkness with its sopping weight.

"The door!" She waves his hands off and he lunges over to open it. Gemini's running alongside them and Teo reaches out a hand, helping him swing in.

"Is that Phoenix?" Gemini asks Teo, who holds out his wrist. Gemini grabs the wrist and speaks into it, "Phoenix, don't worry about us. We'll meet you at the ship."

"I'll take care of Denmark," Phoenix says and hangs up.

"We good?" Gemini asks. The car's speeding so fast, every little bump sends all of them airborne.

"I'll live," Cass says shortly around a mouthful of her shirt. She rips off a strip and wraps it sloppily around her arm.

"You can't wrap your own arm!" Teo snaps, taking over for her.

"That's why you don't yell an invitation before jumping into the fight," Gemini says.

"Jesus, Gem," Cass says.

"And the Holy Ghost," Gemini finishes for her.

Cass yelps as Teo tightens the strip around her arm. "I got shot, Gemini. A little sympathy?"

"Did the bullet go through or is it still in there?" Teo asks.

"Beats me." Sweat beads on her upper lip, glistening in the dark. "You jake, Alliance cap?"

"One piece," Dae says unsteadily from the back.

"How about you?" Gemini asks Teo.

"Me?" Teo says in astonishment. "You're the one slitting throats left and right with bullets flying. You and Cass and Dae! Cass is the one who got hurt!"

"Yeah, Gemini!"

"Phoenix would kill me if anything happened to you," Gemini says brusquely as he leans forward. "Aries, head back to our ship. We're meeting everyone else there."

TWENTY-FOUR

THE CAR PULLS into the alleyway, coming to a stop before them. The headlights' glare fills Ocean's vision. The stench of street grime coats her shallow wheezing. But she's more acutely aware of Sasani's arms around her. He cradled her head with his hand so it wouldn't hit the ground.

"Thank you," she says.

He says, "Just returning the favor."

It's not until he speaks that she realizes how close his lips are to her skin, his breath tickling her neck. His body has molded tightly to hers, the spread of his fingers against her ribs. He seems to realize it the same moment she does, and he immediately lets go and she rolls to her feet.

Ocean quickly scans around to any other place, any other person. "Anyone hit?"

"Who even knows?" Joonho groans, which Ocean decides to take as a no.

"I don't think so," Sasani says.

"Ocean Yoon. Nice to see you again."

She can't see who's talking, but the car's idling and it's an open top, making it easy for her to hear their words. Her thoughts sprint after one another. If she can distract them long enough, Sasani and Joonho could run back into the cover of the kitchen.

Bullets blast to the right of her, glancing off the handle of the door as if they could guess her thoughts.

"I'm going to enjoy killing you," the person says. They have a contralto voice. "I have orders to do my best and keep Joonho Park alive though. Corvus is interested in acquiring him."

"What the hell does acquiring mean?" Joonho mutters under his breath. "As if I'm a rare bird."

Footsteps crunch as the person jumps out of the car. They cross in front of the headlights and Ocean has the briefest glimpse of a woman with long dark hair gathered into a ponytail. Alessa Papanikolau.

"We didn't get a chance to chat last time," she says. "I didn't realize then that you were the one who shot Amell."

"I think we can call it even now," Ocean says.

Thankfully Alessa's a talker, because otherwise they'd already be dead. Sasani and Joonho are plastered to the ground. Neither is armed, and Sasani raises his eyebrows at Ocean in a *Now what?*

"I'm standing up."

Ocean twists her head to see Joonho slowly doing just that.

"Stay where you are, Diplomat," the woman says.

"I'm unarmed, I'm moving slowly, and you said you didn't want to kill me," he says.

"I reserve the right to change my mind."

"Oh, but I'd be so interesting to acquire," Joonho says. "I'm a Diplomat, and we do much better when we're able to talk it out with people. I could offer you a trade."

"A trade?" Alessa laughs. "I already have everything I want from this current exchange."

"What did Yeonghui want in return for giving us up?" Joonho tosses out lazily.

Sasani huffs in surprise, but Ocean's come to the same conclusion. Yeonghui brought Joonho here, and she's the only one outside their group who knows where they're all hiding. The question, then, is why she waited this long.

"What anyone ever wants," Alessa says. "Power."

Ocean thinks back to the small amount of information she gleaned about Yeonghui from their dinner. How she was constantly trying to extract something from Teo.

"She's always wanted a seat at the table," Joonho clarifies.

"She wants *your* seat," Alessa says.

"Someone who hasn't trained as a Diplomat can't take my place," Joonho says dismissively.

"Ah, but no one would know she hasn't trained as a Diplomat. Not if she has your face."

Joonho goes very still at that. "I like my face," he says. "I would like to keep enjoying my face, and I don't think anyone else should have the right to use it."

Alessa laughs with glee. "Marv, I love hearing people panic."

"You're giving her a deepfake suit?" Ocean asks. In someone else's hands, that technology could be reverse engineered. "That's..."

"Stupid," Joonho affirms.

"What do you know?" Alessa snarls. "You arrogant Koreans. Yeonghui gets a suit. She uses it to impersonate you, Diplomat Park. And then we expose her, and let everyone in the solar know that this technology not only exists, but it's in the hands of Koreans. And the Alliance by association."

What would it mean for the Alliance to have access to the chameleon deepfake ability, or whatever other technology the Alliance could glean from those blueprints? Ocean swallows. It wouldn't even matter if the Alliance used it; the knowledge that they had it would tip off a line of hostile dominos. What happened on the *Shadowfax* has been streamed, seen a million times, all over the solar. Anyone can grasp the capabilities, can think up even worse ones. At best, it would spur them to develop their own type of similar technology to combat it. At worst . . .

"Interplanetary war," Joonho whispers.

"The genius of Corvus," Alessa says, her voice dripping with ardor, "is that it's just Koreans destroying themselves. Yeonghui has the choice to do what she will with the technology. But we all know that she's going to end up destroying the Alliance. Koreans can't help crawling over one another in a bid to get ahead. They're only getting what they deserve."

Ocean tracks Alessa's voice, checking to see if it comes closer or moves to the side. Does she have her knives today as well as a gun? She could be packing anything. She could have a shield, she could also be wearing an augmented suit like Emory was.

"Revealing Yeonghui would reveal the existence of the suits," Ocean says. "It would mean Teo could come forward. We'd expose Hadrian."

"Oh, we don't really need Hadrian to pretend to be Declan for much longer anyway."

"That's not how information works," Joonho says. "Give it away freely without staring down the consequences, and you'll end up chained to a mountain with an eagle eating out your liver."

"I bet you're a lot of fun at parties," Alessa replies.

"I'm *delightful* at parties."

"He's not," Ocean says.

Suddenly, the restaurant side door slams open and Phoenix rolls out. Bullets bombard the ground in his wake, and Ocean dashes to the side of the car. She skids across the dirt, picking up a handful, and flings it in Alessa's direction. Alessa curses and stumbles back in direct view of the headlights. Ocean brings up her gun. She has the shot; it's clear as day. But before she pulls the trigger, she somehow finds Sasani. His eyes lock with hers. And she falters.

"Ocean!"

Phoenix tackles her as Alessa shoots. They slam into the wall behind them. Her head knocks back so violently that a supernova of pain explodes in her skull. Sasani and Joonho have scrambled behind the door Phoenix opened. Sasani's yelling at Ocean, but she's distracted by the warmth spreading over her. She checks herself, but it's Phoenix who slumps, clutching his side.

Phoenix grunts. He rolls and fires back at Alessa. A bright blue flash lights up the alleyway.

"Shibal," Ocean swears.

Alessa puts up her gun and laughs. She's back in the darkness now, that burst of a blue shield the last glimpse Ocean saw of her. "Do you think after last time I'd come at you without a shield? They take a lot of time and money to make, but we just finished this one. Corvus had me make one for Emory first, but he said *I* should have the next one. I'm the one who financed the development of them, after all."

"Keep her talking," Ocean whispers to Phoenix. It shouldn't be hard.

They're on the other side of the car now. Phoenix bobs his head in assent, and then grimaces. His shirt is torn and he's bleeding from his side. Already, his skin is pale, but when he speaks up, it's with all the bravado of an actor on the stage of the Globe Theatre. He even runs his hand through his hair, and his Phoenix Toss catches the glimmer of the streetlights.

"So, you're the financier, are you?"

"Is that Phoenix?" Alessa inquires. "I've been curious about you."

"There are less dramatic ways to ask someone out on a date," Phoenix drawls.

A smattering of bullets tear up the ground, pelting a path toward him. She has no way of hitting him on the other side of the car, but he's obviously touched a nerve. Phoenix's mocking laugh rings out. Ocean uses the noise as cover to crack open the passenger door. She slithers into the car as Phoenix and Alessa continue talking.

"What a waste," Alessa says. "I'm glad Corvus has finally seen the light."

"Is that what you call it?" Phoenix volleys. He pops his head up and fires at Alessa. Even though she has a shield, she ducks behind the other side of the car. "He's always been obsessed with me, hasn't he?"

"He's *not obsessed*—" Alessa shrieks.

The door next to Alessa is still ajar and Ocean kicks it violently. It flies open into Alessa, cutting her off mid-sentence. Ocean dives out of the car at Alessa. The discharge of bullets flares the darkness. Ocean's hearing goes fuzzy as she unloads into Alessa, to activate her shield. It glows blue every time she's hit. Alessa's shield blazes again; not from Ocean now, but Phoenix.

The light-up briefly reveals Alessa's face, the dark eyes and olive skin. Her shield covers her whole body, even coming up over her head. It's hard to tell whether it has any vulnerabilities. She grunts at each impact, but remains upright.

Alessa aims at Ocean's face, but Ocean rushes her. She turns her head and ducks her shoulder under Alessa's outstretched gun arm. The gun goes off, shooting behind her. Ocean grabs the gun wrist. She yanks Alessa forward and pins the other woman's arm behind her. When Alessa struggles, Ocean slides her body snug against hers, like a finger trap that pinches tight with effort. Alessa yelps as Ocean twists her arm hard, locking their positions.

A blue light blazes up again, searing her vision, as Phoenix shoots Alessa point blank. Before Phoenix shoots again, Ocean widens her stance, planting one leg in between Alessa's, and then centers her own gravity. She wrests as Phoenix's next bullet hits Alessa, throwing her back. She takes Ocean with her. They fall onto the hood of Alessa's car. The headlights dim as Ocean's grip loosens. Alessa rolls and pistons her legs into Ocean. Ocean hits the ground sideways and skids backward. She crashes into another body that bolsters her. Phoenix.

"A fancy restaurant like this probably has insurance, right?" Phoenix asks.

Phoenix opens his palm to flash an item at her, and then he slings it into the darkness. Only then does Ocean register his muffled words, what the item was: the same device Hurakan planted all around the *Ohneul*.

Ocean glances around to check that they're clear. She drops to a knee. Bullets pump out of her gun. Each ping throws Alessa back a step, two steps. Phoenix joins her. Their barrage jostles Alessa off-balance, like she's an angry drunk being ushered backward.

"How stupid are you?" Alessa snarls. "I told you, I'm wearing a *shield*."

"We know," Ocean says.

And then Phoenix trips the detonation. The wall behind Alessa explodes. Bricks and rubble fly everywhere, burying her. Ocean throws up her arms at the same time Phoenix throws himself on her. They collide on the ground, a mess of limbs and dust.

A pair of headlights glint from the other end of the alley. The new car jerks to a stop in the middle and the door opens. Maggie jumps out and gapes at all of them.

"Carla is going to *kill* us."

Ocean props herself up on her elbows to speak, but only coughs in the dust. Then hands are helping her up. It's Joonho, who damn him, still appears as if he's fresh from the jjimjilbang.

"Are you all right?"

Ocean registers Sasani's frantic tone better than his words, and then his hands are on her face. His fingers swipe up her neck before they lift her chin, angling it to the side. Her nerves are extra jangled—her ears ringing, her skin scraped raw. The touch is a wire to her skin and she bites back a gasp.

Sasani snatches his hand away, his fingers coated with pale dust. "You're bleeding."

"I guess you'll have to patch me up again," she says.

"I'm fine, by the way," Phoenix speaks up from the side.

Sasani lifts Phoenix's shirt, or what remains of it. "No, you're not," he says.

As Phoenix's chest heaves, a shallow rivulet of blood pumps out of a wound. Sasani's expression darkens.

"Is she dead?" Joonho asks sharply, drawing their attention back to the rubble.

Ocean rubs her ears. Everything comes through as if her head's been wrapped in cotton. "Probably not," Ocean says. "She was wearing a shield. But this will slow her down, at least."

"We should hurry out of here," Phoenix says.

Maggie gestures widely at the car. "Ocean, you wanna do the honors?"

Despite everything, a smile wells up in Ocean.

"Do I ever."

TWENTY-FIVE

"**D**EAD END, DEAD end!" Park screams, and it's probably the most harried Haven's ever heard him.

The thought satisfies him, but only a little. He sits behind Yoon in the driver's seat as he attempts to administer first aid to Phoenix. He has, as always, his mini kit in the front pocket of his suit, but he needs Phoenix lying down and stable to properly treat him. For now, he stems the flow of Phoenix's wound as best he can and wraps it up while Yoon speeds through the streets. Thierry, on the other hand, is on Phoenix's other side, clapping her hands with delight.

"Slow down!" Park yells. "You're coming up on it too fast."

Haven peeks over to the side-view mirror in time to catch Yoon's smirk before her hand comes down to the gear. She spins the wheel, the car skating to the side to make the sharp corner. The metal crisscross of the fence at the end of the road looms up against the window in front of Haven's face.

Park lets loose a string of expletives.

"My brother," Yoon says lazily, only one hand perched on the wheel now, "once described drifting as controlling the uncontrollable. I always liked that thought."

"Where are we going?" Thierry pipes up.

"Home," Phoenix wheezes. "I talked with Gemini. We're reconvening at the *Pandia*."

"Are they all right?"

"They were also hit, but they're jake. I didn't get all the details though. Yeonghui was next to me when Teophilus called and I think he was worried about what she might hear."

"Where is Yeonghui?"

"Tied up," Phoenix says with grim satisfaction. "Teophilus said 'Something is rotten in the state of Denmark,' which means he suspected corruption in the government. It could have pertained to either Park or Yeonghui. I don't think he was sure which one. I couldn't be sure either so I tied Yeonghui to her chair. Although it was pretty clear once I saw her reaction to the gunshots outside. Carla kindly offered this car and Maggie went to fetch it while I came to help."

"It's a very nice car. Don't you think?" Yoon asks Park, whose pinched lips could be to keep back the contents of his upset stomach or a show of his regret at claiming the passenger seat, even though he did it to guide her through the streets. Before he can answer, shots pelt down on the roof of their car. Haven ducks.

"What is it? Where is it?" Thierry yells, hands over her head. The delight at having an unobstructed view of Yoon's driving has dissipated immediately.

"Behind us," Yoon says.

"Above," Phoenix amends.

Haven verifies through their back window. "Behind and above." He squints at the solo blue jet trailing them. "I think it's Alessa."

"Wow, they're made of money, aren't they?" Phoenix says.

"That's a Pull-100s model." The note of hilarity in Thierry's tone is of someone grappling at a situation. "Not great on maneuverability, but it packs a punch with its heat."

"Thank you, Maggie." Yoon spins the wheel and drives up on the curb. "I guess we didn't need to worry about that explosion hurting her too much."

"Where are you going?" Park hollers.

"This alley leads out to the next street. It has more cover," she says.

"How do you know all this?"

Yoon skids the car down a side street Haven could have sworn was barely wide enough to fit them.

"I went to go pick up Sasani once, remember?" She says, "I paid attention."

The car spits out into the next street and Haven lowers his window. "Out of the way!" he shouts, although if people aren't already jumping out of the way of the barreling car, he's not sure what help it will be. It can't hurt, though. Yoon smiles at him via the side-view mirror.

"Any weak spots on the jet, Maggie?" Phoenix asks.

"The windows?" Thierry's ducked her head between her knees, her fingers locked and shielding the back of it. "I don't know!"

Phoenix hoists himself up. "Hold on to my legs, would you?" He crouches up on the seat as he lowers Haven's window farther.

"You shouldn't be moving!" Haven says, but Phoenix flashes him a grin before he rises from his position.

Haven is barely able to jam the release for his seat belt so he can lunge forward to grab Phoenix's legs. Phoenix is already leaning out of the window, aiming his gun back for the jet, which is diving down from having to fly over the alley that had been too narrow for it.

Shots rain down on them, and Yoon zigs the car sharply. Phoenix yelps and Haven tightens his grip on his legs as he teeters. Thierry falls against them and immediately burrows underneath. Phoenix recovers quickly, firing back at the jet.

"I don't think you're doing very much!"

"Constructive criticism only!" Phoenix yells back at Park.

The jet maneuvers to avoid Phoenix's shot, swerving in the air before straightening its course. It might not be very much, but it's keeping the car and the people inside it intact.

"This is *not* what I signed up for," Thierry mutters from underneath Haven, and he couldn't agree more.

Even pressed up against Phoenix, Haven hears Thierry sucking in air. Rapid, high-pitched squeals. Too rapid. She's going to hyperventilate.

"Slow down," he tells Thierry. "Deep breaths."

"You try deep breaths!" Thierry snaps at him. "People are shooting at us!"

Haven lets that skim past him. "Take in a breath. Hold it while you're counting to ten."

The car slides back and forth, and Park's colorful oaths accompany each sudden swing. All around them bullets whiz down like a malicious hailstorm and Haven squeezes Phoenix's legs. The raider crows ecstatically, giving back as good as he can. Outside, the scenery flickers by, no longer streets and storefronts but an off-ramp joining a larger road.

But Haven concentrates on Thierry's body underneath him, mentally counting with her. "Good. Now exhale and count to ten."

"You all right, Sasani?" Phoenix calls down to Haven.

Haven inspects Yoon's reflection again, and he flinches as Phoenix lets another round of bullets fly. He wouldn't say *all right*, but Yoon's serenity in this mayhem is like a dampener on all the noise. He tilts his head up to respond to Phoenix, and only then sees how pale he is, the strain on his face as he raises his gun again to aim back.

"That road, take that road!" Park points to the road going the opposite direction, hitting Yoon's arm as if he doesn't think he's shouting loudly enough to grab her attention.

Yoon *laughs* as if he's thrown down a challenge. The engine revs and the car zips forward. Something must be wrong with Haven because every time they're in danger, he has to check on Yoon, and—

Above them, the sky goes dark and Haven blinks in the darkness at the understructure of a bridge.

"What are you—"

Before Park can finish the sentence, before Haven can finish his thought, Yoon slams the brakes and her right elbow comes up and over as she rotates the wheel. The car's rear fishtails out. Phoenix falls back into the vehicle, and they all list over to the right while Yoon executes a U-turn, driving out from underneath the bridge again. The jet soars past them, still going the same direction. Yoon's used the cover of the bridge to pull her reversal, buying them time. She drives them over the grassy midway and then onto the next road, which curves to the right and away.

"Once we enter the base, can you drop me off?" Park has one hand on Yoon's headrest as he twists his neck back, assessing the jet as it curves around, realizing its error.

"Where?" Yoon asks.

"See up front?" Park points to the right.

"You're going out there?" Thierry wheezes.

"Leaving us so soon, Diplomat?" Phoenix's whole body trembles, belying his light words.

"Unfortunately," Park says. "Someone has to get you clearance to leave Artemis. Ocean, drive me up against the door, under the awning?"

"Phoenix, if you're visible," Yoon shouts over her shoulder. "I don't think she'll bother too much with following Joonho."

"Got it," Phoenix grunts. "I'll cover for you, Diplomat."

"Get ready," Yoon says to both. "Thirty centimeters?"

"What does that—Are you sure?!" Park shouts as Yoon shifts gears.

Yoon makes good on her announced measurement when she slides to a halt next to the warehouse Park indicated, right under the overhang of the front door. Yoon's angled the car just so, and when Phoenix pops up through his window again, Park flings open his car door. It bangs against the wall as he leaps out, but Yoon's already driving away as Park waves his wrist over the pad at the entrance.

"We're almost there," Yoon says. "Hold on, everyone."

She says everyone, but she directs it at the mirror reflection of Phoenix, her mouth a tight line. Phoenix has chalky skin, and his mouth hangs open as he labors to drag air in. The trickle of his sweat mingles with Haven's. Even if they make it to the hangar, they have only Phoenix and Yoon with guns against Alessa's massive jet trailing them.

"Gemini says—come around—the back." Phoenix coughs intermittently between his yells. "They're ready."

Yoon doesn't answer, but when they reach a familiar hangar, she skirts it. She rides the curve to the back of the building, which is one large garage door drawn up. While she zooms toward it, Haven hears the jet behind them.

And out of the garage steps Cass, outfitted with a large shoulder holster. She's yelling at them, but it doesn't even matter what because she opens fire at the jet, bullets spitting out of the weapon resting on her shoulders. The car screeches to a stop behind her.

"Now! Let's go!"

Once Haven's out, he helps Phoenix, whose legs collapse like jelly the moment he steps out. Haven doesn't like how cold and clammy his skin is. He staggers to the side to make room for Thierry to exit, but she's frozen in her seat.

"No no no. I'm not going. You can't make me!"

"Maggie, we have to go!" Yoon says from Haven's side.

Phoenix swipes for Thierry, but the movement's weak and she flails, scratching him. "No, you can't make me!"

"What's the hold up!" Cass screams back at them. "I can't do this forever!"

As if on cue, bullets ping all around them. Haven doesn't know where to go. Phoenix makes as if to get back into the car, but his body folds up. He goes down, taking Haven with him. Haven skins his elbow on the cement. It leaves a salmon pink abrasion that he can't feel at all.

"You're losing too much blood," Haven says desperately. "I need to get you inside."

Thierry has rolled into a tight ball, clutching at the seats.

"Maggie, we're not leaving you behind." Phoenix strains against Haven's arms.

"Help!" Haven yells, not even sure what help he can get. But if he's struggling to hold Phoenix, he can't drag him *and* Thierry.

Yoon pushes past Haven and crawls into the back seat. She clasps Thierry's shoulder. "Maggie," she says. Haven barely hears her over the mayhem. "I'm on your side."

Thierry is taut for a second more, and then she goes limp. Yoon pulls her out of the car. They all run back toward the *Pandia*'s open bay, Yoon helping Thierry and Haven supporting Phoenix.

"Cass, fall back!"

"Finally!" She blasts shells as she runs backward.

"We're in!" Phoenix says into his wrist as he grabs a handful of Cass's shirt and yanks her back. He slams the button to close the door.

The *Pandia* rises from the ground and flies straight at Alessa's fighter jet, which swoops out of the way before it darts after them, firing away.

"Everyone in?" At Cass's nod, Phoenix slumps to the floor. "Cass, I need you on defense."

Cass coughs weakly. "That might have taken it out of me, boss."

Her shoulder gun drops to the ground, revealing her bound up arm, drenched and bleeding out. Phoenix's mouth goes flat.

"Leave it to me," Yoon says. She carefully hands Thierry over to Haven.

Thierry sways on her feet, and Haven scoops her up into his arms. Her warm body goes limp.

"No, I need you at the wheel," Phoenix says. "Help me to the cockpit, Ocean."

Yoon raises her eyebrow at Haven and he shakes his head. It's not a good idea.

"Phoenix," Cass says. It's in that familiar two-note cadence everyone uses on Phoenix, although Haven doesn't know why they bother.

"This is my ship," Phoenix snaps. "Sasani, I promise you can fix me up after, but *not now*."

Cass leans against the wall, her head down. Yoon's already ducked her head under Phoenix, resting his arm on her shoulder, but she waits on Haven. He finally nods curtly. He'll worry about his job; they'll do theirs. At that, they're all hustling back into the body of the ship. Phoenix and Yoon shamble toward the cockpit, leaving Haven to make his way to the med bay, Thierry slack and trusting in his arms. Cass rests her hand on his shoulder, leaning on it as they move as quickly as possible. At the infirmary, he lays Thierry on one cot and helps Cass up to another.

"What is it?" he asks.

"Bullet."

He washes his hands, gloves them, and unwraps the bandage around her upper arm. No exit wound. It's still in there then. And the rate at which she's bleeding isn't great. He keeps his eyes on her arm as he opens up the second drawer from the right. First, clean the wound. The speaker in the room beeps from the med bay's top corner as he brings out the gauze and sanitizer from the drawer.

"This is your captain speaking," Phoenix's voice comes through it. "We're expecting some turbulence as we leave the Artemis troposphere, but don't be alarmed."

"Great," Thierry says.

"Gemini is now in the gun vestibule and has us well covered from the back."

"You're welcome, Cass," Gemini calls, and from next to Haven, Cass groans.

Haven's already cleaned Cass's wound, and he affixes his headset that has an X-ray lens that he can swipe over his left eye. *Godsdamn.* He can't leave the bullet in there after all.

"This is going to hurt," he says calmly.

"It always does."

"We're waiting for the Artemis shield to open up," Phoenix says, "and ah . . . speaking of! Let's patch on through our guest for the evening: Diplomat Joonho Park!"

"You're clear," Park's voice sails through. "I'm sending you the coordinates now. I'll give you a bigger window this time."

"Thanks," Yoon's voice comes over the intercom, sounding anything but impressed.

"Can you cut it off after us again?" Anand, now. Even with the rustling, Haven's surprised to find he's able to easily identify everyone's voices.

"I'm insulted you asked," Park says. "I'd say you're welcome back to the Moon, but that would be a lie. I hope you don't return for a long long time. It certainly made my life more difficult." He pauses, then says, "Ocean, I suppose we won't keep in touch?"

Haven finds himself listening intently even while his tweezers are poised inside Cass. His hand is as steady as Yoon's control of the ship while he references his lens. Cass clenches her teeth, growling under her breath.

"I'm not good at that," Yoon says. "But I think we'll be all right."

He feels the metal of the bullet between his pincers and squeezes it.

"Sure," Park says. "But you owe me now. Don't forget that; I won't."

TEO'S DURUMI

Haven drops the bullet and it clatters onto the metal pan.

Phoenix whoops so loudly that Haven winces. "We're through! Everyone, we are through and we are kissing the Moon goodbye, and I for one don't intend to go back, cemetery honey or not."

Haven lets out a long breath. The hard part's over.

"You're not bad at this, doc," Cass says.

The warmth from that statement surprises him. Only now he registers the last minutes, Thierry in his arms, Cass's hand on his shoulder. He sews up Cass, disposes of his gloves, and washes his hands again.

"Holding up, Thierry?" he asks.

"You know, I'm a lot better now we're inside," she says feebly. "I thought working back of house during the dinner rush was stressful, but I guess it's all relative."

Haven stretches out Thierry's legs and then elevates them. He pulls open another side drawer and removes a blanket. He carefully wraps her in it. As he's tucking in the corners, he sees Cass scrutinizing the drawers and the trash can.

"Not bad at all," she mutters.

The last time he was in the infirmary, he had given it a much-needed cleaning and organization. He had thrown out anything that he deemed to be dangerously expired, and ensured everything would be on hand in the closest drawers when he needed them. There's now a clear path from the door to the first cot, although it might be better to move the two cots so that the sink is in the middle to make cleanup easier when working with more than one patient.

The infirmary comm beeps. "Maggie, you good?" Gemini's voice comes through. "Some of these repairs are *not* holding up, and I could use you."

Thierry immediately straightens. "I knew I should have supervised those mechanics."

"Don't force yourself," Haven warns.

She inches off the cot, keeping the blanket tight around her. "From my recollection, Ocean and Phoenix were a smidgen more banged up than I was. Who knows what happened to everyone else too . . . I'm making room for your next patients." She waits at the med bay door. "Once I fix this mess, I'm making hot chocolate for everyone. You do want some, right?"

Haven thinks about it. "Yeah," he says. "But take it easy, won't you?"

She waves a hand at him and toddles off while he stretches out his arms and cracks his neck. Next patients, huh? He settles back in his seat to wait.

TWENTY-SIX

TEO LISTENS TO the line ringing in the *Pandia*'s common room. The large room is still set up from the crew's last on-ship *Cemetery Venus* viewing, with two rows of seats. One long wall is a window, showing the depths of space they're flying through. Teo's held more than one important conversation in this otherwise nondescript space. And now when the call goes through, his comm throws up a screen to show a woman he doesn't recognize, a Korean with large brown eyes and thick black hair braided back and tucked under a bandanna.

"Teophilus Anand?" she asks. "It's about time you called. What do you want me to do with her?"

She pulls back and the screen goes to Yeonghui dressed in an elegant hanbok, tied even more elegantly to a chair. Her breaths come out in white huffs and a menagerie of meat dangles from the ceiling all around them. Teo recognizes the walk-in freezer of Yeonghui's manor. He couldn't have asked for a better backdrop.

Teo sighs. "It's Carla, right? Thanks for holding her."

"Anything for Maggie," she says. "Although I didn't think that *anything* would include kidnapping a Jang in her own home." Carla says dubiously, "I know Maggie wouldn't ask me to do anything bad, but..."

"Did you have any trouble bringing her back there?"

"No, I had another car," she says.

Ah, the perks of being a Sonamu celebrity chef. He hopes it eases the pain of whatever damage Ocean wreaked in what sounds like an extremely eventful escape run.

"The main part of her house isn't in great shape..." Carla trails off. "But Yao here was happy to help tie her up in the kitchen. Never a good sign, if your staff is willing to aid and abet."

Teo rubs his forehead. He's not surprised that Yao was quick to help. "Would you give me a few minutes to speak with her?"

"Want me to get rid of her gag?"

"If it's not too much trouble."

Carla must deposit the bangle on a shelf because the video shudders with a click. Teo watches Carla free Yeonghui's mouth. Yeonghui expresses her gratitude by spitting.

"You can't do this to me!" she shouts. "Do you know who I *am*?"

"Obviously." Teo stretches his legs out and crosses his ankles while he leans back in his chair. "It meant so much to me when you told me you believed that I hadn't killed my family. But that was before I figured that your response was less about you believing me, and more that you didn't *care* whether I had killed them or not."

Yeonghui rolls her eyes. "As if you had it in you to murder your family in cold blood."

"I was naive, I guess," he says offhandedly, as if she hadn't spoken at all. "But I don't think you really understood those dinners our fathers had together."

"You had no idea what a privilege it was to sit in on those dinners." Yeonghui sniffs. Teo chooses to believe it's to keep the snot from running down her face in the frigid freezer rather than out of superiority. "Did you even sense the matrix going on under their words, why they asked to pass the sauce or handed each other certain plates? God. You were too busy thinking about yourself, your money, your hair probably. No wonder your father was so disappointed in you."

Everyone always talks about his hair. He supposes that should be gratifying.

"My father was in a constant state of disappointment over me," Teo says. "Everything was always a teaching moment, and I admit most of them didn't stick. But he did tell me a few things about you and your father."

"Oh, and what's that?"

"He said that in our dinners, we were always in a place of power over you." When Yeonghui's face contorts, he continues, "He said your politics are clumsy and your family always goes for the quick buck. You think I didn't pick up on what you were getting at when you were talking about wine vintages and sugar?" He holds up a finger. "'16, not a great year for the Jangs on the Moon because you angled Anand shares to ultimately lose out on the terraforming initiative, correct? Your family wanted to carve out more land on the Moon. You should have brought out a '21, which is when my father helped procure a plot on the Moon so you could cultivate your own vineyard."

"Why would you pretend you didn't know what I was talking about, then?" she asks incredulously.

"You've always assumed you're above everyone around you. In money, in influence, in intelligence." Teo says, "It was easy to feign ignorance when all you expected from me was a desire to get into your bed or to find the next place to party." Yeonghui huffs, and Teo continues, "I was happy to pay you any amount of money for your help on the Moon. You know that the Anand family motto might as well be that there's very little we can't afford. But I wasn't willing to sign over shares involving Anand Tech, and that's what you were getting at with your wine vintages, weren't you? Still, I didn't think you'd resort to this."

Teo shrugs. It's not the Alliance shrug, the tap on the shoulder that conveys the idea even if you're in a spacesuit. It's his approximation of Sasani's *fuck you* shrug, so Yeonghui will get the full benefit of it.

"I don't know how long Corvus was courting you. I'm grateful you didn't give us up right away, although you certainly could have handed our location over to Alessa at any time. You were keeping your options open. But I guess when you figured out that our connection wasn't going to benefit you, you finally cut a deal. Corvus offered you the blueprint to his deepfake suits. And you were willing to give up who you were to impersonate Diplomat Park, to sit at the cool kids' table, to speak in your coded language of tea and wine. You were going to pretend to be Diplomat Park to afford your family more money and more power. But you never saw beyond yourself, did you?"

"I was willing to do what it took to help my *family*," Yeonghui snaps. "What do you know about it?"

"Your family, at the expense of the solar," Teo says. "Did you even think about the repercussions? Or is it that you just didn't care? That wanton use of technology was why I wasn't comfortable offering you anything of Anand Tech in the first place."

Yeonghui's bent over, but her shoulders shake. And then she throws her head back as she laughs. "What are you going to do about it, Teo?" she asks. "You've backed yourself into a corner. Are you going to keep me in this freezer forever? I already have the blueprint."

"The blueprint doesn't have any worth to you if everyone else knows your plan." But hell will break loose if word gets out that she has the blueprint. Teo says calmly, "So you might as well hand it over to me."

Yeonghui cuts off mid-laugh. "Why the hell would I do that? Are you—"

"What do you think I was doing while I was on the Moon?" Teo asks. "You think I was lazing about, eating Shine Muscat grapes out on your back patio? No, I was busy."

"I heard you went out to meet Diplomat Park."

"I did. Once," Teo says. "But I also paid my respects to Lee Taekwan's family."

Yeonghui's face goes pale, although she's too controlled to reveal anything more. "I have no idea what you're talking about."

"It's funny that you mentioned what you were willing to do to help your family. But I guess you just meant your immediate family? Sasani told me that you mentioned how you had some sort of relationship. That he saw you at his funeral. You really have *no idea* what I'm talking about?" Teo asks. "We both know you don't care about the tech in and of itself. You only care that it'll give you power. But if you don't give that tech to me, I can release other information about you that effectively wipes out your reputation, your goodwill, your potential to have a seat at any table."

"You're bluffing. You don't know anything."

Teo honestly wasn't certain whether he had gone to that family to pay his respects or to find out more of how Lee had gotten linked to Corvus. But the same day Teo had been shot by a known enemy, he had found out enough to garner suspicions about his supposed ally. And then he had taken those suspicions to Diplomat Park.

"It would have been easy to think that Lee was independently approached by Corvus. That Corvus promised him something in return for what he did at the hangar. But it seemed like such an odd way to reveal a trump card. As my friend Cass said, it would have been simpler to have knifed me in my sleep. But I did consider whom that move possibly benefited." Teo scratches his temple. "Because of that assassination attempt, I asked you to house us rather than Diplomat Park. I distrusted the Seonbi and their seowon. The thought had occurred to me that you were connected, but again . . . I was naive. You say you knew I didn't have it in me to murder my family in cold blood. I had thought the same for you."

Yeonghui has pressed her lips so tightly together that they are a white line on her face.

"You're smart, Yeonghui," Teo says pleasantly. "You've always thought you were as good as any Diplomat, so I'm sure you mark anyone's tells. You've noticed my hands quiver when I'm nervous." Teo holds up his hands to show how steady they are. "To you, everyone is expendable. Your servants, your business partners, your own *cousin*. I found out from Lee Taekwan's family that you two were actually quite close. He looked up to you while you were growing up together, so it would follow that you could have easily persuaded him to the dark side. But when it came down to it, you used him and then when he became a liability, you eliminated him, didn't you?"

Teo drops his hands and then says slowly, evenly. "Send over the blueprint within the hour, or a prepackaged media file will be sent to all the net outlets I know. And trust me, I know a lot."

"Why . . ." Yeonghui's chest heaves. "You talk about my desire for power, but what are *you* planning? You're an *Anand* and part of the Alliance."

"I don't know that I align myself with either anymore," Teo says thoughtfully. "But let's say I have a professional curiosity. Not that it matters since, again, I have an arsenal to unleash on you if you decide not to share."

Then he says, "Carla? I think that'll be all. And you can let her go now."

Carla comes back onto the screen and picks up the bangle his image must be projecting from.

"Would you send me the bill for anything damaged at your restaurant? If you can't get ahold of me, Maggie will be able to."

"My insurance is pretty solid, but you know I'm losing out on business while we rebuild?" she asks bluntly.

"You should certainly add in that expense," Teo says. "And let me know if Yeonghui gives you trouble, will you?"

"Sure thing, Teophilus." Carla makes the motion over her lips of zipping them closed. "I have to head back to the restaurant now to answer to the commotion. Tell Maggie to expect a call from me soon."

He grins at her and then the screen closes up. Once it does, Teo slumps back on the chair and lets himself deflate, as if all his bones are liquefying.

"Nicely done," a voice says from the side.

Phoenix leans against the doorway, the concern on his face warring with affection. He has his hand pressed up to his side, where

Sasani bandaged him up. Teo stretches out his hand and Phoenix comes over, folding it in his as he sits next to him. Teo closes his eyes as he leans his head back on the chair again, focusing on the solidity of Phoenix's hand.

"I was never a fan of hers anyway," Phoenix says.

"Jealous?"

"A little."

Teo opens one eye to peer over at Phoenix, who has a decidedly serious expression.

"You had no reason to be." Teo closes the eye again. "I admit, I thought it more likely that Park was going to betray us, but the motives were murkier."

Phoenix asks, "What are you going to do with that file on her?"

"I can't hand it over to the media outlets. I made a deal with Yeonghui," Teo says. "But once we get the blueprint from her, I'm going to send the file to Lee Taekwan's family. They can decide what they want to do with it. With her."

Phoenix traces the lines of Teo's palm. "They might forgive her."

Teo doesn't know about that, but it wouldn't have been right to keep the information from them. Yeonghui is part of their family, but Taekwan was their son. Family is so important to Koreans. Well, not just Koreans. Teo rubs his eyes. "Yeah, they might."

Teo tugs Phoenix by his hand and Phoenix draws close to find all the right spaces. He pushes his head onto Teo's shoulder and tucks his nose into Teo's neck, breathing against his skin. Teo keeps one arm wrapped around Phoenix while he strokes his hair back slowly.

"Is this all right?" he asks quietly.

"Mmm." Phoenix's arm snakes around him and he squeezes Teo closer. "Thank you."

A rush of warmth floods Teo. Nothing is solved, and they're haunted by demons. But still. This. This is so good.

"What have I done to deserve this?" he asks, his fingers in Phoenix's hair.

He says it softly, not asking for a response, but Phoenix goes still under him. "I can't tell if you're saying I'm a blessing or a curse."

Teo thinks back to when Phoenix stumbled into the cockpit, supported by Ocean, his body bleeding and his face pale and sweating and how everything else had stopped for Teo.

"I think you might be both," Teo confesses.

Phoenix's hand comes up to hold the one Teo has in his hair. He straightens as he brings Teo's hand to his mouth and kisses the inside of his wrist, his eyes on Teo. The touch of his lips ignites a hot, molten core deep in Teo.

"If I believed in the idea of people deserving anything, I'd say you deserve the solar. If you want it, I'll bring it to you. I'll steal it piece by piece." He leans forward slowly and kisses Teo on the corner of the mouth.

"I don't want the solar," Teo says roughly.

Phoenix lifts Teo's hand and kisses down the arm, the barest touch of his tongue against Teo's skin. The whole time, he keeps his eyes on Teo. He doesn't say anything aloud, but Teo hears his question anyway.

"If you're a curse," Teo says, "then let me be ruined."

He cups Phoenix's face to bring him in for a kiss. Phoenix presses up against him, their mouths moving against each other, his tongue dipping in. Teo wants every piece of him, wants to touch everywhere.

But every touch, every gesture, is a question he asks Phoenix. And as Phoenix answers *yes*, Teo places his hands on Phoenix's hips. Phoenix moves forward, straddling Teo in his seat. Teo groans as they come together. He tugs Phoenix's shirt up to touch him, tracing the bare skin below and above his bandage, and Phoenix rolls his hips forward as he arches back into that touch, leaving his neck open for Teo to taste, for Teo to tongue, for Teo to bite.

"Wait."

Teo stops immediately, his teeth on Phoenix's shoulder, which he's bared after unbuttoning his shirt.

"Did I get too carried away again?" His voice is unsteady. Of course he did. His whole body is straining with his want.

Phoenix laughs weakly. "No, I mean, god yes. But—" He shudders in a breath. "We're still in the common room."

It's difficult to recall that they were *anywhere*, to be honest. Teo's existence had been Phoenix's body in his hands, his lips . . .

Teo clears his throat. "Right."

The common room's door is open to the hallway. He tries to recall exactly how loud he had been. Probably very. Phoenix's hair is completely disheveled, his swollen lips parted. Teo wants to trace his brow, glide a finger down his broken nose.

"You're so beautiful," Teo says wonderingly. At the form of Phoenix before him, and the form of Phoenix's self that has become clearer and clearer to him.

Phoenix closes his eyes. He touches his forehead to Teo's. "If you want," he says, his breath hot on Teo's skin, "you could come back to my room."

Teo pulls back. Phoenix's face is solemn, but searching too.

"Are you sure?" Teo asks.

Phoenix kisses Teo's cheek, next to his eye. And then back on his temple.

"Yes."

TWENTY-SEVEN

HAVEN FINDS HER asleep in his usual spot, her head leaning against the window in the common room. They sat together on another night like this one, and that could be what led her back here, or it could be happenstance.

Haven sits next to her. Her hair's fallen over her cheek, failing to hide the red line she got from the explosion at the restaurant. Phoenix got by with some stitches, although he's been on his feet more than he should be. Yoon's cut didn't need to be sewn up, and probably won't leave much of a scar. If anything, it'll be a hyphen in her skin to match the one on her eyebrow he never learned the story behind.

"I'm not always going to be around to patch you up," he says. "Could you please try and be more careful?"

Yoon stirs in her sleep. He wants to brush the hair back from her cheek, but he touches her shoulder instead. It's rounded, hunched to protect herself in a way her posture never allows when she's awake, small underneath his hand that is suddenly too large, too clumsy, in comparison.

"Yoon."

Her eyes open and then focus on him. "I fell asleep," her voice scratches out.

"Yes." Haven sits back. "You should sleep in your room. Your body needs to recover."

Yoon stands slowly, and a few of her joints crack and pop. "Did you find a flight from Seoul to Prometheus all right?"

"It wasn't difficult."

"Good. That's good." Yoon nods—to herself, to the distance his polite tone has imposed, maybe to whatever is on his face. She's already half turned away when she says, "I never wanted to take your future from you. I hope you know that."

The sight of her back fills him with a grief. It pours into him like smoke, this awareness that his future is going to be full of her absence. It's so hard to let her go this way. He knows he'll fade from her, and even the memories he wants to hold close will opalesce with distance. You can never choose how someone's going to remember you, or if they'll remember you at all. But selfishly, he wants to believe their time together has made some difference, even if she forgets him and moves on. You don't always remember what changed you, after all.

"Yoon," he says, against his will.

She halts. He's always surprised whenever she stops for him. This might be the only chance he has to say goodbye to her. They're landing on Earth, in Seoul, in the next cycle, and he's catching a flight to Prometheus from there.

"I hope you know too," he says, "you've never disappointed me. Not once." For all that she's tried to. For all that he's tried to convince himself she should have.

"That can't be true," she says, but she's listening. Even if it wasn't just the two of them in the room, he'd be able to tell by the set of her shoulders. She faces him. "How do you see me?"

He doesn't know how he can possibly answer such a loaded question without exposing himself.

"When we were back on the Moon and we were being chased and shot at and you were driving down alleys and side streets and spinning around"—he swallows—"even then, I felt safe."

Her eyes have always drawn words from him, and not entirely against his will. He's always had truths he'd share if anyone would listen, if he'd had the courage to say them.

"It's not that you were a good driver. Any idiot could tell that. But I trusted you. And that's how I see you. You have always been someone who keeps others safe."

He has, at some point, become less accustomed to what's on his own face and more familiar with how Yoon reacts to him. She covers her face briefly with that hand that has the crane etched on it.

"I'm afraid to believe you," she says finally, "because I think it might destroy me."

And oh, he's a fool. She drops her hand and offers Haven a crooked smile. The pain in his chest is so acute it makes his body insubstantial, as if he's transparent with want. He has to put his hand to his heart. He can't stay here, but he can't leave her like this either. He's a fool and maybe the damage is already done.

"It's fine," she says. "You don't have to respond to that."

He pulls out his player from the folds of his pocket, his earbuds carefully wrapped around it. In the end, this homage to the memories they have together is all the response he can offer her.

"Want to listen to one more song before we head in?" he asks.

When she takes the earbud from him, she's careful not to touch his fingers. He places the other one in his left ear as he scrolls through his player. There's a deep, low ache in his body at how close she is. His fingers pause over the title of a song. He taps on it, and the guitar strums in his ear. They listen for a few bars before Yoon goes still next to him.

"I've heard this song before," she says. "How do I know this song?"

He's about to tell her who it is, but the tears brimming in Yoon's eyes steal his words. He's as familiar with grief as he is with death, and as he watches, a tear spills down her cheek. Haven instinctively reaches out, wiping it away with his thumb. His hand frames her cheek. But when he touches her, her eyes go to him, startled.

He could stay frozen here for years, or it could be one second drawn out, and he wouldn't know the difference. Haven bends his head next to her face. He puts his mouth to her ear, the one without the earbud.

"Ocean."

He wants to give her at least this. To pour everything he feels into her name, to somehow comfort whatever sorrow she holds, to give up this piece of himself for her to keep or to do with what she wants.

Then, gently, he pulls away. Now that the song is done, he removes the earbud from her ear, his fingers from her face.

And because to do anything else might make his will crumble entirely, he leaves.

· · · · ·

Much later, somewhat sated, they lie on the bed in the darkness. Phoenix is on his stomach and Teo grazes his fingers over his back and traces up the ladder of his spine.

"You've got so many scars," he says.

"Hazards of the job," Phoenix replies drowsily. He shivers as Teo skims over his skin. "I have to say, though, I wouldn't mind a vacation after this."

"Mmm . . ." Teo agrees. "Venus, maybe?"

"Anywhere but the Moon."

Teo laughs softly. "It's a unique place. I was studying up on the terraforming while we were there," he says. "A different approach than the domes in Mercury. The Moon's significantly smaller, but if we were thinking about terraforming Mercury, we'd have to factor in the existing day-night cycles. Engineer crops to match." There's no answer from Phoenix so Teo thinks he's dropped off to sleep. He strokes the curve of Phoenix's shoulder as he murmurs, "Something to think about with Mercurians. Like you. Or maybe you know people." He'll have to ask some other time.

"Teophilus?" Phoenix's voice is alert, surprising Teo.

"Hmm?"

"What's going to happen to Anand Tech after the summit?"

"We'll expose Declan, and we'll get the company into capable hands. Hands that can shape what my father originally intended Anand Tech to do."

"Those are your hands," Phoenix says in the dark.

"I'm a wanted murderer."

"Not after the summit, you won't be. If all goes to plan."

Teo props himself up on his elbow. "What are you saying?" He hears the sharpness in his voice. Phoenix's head is still turned away from him, but he wants the other man to face him.

"How many board members does Anand Tech have?"

They've gone over this multiple times. "Nine."

"And what's the name of Hodgson's second-born?"

"Percival," Teo replies without hesitation. "Which, as I've said, is really a mistake. You'd think they would have learned after naming his older sister—"

"And how does Cixin take his coffee?"

"He likes tea, actually. He has a cabinet in his office and a custom water boiler that—"

"Teophilus." Phoenix finally shifts in bed to meet Teo's gaze. "You're always selling yourself short. But you're good at this. Really good."

"Phoenix, my father dragged me to board meetings just so he could prove how useless I was in that space. Just because I know that a board member doesn't like coffee—"

"It's so much to give up," Phoenix says.

"I've never thought that," Teo says dismissively. "This was never me. I'm more than my money."

"You said you wanted to take responsibility." Teo hears Phoenix swallow. "I think . . . that can be about more than the bad things."

"Responsibility . . ." Teo repeats. "Et tu?" He tries to laugh, but the effort squeezes him instead. He thinks about Anand Tech and what his parents did or didn't do. It's so much power, and the thought of it in his hands terrifies him. He wants to say *I can't do this.* But instead, he manages, "I thought I was joining your crew."

A hard block forms in Teo's stomach when Phoenix doesn't answer right away. Then Phoenix says, "If I were being selfish, that's what I would ask."

"You can afford to be selfish," Teo says desperately.

"But you can't," Phoenix says. With those three words, the block inside Teo disintegrates. "I know you don't want to be. Not really."

"No, I don't." Teo's the one to break his gaze this time. "Are you pushing me away?"

Phoenix pulls Teo close as if to counter those words. "I think we're past that, don't you?"

TWENTY-EIGHT

HAVEN'S PERFECTLY CAPABLE of going to the Incheon shuttleport on his own, but Gemini insisted on accompanying him. Anand can't show his face in Korea for obvious reasons, ditto with Phoenix. The *Pandia* is docked at one of Phoenix's usual trusted locations, and the crew is ensconced, laying down their plans. Captain Song left first to visit her parents before ushering them to her Alliance medal ceremony, which she seemed rather unenthusiastic about. Thierry was gone soon after with excited plans involving a list of restaurants, and Kent went to reunite with Sumi, who had docked her ship to meet him. And Ocean . . . well.

If he could have protected himself from finally uttering her name, he would have . . . but by then it was probably too late anyway.

"I don't think she does goodbyes," Gemini says.

Since they're back in Korea, they're back with automated cars where everyone inputs their destination. All the more reason for

Haven to make the trip alone, and yet Gemini's sitting next to him, his elbow propped up as he gazes out the window.

"No," Haven says. "I don't think she cares much for ceremony." Which, ironically, makes up so much of his life.

"Are you fine leaving like this?" Gemini asks. He leans forward to activate the screen between them. He flips the channels until it lands on the news, the anchor now talking about the weather. It's going to rain later this week.

"I'm at peace with my decision." Haven cradles a small glass encasement, which holds a carefully packaged lotus flower.

Gemini doesn't respond for a while, but at least he doesn't contradict Haven.

"I have a good instinct for whether two people will get along or not," Gemini says suddenly. "It's what's guided a lot of my decisions for our crew. And I think if Ocean and Teophilus ever got together, they'd be all right as more than friends. They love each other, you know. They have good chemistry, but they wouldn't be so passionate it would destroy them."

"I think Anand's chosen another path," Haven says.

"Yeah. Phoenix was pretty much doomed the moment Teophilus stepped through that door reciting Shakespeare." Gemini sizes up Haven before talking to the window. "I think Ocean and I would get along quite well as lovers too. If she'd have me. I'd be very happy at least, and I'd try my damndest to make her happy."

Haven ignores the sudden twist in his stomach. Gemini's never hidden his interest in Ocean, after all. "I hope you do make her happy," he says. "Either way." He focuses on the screen before him and frowns. That's . . . Anand's older brother.

". . . think we'll bring positive change to the solar. I'm looking forward to an open discussion tomorrow."

"Tomorrow?" he repeats. "Is this why you're all here in Korea now?"

Gemini moves over to the center seat. He slides a file from his wrist and throws it over to play on the cab's screen before them.

Corvus slaps his hands on a man's head. He radiates a blurred euphoric visage. The camera shakes as he yanks his hand back and that man drops to the ground. Screams jitter through the video. As Corvus lunges forward to grab another person, Haven averts his eyes.

"This . . . this is horrible."

"Yes. This is recent footage that Lupus found of him in Singapore. We found a similar occurrence before this in Brazil. He's been busy."

"What is he doing?"

"That's the problem. We don't know exactly what's happening, and we can't discern a pattern as to where he's hitting. It might as well be whim."

"But these people . . ."

"Dead. All dead now."

Haven says slowly, realizing, "Phoenix showed me medical records from some hospital in São Paulo."

"Cass has been dissecting the tech as best she can, but his glove wasn't included in the deepfake suit blueprint we obtained from Yeonghui. I think this might be more biological, which is more your wheelhouse."

Haven shakes his head. "I couldn't figure anything out from the medical records."

The video's on a loop and the screen's gone back to the beginning. Corvus moves through what looks like a street market. He hasn't yet attacked his first victim.

"You think Corvus is going to be at the summit," Haven says. "Here in Seoul."

"He's probably in Korea already," Gemini says. "His path has been so erratic, this might be the only chance we have of catching him."

Haven studies the screen again. "You planned this."

"I might've had a hand in what we're doing at the summit tomorrow."

"No." Haven shakes his head. "This is why you wanted to escort me to Incheon, isn't it? You put on the news because you thought they would play a clip of Declan Anand."

A brief flash of teeth. "Now why would you say that, Sasani? You think I'm that manipulative?"

"Why do that and then show me what Corvus did?"

"Because you have a strong sense of justice," Gemini says. "I was counting on that."

"Why?" Haven asks again, and a helpless anger rises in him. "What do you expect me to do about it?"

"Ocean and I have talked about Sinis-x," Gemini says. "You know, when she was hanging off the bridge and you picked up my call."

"When she met you."

Gemini smiles and Haven places a softness in him before he moves on. "You had no combat experience, and you had no training. But you followed her out there. Even when you had every right, every excuse, to stay behind and hide."

"It might have been the smarter decision," Haven says. "I wasn't any help out there."

"You're not a fighter," Gemini says. "I don't think anyone has ever expected you to be, whatever your progress with Cass. But I don't know what's going to happen tomorrow, and I'd feel a hell of a lot better if a medic was close by." Gemini cracks his knuckles. "I won't lie to you. It'll be dangerous."

"Why didn't you ask me before?" Haven asks. "Why didn't anyone else tell me or show me this video?"

Gemini scoffs. "Do you know how frustrating it is to watch you all? Teo already dragged Ocean into this mess, and you think he was gonna add you to that? And you and Ocean . . ." Gemini sighs.

"What does that mean?"

Gemini regards him with pity. "What do you think it means?" He shrugs. "Me? I believe everyone has the right to decide for themselves, and I'm all about what's best for the *Pandia*. I'd like to stack our success rate for tomorrow higher."

Haven could try to ignore the images on-screen, but they still flicker at the edge of his vision. Running home, running away from home. Neither are necessarily aligned with easy or hard or right or wrong. He considers the flower in the glass case in his lap.

He says, "I want to help."

Gemini nods. "I thought you might say that."

He leans forward and touches his wrist to the middle screen, altering their destination. As the car switches lanes to exit the freeway in order to go back, he also pulls up another video.

This one isn't a capture of Corvus, but an older news report. There's a warning about graphic images, but it still doesn't prepare Haven for what comes next. The bodies are mangled, ripped open. His mind slides to a clinical approach to protect itself. Serrated edges; the wounds must have occurred while the victims were still alive. His hand goes to his chest, and only then does Gemini stop the video.

"What was that?" Haven asks.

"That's the work of one of Corvus's followers," Gemini says. "He apparently taught her how to wield a knife."

Haven shudders, but Gemini's face is unperturbed. Gemini's letting the video do all the talking for him, not only putting on display the violence they're capable of, but also the risks Haven is coming up against if he joins them.

"Actually, you met her outside of Sonamu. Her name's Alessa."

Outside of . . . Haven realizes what Gemini actually meant by playing the video.

Gemini's mouth is a harsh slash on his face. "Ocean respects you. And that respect almost got her killed. I heard it from Phoenix. She stopped because of you. And now we'll probably meet Alessa again tomorrow."

"I get it," Haven says.

"And what do you 'get'?" Gemini asks in a low voice.

The atmosphere in the car has suddenly gone frigid, and for perhaps the first time, Haven fathoms how dangerous Gemini is. He swallows hard. "You think it would have been better if she were dead? That Ocean should have killed someone who's capable of . . ." Haven gestures at the screen.

Gemini laughs. "You're the one who's so concerned with morals. Right or wrong, I *don't care*. Ocean stopped because of you. And what if she stopped and got killed instead? Are you good with that?" Gemini stares at him, his face bleak.

"No," Haven says finally. Gods help him.

Gemini doesn't speak for a while, and after a long, tense moment, he settles back in his seat, as if he was testing to see whether Haven would leap over this final hurdle.

"What would you have done if the summit news hadn't come up on the screen?" Haven asks.

"It seemed unlikely. So unlikely that if it happened, I woulda chalked it up to fate," Gemini says lazily. "And waved you off at the shuttleport. Happily."

"Really?"

Gemini slouches in his seat and reassumes his position, elbow up on the window ledge and the heel of his hand shoved into his cheek. When he speaks again, the words drag out of him.

"I don't know what I'd do to have her look at me the way she looks at you. And maybe you're right to run away from it."

Haven could ask what Gemini means, but he doesn't want to go further down that path. Gemini taps the screen again, drawing out the transplanted video. The display switches back to the news sharing a much older story about a cat crossing over the Han River when it was frozen over for the winter. They don't speak for the rest of the ride back.

• • • • •

Teo is not, despite what popular opinion may believe, a meddler. Not anymore, at least.

"Joonho turned out jake in the end," he says as he loudly slurps his Yakult. "Surprisingly."

Ocean raises an eyebrow. "Where did that come from?"

"I never liked any of your ex-steadies," he says. They're sitting at a table in the common room, slumped over the surface, knocking back Yakults in the quiet.

"You never even met any of them," she replies. "What do you know about it?"

"I never had to meet them," he says. "It wasn't who *they* were that was the most important to me. It was how you were when you were with them. So, I guess it's not that I didn't like them as people, per se. I didn't like them with you."

Her mouth tightens before she forcibly relaxes. "You were never around when I was dating someone."

"I didn't want to intimidate anyone," he says loftily.

"Conceited."

Teo laughs. He has always wanted to respect Ocean's space. And if anyone was ever that important to her, he would have met them. "But I always keep an eye on you, Hummingbird."

A corner of her mouth goes up as she fiddles with her Yakult. "I've always . . ." She thinks about it. "I've always tried to be in relationships that made sense." She taps her shoulder. "But somewhere along the line I figured out I was the one not making sense. I was the wrong one."

Teo immediately stems her words with a hand on her head. "Ocean." Her name barely makes it through the tightness of his throat. He clears it as he drops his hand in his lap. "You're not *wrong*. Except about one thing, maybe. Relationships aren't always about what makes sense."

Ocean is all about control. Not over others, but herself. It's not that she drives faster, flies higher, or shoots better. It's her control that makes her good. But the problem comes when she applies that same control to other areas of her life.

Teo spears a straw into another Yakult and places it in front of her. "Sometimes relationships don't work out. We're not always going to be the hero. We can't be if we want to grow." He wavers. He's not a meddler. He's not. "Relationships are complicated. But what that boy feels for you is not."

"Joonho?"

"Ocean," Teo says. "You know that's not who I mean."

Ocean is systematically peeling off the foil caps of all the discarded Yakults, collecting the silvery red pieces in one pile. Teo puts a hand over hers. He wants to say *Your hands give you away*, but she knows better than he does. Her fingers are cold from the drink.

"I think I've always depended on you too much, Ocean," he says.

Ocean leans her head down, resting it in the crook of her elbow, although she keeps her other hand in his. "I think I needed that."

Ocean has always been there for him, without fail, without censure. Teo scratches his temple. "So," he says. "Tomorrow . . ."

"Tomorrow," she agrees.

He brings up a fist and as she bumps it with hers, Teo hears the entry open and close heavily. That must be Gemini, although it's too early for him to have gone all the way to the shuttleport and back already. Gemini walks by the doorway, followed shortly by another familiar figure.

"Sasani?"

Sasani comes back to the opening, his bag slung over his shoulder. Teo gets up and strides forward, alarmed. "Did you miss your flight?" Teo asks. "I told Phoenix you should have left earlier. You can never tell what's going to happen on the road and the security is outrageous these days."

"I didn't miss it," Sasani says, then amends, "I mean I did, but it was on purpose." Sasani hitches his bag up higher on his shoulder as he faces Teo. "I want to help, Anand."

Something crumples in Teo. "Sasani," he says. "Oh, no. I never wanted you to get mixed up in this. I never wanted anyone to."

"I couldn't in good conscience turn away," Sasani says firmly. "I want to do this. This was my choice."

Teo's actions, his words, his decisions will always have consequences. But he's loathe to steal away someone else's choice.

"Thank you," Teo says, as warmly as he can.

Sasani's expression softens, and his arm moves a fraction. But he shoves his hands in his pockets and looks past Teo. The table is now uninhabited save for a few empty Yakult bottles. When Teo turns back to Sasani, the other is rubbing the back of his neck with his hand. Teo marks the line of his hair and the meticulously kept undercut.

"You cut your own hair, right?"

That distracts Sasani from the Yakult bottles. "Yes."

"Do you ever cut anyone else's hair?"

"When I'm home, I cut my father's." Sasani frowns.

"Would you cut mine?" Teo asks. "I'd like my visuals to be in peak condition tomorrow, and my hair's been getting a little long." And apparently a lot of people pay attention to his hair.

"You want me . . . ?" Sasani trails off. "I don't think . . ."

"Please," Teo says. "I would be honored."

Teo thinks Sasani is probably one of those people who caves when he's asked to do anything nicely, like Ocean does when someone she cares about tacks on *please* to anything.

Sasani sighs. "Only if you're honest about the results. When do you want to do it?"

Teo ponders whether Sasani has it in him to purposely give Teo a bad cut so Teo will be forced to get it redone. "How about now?" Teo gestures at the table he was sitting at with Ocean.

"Right," Sasani says. "Well. I suppose I have all my gear with me."

He puts his bag down on the table. As he's shuffling through it, Teo picks up the discarded Yakult bottles and throws them in the trash receptacle. It's not like Ocean to run. Not like that, at least.

Sasani leaves to gather whatever he's missing. When he comes back, he ties a sheet around Teo's neck before he arranges a plastic sheeting underneath them. He must have some innate ability to find the requisite materials for any task in the common room, whether it's a funeral or a haircut. His thoroughness is endearing—he not only has shears and clippers, but a spray bottle of water, a comb, a hand mirror, and a pair of gloves. When he straightens, he reaches for those gloves.

"Out of curiosity," Teo says mildly, "are those gloves for you or for me?"

He didn't miss Sasani's twitch earlier. He might be wrong about what that meant, or it might have been that Sasani was going to . . . what? Offer a hand to shake? It would probably be going too far to say Sasani was going to embrace him like a brother. Sasani rests one long finger on the gloves rather than answering.

"You wear those when you're working in the infirmary," Teo says. "It's good to be sanitary. And if it's your preference, then by all means please don them. But if not . . . I don't want you to miss out on how soft my hair is. That's all I'm saying."

He lifts the hand mirror to check himself out, although he's just giving Sasani space.

"You wouldn't mind?"

Only then does Teo angle the mirror back up to Sasani, who avoids his gaze. "Mind?" he says. "To be frank, I'd prefer it. I don't love biodegradable gloves on my skin. But only if you're fine with it, mind you."

"Well," Sasani says. He slowly picks up the spray bottle and comb, as if he's allowing Teo to change his mind. "In that case."

As he spritzes Teo's hair, he places his hand on Teo's forehead to shield his face from the requisite spray. Teo settles comfortably in his chair. A contented sigh escapes him.

Sasani pauses but doesn't comment directly. "How would you like it cut?"

Teo should probably have an opinion on that. He suspects hairstylists abhor it when you come into their salon and say *Whatever you think. I don't care.* "Maybe cut it like your father's?"

Sasani makes a noise from the back of his throat. "No, I don't think that would suit you."

Teo snorts. "I don't need it to be very different. I usually keep it maintained regularly; I haven't had the chance to do that lately."

"I'll see what I can do," Sasani says. "Do you want to use a mirror to watch me?"

"No, I trust you."

Sasani's fingers rest in Teo's hair. "That's generous of you."

TWENTY-NINE

OCEAN'S NAME IS in Common, but the way her mother says it is in two straight syllables: 오션. In all its incarnations, whether her mother is calling her home or saying it with affection, annoyance, or anger, the inflections are always angular. In her mother's mouth, it sounds like a Korean word she doesn't actually know the meaning of.

But when Sasani says it, the simple act of calling her by name reveals the nuances of how he feels for her. She'll probably always associate it with the memory of his mouth against her ear: tears spilled from her eyes, a hand on her face, her name in her ears. If you're lucky enough, you'll find someone who understands you beyond words said or unsaid.

But you can't have that kind of relationship with everyone, which is what Ocean thinks as she dials the number on her nimbus and places it on the surface before her. The call rings and rings, but the opposite line does finally pick up. The screen opens from Ocean's nimbus.

"Hey."

Dae's hair is down and she's in civvies. It's rare for Ocean to see Dae's hair undone. Even after living together on the same ship for years, she's used to it tied back or in a modified daengi meori, the braid so tight it could be a hairpiece glued in place.

Ocean tucks her own hair behind her ears. "I got your apple," she says. Von had actually given it to her, telling her that it was from Dae, with the message that she wanted to try again. "What did it mean?"

"What do you think it meant?" Dae's forehead wrinkles.

The challenge is almost enough to push Ocean to hang up. If she stays on the line, it will only be admitting that she cares about the answer.

But instead of pressing the end button on her nimbus, she touches her shoulder. "It could have meant a lot of things." She hesitates. "I wasn't sure."

Something flickers across Dae's face. "It's not complicated, Ocean. I just wanted to apologize. I went too far in our last conversation."

"You were only saying what you felt."

Dae kneads her forehead. "I think you misunderstood me, Ocean," she says. "I said I wish he hadn't died, but that doesn't mean I wanted you to be dead instead." She pauses. "I can miss him without having to resent you, can't I?"

"Can you?" Ocean asks softly. She hopes it's a question that her mother asks herself too.

"Did you eat the apple?"

Ocean reaches next to her nimbus and holds up the apple. It's still intact, although at this point it's shriveled. She had to protect it from Maggie that morning.

"I see," Dae says and sits back. Normally, Ocean would expect the other woman to flare up, to take some offense, but she just worries at her lip. "Back in Artemis, Phoenix asked me why I joined the Alliance."

"Why did you?" Ocean asks, although she thinks she knows the answer.

"I said it was every Korean's dream." She meets Ocean's eyes. "Right?"

It's both exactly that and more, but for the first time, Ocean thinks Dae might get that. She knows that Dae meant everything she said in their last conversation. She and Dae have twisted words and intentions between them, but if she's being honest, her problems and her hopes with Dae have never been entirely about the other woman. And that was as unfair to Dae as it was to Ocean.

Ocean brings the apple to her mouth and sinks her teeth into it. The flesh of it is grainy, but she chews the first mouthful and then bites into it again. Dae watches her silently. It takes a long time, actually, for Ocean to finish it. Juice runs down her chin and she wipes it away with her arm.

"That was awful," she says.

"I can't believe you finished it," Dae says and then bends over as she laughs.

It releases a knot in Ocean's stomach, and she tips her fingers in a last salute. "Dangyeol, Captain Song."

• • • • •

"Can I tell you how thrilled I am to have a healer in the party?" Phoenix asks.

"Phoenix, your *Final Fantasy* is showing again," Cass pipes up from the other bed in the med bay. She's already been inspected by Haven and she lounges back, hands folded behind her head while waiting for Phoenix.

Haven lifts up Phoenix's shirt to check on his bandages.

"And have *you* ever experienced the pride of playing through *Final Fantasy I* with a party of all white mages?" Phoenix shoots back at her.

"No, because I'm not a masochist," she replies.

"You're healing up nicely." It's hard to believe it's been only a couple of days since they landed in Seoul, although Phoenix had time to heal while they were traveling from the Moon too. Haven peels off his gloves. "I'd tell you to take it easy, but that's been an ignored request for as long as there have been medics."

"Don't worry," Phoenix says. "I'm supposed to stay out of sight tomorrow. Like you. I'll be hiding while everyone else does all the heavy lifting." He pulls down his shirt. "You nervous?"

Haven considers that. "Nervous for everyone else? Yes."

"You do well under pressure." Instead of leaving the infirmary as Haven expected him to, he leans back on the cot like Cass. "These are the things you pick up on when you ask someone to hold on to your legs while you're blasting bullets out of a car being driven by someone acting out the literal definition of highway to hell."

"I wish I had been there," Cass complains.

"No, you don't," Phoenix and Haven say at the same time.

"Ocean promised me she'd take me driving, though," Cass says. "After all this."

At first, jealousy lances through Haven. But that subsides immediately with the memory of her driving, of her smile seen in profile.

There's a knock, and from the doorway Lupus holds up a black object. "Cass, I need some help with the cameras for tomorrow. This one loses signal intermittently."

"Sure, sure." Cass shimmies off the bed, following Lupus out.

"I *am* grateful for your help." Phoenix sits up and folds his legs in a lotus position.

"Hopefully you won't even need me tomorrow."

"But you've already been an invaluable aid," he says. "Even if you twiddle your thumbs tomorrow, and hopefully that is the case, we couldn't have done this without you."

"I regret not offering my services earlier," Haven says.

"Oh, let's not do that," Phoenix says. "Then I'll have to apologize for not asking you sooner, which I'm also sorry about, by the way, and then we'll end up bowing to each other for the rest of the night."

"Why didn't you?" Haven asks. "I mean, ask me sooner."

"Oh, so many reasons," Phoenix says. "If you were Teophilus, you would probably want to hear them all. If you were Ocean, the reasons wouldn't matter so much as the fact I did or didn't act, am I right? And Gem, well, he probably would have figured out all the reasons, along with a few I wasn't admitting to myself. But I thought you might be wrestling with yourself, and I didn't want to add my bumbling interference into that. You strike me as someone who might be burdened by a request."

Haven pauses putting away the gauze in the drawer. "I hadn't realized you were paying much attention to me."

"Just because I seem to be paying more attention to certain people on my ship doesn't mean I don't notice everyone else."

"You and Anand are very good together." Haven places the gauze, and feels a slight comfort in the clear organization of the drawer.

"You're about as good at deflecting as I am," Phoenix says, and Haven flinches. "But I appreciate you saying that. Sometimes you can't help how you feel when a certain person walks into the room. You understand?"

Heat prickles at the back of Haven's neck. He ignores it, though, hoping it isn't as obvious to the eye as he fears.

"Teophilus has been good . . . so good to me," Phoenix says. "I don't know that we'd be very good together on paper, but he's been showing me, slowly, that doesn't mean I have to change. I think, maybe, we've been showing each other."

"How do you reconcile that difference?" Haven wants to ask more, to specify what he means, but he finds he can't, that it's too hard to put to words.

Because at some point, aren't certain differences insurmountable? Or are you able to continue on only if someone cedes a part of themselves? How can he contend with it, this warring of his father's sensibilities and his mother's image, the way everyone no matter where he goes marks him as an outsider, the conflict of his insides with his outsides, the way his desires pull him in every direction?

"I'll never be fully aware of what it is to be him," Phoenix says. "The same way I'll never fully appreciate the challenges you must face. And I wouldn't expect you to relate with every facet of my existence. But I hope that won't keep us from trying to understand each other." Phoenix presses a hand to his side as he regards Haven. It reminds Haven of his father suddenly, how he winnows out the entanglements of Haven's thoughts. Phoenix pushes himself off the cot. "I'm glad you're here, though, and I know I can trust our lives to you tomorrow. Am I right?"

"Yes," Haven says as they stand before each other. "You can."

THIRTY

TEO SLIDES INTO the seat across from him. Gibson raises his eyes to briefly acknowledge whoever's sharing his table and then his whole body jerks like his inner mechanism has halted. Teo could laugh, but he only scratches his temple. Gibson's older, with stark white hair and a beard contrasting his dark skin. It's been a while since Teo saw those laugh lines around the eyes in person, but the sight of Gibson soothes Teo, reminding him of how he was always ready to throw a snarky aside in board meetings.

"Teophilus Anand?" he says with shock.

Teo leans forward on the table and tents his fingers. "Good morning, Gibson," he says pleasantly. "Care to chat?"

The man's eyes dart back and forth, and his hand tightens around his to-go cup. The iced Americano sloshes, and Teo half expects him to hurl it at his head.

But he doesn't, which Teo had hoped for. It's one of the reasons why he chose Gibson. Of all the people on Anand Tech's board, he's the calmest, the least likely to pull the trigger rashly.

"How did you know I'd be here?" Gibson asks.

"This is your favorite spot in the library," Teo says. "After perusing the nature section, you always come here. I'm the one who told you about it."

They're seated at the one table in all of Starfield Library in a white noise spot. It's why he likes this seat, and it's why Gibson would come here for a moment of quiet. After all, Declan is giving his speech in the library today, and Teo counted on Gibson dropping by beforehand. All around them bookshelves stretch up to the enormous ceiling. To the right, around the astronomy bookshelf, you can peer over the railing that encircles the interior and down to the bottom floor where the presentation will be held.

"How did you get in here?" Gibson asks.

"I have my ways."

Ways that include Gemini scaling the outside of the building and hoisting Teo up. Lupus hacked into the system to find out the schedule, the layout of the building holding the summit, and where they had placed everyone. They'd been able to pinpoint the exact route for them to take to avoid detection. Gemini is currently keeping a lookout from outside, but the time window is indefinite.

"You sound like a villain of a B-holo." Phoenix's voice tickles in Teo's ear.

He's not in the room with Teo, but he's nearby from his own vantage point. It was bad enough that Teo was purported to have gone on a killing rampage, but to show up with Phoenix, the Mercurian Murderer, at his side? Not only that, it would have endangered Phoenix. Phoenix had protested vehemently until Teo said *Phoenix*. Then he had subsided, although he insisted that Teo have backup, even if it was hidden backup.

"Will you hear me out?" Teo ignores Phoenix because that's all he can do right now.

He's put himself in an extremely vulnerable position. He has a cap on, but not much else disguises him. Gibson narrows his eyes but he slowly inclines his head for Teo to continue. Teo leans on his tented fingers, hiding his relief.

"Let me ask you this, first," Teo says. "Has Declan been acting oddly lately?"

"He has suffered a tremendous trauma," Gibson says carefully. "At your hands."

"Gibson," Teo says, equally carefully. "Do you think my hands were capable of that?"

"I don't know," he says flatly.

Fine. Backtrack.

"There are only two reasons why I would kill my family," Teo says. "Either I went insane, or I had motive. As you can see, I'm of sound mind." He spreads his shaking hands. "So I must have had motive. Do you think I would have had any reason to kill them? That I was ambitious enough? Or that I was angry enough that I would have disregarded the cameras in the room? You know me, Gibson. I have always been the most aware of how I am seen. It's my brand."

"If you're so aware of how you're seen, you'll admit how difficult it is for me to believe anything other than what I have been seeing. From all angles on the net."

Teo pulls a tabula out from his back pocket and unfolds it so it lays flat on the desk between them. He taps the screen and a display opens up, the blueprint spinning in the air between them.

Gibson frowns at it, then taps his temple where a pair of glasses unfolds. His reading glasses, which also have a built-in glare protector since he stares at displays all day. Teo analyzes the floating display too, so he's studying along with Gibson.

It's a projection of what Corvus named "the deepfake suit." Gibson, along with being levelheaded and part of the Anand board, is also the head of the tech division. He'll be able to verify the veracity of the technology before him.

"Gibson, that wasn't me in the hospital," Teo says.

"Where did you get this?" Gibson taps his temple again and the glasses fold back up.

"It took some bargaining," Teo says. "It's not enough evidence to clear me, unfortunately. But I thought it might sway you. And also it might explain to you why . . . if . . . Declan has been . . . off lately."

"Are you saying someone is using this technology to pose as Declan?" Gibson asks. "You know this for certain?"

"We had a talk," Teo says coldly. "The impostor and I. Not long after my parents had died." And as Gibson studies him and the silence stretches out, Teo continues offhand, "You didn't bring your seat cushion with you? You know how hard the chairs at Starfield are. You said that when you came for an author event. Ryuichi Iwaizumi? And you've always claimed that chair in the corner of the boardroom. The one with the coffee stain? I don't know how many times I kept Leigh from throwing it out."

Gibson lets out a long breath, and his body deflates as he leans back in his chair. "Why haven't you gone to the Alliance with this?"

"Part of it was timing," Teo says. "And part of it is because Declan, the person who's pretending to be Declan, isn't the end goal. The person behind Declan is. And I could only be sure of where he'd be today."

"The summit?"

Teo dips his head. "The person responsible, Corvus, has reason to hate Anand Tech and everything my father stood for. We think he's going to take everyone connected down in one fell swoop. I need your help, Gibson."

"Mine?" Gibson shakes his head. "What do you want me to do?"

"Things will get hairy," Teo says. "I need someone on the ground to manage the room."

"What does that mean?"

"I'm planning on drawing out Corvus," Teo says. "But to minimize any damage, I need a trusted face. Someone people will listen to, who can usher people. Right now, my face is . . . well, it's as devilishly handsome as ever, but not particularly trustworthy."

Gibson doesn't say anything for a long moment and Teo matches his scrutiny.

"It's risky," Gibson says finally. "Wouldn't it be better to evacuate everyone instead? If Corvus is as dangerous as you say, then aren't you endangering people's lives to clear your name?"

"You think this is about clearing my name?" Teo shakes his head. "I may be selfish, Gibson, but I'm not that self-serving. I don't know what Corvus will do next or where he'll go. He's planning on sparking an interplanetary war by *giving* the Alliance this technology. You know how the rest of the solar will react once they hear the Alliance has these capabilities."

The cubes collapse in Gibson's drink. Gibson is levelheaded, part of the Anand board, head of the tech division, but there's yet another reason why Teo's sought him out.

Teo continues grimly, "You're right. We will be endangering people's lives, but I don't make that decision lightly. When you and my father started this company, it was with a simple idea: to make space travel feasible with affordable technology. It was about exploring the solar without taking away from it." Teo pauses. "Even if he lost his way, even though his thinking was flawed, even if he has caused irreparable harm, he wanted to do good."

Gibson's face folds over in regret. "You know," he says.

"Yes. Finally," Teo says. "And in the future, we'll talk about whether we want to move forward with that terraforming initiative, and what that will mean for Mercury and the solar. I'll address what my father did in Penelope and how he wasn't held accountable. But today I need to take care of something, someone, he helped create."

Gibson stares at him for a long while before he says, "I wish Ajay could see you."

"So he could see me break apart everything he worked for?"

"So he could see you're a better man than he was."

Teo clenches his eyes shut. This isn't the time or the place to lose his composure.

"But I think somehow he knew. It was why he tried so hard to keep you out of the business."

"I knew my place," Teo says. "I was never needed to be anything more."

"Teophilus, it's precisely because you lacked something they had that you're wrong about that." Gibson shakes his head. "I'm sorry it came too late."

"He was not a bad person," Teo says, trying to believe it as he says it. "That's why you continued to follow him, isn't it?"

"When your parents started Anand Tech, he had a vision. Ideas. You said it yourself."

"But a vision only exists if it has other people to see it," Teo says. "And followers should never be so devout that they continue to follow even when the vision turns. But maybe we can both own our culpability today."

Gibson cradles his drink in his hands as he stares down at it. "I assume you have a plan to keep us all from being murdered in cold blood."

Teo nods, hardly allowing himself to hope. As he waits, he realizes his hands have gone still.

"All right," Gibson says.

Teo grins. He pockets the tabula as he stands.

"Teophilus," Gibson says. And when Teo waits, he says, "I'm sorry. For your family."

The apology, even if Teo has heard it before, even if he will hear it dozens, hundreds of times in the future, still guts him. It reminds him there is something to be sorry about: he's alone, his family is gone. He'll be sitting in the kitchen, drinking tea and thinking about how much his mother loves—*loved*—Darjeeling. He'll poke at the thought, at the feeling, and think, *I can do this.* But then he'll be before a tabula, remembering suddenly the way his father left crumbs in the crevices of every keyboard and he'll be completely overcome.

"Me too," he manages.

He knows where to stand, where to walk to hide from the cameras. He leaves the table to skirt around a bookshelf and shimmy through that narrow space. At the window, he knocks. Gemini's head pops up, although he's masked and hooded. He's been casually waiting for Teo, plastered against the side of the Coex convention and exhibition center, which houses the Starfield Library among other retail stores. Not too far from them is the large ballroom where the Alliance held its gala before this all began; the party he and Ocean ditched so he could exercise some rebellion against his father.

"You all right?" Phoenix's voice is warm in his ear.

"I would be if there was an easier way to get around," Teo says. But in truth, hearing Phoenix is assurance enough. It eases the ache in his chest.

"Easier? Sure," Gemini says. "Take the escalator. I give it twenty seconds before someone IDs you."

As his makeshift window opens, Phoenix speaks into his ear again. "One down."

Gemini offers a hand up to Teo that he grips. He's not afraid of heights, but . . . come on.

"Don't talk to me about down or up," Teo says breathlessly, and Phoenix laughs. Gemini's stuck to the window and he lashes Teo to him.

"Have you ever been to Starfield, Phoenix?" Teo asks, more to distract himself than anything.

"Never had the pleasure."

"We can come back some other time. Although it's always been touristy. For my money, I'm a fan of the Cheongun Literature Library. Let's go to that one too."

The answer is soft in his ear. "I'd like that."

• • • • •

"What periodical did you say you write for?" Yeseul, the chef, asks Ocean confusedly.

Luckily, a pan clangs on the other side of the kitchen and flames erupt. Yeseul runs over and by the time she has the presence of mind to remember Ocean and Cass, Ocean has a transparent tabula up and is typing away as if taking notes. Cass doesn't even try. She leans back against the wall as chefs and servers scurry back and forth. No wonder Yeseul is confused. Maggie got them an in, but Ocean and Cass probably don't match the profile of journalists for the high-end food periodical advertised. Cass is dressed for battle, and her sleek catsuit is actually a Teo creation. The lines of her sleeves hook over her fingers, and her oversize power gloves fit right over them.

Teo has decked out most of the *Pandia* team today. Somehow, somewhere, he took the time to design outfits for all of them, and then got the help of a shop in Artemis to fashion them. On the trip back from the Moon, he was holed up adding the finishing touches himself.

And Ocean? She's wearing her red flight suit, the one Teo made for her, the one he saved for her for years. It's . . . flashy for her taste. All red, with the leather jacket. But she knew it was the right choice when she walked into the *Pandia*'s cockpit and saw Teo with his trembling hands and taut shoulders. His whole face had lit up as he said "*Red.*" It's in good condition and it molded to her body as if no time had passed at all. She ripped off the Alliance patch that was on it, but otherwise it's the same as before.

"Hot! Behind!" Someone to the left of her whips around the corner holding out a sizzling pot.

"He talking to you, Red?" an amused voice drawls into Ocean's ear.

Cass rolls her eyes. They're all connected via their ear comms now, although Teo's on another channel with Phoenix currently.

"You calling me Red now too?" Ocean asks, subvocalizing, although it probably doesn't even matter. The kitchen's such mayhem no one would even notice her seemingly talking to herself.

"The name's got a certain allure," Hurakan says. "Teophilus has good design sense."

"My vest has shoulder pads," Aries announces, reminding Ocean of his position. He has a separate vehicle, parked near a van holding Sasani and Lupus. Hurakan always likes having multiple escape routes; he's currently standing by with Teo in a secluded spot on the lower level of the Starfield Library where Declan will present.

"I like your flight suit," Cass says.

"Thanks," Ocean replies. "It has pockets." She demonstrates for Cass as she says it. "I like yours too."

"Cass and Ocean." This time it's Lupus. "Can you adjust the frequency on your comms? I'm getting too much extraneous noise from your end."

Ocean cups her ears as Yeseul bellows, "Where are the gyeran jjim?"

"It might be hard to block all of it out," she says.

"It's part of the territory," Cass says. "We knew that coming in."

Cass and Ocean are running backup for Teo. And Maggie's connections had gotten them pretty damn close—right in the kitchen where they are prepping the food for the conference.

"Ocean, switch to channel 3 for me?" Hurakan says. "For a moment."

Ocean puts her hand up to her comm to do that, switching over to the private channel with him. "What's up?"

"I got you a little something."

TEO'S DURUMI 307

"What's that?"

"Check your ear."

Ocean touches her left ear and then her right ear. They both have earrings in them now. "You gave me back my earring?"

"Nah," he says. "I got us another matching set."

"When did you do that?" she says with exasperation. "How?"

"Tell you what," he says. "I'll let you in on my secret when we get back from this."

"Aren't you tempting fate?" It's like calling this his *one last job*.

"I'm flattered you think I'm enticing enough to lead fate astray," he says. "I wanted to make up for stealing your earring in the first place."

"I thought it was on loan."

"Ah, well . . . I decided I want to keep it. If that's jake with you."

"What's the second earring?" She touches it again, but can't tell.

"It's a crane," he says. "Your old call sign, yeah? Matches your tattoo and your gun. I figured it was appropriate."

Her hand drops.

"The red-crowned crane, the symbol of Incheon, and probably another reason why Teophilus calls you Red, eh? It's a point of honor to be given that call sign by the Alliance, a Korean agency. Not only that, but it's the symbol of Korean unification since the DMZ was converted into a crane habitat."

Ocean falls silent for a few moments. "You always take your vetting this seriously?"

"When it involves you, yeah. Anyway. I couldn't let you go into battle with one ear bare. I'll see you on the other side, Ocean."

A half-incredulous laugh chokes out of Ocean as the click indicates that she's alone on this channel now. She shakes her head as she taps back on the main line.

"Pep talk?" Cass asks her.

"Yeah." In a way, it was.

"Marv." Cass motions to herself with her gloved hands. "Your turn. Lay some wisdom on me."

"What?"

"This chaotic kitchen is our green room," she says. "This is our moment of zen before we go out and deal some hurt."

"*This* is our moment of zen?" Ocean says skeptically. She has to wait to speak until after several carts roll by. They rattle along with mini black pots filled with the fluffy gyeran jjim Yeseul was yelling about.

"Very soothing," Cass says.

"We might all die today," Lupus says. "You might as well take a moment."

"Lupus!" Cass scowls and raps her knuckles on the table next to her.

"That's not wood," Ocean says as she traces the red crown of the crane tattooed on her hand. "Maybe we should prepare to go to our deaths now."

"You are so bad at this pep talk thing," Cass says.

"My mom's a haenyeo, a Jeju female diver," Ocean explains. "She says each time they dive, they go to their deaths. The surface of the water is the line between the world of the living and the dead. Haenyeo make money in the death world, and if they're lucky, they come back to the world of the living to spend it."

She lets the bustle of the people around her fill the space. All of them moving in the kitchen, focused on their tasks yet hyperaware of one another. "Haenyeo have been diving for centuries, but even with all that experience, they know the sea is a dangerous place and they're acquainted with the idea of death."

"*Go deeper and deeper, it seems like the way to hell.*"

"I always wanted to be a part of that," she says. And even though Cass is next to her, she's talking to everyone on the line. She's talking to Teo and Phoenix too, even if they're not listening right now. "Because they die together, but they depend on each other to bring one another back to life." She tilts her head at Cass. "So maybe we should prepare for our deaths. But I trust you to bring me back to life. And you'll do the same."

Cass has folded her arms as Ocean talks. "Well," she says wryly. "We've aimed guns at each other, we've shot down another ship together, and you've even knocked me out. Resurrecting together's not a bad next step. Our leader's name, after all, is Phoenix."

The line clicks once, twice, as Phoenix and Teo join back in.

"How'd it go?" Aries asks.

"Teophilus is very, very good at this," Phoenix says.

"I don't do the humble or bashful thing, so I'll just say we're in." Teo's voice is unwavering. "For better or worse, we're moving forward."

It tremors through Ocean, like waiting in the wings on a stage and being told they're next.

Cass holds out her fists to Ocean. "We die together?"

Ocean bumps them with her own. "We come back together."

• • • •

Haven monitors the screen before him, a layout of the vitals of all the team members inside the Coex building. Nothing too alarming yet, although Anand's heart rate is the most erratic, sprinting up and down through what Haven supposed was his conversation and then jumping when he climbed out the window. Gemini's has remained a steady blip, except when he was talking to Ocean and then asked her to switch to a private line.

Not that Haven blames him. When Haven walked in and saw Ocean in that famed flight suit, his heartbeat hitched up a few notches too. It was undeniably tailored to fit, but more than that, her stance in it was relaxed, confident.

And everyone's heart rate jumped when Anand came back on the line and said they were moving forward.

They are in a large van, and behind him, Lupus is overseeing all the other tech. They're tapped into the security feed of Coex, allowing them to see into the building. Lupus also controls the camera drones, and looked possibly the most gleeful that Haven has ever seen them at that prospect. Phoenix had said somewhat fondly that it was Lupus's big directing debut. Everyone on the team has a camera fixed on their bodies, even Aries, who's on reserve duty. He's also armed with a mini-arsenal, ready to leap into the fray to supply the team.

"Any sign of Corvus or his minions?" Aries asks.

"Declan is in the dining area with everyone, and they're scheduled to move into Starfield soon enough," Lupus says.

Haven sees it on the screen as Lupus does, and they lean forward.

"We've got a visual, but you're not going to like it."

THIRTY-ONE

OCEAN LISTENS AS Lupus continues over the line, "Pretty sure it's Alessa. But she's not in the Coex building with you. She's across the street, at Bongeunsa."

"Bongeunsa?" Ocean says, "The temple is probably crawling with tourists."

"She's not trying to hide. But she's in an area that's cordoned off for repairs. She's next to a huge Buddha statue covered with scaffolding."

The Maitreya Buddha then. The statue is one of the tallest in Korea and it's to the back of the park area of the temple.

"What do you think, Phoenix?" Cass pushes off from the wall.

"If we confront her, we might tip off Corvus we're here," Phoenix says in their ears. "But I don't doubt Corvus is expecting confrontation. It might be he's luring us."

"A trap, then?" Aries asks.

"It's a trap for me," Teo says.

"I think so too," Phoenix says. "It's up to you, Teo. I can't decide for you."

Each breath drags Ocean's lungs in crushed glass as she waits for Teo's answer.

"I can't go," he says finally. "Obviously. I have things to do here."

"Right," Phoenix says easily, as if he knew Teo would say that. He moves on. "But we can't ignore her either. She's in a place with lots of bystanders."

"Where aren't there innocent bystanders?" Ocean asks. "With the Alliance Con today, it's the busiest place in Seoul. Between the temple and Coex alone, that's hundreds of people."

"Cass, you and Ocean go check," Phoenix says. "It's not far; it's literally across the street."

"I don't like it," Cass says. "It takes us away from you and Teo."

"I'll chaperone them," Aries says.

"Me too," Hurakan chimes in.

"If you remove her from the game, that's one less player we have to worry about on the board," Phoenix says. "And she's a dangerous player."

"It's your call, Phoenix," Cass says. She asks Ocean, "You know the way?"

"More or less," Ocean says. She cocks her head as she heads out of the kitchen, down the hallway, and to the stairwell.

Contrary to her work ethic involving the countless missions she completed for Dae and the *Ohneul*, Ocean closely studied the maps and the layout of the Coex building and its surrounding area. Most Koreans have a passing familiarity with the area—the Hyundai mall, the museum that used to be an aquarium. But she's only made the trip a couple of times, and she's even less familiar with

Bongeunsa. She's been there maybe with an ex-steady for tourist reasons, although the memory is hazy.

"Bongeunsa," Aries intones over the comm, and Ocean jumps. "Originally known as Gyeongseongsa, but reconstructed and renamed during the Joseon dynasty by Queen Jeonghyeon who helped revive Buddhism in the country. Word is that the restoration of the Buddha statue is quite extensive. They hope to be done late summer of this year."

Ocean raises an eyebrow back at Cass.

"Ignore him," Cass says as they hurry down the stairs, their steps echoing. "It's how he diffuses nerves. He's probably reading from the temple website."

"Don't interfere with my de-stressing process," Aries says.

"Last time I was in this area, it was on a very nice date at Han Oak," Teo says brightly.

"What did you eat?" Lupus asks.

"*No*, don't talk about food," Cass says. "You're going to make me hungry."

"I'll treat you after this," Teo says. "If we don't all die."

"Don't say that!" Cass snaps as she raps her knuckles on the doorway before she and Ocean pass through it to the outside. The doorway has deposited them out of the northwest end of the Coex mall. They can see the temple from there.

"Was that even wood?" Aries asks.

"Don't interfere with *my* de-stressing," Cass shoots back.

"Please pay attention to your surroundings everyone," Phoenix says mildly.

It's good advice as Cass and Ocean are crossing the street now. They stride across the road and then into the parking lot of the temple grounds, the dirt gristle chuffing with each step.

"Who were you on a date with?" Cass asks. "Should Phoenix be jealous?"

"Kim Minwoo. And no, never," Teo says. "No matter how pretty he is."

"Gasp," Phoenix says. "I thought I was the prettiest one."

Ocean and Cass run up to the temple gates, passing under the sloping roof and the intricately designed border above the tall pillars. The words over the gate are in hanja, and Ocean doesn't know what any of it means, or what symbolism is carved, although she wouldn't be surprised if Dae knew. Maybe she'll ask someday.

"Sasani might be the prettiest out of all of us," Teo muses. "Gemini gives him a run for his money though."

"Oh Teophilus, you can't handle me," Hurakan says. "You can barely handle scaling the side of the Coex building."

The temple grounds, unsurprisingly, are packed full of people. To their left, a man poses for a picture being taken by a floating tabula.

"Buddha statue's in the back and to the left," Ocean says to Cass.

Cass punches her fists together and her gloves light up. "Lupus?"

"Alessa's holding her position. You'll see her soon enough."

"Teo, Gem, Aries. Switch to channel two with me," Phoenix says. "We're about to head in."

"We'll be on channel three," Cass says, putting a hand to her ear.

"Vitals are good for everyone," Sasani says. "I'm keeping an eye on them."

The surround sound of voices in Ocean's ears is like a chorus of support, a call and answer, all of them bolstering one another before they dive in.

"Ocean and Cass, be careful," Phoenix says.

"You too, Phoenix oppa," Ocean says.

Ocean hears the hiss of the line, a surprised gasp before she switches over to channel three with Cass.

They pass a smaller temple where a crowd has gathered. A monk stands on a platform before an enormous drum, pounding away at it rhythmically.

"What's that about?" Cass asks.

Ocean spares another scan as he finishes his routine and another monk moves forward, ready to ring an enormous gong with a wooden ram hanging from the ceiling.

"I have no idea," she admits.

Whatever it is, it's drawn the bulk of the people from the surrounding area, so there are fewer people when she and Cass head up the path leading to the Buddha statue and then duck under the cordons flagged and stickered with specific instructions to not do exactly what they're doing.

"Is it just the two of you?"

Alessa crouches on a platform above them, on one of the lower levels of scaffolding surrounding the stone Maitreya Buddha statue, which stretches high into the sky, probably close to thirty meters. Rows of buddhas are etched into the surrounding white walls, serenely gazing out.

Cass says, "This doesn't seem very respectful."

They stand on top of a glossy red stone square, the shiny surface reflecting Ocean, Cass, and the sky above. When Ocean was last here, people were kneeling in supplication on this same ground, faced with their reflections, as if praying to themselves. Cass squints upward. "You coming down or what?"

"I'm not going to prostrate myself," Alessa says. "You come up to my level or not at all."

In the distance, Ocean hears one last gong reverberate through the air. As the sound shivers around them, the silence settles on their shoulders.

"How apt," Alessa says, her face angled as if chasing the last echoes. "That means they've started evening prayers. I'll say one for your souls after I'm done here."

"Now *that's* disrespectful," Ocean says to Cass.

"Don't worry about us," Cass calls up to Alessa. "After all, we already planned on dying today."

Ocean pulls out her gun from her jacket.

· · · · ·

"She called me oppa, right?" Phoenix asks.

In spite of everything, Teo smiles at Phoenix's stunned voice. "Can you give us a visual?" Teo asks into the channel.

Not too long after, a notification opens up on his tabula. He taps it to open the link sent from Lupus, and he and Gemini lean their heads together to watch it. It's a live feed of the event that's being broadcast on AllianceVision.

Even if he was expecting it, his stomach lurches when Declan steps up onto the platform. Starfield Library is not a particularly defensible spot. The sunken basement level is typically used for author talks, and there are easy sightlines from the levels above. Spectators mill the section behind several rows of chairs. The platform is situated between two sensored entryways that lead into underground stores, while opposite them is Starfield's main area. The front doors go out to the street, and escalators lead to other levels of the library.

It's not very secure, but it makes for great dramatic flair. A private conference wouldn't have nearly as much media coverage or public eye. A large living art installation looms between the chairs and the front entrance, a riotous collage of flora from all over the solar. Von would've loved it, but his presentation is on schedule elsewhere.

Phoenix, who knows Corvus best, thinks he plans on laying it all out here. He's not going to hide the decimation of everyone who's come to the summit: the Anand Tech board, Alliance members, and other political and business people who want in on the Anand line.

They only need the visual from Lupus, because Teo and Gemini are on the other side of the platform's wall and Teo can hear Declan's amplified voice without too much difficulty.

". . . My father wanted to scale back on terraforming because he thought of the harm it was doing to the solar. But what of the plight of our common man?" Declan asks.

He's never been one to stand behind a podium, and true to form, he strolls leisurely back and forth on the platform. He gestures to the screen set in the bookshelf behind him, showing pictures from terraformed planets and moons. Hadrian must have studied Declan extensively, religiously, to portray him so accurately. His heart twists at the way Declan's hair artfully falls into his eyes, before he flicks it back again.

Teo hears a click and then "Anand, you jake?" Sasani's ever-soothing voice.

"Oh, great, you know?" Teo says blithely. "Are you asking because my heart rate is galloping away?"

"I'm asking because I'm concerned for you," Sasani replies.

Teo considers the department stores around them, the people walking in and out of the Fritz Coffee diagonal from them. As the sign shifts to display the latest seasonal flavor of yuja butter latte, he briefly, for one last time, ruminates on running away. He sighs.

"You know what would make me feel great, Sasani?" Teo asks.

"What's that?"

"If you called me by my first name." Teo folds the tabula and slips it into his back pocket.

There's a long silence at the other end.

"Nongdam, Sasani," Teo says.

"I could do that," Sasani says. "You said all your friends call you Teo, didn't you?"

For once, Teo has no words ready.

Gemini grins. "Teophilus looks like Shakespeare came back from the dead to shake hands with him."

"As Thierry would say, I'm on your side, Teo," Sasani says. "We all are."

Oh god, all these warm feelings. Ocean even calling Phoenix oppa. This isn't like a setup to a last stand at all.

"Then, Haven," Teo says. He can't help the grin as he says the name. "I guess we may as well get started. Thank you, everyone." He clicks over to another line. "Lupus, how's the feed on your end?"

"We're set here. I'll dampen the other comms in the room," Lupus says. "It's time to make a dramatic entrance."

"My favorite words," Teo says.

His heart is hammering so hard his body might not contain it. Gemini pats him on the shoulder. The former thief is also wearing Teo's design today, the original one he showed Phoenix. Gemini slides up the mask and the hood, so the only part of his face showing is the space around his eyes. Teo's not altogether sure who else put on their new outfits. Lupus snuggled into their hooded uniform almost right away, but he doubts Phoenix put his on since it's far too attention grabbing for their purposes today.

Seeing Ocean in her original flight suit, though, had given Teo a joyful jolt. He lets that image settle in him now.

The doorway is large and faces the audience members of the event space. As Teo passes through, he walks between its sensors. They stay silent, and he pulls off his cap and throws it to the side.

As he strides forward, he tousles his hair lavishly like he's a shampoo model. But it's not a shampoo model he has in his mind as he imitates that exact toss of his head, the cocky set to his chin. A gasp rings out so loudly that it has to be the culmination of several exclamations happening simultaneously, and then all eyes in the audience are on him. Some people stand and point at him. He blows them a kiss. One man has his comm out and he spits out words rapid-fire before he pulls his wrist away, confused. Teo hides his grin.

Then he slowly faces the stage.

"Hello, brother."

THIRTY-TWO

TEOPHILUS STEPS OVER the threshold like he's a descending god and Phoenix's heart tightens. He knows Teophilus doesn't want to do this, doesn't want to face the man who wears his brother's skin, but none of it shows on his face as he tosses aside his cap.

The movement, as intended, draws the attention of most of the audience. Even if he hadn't done that, Phoenix thinks they wouldn't have been able to help but notice him anyway. Teophilus has always had a magnetic charisma. He flashes that megawatt smile as he runs a hand through his hair, showing off his new haircut, tossing his head. Phoenix recognizes the movement before he identifies it.

"The Phoenix Toss," Gemini murmurs into the comm line to confirm it.

God, Phoenix loves Teophilus.

Phoenix leans over the railing. Gemini got him onto the second floor undetected, but he doesn't need to worry anymore about anyone spotting him because they're otherwise preoccupied. More than one person has pulled up their comms to call for help, but they end up staring at their wrists or tapping them to shake their comms. It's no small effort to dampen comms but let the *Pandia*'s work freely. But Lupus has always been a talented kid.

Teophilus blows a kiss at someone before he faces Declan.

"Hello, brother."

It's in Teophilus's hands now. Phoenix is here only to back him up.

Phoenix wanted to be selfish. If he wakes up in the middle of the night, he wants to have Teophilus's face near his. He wants to provoke that wicked laugh, to toss out any obscure reference, quote, repartee, and have Teophilus effortlessly lob it back. He wants Teophilus there to challenge him. He wants the comfort and security and the surprise that Teophilus gives. And he wants Teophilus's mouth, the arch of his neck when he throws his head back, that divot in his hips where Phoenix's thumb fits perfectly.

If Phoenix asked, Teophilus would drop his entitled life and his money in a heartbeat. But it would have been selfish because it would rob Teophilus of the good he could do, the good that other people need.

"Are you here to turn yourself in, babu?" Hadrian asks.

His question reminds Phoenix to focus. He homes in on Hadrian's carefully modulated tone, the voice of a concerned older brother who's magnanimous even before the man who has murdered his family.

Dozens of people have their tabulas out, recording. They were counting on that ingrained habit: the more cameras, the better.

Teophilus slowly puts his hands up and rests them on his head. He wants to appear as harmless as possible. It's why he came in through the side doors in plain view, so everyone could see that the sensors didn't go off, that he doesn't have a weapon on him. Everyone is so enthralled, Phoenix easily sidles over without drawing attention. He descends down the escalator to the first floor.

"I'm so sorry," Teophilus says. "I have been so lost."

Hadrian blinks, taken aback. He likely anticipated Teophilus to accuse him off the bat.

"Why did you do it?" He darts a survey of the situation: cameras everywhere, but no security guards. Phoenix smiles grimly. He and Aries took care of that already.

"Do you remember when we went to Venus for a family vacation? It was when we were kids." Teophilus steps forward, keeping his hands on his head.

Hadrian frowns. "We never went to Venus on a family vacation." Hadrian shakes his head, and his shoulders relax. He thinks he's onto Teophilus's game. "What are you talking about, Teo?"

Teophilus wavers, as if confused. "It wasn't Venus?"

By now, the whole solar has witnessed the footage of Teophilus murdering his parents. It's been seen from every angle, dissected by every news and gossip station. It was hard for Teophilus to sift through that, but necessary. The prevailing opinion, given Teophilus's public persona, is that he lost his mind. Maybe the trauma of what happened on the *Shadowfax* unhinged him.

Teophilus Anand, the pampered prince. It's what the whole solar has thought of him, and honestly what Phoenix pegged him as. And Teophilus, who has always talked about how he's used to being used, has perfected the art of using himself. Everything hinges on that today.

"Do you mean when we went to Hawaii?" Hadrian asks. Of course he knows the family history. They were never expecting him to make an amateur slipup.

Teophilus's forehead crinkles. "Yeah, I guess that might have been it."

"What about it?" Hadrian asks and directs a wide-eyed plea at the audience.

A couple of people from the audience take the cue and peel off to find help. It's only a matter of time before they're interrupted.

"I wanted to swim in the water, but baba said I wasn't strong enough," Teophilus says as he steps forward again.

Gemini enters through the side door as if he's a bystander who happened by. He also doesn't set off the sensor so there's no cause for anyone to notice him.

The event Teophilus is talking about might be too specific for Hadrian to know. Or it could be that it's not even a real event at all. But before Hadrian can respond, Teophilus continues.

"But I went out anyway and then got swept out." Teophilus's voice is low, full of emotion. "You came and you saved me."

The whole room is hushed. Phoenix is close enough now to see tears overflowing in Teophilus's eyes. *Oh Teophilus.*

"You always came to my rescue, Declan," Teophilus says. "You always took the fall."

He lowers his hands and although some people in the audience tense, Teophilus only holds them out as he approaches the stage.

"Please, Declan. Help me now? Please."

Corvus undoubtedly has plans, but at least for now, Hadrian has to keep up his charade in front of all these people, all the cameras. He can't possibly reject his younger brother, the one everyone thinks went insane, who has no weapons now and is no harm to anyone.

Teophilus steps onto the stage, his palms up in a plea.

"I'm so tired. Will you save me again?"

Phoenix holds his breath along with the rest of the room. And then, finally, Hadrian does what any older brother would, should do. He holds his arms open for an embrace. Teophilus stumbles forward and collapses into them so forcefully Hadrian staggers back a few steps. Hadrian wraps his arms around him as Teophilus cries, clutching at him. Phoenix doesn't doubt they're real tears. Hadrian pats Teophilus's back as he scans the room.

Teophilus lifts his right hand and cradles Hadrian's neck as he buries his face into the shoulder of the man impersonating his brother. The man who, in actuality, killed his brother. His other hand comes up, the palm cupped, ready to hold his head.

Very few people will catch what happens next. But Phoenix does.

From across the room, Gemini clicks his shoes together and a knife pops out of his custom heel. In one fluid motion, he removes it and hurls it with pinpoint accuracy into Teophilus's upraised hand.

Before the eyes of the whole solar, Teophilus takes that knife and plunges it into his brother's back.

THIRTY-THREE

THE DAY BEFORE, Haven had taken Teo's hand and led it to the back of his neck so Teo could feel the ridge of Haven's spine.

"C7," Haven said, his serious eyes locked on Teo's. He wanted to make sure Teo was certain. "The last bone of your cervical spine."

And although Teo should be concentrating on that as he steps onto the stage now, as he says, "I'm so tired. Will you save me again?" it's all wiped away when he falls into Hadrian's arms.

Teo lets himself indulge in this, even if it's a lie. A sob wrenches out of his throat as he clutches his brother. He even *smells* like Declan. He must be using his cologne, and even if something rises in Teo like bile at the thought, he could cry, too, for this last moment he has with his brother.

This Declan looks like his strong, tall, ever-capable brother. The brown skin, the Roman nose they share, the thick eyebrows, the deep indents in the forehead drawing frown lines that will never have a chance to become permanent. He smells like memories that will slip out of Teo's fingers.

Declan pats Teo on the back, the familiar counterclockwise rub with the two pats. In response, Teo angles them slightly so Declan's back faces a camera. Then, he reaches up for Declan's neck and feels the nub.

C7. The last bone of the cervical spine.

Teo inhales one more time and then lifts his right hand. To his left, he sees Gemini. He keeps his head shoved into his brother, but their eyes lock and Gemini mouths a word and clicks his heels together.

One.

Eighty beats per minute, which Maggie says is the tempo of the andante portion of Tchaikovsky's *1812 Overture*. They mouth the next word together before Gemini bends down.

Two.

On the count of three, Teo snaps his hand shut as they've practiced, and his hand closes on a knife. Even if he's prepared for the force of the shot, the violence of it snaps his hand back.

When he first met Gemini, he had noted the built-in custom heels of his shoes right away. But he had been wrong in thinking it was meant to bolster his height. Today, the right heel holds a very specific knife, one made from a Brazilian walnut tree, one of the strongest woods in the world and a kind of material that will pass any sensor. It's small and not the sort you use to kill someone, but then again, that's not Teo's intent.

He stabs straight into Hadrian's back.

Hadrian screams and Teo digs the knife in. In his desperation, Teo jerks the other man around. The crowd has erupted into pandemonium. Teo has his hands full, but Gemini jumps onto the platform, deftly blocking and taking down anyone trying to interfere. From the corner of his eye, he sees Gibson jump up from his seat, his arms out, trying to allay the crowd.

This was Teo's *professional curiosity* when he demanded the tech from Yeonghui. He didn't need it to convince Gibson, he didn't intend to use it to bolster Anand Tech. Teo knows, maybe better than most people, all clothes have a seam. You can conceal it as cleverly as you want, but it all comes together at a point. And for the deepfake skinsuit, it's this point here.

Teo rips the knife down and the suit breaks open. His hands maul it. He's crying, yelling as he rips it apart, rips apart this facsimile of his brother. Wires spill out like nerves and liquid gushes forth, until another body emerges from the mess and slops to the floor.

Hadrian. So, this is the face of the man who was hiding in his brother this whole time.

In the complete silence, the screen behind Teo flashes over to what's playing on the news, courtesy of Lupus. It's an overhead shot of the platform that shows Teo standing over Hadrian's body.

Hadrian is a pale man, and he lies sputtering on the ground, gasping air in like a sallow fish flopping on a boat deck. It was probably excruciatingly painful to be ripped from the suit like that, but Teo can't muster up much sympathy for him.

The screen splits then, as Lupus brings up a playback of Hadrian onstage, embodying Declan so perfectly it's impossible to tell them apart. It plays side by side with Hadrian on the ground.

"This is not my brother," Teo announces to the frozen audience. And even as he addresses Hadrian on the ground, he keeps his chin lifted enough so his words resonate. "Did you kill my parents too?"

Teo asks more for the dramatic effect of it, and also to remind the audience this man, *this man they were just convinced was Declan*, is not. Their eyes are not to be trusted. It doesn't hurt that he lets his voice hitch at *my parents*. Once people realize that Teo's not the actual killer, as they've thought the whole time, it should be reinforced that Teo also lost his parents. Teo has also been grieving.

They don't know that the person who killed his parents is at Bongeunsa, facing Ocean and Cass. He had a chance to go to Alessa, and Phoenix gave him that chance. He wanted to kill her with his bare hands. But what would that have accomplished? Teo puts his foot on Hadrian's chest and presses down.

"What did you intend to achieve by framing me?" Even though he says it down to Hadrian, he makes sure his voice carries.

He doesn't expect Hadrian to answer. The other man is incapacitated, his body jerking around from having the suit ripped from his skin. His mouth gapes open and his hands claw at Teo's foot. He has bright-green eyes, the most vibrant feature of his pasty face. But Teo's ever aware that their quarry is much larger, and they need to lure him out.

The screen next to Teo blinks again so the split screen is no longer playing the Declan playback, but an interview.

"Teophilus Anand? Yeah totally, I know him. We've spent the last few weeks together," one of the people on-screen says cheerfully.

"Really?"

The other person on-screen, Kim Minwoo, leans forward in his seat, sounding totally fascinated. "The last few weeks? How is that possible? Did you pick him up after he murdered his parents?"

Behind the two of them, the blue Shinjeong Co logo is huge on the wall. Kim Minwoo, a surefire draw for any net segment. Also, a shrewd businessman. Today uses up both favors that Teo's long-ago publicity stunt with Minwoo won, but he figures this is well worth it. There's a reason why Kim Minwoo is highly sought after for CFs, whether to peddle skin cream or Shinjeong's latest massage chairs. The audience at Starfield is now entirely captivated by the screen for another reason.

"What? No!" Maggie, seated next to Minwoo in the video, flaps her hands. "That wasn't him! He was on *our* ship when that happened."

"How do you know that? Are you sure it was really Teophilus Anand with you?"

Maggie scrunches up her face. "Do I know if it was Teo? If it wasn't him, then who always used up all the hot water and ate all the Moon Bars? He stole my special soap too. If it wasn't him, then why did people keep trying to blow up our ship to kill him?"

"I met him once before, you know. We went on a very pleasant date." Minwoo muses thoughtfully, "I never thought he was actually capable of it . . ."

"Capable of it?" Maggie *tsks*. "I don't know if he'd harm a fly, but he did stop me from killing a spider. He chased it around the room before he caught it in a cup to release outside. And even then, he made Von message the local university to see if it would survive in the ecosystem." She breaks off. "I have to tell you, though, I'm a *huge* fan. Our whole ship has been watching *Cemetery Venus* together and I have a theory that I was hoping you could—"

A high-pitched beeping is loud enough to draw everyone's gaping attention away from the screen. It's the sensor at the front of Starfield.

A man flares out the edges of his coat as he walks down the aisle toward Teo. He claps his hands. He's so pale that the light coming in through the glass ceiling practically makes him glow. He's tall and lithe and although his mouth twists sardonically, his gray eyes hold only a horribly empty vagueness. His right hand is encased in a blue glove that goes up to his elbow. Behind him, a woman with dirty blond hair follows, and even if she hadn't had a weapon in her hands, she would have set off that alarm on her own because she *is* a weapon, if he's identified her correctly as Emory. He hears the whir of her movement, even though she moves smoothly.

"Well done, Teophilus Anand," Corvus says. "You've brought me out. Now what?"

Time has a funny way of elongating and speeding up. Teo's thudding heart shakes his whole body. Corvus's steps echo in his ears. But now Corvus is before him and it's too much, too soon.

Corvus has combed his hair elegantly back from his forehead. He wears a long white leather duster over a black ensemble, as if he's some avenging angel, and Teo has no doubt he dressed this morning to be seen.

"Corvus Laurent," Teo says. "So kind of you to come out of hiding. It's time to turn yourself in."

Corvus raises his palms up. "For what crime, may I ask?" His voice carries like Teo's. Not only is everyone around them hushed, the two of them know they're playing for a larger audience. All the world's a stage.

"Murder," Teo says. "For the mass murder of people in Brazil, Singapore, and on Mercury in Penelope and Circe, as well as numerous others."

"Murder?" Corvus bares his teeth. His tongue comes out to touch his pointed canine. "But I wasn't *murdering* anyone, Teophilus Anand."

"Footage from numerous sources would disagree," Teo replies, struggling to keep his words steady.

"Oh, but we're beyond trusting footage for anything anymore, aren't we?" Corvus keeps walking forward, with Emory close behind. "The evidence stacked against you is rather damning in that aspect. But you're mistaken. I haven't killed anyone. They live through me."

Corvus raises his hands; his nonsensical words are clearly meant to segue into a monologue, but Teo didn't create this stage for him.

"Corvus, this isn't the way," Teo says. "I know why you're doing this. And I know my father was responsible. But this isn't the way forward."

"You know?" Corvus snarls. "What do you know about me?"

He extends his gloved hand to his right and beckons.

"Corvus . . ." Emory says, a hesitant tremor in her voice.

Corvus rotates his head like a robot tracking a voice, and Emory shrinks back from whatever is on his face. She drops her gaze and pivots. Quick as a rattlesnake, she nabs the closest person to their right from the audience. Pavesi, another Anand Tech board member. She screams and the people around her scramble away, although one, Cixin, goes for Emory. But Emory sweeps out her right arm, the mechanized one, and sends him hurtling, while her left arm clamps around Pavesi's neck. The rest of the crowd disperses in a flurry of mayhem.

"Let her go!" Teo promised Gibson no one would get hurt. "You have nothing to gain from harming her."

Corvus cocks his head at Teo. "Harm her? Why would I do that?"

Then he slams his hand down on Pavesi's forehead. And like those newscasts, Pavesi screams. Only now, Teo has a front-row seat to it. Corvus's glove lights up, and brilliant blue lines sink into Pavesi's head and race through her veins.

"No!" Teo leaps forward off the stage. He has no weapon, no plan, but he needs to stop this.

Emory drops Pavesi and kicks Teo in the stomach. The weight of her mechanized leg condenses all at once, knocking the air out of him. Teo's body slaps the ground. She sustains her pose, as if she's a martial artist. Gemini flies past him, alighting on Emory's leg to launch at Corvus, but Emory scissors a kick, dropping Gemini with one leg to slam him with the other. Teo wheezes as he tries to push himself up and falls on his face again.

"I need a clear shot!" Phoenix shouts through the line.

Gemini and Emory are flat against the glossy wood flooring but he clutches her arm. He heaves against her, but Emory hikes up her knee and digs it into Gemini's back. Her augmented strength is too much for him.

Corvus is already wrenching his hand back. Pavesi flows over the floor. Her brown hair falls over her face, her eyes gape open but the pupils are two empty holes. Corvus falls to his knees, with his head dropped back, his mouth ajar. He quivers.

"Esther Pavesi." His eyes flicker back and forth rapidly, as if he's reading the dreams inside his own head. "Teophilus, when are you going to let me set you up with my niece? She'll help you settle down, no?"

As Corvus speaks with a particular accent, he brings his hand up to his chin, the index finger tapping on his cheek. He stands, smiling maternally at Teo.

"How . . . What . . ." Teo stammers.

TEO'S DURUMI

"You're quite the handsome devil; you need someone to balance you out. You have too much fire in you. My sweet niece Sophie would be the person, I think."

"Stop. Stop talking," Teo says. He gapes at Pavesi, the real Pavesi. She's slack-jawed, but her back moves slowly as she breathes.

"I haven't murdered anyone," Corvus says. "I've given them a new home. I've become a vessel, you see. I have become more than myself. It is the ultimate act of sacrifice and empathy."

"What are you *talking about*?" Teo sits up.

"How will we improve as a society, as a solar, if we don't *truly* understand one another?" Corvus asks. "The pitiable thing is, no one will ever understand—*do* anything about—your suffering unless they experience it themselves."

Teo hears his own shallow breathing, and a whiteness threatens to encroach his vision. *This* is what Corvus was doing? This tech wasn't included in what Yeonghui sent them, but he doesn't think she kept it hidden. He doubts Corvus planned on sharing it with anyone else.

"I don't care what you call it," Teo says shakily. "You're killing them!"

Corvus sneers. "You and your family have had a far more direct hand in killing people, Teophilus. And why? Because your actions have never taken into account the utter destruction of others. Because you could never think outside of yourself."

"Is that why you killed them?" Teo asks hollowly. "You didn't even try to do this, this *thing*. You murdered them in cold blood."

"What would I do with the memories, the essence, of a whole family fine with letting Mercury bleed out because they didn't want to share their wealth, their technology?"

"You're not wrong," Teo scrapes out. "We were wrong. My father's way forward wasn't right, and neither is this, Corvus. We can—"

"We?" Corvus tilts his head, so like the bird he's named for. "You don't care about *we*. None of you did, but maybe I can make *you* see. I had your parents killed. I had your brother killed. But you wouldn't submit so easily, and maybe I should reward you for that." Corvus sweeps an arm around. "I'll make them *all* see. What need do we have for your Anand Tech board when I can absorb them all? Their information, their knowledge? And that will be subsumed in me, a Mercurian who can put all of that to actual good use."

Teo subvocalizes, but even his inner voice is dull in his mind. "Is that enough?"

Lupus says over the line, "More than enough."

He can't work out the exact mechanisms of Corvus's glove. But Corvus has been somehow siphoning the memories or some such out of people. Teo hadn't wanted anyone to get hurt, but his decision, *his decision* led to this. To the end of Pavesi's life. Like his father made the decision leading to countless tragedies, like all of Teo's decisions have toppled over dominos, involving the people he loves, forcing their hands, bringing death.

Corvus's words *"because you could never think outside of yourself"* are entirely correct. As if on cue, the screen next to them splits again and now along with the interview and Starfield, it's showing footage from the Bongeunsa grounds across the street. Teo recognizes the enormous Buddha statue looming on the screen. Lupus wouldn't have added the screen unless it was important, but he can't pay attention to it.

"I'm sorry for bringing everyone into this," he subvocalizes over the line.

"So typical," Gemini grunts, his face still against the ground. "An Anand making this all about himself."

"I'm with you, Teophilus," Phoenix says. "Today and always."

"You're mine, Teophilus Anand," Corvus says slowly, as if he's savoring each word.

Teo speaks aloud now. "Like hell I am."

• • • • •

It was easy enough to pull schematics for the deepfake skinsuit from the blueprints they got from Yeonghui, even if Cass found Corvus's notes meandering and abstruse. Scrawling. She wouldn't have guessed that from what she's seen of the guy, who looks like the embodiment of champagne. Insubstantial froth that goes with caviar.

But she'd stayed up all night to rig up a projection of the shielded suit for their team meeting (and geez, yes, Phoenix, she finally admitted it was a *team* meeting). Alessa and Emory both seemed to have some version of this armor. There weren't any apparent vulnerabilities, though that probably went without saying.

But Teo had tilted his head as he studied the rotating 3D hologram. "Every suit has a seam."

Cass pointed out, exasperatedly, "Their shields must have an anchor point, but it could be anywhere. It might not be the same for the two of them either."

"It's not made of mithril," Phoenix said. Cass usually hated whenever he made some sort of hoity-toity reference as if he hadn't grown up rolling around in the same Mercurian dirt she did, but he continued, "Hit any shield in the same exact spot over and over and it's bound to crack." He measured up Cass and Ocean. "And I can't think of any two people who are better matched to do that."

And now, in the midst of battle with Alessa, Cass thinks that Ocean might actually be her favorite person.

Alessa's suit lights up blue as Ocean's bullet hits it, illuminating a target over Alessa's heart for Cass.

"Your move," Ocean shouts from her position on the upper level of the scaffold.

Her challenge has a laugh in it, and Cass growls in response, the excitement sparking in her chest. She's not going to let Ocean down. Before the suit's light fades, Cass is in front of Alessa. Her lit-up glove is a blur of green light as it repeatedly slams into that spot.

As Cass puts her shoulder into her next punch, she feels her left foot connect with the ground, drawing up strength through the solid plant. At this point it's all muscle memory, so she flourishes it with a spin.

"Aw, poor little armadillo," Cass taunts as her feet weave. "Can't do anything even with your shell?"

Alessa raises her gun, but Ocean shoots at her wrist. Alessa's shield may be impervious to bullets, but Ocean can throw Alessa off-balance by pinpointing shots against the wrist, the hand, the knee. A snake of appreciation threads through Cass. It intertwines with her buzzing adrenaline. Alessa yells in frustration as her next attempt goes wide, the bullets hole-punching an arc into the plastic tarp next to her. Cass uppercuts into Alessa's chin, knocking her back a few steps. The moment she lets up, Ocean hits Alessa in the original spot. Double whammy. Precise, beautiful shots. Damn, she's good.

"Why are you even here?" Alessa yells as she swings at Cass, who dodges her easily. "Teophilus getting other people to do his dirty work again?"

"Dirty work?" Ocean repeats as she shoots at Alessa's chest again, causing her to step backward. Cass dances into that opening with a roundhouse kick, sending Alessa flying through the air. "That's a harsh estimation of yourself."

Alessa barks out a laugh. "That pampered prince."

She's distracted, but Cass and Ocean aren't there just to run interference.

In her ear, Cass hears Ocean click into the main channel and follows suit. "Are you getting this?" Ocean subvocalizes.

"Loud and clear," Lupus replies into their ears. "But Ocean, aim your camera at her. The audio's good, but we want an unobstructed view. You're competing with Kim Minwoo's screen right now."

"Oh, in that case, you might be doomed, Ocean," Aries says.

Alessa twists past Cass, and bullets drill through Ocean's floor. "Thanks for that vote of confidence," Ocean mutters. She says loudly, "Pampered prince? How is Corvus any better?" She drops down to the same level Cass and Alessa are on, so she can give Lupus that better viewpoint from the camera on her shoulder.

Alessa laughs exultantly and she slaps her hand down on her gun. The machinery on it rotates outward, transforming it from a pistol to a much more unwieldy weapon. "What we do for Corvus is saving the solar."

And then she aims the improved gun at Cass. Cass glimpses the Buddha statue next to them, its huge face staring out from behind a plastic sheet curtain. She dives away from it, to the side, and bullets pump out like a machine gun as Alessa sweeps her aim. Cass hears a thump from Ocean hitting the floor.

"Ocean!" Cass yells as she darts forward and pummels Alessa.

"Just clipped," Ocean says over the feed. "But my suit's torn. Teo's going to kill me." When Cass whips her head back, Ocean's out of sight.

"Try to stay alive long enough for him to do that, yeah?" Aries says.

That's up to Cass. Her fists fly into Alessa's face. She covers every angle; slaps Alessa when she tries to raise her gun again. Cass appreciates the clarity of a good fight. She just wants her fists to connect. She's not like Gemini, who loves getting into people's heads. She couldn't care less.

"You call murdering people saving the solar?" Ocean yells around the corner.

Alessa only grunts in answer, as her head snaps back from another blow from Cass. She can't deny how satisfying that is, the candy neon of her gloves sparkling in her retinas, but then she hears Ocean subvocalize: "Let up enough for her to answer, will you?"

"You're asking for a lot, Ocean," Cass replies over the channel. But she does what she's told.

When Ocean speaks aloud next, Cass registers it as coming from her other side. Ocean must have looped around the scaffolding. "Did you kill the Anands to save the solar?"

Cass drops her elbow into Alessa's back, but she makes the movement slow enough for Alessa to catch it. Alessa grabs Cass's glove and jerks Cass forward, into her knee. Cass has her stomach muscles braced for it, but she groans loudly and goes to the ground like a football player hoping for a penalty.

Above her, Alessa raises her gun at Ocean. "The Anands were killing the solar. You stupid, arrogant Korean. The Alliance and

Anand Tech. So self-important that you were blind to your imminent downfall." She sneers. "I enjoyed every moment of stabbing the Anands to death."

Cass hears Ocean over the channel again: "We got it."

Cass flips up onto her feet nimbly, but just as she's aiming a kick into Alessa, screaming takes over the main channel. It's Phoenix's voice.

"Sasani, I need you!"

Phoenix would never scream like that for himself. Cass glances over at Ocean, whose face has gone completely pale. But it's distracted them at this crucial moment and Alessa uncurls from the ground, raising her arm to aim the gun at Ocean. Cass rushes forward, but all Alessa has to do is squeeze the trigger.

Their world explodes in sound and light.

THIRTY-FOUR

TEO LUNGES FORWARD, distracting Corvus and Emory. Gemini uses the opening to slam his heels down on the ground and another wood knife pops out of his left shoe. He kicks back, his leg coming up to slice away at Emory's face. It skids across her in a streak of blue, not enough to penetrate the shield, but forceful enough to adjust her center of balance. Gemini thrusts his hips up from the ground in a push-up. She tumbles from him. He's up and leaping on overturned chairs, flying through the air at her. Emory claps her hands together around his kick, clamping on to hurl him through the air again.

Suddenly, a red flash arcs down and hacks at her mechanized arm. The screech of metal against metal squeals through the air and Emory falls backward. The red sword is wrenched upward to reveal Dae.

"Sorry I'm late," she says. "I was attending an algae presentation nearby." She brandishes her bonguk geom. The red light flares in the air, reflecting off her face.

"A *sword*?" Emory snarls.

"Daebak," Teo says.

Dae grins in acknowledgment of the word before she swivels the sword around. "Didn't you hear?" she asks Emory. "The Alliance says I'm a national hero now."

A knife slices through the air right in front of Teo. "You should be paying attention to yourself, don't you think?" Corvus asks.

Teo stumbles back, right into a row of chairs and he goes down in a tangle of limbs and chair legs. Corvus stalks forward, while behind him, Dae presses Emory, the air a crackle of energy and sizzle of ozone. Gemini rolls to his feet, now pulling out the knife from his heel. As he winds back to throw, the sensor goes off again.

Corvus freezes in place. He had to be expecting this, but shock ripples through the other man's form. It's Phoenix, striding forward.

"Hi, Corvus," he says pleasantly. "I think there might be a dispute about who belongs to whom."

Corvus's eyes narrow. Phoenix shrugs off his jacket and spreads his arms, showing off his flamboyant ensemble. The shimmery red, orange, and yellow feathers flutter with the motion. Phoenix pulls out a gun from his coat.

"You wore it," Teo says from the ground. He thinks his heart might burst. It's better than he could have possibly imagined.

"Garrett?" Corvus's voice is confused.

As Teo pushes himself off the collapsed chairs, he sees Phoenix's eyes snap to him in surprise. Teo drops on reflex and a fist arcs in the space where he just was, moving so quickly the air whistles. He rolls to his back, and Hadrian stands above him.

"No hello for me, Garrett?" Hadrian growls.

"Don't kill him, Hadrian," Corvus says. "I want to take him alive."

"Yes, Hadrian," Teo says from the ground. "By all means, you should leave me unsullied for your master."

Now that Hadrian is sensible again, now that he's himself and not clothed as Declan, he takes stock of Teo without a hint of amusement. He's wearing some spandex or latex material, likely to fit into the deepfake skinsuit, and the material stretches over his form, showing he doesn't have a gram of fat.

"Oh, don't worry," he says. His voice still sounds like Declan's, has the same timbre, but he speaks with a completely different accent. "I can do plenty while keeping you in good condition for Corvus."

Hadrian at least doesn't have a weapon. Teo can work with that, or he thinks he can, until Hadrian's fists come down. Hadrian's hands are on Teo and he lifts him as if he's nothing, as if he's a toy poodle.

"Aries!" Phoenix bellows.

Teo's senses are heightened now as he waits for Hadrian to destroy him, and so he hears the click before the chairs behind Hadrian explode. Hadrian roars and drops Teo. Teo hits another chair on the way down, but as he falls, he sees Aries from across the room, his hand up, a detonator in hand. It's a trigger for one of the many traps he laid around Starfield earlier, in case. Now that the civilians have dispersed, it's their turf. Hadrian's arms drip blood and his eyes are murderous now.

"Teo!" Phoenix is yelling for him this time.

Something hits Teo's foot. A gun spins on the ground next to him. Teo snatches it up. Hadrian charges forward and Teo squeezes the trigger. Hadrian cries out as he's hit in the shoulder. Someone else screams and Teo whips his head toward the sound. Across the room, Dae's hit the floor, sword clattering from her hand. Hadrian collides into Teo at the same moment. Teo grips his gun as they go down, but Hadrian isn't even trying for it. He punches Teo in the face. He rains down blows like a fighter whaling away.

Teo wishes the shock would settle in. He wishes he could black out. But each smack is a starburst of anguish, waking Teo up again and again. It's his whole existence. Hadrian grunts and heaves for air. He sounds like Declan. Like when Teo would go running or lifting weights with him. It's bizarre to recognize someone's grunts.

Declan is dead though. Declan is dead and his parents are dead. Teo's going to join them soon. He's been struggling, trying to keep up, trying to figure out what to do, how to avenge them, how to *be*. And now, he doesn't have to worry about anything anymore.

"*You said you wanted to take responsibility.*"

Phoenix's voice pierces through the blackness. Teo chokes in a coppery breath. Fluid gurgles in his mouth like some hellish mouthwash.

Hadrian's fist smashes into his face. His head slams back against the floor. The gun's on the ground next to his hand. He clutches it as Hadrian hits him again. He hears a bone crack, probably his rib? He's learned what C7 means, *Thanks, Haven*, but other than that, he doesn't know anything.

He can't die like this. He hasn't lived a life worth anything, that gave anything to his family. He can't die like this when he hasn't atoned for anything or anyone, least of all himself.

Hadrian's consumed, like a predator with the taste of blood. Maybe he doesn't intend to keep Teo alive at all, despite Corvus's order.

"You greedy bastard," Hadrian pants out, and maybe he's too used to playing Declan's part these past few weeks or maybe Teo's delirious, but it sounds like his brother is saying these words. "You selfish son of a bitch."

"I'm sorry," he gasps out.

That brings Hadrian to a stuttered stop before he brings his hands together in one fist and pounds down on Teo's chest. "You're sorry? You're sorry? What good will that do me?" He laughs riotously. "I'm going to kill you. I'm going to kill you and everyone you've ever loved."

Even as Teo thinks *You've already taken away everyone I loved*, he knows it's not true. He sees his hands seeking Ocean, he sees Phoenix kissing his palm.

As Hadrian cocks his fist back for another blow, Teo squeezes his gun's trigger.

Hadrian flinches as if he's been stung by a bee. Teo re-aims and pulls the trigger again. Hadrian's body convulses as if hit by a hammer. As Hadrian falls backward, Teo pushes off the floor with his left elbow.

Hadrian jitters on the floor. Teo struggles to sit up and lets the gun drop. He drags in breath after breath. Air whooshes in his ears. Sparklers of agony fizzle all over. He has to get up. He has to help.

But then blue light blazes before him and a claw clamps onto his head. It's like someone's ratcheted up a lever on all his agony. It's like metal screws twisting into his head. He screams as his hands come up. His fingers scrabble against a smooth surface. His nails rip.

"I'm going to enjoy this," Teo hears above him.

He's completely overcome.

"Shhh, stay here."

The urgent whisper, the fleeting ripple of someone's coat and the harsh dry taste in his mouth before he's shoved underneath a desk, his shoulder digging against the hard edge of its inside corner. His knees scratch the rough rug.

"What are you doing?" A woman's voice, a voice he knows so well, a voice that sang Il y a longtemps que je t'aime. *"Stop!"*

Screaming before the sickening sound of a voice halted in life, the slop of fluid and something else . . . something more solid . . . hitting the ground.

Teo shudders before he's slammed by another sensation. The memories flick by faster, some familiar, and others alien. *The dust coating his tongue as he surveys a sky encased in a glass bubble and distaste chokes him like bile*

before he

holds out his fist and Ocean bumps it, her eyes on him and the quick, immediate response of his body to that, the warmth enveloping him

like

the clammy smooth underside of his bare foot brushing the supple skin of another. He follows the line of that foot, that long leg, up to a man lying in bed, his hair shorn short but . . .

But Teo knows if the man opened his eyes, they'd be a vibrant blue and it's not his memory, it's not, but he sees *a pale hand traces Garrett's shoulder. Garrett murmurs, his arm coming up over his head as he rolls over to sleep on his stomach again. He can taste that skin, the comfortable warmth of him and*

as if that opens Teo up, now he sees

Phoenix in the dark, underneath him, opening up, his mouth in a gasp and Teo's hands exploring. Phoenix's fingers in his mouth. "Please," he begs. And out of Phoenix's own mouth is a moan: "Teophilus."

No, no, no. This is Teo's memory. So much of his life hasn't been his, but this—he doesn't want to share it. No, *no, no*. His hands come up to the gloved arm stuck to his head again as he sobs. But he's not the only one to balk this time.

"What is this?" Corvus's eyes snap open, his face contorting. "Why is he in your head? Why is he in *your* head?"

Teo only wrenches at Corvus's gloved hand. His head is coming apart as if he's pulling himself out, as if he's ripping out his own veins. He wants Corvus away, he needs him gone, he needs to keep that for himself.

"He's *mine. Not yours*," Corvus howls.

But his cry is answered by another devastating one. A burst of red light stuns Teo. Screaming comes from all around him. He nearly sees that screaming, in smears of red and blue light, in white even, as he falls back.

"Sasani!" Phoenix's voice is frantic, wild. "*Sasani, I need you!*"

His fall backward stretches into an eternity. Time is a funny thing, and now it slows. His whole life stretches out before him as he waits for his body to connect with the floor.

THIRTY-FIVE

HAVEN NOW HAS more than a screen full of vitals to pay attention to. There's a live stream of the interview between Kim Minwoo and Thierry, a stream from Ocean's camera at Bongeunsa, and one of various camera angles at Starfield Library controlled and maneuvered by Lupus.

On-screen, Captain Song handles her Alliance-grade sword with finesse, the blade a ray of red light and metal as she stabs and parries Emory. Gemini's everywhere Captain Song isn't, sliding up, slicing in with his knife, shooting at Emory at every opportunity. While Captain Song moves with precision and clean lines, Gemini uses the landscape, leaping over chairs, kicking them so they go charging against Emory while he uses them as screens.

"Her mechanics!" Gemini shouts as he bombards her legs.

Her legs don't give off blue sparks like the rest of her body, which is covered in a shield. Gemini runs forward and then slides on his knees. As he skates forward, he hunches his body down to a protective huddle before he hurtles into her legs.

But Emory keeps her legs firmly planted, rock steady. She brings her gun down before Gemini, agile as always, grabs her wrist and yanks it downward, holding her body taut. It leaves her left leg in a straight line, completely exposed and Captain Song leaps in, sweeping her sword down at the juncture where Emory's mechanical leg meets the rest of the body.

Red and blue lights glimmer as Captain Song's sword shimmies in. She shouts in triumph, but then she grunts when she tries to yank her sword back. Emory closes her hand around Captain Song's hand on the blade, so she can't escape. While Captain Song fights to free herself, Emory violently wrests her gun from Gemini's grip and then shoots once, twice, into Captain Song's body.

Haven's already moving. He jumps out of the van and says into his comm, "Aries?"

"I'll meet you there."

He doesn't wait for what else Aries might say before his shoes are slapping the pavement, running straight for the doors of the Starfield Library. People are streaming out, terrified faces calling for help left and right. Haven pushes past them, going the opposite way. As he does, he hears shrieks and gunshots. People hit the pavement to protect themselves. The gunshots are unbelievably loud—he can't even tell if it's next to him or if the bullets are being aimed at him. Haven's knees buckle before he forces himself forward, gritting his teeth.

At the door, he's carried back several steps by the onslaught of people escaping, and he has to shove his way through to emerge inside the library. The sounds from the video are this much closer, and his mouth is dry, his legs shaking even as he orders them to sprint forward.

Captain Song's collapsed on the ground while Gemini and Phoenix are fighting Emory now. Aries is already there, gun out as he hovers. Haven runs toward them. He drops next to Captain Song, who's in a puddle of blood.

"Captain Song."

"Always so respectful," she says from the ground. "I'd salute you, but... well..."

Her clothes are sopping red already, and in person, it's worse than he thought. Haven has his side bag open. The gauze there mocks him. Pressure. He has to apply pressure to it. The thought calms him. These seconds are crucial, and he needs to do everything he can to stretch her time out.

"She's losing a lot of blood," Haven says as he works swiftly. "We need to get her to a hospital now."

"I hailed an ambulance," Aries says. "But..."

"It'll be too late."

"I'll take her." Aries lifts her and he's already off.

Haven wants to supervise how she's being carried, but his attention's suddenly drawn to the other side of the room where Corvus stands. Corvus brings his right hand up and its blue glow casts lines on his face. Teo is a blood-streaked and pulverized crumple at Corvus's feet. Teo struggles on the ground. Corvus moves to meet him.

"No!" Haven yells.

Corvus smacks his palm against Teo's forehead and those blue lines light up, sinking into Teo, and they both convulse.

"No!"

The raw scream comes from Haven's side. Phoenix scoops up something from the ground and sprints past Haven, his movements a blur.

"What is this?" Corvus snarls at a helpless Teo, stuck to him. "Why is he in your head? Why is he in *your* head?"

Teo only responds by grasping wildly at Corvus's arm, struggling to pull him away and Haven's frozen at this echo before him of every other victim Corvus has attached to, sucking them dry.

"He's *mine. Not yours.*"

Phoenix leaps from a chair at them, screaming, the muscles in his neck and arms tense and bulging. He has Captain Song's bonguk geom, her glowing red sword, in his hand, and he slashes down in a blistering arc.

The sword goes straight through Corvus's right arm, the one with the glove holding onto Teo, who has been trying desperately to wrench free.

Teo falls back to the ground and Phoenix yells as he dives for him, oblivious to all else. Corvus shrieks in agony as blood gushes from his arm.

"Sasani!" Phoenix cries out, so heedless he hasn't even realized Haven's already in the same room. "*Sasani, I need you!*"

As Haven runs forward, Emory throws Gemini from her with a cry. She bolts to Corvus. Phoenix grabs on to the remains of Corvus's gloved arm and rips it from Teo's head. The detached arm spins in the air, throwing an arc of blood. Emory's hand snatches out to grab it in mid-flight. She gathers Corvus up in her arms and then sprints away, moving impossibly fast.

"She took the fucking glove," Gemini snipes. "I'm going after them. Lupus, keep a camera on them, will you?"

Gemini takes off, hurtling out of the building. Aries is already gone with Captain Song, and Haven can't do anything else for them. He runs over to where Phoenix is cradling Teo to his chest. Not too far from them, an older woman lies on the ground, her eyes open but unseeing. Hadrian's lying in yet another dense pool of red. Phoenix's head snaps up at Haven's approach. His hair is disheveled. His coat's feathers hang limply, drenched in blood. He wipes an arm across his face, for sweat or for tears, and red blurs over his forehead. The vibrant color is stark against his gray skin.

"Please," Phoenix begs Haven. "He's still alive. He's still breathing."

Haven's saved from a response when Teo coughs in his arms. Phoenix freezes. Teo's eyes flutter. Several holes in his forehead are pulsing blood. But unlike the woman on the ground, when his eyes open, they focus on Haven. One of his pupils is blown out, the other one shrunken to a tiny point. A concussion then, at the very least.

"Anand?" Haven ventures. "How are you feeling?"

"My head . . . hurts . . ." His hand twitches at his side as if he wants to lift it.

"Can you tell me who you are?" Haven has his med kit out again. Teo's head wounds aren't a full-on gush, but he should still stanch them. If it's anything like the other medical reports he saw, the wounds shouldn't be too deep.

Teo struggles. "I wish . . . I wish you would."

Phoenix's hands hold Teo's head to his chest, but they're not sure whether they want to clutch at him more tightly or to lessen their pressure. His eyes dart back and forth from Haven to Teo. "Is he going to be all right?"

"You don't know your name?" Haven asks calmly. He holds Teo's arm out as he assesses the rest of Teo's wounds, which are substantial.

"Do you?" Although the words are faint, Haven hears the acidity in them. "I thought you were calling me Teo now."

Phoenix's laugh, weak, spills out of him. He buries his head in Teo's hair.

"Ow," Teo says.

• • • • •

No hesitation.

Garrett's movements had held no hesitation. One moment, exquisite misery had racked Corvus as Teophilus tried to wrench his hand from his forehead and then the next, he had heard familiar screaming.

A flash of light cut through his peripheral vision before slicing cleanly through his arm. Garrett, hacking off his arm with a sword, his eyes wild. Not even bothering with Corvus as he fell forward to cradle Teophilus Anand. Then Corvus's world had imploded.

Corvus's vision keeps cutting to black. He can't even tell what's up or down anymore, but he's grasping consciousness. All he gets for his efforts is the image of Garrett's face as he cut into him. In Teophilus's memory, Garrett's moan was desperate and Garrett's eyes were soft in a way Corvus never knew in all their years together.

Corvus weeps at the emptiness yawning wide in his body, threatening to eat him alive. The loneliness tears its teeth into his soul and the wail building in his chest could be because of the agony from his arm, or the complete lack of Garrett's regard.

"Corvus, I can't—" He barely hears Emory through his despair. "There's so much blood, I can't—What do I do?"

"He chopped my arm off," Corvus says hazily. The words release like a balloon into the air.

He should examine the damage. He tries to wiggle the fingers of his right hand to no avail. His right arm now ends in a stump at the elbow. Emory blocks his view.

"Don't look. Don't look at it."

"I'm dying, aren't I?"

"No," she says fiercely. "If we get you to a hospital, we can cauterize it."

Corvus laughs, but the sound is so empty he practically hears it echo in his own mouth.

"You can't die," Emory says. "You can't. We have to change the world, the solar, Corvus. You promised. You said we could do anything."

"I have nothing." Corvus closes his eyes.

As he does, the voices clamor in his mind. The constant barrage of memories that aren't his. His face twists from the strain. So many, and yet he's left so barren. Each forehead, each rush of emotion into him had been such a thrilling jolt in his otherwise empty life. He had been so sure Garrett would come back to him.

That softness in his eyes, the complete abandon.

But that wasn't his memory. It was Teophilus Anand's. If he was being honest, the only times Garrett had gotten that close with him, the most vulnerable he had gotten, it hadn't been with that kind of tenderness. It had been wrapped more in a fear.

"He took him from me." Corvus weeps now. "He's taken everything from me."

He's so weak that the memories assail him. Teophilus's are the most potent since they're the most recent. Teophilus with his parents, with his older brother, all alive, all showing their love to him in infinite small ways. Teophilus, who has been blessed from the beginning.

"*So you're the one they call Headshot?*"

The stiffening of the shoulders even as the girl lifts an eyebrow at him. His facial muscles freeze, and he only then realizes how silly the smile feels on his face.

"*You're the one they call the useless son?*"

A pang stabs him in the gut, even as an unfamiliar emotion rushes into his limbs. Relief. Yeah, that is what they must say about him when he's not around.

"*Is that what they call me? The useless Anand?*"

"*No.*" *The girl shakes her head.* "*But it's what you call yourself, isn't it?*"

"He doesn't have everything," Emory insists. "You have me, Corvus. You'll always have me."

That's what they always say before they abandon you. Emory's desperate face is so hopeful though. She believes her own words so much that he wants to believe in them equally.

"He doesn't have everything, does he?"

"Hold on, Corvus. We can make it through."

"I'm going to bleed out, Emory."

Emory's face tightens. "I'm not going to let you."

"You foolish girl."

Emory deposits him onto the ground. She's probably being as gentle as she can, but there's no being gentle when your arm is a gushing stump. He can't tell where they are or how far she's run. They're inside somewhere now, and he's leaking, literally pouring his life's blood, out on a wood-paneled floor. Next to him, Emory puts down a glowing red sword, the sword that did this to him. And next to that, like some grotesque trophy, is his arm, still encased in the glove.

He hears a grunt. Emory wraps her left hand around her right mechanized bicep. One of the augmented parts he designed for her. She puts her fingers in the grooves under the armpit and it beeps and clicks as she enters the pressurized code.

Her face goes white as her arm juncture releases and she wrenches it free.

"Take my arm." She strains out her words. "If we line it up correctly, we can cauterize your wound. It's not the right size for you so it won't be a perfect match, but it'll close up your wound at least."

Emory, since he found her, trained her, has been groomed to be his right hand. Now literally. Corvus could laugh, but his mouth is full of blood and tears.

"Emory," he says. "Your arm attaches at the armpit. My arm is cut at the elbow."

She doesn't answer right away, but she looks over where his discarded arm is. When he follows the line of her gaze, though, he finds he's actually mistaken: she's not looking at his glove. She's looking at the cursed Alliance captain's sword. Oh.

"Do it."

She picks up the sword with her left hand and holds it over his arm, right at the shoulder. Despite his command, despite the fact she's the one who brought the sword so she must have known this might happen, she quavers.

"Emory," he says and catches her eye. "I don't consider it a loss. You've shown me I can be stronger without it."

A tear slips down her face. "You can hold on to me if you want," she says. "I'm sorry, Corvus."

She pushes the sword down into his arm before he can respond and his mind erupts in agony. He's howling and screeching. His free arm goes to clench Emory, and then senselessly beats at her. *Stop. Stop it.* But she's straddled him and the work of going through his arm probably takes merely seconds since it's such a sharp sword, but it's like the suffering stretches for years, his mind going to pieces, blistering and fracturing.

He barely has time to suck in a breath as Emory throws aside the sword. She jams her metal arm into his stump and the waves of pain assault him again as the arm whirs and sinks into his nerve endings. As he shrieks up to the ceiling, he smells burning flesh. Over it, he hears Emory repeating *I'm sorry, I'm sorry* and she cries as if that's supposed to console him. He briefly, overwhelmingly hates her, hates her as the one torturing him.

Only for a fleeting moment, though, and he instead latches on to who's at fault: Teophilus Anand. Anand Tech took away his parents, shackled Mercury from its infancy, killed the one who took him in after his parents died, and now Teophilus Anand is responsible for this, for taking Garrett, for taking his arm. How could he have done it? That asinine, completely empty man sitting at the bar, licking his lips at Corvus without a thought in the world?

But even as Corvus thinks that, other memories push against his brain, ones of bending his head down into hands, of doubting his own worth, of horror at hearing what his father has wrought, of desires to do better—

"How do I change what my father did, Phoenix? I don't know how to make it better."

No, it's not true. Corvus wrenches away. *That's not him, that's not what he was thinking, what he was going to do. People lie to themselves all the time! People—*

The metal arm connects, and Emory punches another panel in it frantically. Cool, blessed comfort seeps in from it. A silvery cold painkiller numbs him and it's like slipping into calm waters again.

When Corvus comes back, his throat is scraped from screaming and he's drenched in sweat and blood. He blinks up at the ceiling, the sound of his panting filling his ears. He tastes blood in his mouth. His fingers spasm, clammy with fluid. His left hand's fingers.

He experiments then and tries to move his right hand. The mechanical fingers twitch. He moves to roll over, but the arm at his side is like a bag of ore and it barely shifts.

"Careful, Corvus," Emory says. "It's going to be a lot heavier than you're used to." Her smile is wretched. "You're going to walk tilting to the right for a while now."

"You know," a voice drawls from behind them before Corvus can answer. "I was worried when Lupus's camera lost you. It couldn't keep up with your legs."

Corvus can't even lift his head, but Emory spins on her feet, crouching into a ready position to face the doorway, where a man leans against it. He pulls back his hood, revealing dark, wavy hair and a lazy grin.

"But you made it easy to find you when you screamed loud enough to wake the dead."

"You," Emory growls.

"Me," he agrees. "And now that we've got the reintroductions out of the way . . ."

His next movement is fluid, quicksilver, not that it matters. Corvus simply doesn't have the strength to dodge the knife thrown his way.

· · · · ·

When Gemini throws the knife at Corvus, Emory leaps to intercept it, but he expected that. He jumps forward to slash at her head. His knives ricochet back from a shield. Gemini bolts backward to avoid Emory's sweeping kick, her leg so heavy it *whumphs* in the air. One blow to the head and he's a goner. But she's missing her arm now; he can see it's been attached to Corvus's body and there's enough blood in the room for the packing floor of a slaughterhouse. The monks are going to love mopping this up.

"Corvus, get out of here!" Emory shouts.

Corvus has sat up, and Gemini can't even believe he has the strength to do that, although he's listing to the side from the weight of his new arm. He's pale to the point that Gemini half expects him to go translucent. Emory is up on her feet. She fires at Gemini. He tumbles for the door. Emory's bullets peck the screen full of holes.

"I'm sorry you have to put up with me," he calls through the opening.

Gemini had been severely limited back at Starfield Library since he had to contend with the sensors and wasn't able to bring in his arsenal. But while running from Coex, he made a quick detour to their van. When he flung open the door, Lupus already had his holster held out. It made sense that Emory would make her way here to rendezvous with Alessa, but they hadn't made it far enough into the Bongeunsa grounds. Gemini had followed the screams to a temple off the side path.

Gemini picks out his next item from the holster and pulls out the pin with his teeth.

"But Phoenix was preoccupied taking care of Teophilus," he says and throws the smoke grenade through the paper screen door.

It explodes with a puff and a flare of light and Gemini uses that as cover to bust down the screen. He pulls out his gun and shoots through the haze. When the bullets hit Emory's shield, she lights up blue. He runs toward that and leaps through the smoke. He tackles her to the ground. Her left hand comes up to cover her right shoulder and he adjusts, flipping around until he's straddling her head with his thighs. He grabs another knife and then jams it into the juncture where her mechanical leg meets the shield, where Dae already got a good hack at it. He stabs it ferociously three times before her other leg comes up to knee him in the head. It's not a great angle, but it jostles him, knobbing him in the cheek. He has to roll off to avoid it.

"Corvus! Go!"

But Corvus only leans against the wall. He's up, but he hasn't moved otherwise. His attention is on Gemini and his face is contorted in hatred. Got him.

"Poor Corvus," Gemini says. "Gained the whole solar, but lost the only one who matters?"

Corvus's face snarls, like he's a wild animal stuck in a trap. Emory's elbow cracks down onto Gemini's back, and against his will, it arches sharply. He hacks out a gob of spit. He spins to his feet as he crouches back, his elbows up in a ready position, one hand with a knife and the other with a gun.

"Alessa," Emory says. "I need you. Where are you?"

Gemini can't hear the answer over their comm, but he assumes Corvus is on the same line, because his face smooths out, completely changes, as he listens.

Gemini doesn't like that at all, but he has no time to decipher it because Emory is blasting at him. He fires back as he dashes around the room. The bullets dissipate the smoke. They embed themselves in the wood pillars, the ornate chairs, and lacquered furniture. He'd be regretful, but if he has to choose between himself and a Joseon-era seat, it's not a hard call.

All through it, he hears Emory begging, "Corvus, please go. If you die, this is all for nothing."

"What *is* all this for?" Gemini shouts from behind the stand.

No one ever does everything for a grand cause, for the *solar*. Anyone who ever claims that is lying to themselves. It's always for one person. If you're lucky enough, or unlucky enough, that person is someone else.

"Don't you dare talk to him," Emory snaps, "as if you *know* him."

"Do you?" Gemini asks. She's too emotional.

"Shut up!"

She punctuates her words with a barrage of bullets. It's sloppy work. As the bullets go wide, Gemini takes in a deep breath. Holds it. Whirls and throws one knife. He hears a grunt as it hits.

"Corvus!"

Corvus ponders the knife sticking out from his shoulder. He wrenches it out and studies it bemusedly. It could be that the arm is pumping him full of a painkiller. Gemini sidles back as he raises his gun. His ear picks up the whir and his body reacts before his mind does. The kick that was meant to crush his outstretched arm only hits his hand, knocking his gun to the ground. He's spinning away again, pulling a knife and throwing it.

Emory stands in front of Corvus to guard him, aiming her gun at Gemini with her left arm.

"You're right, Emory," Corvus says, although Gemini can't see him. "He doesn't have everything. I won't let him."

When Emory shoots, Gemini catches how her eyes flinch. Everyone's eyes flinch when they're shooting, and it doesn't matter that Emory's behind a shield or that she may have fired a gun a thousand times before. The only person he's seen who doesn't flinch is Ocean.

His body reacts to that minute movement. The bullet still grazes his right arm as he sprints forward.

Clipped by a bullet. He can't act superior over Ocean anymore. He skids over the ground, aiming for between Emory's legs. Through them, he has a clear view of Corvus limping, running away.

"Alessa, hold her there."

Gemini falters. Emory slams her legs together and the air explodes out of Gemini's body. He scrabbles against her mechanized legs with his knife, sparks flying as he chips away, but she points her gun down and blitzes him left and right as he flops around, trying to avoid the bullets even as she's pinned his body.

Gemini lunges upward and grabs her wrist, twisting it up violently. The break is crisp, like an egg cracked over the pan. As she screams, her clamp around his middle loosens. He keeps his ironclad hold on her wrist, wresting her forward to propel himself off the ground. She squeals again. He swivels around as she finally, *finally* exposes her weak spot.

He spins out his knife and drives it deep into her armpit. The blood spurts and she screams. So he was right; the shield had covered her body up until the mechanized arm, but after the arm was removed, it left a gap for him. He relentlessly stabs into the opening, his only recourse since the rest of her is shielded. Emory's other arm comes to batter him in the head and then she knees him in the rib, the leg heavy enough that he hears the bones break at once.

If he was being smart, he'd play this safe. He'd back off and wait for another opportunity to get at her. Gemini has always been smart. But Corvus is on his way, and he told Alessa to *"hold her there."* So, Gemini clings desperately to Emory as he keeps stabbing her, the blood spraying out onto his face. Emory drops to the ground and he goes with her, the two of them locked as she kicks and knees at him. Every time her leg connects, his mind disconnects with his body, narrowing down to a sickening crunch or a flicker of lights.

"Gemini? Gemini!" he hears through the line. "Where are you?"

"Sasani," he manages through gritted teeth. "I'm a little busy."

Emory's body jerks and her legs collapse. Gemini has his knife hand up, poised, but she doesn't move to stop him. He holds for another minute, his body shaking, before he crumples on top of her.

"This . . . this is good," she whispers.

"What about this is good?" Gemini asks wearily.

"I stopped you," she says. He's horrified at her joyful, beatific countenance. "I bought him time to get away."

"You think he's running away?" Gemini scoffs.

The room fills with the rasping of her breath as she processes that. "What do you mean?"

"He said *I won't let him have everything.*" It hurts to breathe. "What do you think I mean?"

"Gemini, can you tell me how to find you?" Sasani says through his ear again.

"I'm on the temple grounds." Gemini spits up blood. "Corvus got away."

He blinks away the dots spiraling in front of his vision and focuses instead on a misshapen object on the porch, next to the battered screen doors. It could be mistaken for some weird pale fish, but Gemini knows what it is.

"Do you really think he made that glove so he could understand other people?"

Emory doesn't answer, but when he lifts his head, silvery tears are tracking down her face.

"I'm coming to you," Sasani says. "We'll let the authorities handle Corvus. Alliance members are arriving on the scene."

"He's going after her, Sasani," Gemini says. "Don't bother with me."

Dizziness comes over him in a wave. *Inhale. Exhale.* He hadn't realized he was this close to passing out. He needs to hold on. *Inhale. Exhale.* He pounds a fist on the ground and tries to drag forward off Emory, but the slightest movement jars every one of his jagged, broken bones and he groans.

"What are you saying?"

The object on the ground is Corvus's discarded arm. Pale because the glove has been forced off it. It's a right-hand glove, but if Corvus took it, he has use for it. Gemini puts his hand up to his ear. Which channel is she on? He hasn't heard her in a while, but he has to warn her.

"Ocean, he's coming for you."

THIRTY-SIX

CASS IS CLOSE enough to whiff a kick at Alessa. It only grazes her, but it's enough to save Ocean from a full-on shot. Ocean twists away, but the bullets rake her side. As her arm ricochets back, the hand on her earpiece snags and her comm goes sailing through the air. Alessa whirls around to blast Cass, whose flying kick left her exposed. Those bullets hit too, and the scaffolding vibrates as Cass falls.

Phoenix's cry can only have been about Teo, but Ocean's been cut loose from the comm so she has no idea what's going on. Ocean crouches on one leg. She wipes everything out, lets it all go into a void as she aims, shoots, aims, shoots, the bullets a dull thud in her consciousness as she hits the bull's-eye each time.

This is the quickest way out of here, the fastest way she can get back to Teo. At this point, they have everything they need from Alessa. Now they need to get out of this alive.

Alessa doesn't have an opportunity to raise her gun against Ocean, pushed back by the onslaught of bullets. Her back slams against the scaffolding.

"This again?" she asks through her teeth.

But as she says it, it happens. When Ocean's next bullet strikes Alessa, it pings differently and the smallest fracture cracks on the shield. Alessa's eyes gape and her hand darts to the fissure, testing it. She grips the metal piping behind her and then hops up onto it. Ocean keeps up her relentless attack, but Alessa presses her hand over the shield where the fracture is to block it. She clambers up to the next level of the scaffolding. Ocean runs forward to Cass, who's grimacing as she grips her leg.

"How bad is it?" Ocean asks.

"It'd be a lot better if you let me get a hit in once in a while." Cass sits up with a glower. "What do you say? Should we go finish the job? Or should we head back?"

"What's going on on the main line?" Ocean asks. "Is everyone jake?"

As Cass touches her ear, a machine gun fires rapidly above them. They duck down, but the bullets aren't aimed at them but outwards. Alessa ululates.

"What the fuck," Cass says angrily. "She's firing at civs?"

Ocean peers upward, the staccato of bullets ramming her eardrums as they go off. "If we get up there while she's distracted, she won't be waiting for us to pop our heads up to shoot at us."

Cass grabs at Ocean's shoulder to pull herself up. "Help me up the stairs?"

"Maybe I'll leave you down here."

"We go up together or we don't go at all," Cass says. "We need each other."

Ocean slings Cass's arm over her shoulders. "Don't hold me back."

"Me? I should be the one saying that."

They hobble up the rickety steps to the next level, and then the one beyond that to the top of the scaffolding. Ocean and Cass exchange looks, a question and confirmation in one, before they poke their heads up together. Only to immediately duck down as a scatter of bullets smack the floor.

"So much for that," Cass says.

"What are you even fighting for?" Alessa yells at them.

Cass makes a face. "What does she even want us to say?"

"She wants us to ask her back. Typical bad conversationalist."

"I want the simple things in life," Cass says under her breath to Ocean.

"Simple things? Money? Love? Adoration?"

"Simple things, Ocean. I said, simple. Three meals a day, ice cold beer at night. I wouldn't mind a few Miles Davis records on vinyl."

"Miles Davis! *Kind of Blue*?" Ocean asks. "*Bitches Brew*?"

"See, I knew you were a quality person," Cass says. "Once this is done, we are having a listening party."

Ocean knocks her knuckles against the wooden scaffolding above them and Cass grins at her. She then punches one of her gloves over the other, opening a panel in her palm.

"Huh," Ocean says, impressed.

Cass says, "Everything I design has to have as much function as a utility belt. I made Gemini's shoes for him too."

"With the heels?"

"Those boots were made for more than walking." She pulls out a black block before she closes up the panel and asks, "Ready?"

"Whatever you got, wild child."

"Shield your eyes."

Cass tosses the item over and onto the floor above them, then she punches her gloves together again to make them light up green. Ocean has her head ducked and her eyes squeezed shut, but the world ignites white behind her eyelids.

"Cover me!" Cass yells as she stumbles up the steps, rushing forward before Ocean can even protest.

Alessa's kneeling on the ground, her hands scrunched over her eyes. But she must hear Cass rush forward, and her gun arm comes up, spitting bullets. Cass dodges to the left and Ocean shoots at Alessa's wrist from the inside, popping her arm to the right before she runs up on the scaffolding to join Cass.

Ocean aims at Alessa's fragile spot they had been taking apart, but Alessa's wise to that, hunching forward and guarding it even as she squints a scowl, letting loose with her gun to keep them from getting closer. Ocean has to hit the floor to dodge the bullets.

"I'm at the Buddha," Alessa pants out, the words incongruous until Ocean realizes she's not talking to them. "I'll be right there."

Cass is tall, her long limbs able to stretch farther than Alessa's, but she isn't being given a chance to use them. Ocean shoots at Alessa's shoulder. Alessa flinches, but keeps it rounded. Maybe they'll have to make a new target. Ocean aims at her left shoulder, firing three shots at the same spot, the impact blooming out each time.

Cass's quick on the uptake, and she moves in to punch at that spot, her jabs a blur before she has to weave to the side. Ocean uses the opportunity to pop Alessa in the knee, and the leg collapses. Cass sweeps Alessa's legs out from under her. Alessa falls backward, landing with a snap so hard her whole body shield sparks blue. Cass has Alessa's gun arm sandwiched between her legs. She pulls up. Ocean runs forward, launching slug after slug at Alessa's exposed chest.

The fissure cracks and splinters and then the shield's light splutters. With a roar, Alessa's leg comes up, folding her body to smack Cass. As Cass yelps, Alessa grabs Cass's right leg and then digs her fingers into her bullet holes. Cass screams and when Ocean raises her gun, Alessa yanks Cass around to cover her body.

"I got it," Alessa says. "I'll keep her."

Alessa's entwined around Cass as Cass flails, but Alessa's attention is on Ocean now. She smirks. Ocean raises her gun, her hand steady. Cass slams her fist down on the ground as if she's crying uncle. She and Alessa toss like a crocodile roiling in the water with their prey clamped in their jaws. Cass's gloves flash, lighting up every time she punches at Alessa, but they remain locked. Alessa's shield is holding, and the lights confuse Ocean as she tries to find an in.

"Ocean, do it!" Cass yells. "Just shoot!"

"Like hell." Even if she hits Alessa, her shield's in effect, and there's the chance she'll hit Cass, who isn't similarly protected.

Alessa laughs. She rolls with Cass away from Ocean, propelling toward the far edge. She's going to barrel off. When they hit the ground, more than twenty meters down, she'll be protected by her shield, but the impact will kill Cass. Ocean runs ahead of them, jamming her gun back into the jacket. She leaps forward and grips the metal piping, jumping out and swinging around. The old wound in her shoulder protests mightily as she strains it.

Sorry she thinks as she arcs around, using the force of the movement to crash a kick at Alessa and Cass's approaching tumble. She stops them short, but the collision knocks her backward again. Her legs flail in the open air, and her hands strain against the pinched death grip she has on the pipe.

As her legs kick in the air, though, Alessa throws Cass to the side. She fires at Ocean. The bullets zip past her. Ocean swings her legs back and then forward again, and lets go in time for her body to fly forward. While she's in flight, a sharp pain slices through her arm. Another sting blazes the side of her neck. She lands flat on her back, the air clapped out of her body.

She automatically goes for the gun in her jacket. But Alessa's leg eclipses her vision with a vicious kick. Ocean's hands, her fingers, so weak and nerveless from holding on to the scaffolding before, let loose the gun. It skitters on the ground.

When Ocean rises, a boot comes down onto her shoulder where her old wound is. She cries out as it grinds in. She squirms on the ground.

It's not Alessa's foot. A pale man with pale gray eyes looms over her. His right arm is mechanical and his body leans to that side. His left hand is encased in a glowing blue glove.

"Hi, Hummingbird."

She gapes up at him. "What did you call me?"

He ignores her to address to the side, "Thank you, Alessa."

Alessa sits on top of Cass, who's lying down, her face plastered with blood. Ocean's heart plummets until she hears Cass groan. Alessa has a gun to Cass's head as she lazes on top of her, like Cass is a human throne.

"My pleasure, Corvus."

Ocean struggles under Corvus. "Who said," she grunts, "you could call me that?"

Corvus digs his boot in harder and she can't bite back her gasp. "This is where you were shot, right? When you were defending him? Saving his life?"

Ocean's left hand goes to the boot, as if she could shove him off, but her movements are oddly sluggish. Her right hand won't even move. When Corvus shifts above her, he squelches . . . no, *she* squelches. The wetness at her neck can't be just sweat.

"Too bad your efforts came to nothing."

His words stop her. "What are you talking about?"

"He's a part of me now." Corvus raises his gloved hand. "That's what this does, you see. It joins me with people. They become a part of me, I become a part of them. And I used it on Teophilus Anand."

"What are you *talking about*," she snarls.

"Everything your friend was, your *best friend* was, is now in me. So I guess that makes me . . . your new best friend?"

"You're not making any sense," she spits, even as her mind goes back to Phoenix's frantic cry over the comm line.

"Don't listen to him, Ocean," Cass heaves out. "He—"

Alessa cuffs her with the butt of her gun. Cass's head drops, senseless.

"Hummingbird. Red. Finesure. Am I missing one?"

Ocean goes still.

"Oh, right. Headshot. That was the first one he came up with, wasn't it? *I* came up with. I felt bad about that one."

"You're *not him*," she hisses out even as lightning crackles hot through her limbs.

"Third floor of the Alliance gisuksa has a side hallway behind the private study rooms. You've never been there, right?"

TEO'S DURUMI 371

Corvus lets that sink in, lets Ocean think that over, lets her wrestle with how he pronounces *gisuksa* perfectly. Then, he says, "No, you haven't. Because if you had, you'd know that's where a certain vending machine is. One always stocked full of lychee sodas."

Even on a different face, that politician's smile is familiar to her. Her mouth snaps open to deny it again, but what comes out is some broken form of her voice she doesn't recognize. "What did you do to him?"

"What did I do to him?" Corvus asks. "Everything I have ever done to Teophilus is in me now, because I've subsumed him."

He flexes the fingers of his glove. As he does, the blue light in it flickers and he frowns at it until the glow steadies.

"Did you kill him?" Ocean wheezes for air, but none of it's going in. It chips away at her chest.

Corvus crouches down on top of her and he's heavy, so much heavier than he should be. He crosses her left arm on her chest before he arranges his mechanized arm on top of it. The gross weight immobilizes her.

"Do you want to hear what he thought of you?" Corvus scratches his temple and it's so like Teo, she wants to scream. It's not just the cadence of his words either, but the aching familiarity of his tone. "It's rotten, isn't it, Ocean? We're the disappointing second children. You bared yourself to me because you thought I was your friend, but I only bothered with you because you saved my life. But you knew that, didn't you? Deep down, I think you did."

Ocean closes her eyes, but his words are burrowing inside her. They're unearthing her own thoughts, her own insecurities, like he's scraping into her with a metal scoop.

"It's hard being so alone, isn't it, Ocean?" Corvus gives her that wry self-deprecating grin. He traces a finger on Ocean's cheek, wiping away her tears. Her hands twitch, but she has no will to resist. "Don't you want to be completely accepted as you are? You'll never be misunderstood again." Corvus holds up his gloved hand, and the blue light reflects on his face. He tilts his head. "It's such an effort to exist. What's even the point?"

Ocean wants to shut off everything. He's right; she's been tired for a while.

"I'll make it all worth it," he says soothingly. "It might hurt more than usual because I had to turn the glove inside out, but it should work. Don't worry, we'll endure it together."

His gloved palm opens wide, ready to engulf her.

Only to meet the palm of her hand.

With all her strength, she's brought her free hand up to her forehead. Their palms commune, as if in prayer.

"You don't get to take anything from me." Her throat gurgles as she forces the words out. She needs her words to be clear. She enunciates, "You're not him. I don't care what you've pulled from his head."

Corvus's eyebrows come down, color splotching his pale cheeks now. He laces his fingers through hers and crushes her hand. He squeezes tighter and tighter. She bites down on her tongue and if her mouth wasn't already so filled with blood, she'd taste it. But she can't be angry at him and she can't even pity him.

"You're the one," she winces out. "You're the one who molded yourself into other people, so you'd be accepted."

Corvus blanches. He narrows his glittering eyes into slits. "I was being merciful," he hisses. "But now I see that was wrong; I wouldn't want you contaminating me. The best way to get to him is to drag a knife through your belly and let you die slowly while he watches."

He clenches her fingers and she hears the bones break before he flings her hand to the side, out of the way. Corvus lifts his head and then laughs at a drone camera floating in the air before them. Belatedly, she remembers the camera on her right shoulder, that it may have been on this whole time.

"Are you watching this, Teophilus?" Corvus asks the camera in the air.

Ocean's gasp coughs into a wet hack. Teo? He's alive?

"I'm going to kill Ocean and I'm going to draw it out. You'll have the footage forever. And you'll know she's dead because of you."

Corvus flips up a knife, and dazedly, Ocean recognizes that blade. It's one of Hurakan's. Corvus rears his arm back.

A bullet whizzes by and hits the wood floor next to Ocean.

Haven stands at the scaffolding stairs, pointing Ocean's gun. "Get off her," he says.

Alessa stirs from next to them, but Corvus puts out a hand, halting her. He shoves off Ocean and stands with a grunt, bolstering his right arm with his left. Ocean gulps in air and rolls over to her side, but she can't get up. She touches her hand to her neck and it comes away red. She presses her hand to the wound, trying to stem the flow. The pulse throbs beneath her fingers.

"Sasani," Corvus says pleasantly. "You're not going to shoot me, are you? You have morals."

"Ocean, are you all right?" Haven asks, but Ocean can only cough in response.

"Ah," Corvus says. "For her, you might, though? Is that so?"

He faces Haven squarely and throws open his left arm. "Go ahead. Take your shot, Sasani."

"Corvus," Alessa says sharply.

"Shoot me dead, Sasani," Corvus says. "If you don't, I'm going to kill her. And more besides. You know that, don't you? Will you do it to save her life?"

Haven looks to Ocean. He recenters her gun on Corvus. But he stops. He's probably never even held a gun before.

"Haven," Ocean chokes out. His focus darts to her again. "Please," she says, but fluid splutters her throat before she can speak, and the gun wavers in the air.

"That's right, *Haven*," Corvus mocks. "Please save her, save all of us." He pulls out a gun from his waistband. "I'll make the decision easier for you, shall I?"

When Corvus points his gun back at Ocean, Haven goes perfectly still. Even though it's impossible at this distance, Ocean swears she can see it with razor focus, his finger coming up to the trigger. His hand is shaking and the muscles all up his arm strain.

"Haven," Ocean tries again and Haven locks eyes with her. "Don't do it."

It's all she can manage and Haven's face crumples. "Ocean," he says and her name holds so much regret now.

Corvus laughs riotously, startling them. He tucks his gun back in his belt.

"I knew it," he says. "You can't do it. You're like *him*. Not willing to give up what it takes to save the solar. But that's not me. That's not me and it never will be."

"You're wrong," Haven says, and Corvus pauses. "I wasn't trying to decide whether or not to shoot you."

"Oh, you weren't?" Corvus asks, amused.

"I've been told any number of times you shouldn't just pay attention to where your opponent is looking," Haven says slowly. "You should have thought about what I was distracting you from."

Alessa screams then and Ocean jerks her head around. Cass is up, she's dug her fist into the fissure in Alessa's shield and she's wrenching it apart as she incessantly punches in. Corvus dives his hand back into his waistband, but Haven's sprinting forward. He tackles Corvus to the ground. Shots ring out. Haven's head jerks up, even while he's trying to keep Corvus down. Alessa's wildly waving her gun.

"Haven," Ocean calls out. She pushes herself up and holds out her hand.

Haven frees a hand to toss her her gun before planting a solid knee into Corvus's stomach. He launches over to Alessa and Cass. Ocean catches the gun and turns it around on Corvus, who's on the ground. Corvus sits up, his lips stretching into something that's supposed to be a grin.

"Stay down," she commands.

"Now you, Ocean," he says. "You have no compunctions against killing me, do you?"

He pushes himself upright and looms over her.

"Stay *down*," she says and shoots him in his left arm.

His arm ricochets back, and it slices a path of blood in the air. But Corvus only shrugs his shoulder, like a horse readjusting after flicking its tail.

"What's wrong?" He cracks his neck as he flexes it back and forth. "This close, there's no way you'd miss," he leers. "Here." He points to his heart. "Or here." He points to his forehead.

Blood's splattered all over his skin and his nails are ragged. But when his chest expands, it's as if they're inhaling together, as if the breath she hears scraping over the pulse in her ears is his. She traces the trigger against her finger. But instead of narrowing in on Corvus pointing out the perfect bull's-eye, her vision's funneled down to the tears streaming from his eyes.

"Do you think you deserve it?" she asks. "Do you want to die?"

His finger trembles while hers remains steady. He asks in a low voice, "Do you think you understand me?"

"Even if I did," Ocean says, "it wouldn't absolve you."

Corvus's mouth crumples and he lurches toward her. She scrabbles backward, trying to move out of the way, blasting now at his knees. He bulldozes forward, his body hitting hers full on as he shoves.

Her back hits metal and her body distorts as her leg gets kicked back. The sudden gaping absence is unmistakable; her leg is hanging over empty air. He's pushed them all the way to the edge.

She's too weak to do anything except put her arms around him.

"You think that will stop me, Ocean?" Corvus snarls. "That's what I *want*. You and me, Ocean. We'll go together."

When Ocean tries to tighten her fingers, they only twitch. She turns her head to speak into his ear.

"It won't absolve you," she says. "But I do understand you."

For a few moments, Corvus pants against her.

Then he pitches her forward with a scream. The barrier behind them breaks away. She falls backward in the air.

• • • • •

When Teo tossed his gun to Ocean on the *Ohneul*, Haven had marveled at it: how Teo threw it perfectly without a signal, how they moved so seamlessly together after. But now he gets it; Teo trusted Ocean, even or maybe especially without words. He had committed to whatever she decided to do with that gun.

Haven tosses her the gun, and it goes in an easy loping arc. He runs toward Cass and Alessa without even seeing if the gun will land. Ocean will make that connection. One of Lupus's drone cameras zooms in front of him and smashes into Alessa's gun hand, knocking it to the side. Cass rises from the ground, bleeding and beat up. She wipes her mouth with her glove and with the barest glance at Haven, her feet sketch out a pattern he's seen before. She moves in to carve an uppercut to Alessa's chin. Haven zags to the right. He aims and jabs at a point right beyond Alessa's ribs. Molten agony blooms in his bare knuckles.

Alessa's shield is no longer working and she caves from those two blows. But she keeps pumping out bullets from her gun as she goes down. Cass tries to dance out of the way, but her legs are already damaged and the bullets bury themselves in her hips. They blow away pieces of her clothes and flesh. Cass spins on the ground, her movements seemingly erratic, but her fall knocks her into Alessa. Her gloves whine while they power up one last time. She rams them into Alessa's gut. She lifts her right fist to punch savagely into Alessa's head. They collapse on the ground.

Before Haven can check on them, he hears a crash and a scream from behind him. He spins around. The platform is empty. The barrier around this level is destroyed on one side.

"Ocean!"

He scrambles forward, searching frantically before he sees it: a hand grasping at the edge of the scaffolding. The fingers grip into a gap between the last two planks of wood. Haven dives forward and grabs onto the wrist.

Ocean's head pops up from the edge. She's hanging by her left hand. Her right hand comes up to try and connect with Haven's, but when he grabs on to it tightly, she yelps. The fingers are broken. He grabs lower, on her wrist.

"I find myself in this predicament a lot," she says, "don't you think?"

Haven has nothing on the edge to brace against, and when he tries to pull her up, he skids forward. Ocean's eyes go wide.

"Stop," she says. "I'm too heavy. Corvus latched onto me."

Haven hazards a peek over the edge. Corvus dangles in midair. His head lolls back, his mouth slack. He must be knocked out, but his metal arm stretches above him, the hand clamped around Ocean's ankle. No wonder she's so heavy.

"Hold on, Ocean." He clenches his jaw as he desperately casts around for a weight, a crevice, anything he can leverage. Cass and Alessa are on the ground, completely still. Her wrists are sweaty in his hands and they slip before he tightens his grip with a gasp. Haven tries to pull her, but he only slides forward again. "No, godsdamnit *no*." He keeps hold of her as he lies flat on his stomach, stretching his feet back for a purchase, for anything.

"Haven," Ocean says.

He can hear it in her voice. He looks everywhere else but at her. The camera drone zips by. "Help! Oh gods. Please help."

He skids forward, a tiny judder before he locks his limbs violently. She swings her body and he wants to yell at her, to scream at her to stop, before he hears her feet scrabbling on the scaffolding beneath them. She's searching for a foothold, but her legs have nothing to brace on either. Leg. She probably can't even move the one Corvus is attached to. As she moves, they spill forward a few more centimeters.

"He's too heavy," she says. The tendons on their wrists are tight and strained. Her sweaty face is pale, the smeared blood standing out starkly. But her words are detached, a clinical observation. "You have to let go."

"I can't." He means it with every fiber of his being. "Don't leave me. Don't go."

"Haven, please," she says and only now does her calm facade break, letting forth her anguish. "I'm not taking you with me."

"Ocean." He would never have thought her name could scrape his throat like this. The next words tear from him. "You said you didn't want to take my future from me. Please. Please don't."

Ocean's breathing goes ragged. Even as Haven keeps his iron clasp on her wrists, he tries to hold her gaze tighter. But Ocean looks at him like she always has: memorizing him as if she knows she can't take him with her.

"Thank you for seeing me," Ocean says. "I hope you saw how I felt about you." She wrenches her left wrist free from him. The movement slides them forward even more and she stretches back.

"No. Ocean, no," he begs as he grips her right wrist with two hands now.

He's so intent on her that he doesn't register the pounding steps behind him. Doesn't even think about what it could mean until Ocean gapes at something above him.

"Ocean, don't you dare!"

• • • •

It's Von.

His eyes are wild, his hair a bristling mess in the wind. His conference badge flaps in the air as he flops to the ground, holding out his hands for her. And when she stretches for him, he seizes her wrist and yanks her up with Haven.

They drag her up, scraping her body against the scaffold's edge as she scrabbles to help them. Her body's a mess and she's spent, but it doesn't matter because Von's somehow there, has somehow appeared and he's crying now as he pulls up Ocean along with Haven. When she's on the scaffold again, Von engulfs her, his arms wrapped around her. Haven sits back, his chest heaving, and his face stunned but staring at her as if she's a miracle, as if he's never going to stop looking.

"You idiot," Von is saying over and over again.

Ocean feels her body shutting down, the exhaustion finally taking over. She struggles to keep her eyelids open. Corvus's mechanized hand is still clamped onto her foot, and he lies stretched out on the ground. His face is streaked with blood and sweat, but oddly peaceful.

It's only then that she lets herself slump into Von. She says, "You saved me."

Before she finally succumbs to the dark, she hears:

"Us," Haven corrects quietly. "You saved us."

EPILOGUE

"WE'LL RECONVENE ONCE I return," Teo says to the room. "I'll assess the current situation and bring back a detailed report."

"And you think this is the right decision? To hand it over to... to..." Hodgson asks skeptically from the side.

"To the people who live there? Do I think it's wise to relinquish control that we never should have had in the first place?" Teo asks. "'What is the city but the people?' We should have done this long ago, and we'll offer Mercury the assistance that they're owed."

He inspects his hands. At his first board meeting, they wouldn't stop shaking, but he no longer has that problem. When he raises his head again, Gibson nods at him from his usual corner. The rest of the room is gathering their tabulas. More than a few of them were uncertain whether he'd measure up to the task. They've been waiting for him to slip up these past several weeks; he hasn't given them an opportunity to criticize him.

Not that they had a choice in allowing him a seat here. After Teo's parents' and Declan's wills were uncovered, it was found they had left all their shares to him. Teo had wept, although he waited until he was alone to do it. He's not sure anyone would have understood him.

Footage from the infamous summit was broadcast live across the solar, thanks to Lupus and with the help of Minwoo and Shinjeong Co. Everyone saw Teo expose Hadrian and then fight Corvus and his crew, the same Corvus who had been seen all over the solar killing people left and right. The tech behind his glove has been theorized upon widely since, but it's mere speculation. Gemini quietly destroyed the glove itself, although the Alliance has no idea about that.

Confessions were extracted from Alessa during her fight with Ocean and Cass, exonerating Teo. Lupus submitted an entire portfolio outlining Corvus's history and his work over the past decades, all leading up to what had happened on the *Shadowfax* and beyond. Hadrian died, but Corvus himself is in a coma, and Alessa is awaiting trial. Emory disappeared without a trace . . . Well, no, not entirely. She did, after all, leave her arm behind with Corvus, like some modified Cinderella tale. The members of the *Pandia* and former *Ohneul* came through—some a little more banged up than others, and it was touch and go with Dae for a bit—but they're still standing.

Teo walks out of the boardroom and down the hall to his office. When he opens the door, he pauses. Phoenix sits in the windowsill, his leg bent up and the wind ruffling his hair.

Teo closes the door behind him. "Front door too easy for you?"

Phoenix turns his head, and Teo marvels. Will the mere sight of him always hold this power? It's been this way since the first day he saw Phoenix framed in the entrance to the *Ohneul*, reciting *Coriolanus*.

"Gem's not the only one who can scale walls." Phoenix asks, "How did it go?"

Teo joins him on the window seat. "Much less exciting than my first presentation with Anand Tech," he says. "No swords, no murder attempts."

Phoenix takes Teo's hand, skimming his touch over Teo's wrist, his palm. He leans forward and Teo closes his eyes as Phoenix kisses him on the mouth, the cheek, and then once over each closed eyelid. His fingers briefly flutter over Teo's forehead where he has marks from where Corvus's glove punctured him.

Teo hasn't figured out what's gone, how he's changed, how much Corvus shared with him. But the memories he thought he lost, the ones he felt being ripped from him, left shadows in his mind. Memories are tricky like that. You can't excise one cleanly. One is linked to several hundreds of other impressions, other feelings, other scenes.

"How long can you stay?" Teo asks, his eyes still closed.

"Mm . . . I'm giving the *Pandia* crew a break. I think they deserve it."

Teo opens his eyes to take in Phoenix's sun-kissed skin, his radiant blue eyes. He leans forward and kisses Phoenix. "They're taking a break from you?"

Phoenix smiles against Teo's mouth. "Do you blame them?"

"Yes."

Phoenix laughs. "Cass and Aries took the ship to Venus for some upgrades. They found a shop highly recommended by a local."

"Which I'm sure had nothing to do with the fact that the local runs the shop." A local who apparently made a small cameo appearance on the final episode of *Cemetery Venus*.

"Indubitably," Phoenix says. "Lupus snuck into a film festival in Busan. They probably won't see the sun for a couple of weeks, which is to say, nothing outside of the norm."

"And Ocean and Gemini?"

"They're taking care of some personal business," Phoenix says.

Teo twines his fingers with Phoenix's. "You'll watch out for each other?"

Phoenix's eyes soften. "Always."

"And you?" Teo asks. "Don't you deserve a break from playing Hong Gildong?"

"I always fancied myself more of a Robin Hood," Phoenix says. "Besides, I heard someone important is visiting Mercury. He might need some assistance traveling around."

"Someone important? And you know him?" Teo teases.

"'By the elements,'" Phoenix says, "'If e'er again I meet him beard to beard . . .'" Phoenix smiles and Teo has to kiss that smiling mouth again before he finishes the line for him.

"'. . . he's mine, or I am his.'"

• • • •

When Ocean comes back home, her umma opens the door.

It's like two worn puzzle pieces that take a moment to come together, that require a moment of *Does this fit here?* Then her umma opens the door wider.

"Babeun meogeoseo?"

Ocean shakes her head. Behind her umma, Appa pushes up from his seat at the table. His hand goes up to his mouth.

"You're in time for dinner," her umma says.

And that's it.

Later, Ocean goes swimming in the waters surrounding Marado for the first time in years. The first time since she was rejected from the haenyeo. She cuts through the waves, kicking strongly. She dives underwater. Deeper and deeper. Her lungs burn but she pushes against their plea for air. The ocean is vast, timeless, impartial and embracing all at once. Inside of it, floating on its surface, she's weightless.

Ocean-ah. Her mother says it in a particular way, comforting and abrasive all at once. The night before, Ocean took her blanket and pillow into her parents' room to curl up in between them. They had both curved inward toward her. Her father's breaths even and slow as his arm draped over her shoulder. Her mother taking her hand in hers. And as Ocean lay there, she thought about how small her mother's hands had gotten. Ocean's hand could envelope hers so easily.

The next morning, her umma had asked her if she wanted to come along to swim with the haenyeo.

"No," Ocean said. Her mother nodded as if she understood and moved to leave. Ocean said, "But some other day."

After all, the waters are in her name.

"You shouldn't strain yourself."

The voice comes from her right and is accompanied by a splash as a body lowers itself from a small rowboat. She straightens in the water, treading it, and a head emerges from the surface, spilling water from his dark hair as he paddles lethargically around her.

"Neither should you," she says.

Hurakan dips his head underwater and comes up again a ways away. "I think your umma likes me." He glances at her sidelong.

Ocean has to laugh. "She thinks you're very handsome."

"She's not wrong."

Ocean's umma has unsurprisingly taken to Hurakan with all his charm, ever since she noticed him behind Ocean at the door and gaped at him.

"She thinks you're my last hope for marriage." And she's fed him accordingly.

Hurakan doesn't laugh or provide another witty rejoinder, and Ocean assumes he's disappeared underwater again until she finds him studying her. Then he splashes water at her.

"You're very marriageable now," he says. "The whole solar might have fallen in love with you after all that heroic footage."

"I haven't watched any of it," Ocean confesses. She doesn't think she ever will. She lifts her wet hands and smooths her short hair back. "I think you might be mistaking me for Dae. She's the hero of the Alliance now."

Teo's nickname for Dae has caught on: *Daebak*. Dae's been offered another position, another ship, but she's not sure yet whether she'll take it. She did ask Ocean to come along to help her pick out a new ship if she does though.

"It suits her." Hurakan laughs. "You could be an Alliance hero too, if you let them claim you. They'd be happy to."

"No," Ocean says slowly and thinks again of her umma's offer. "I'm not theirs anymore."

Hurakan swims away, his movements deliberate, the water barely swelling as he cuts through it. He pulls himself up on the boat again, the water streaming from his long, lithe back. She follows him, and he pulls her up. He doesn't let go of her arm, though, when she's up on the boat with him.

"I'm going to ask you something," he says. "And you don't have to answer, if you don't want to."

Ocean's aware then of how quiet it is out on the water. They're on the opposite side of the island from where the haenyeo dive, not too far from the shore. The air is crisp on her skin. A drop of water glides down Hurakan's neck.

"What is it?" she asks.

"Can I kiss you?"

The question startles her, but his own face remains neutral.

"Why?"

He lets go of her arm and huffs out a breath to the side. "You never ask why. Why would you start now?" He arches his eyebrow at her. "I promise it doesn't mean anything. Won't mean anything."

They float on the water as he waits on her answer. She focuses on the beauty mark on the tip of his nose, the line of his throat as he swallows.

"All right," she says.

He doesn't ask her if she's certain. He actually doesn't react except to bring his hands forward to hold her face. He leans forward, his eyes closing. Her eyes slide closed too and he kisses her, his thumbs brushing her cheeks. His lips taste like salt, and he opens his mouth against hers, touches his tongue to hers, and it's like he's pressed tears into her mouth. When he breaks away and she opens her eyes, he's so close she can see the moisture on his dark eyelashes, the two earrings in his left ear that match hers, the water droplets on his face.

Then he's gone, picking up the oars and arching backward to row them home.

"I wanted to try it once," he says, his face turned away.

But it's that angle, the profile with his ear, that reminds her finally.

"You said you'd tell me about the earring," she says, taking up the oars as well. "When we were done with the job in Seoul."

"I did, didn't I?"

He finally smiles, that same dazzling smile she saw on top of the bridge.

"I changed my mind," he says. "Some secrets are meant to be kept." He's solemn now, closed off, as they match strokes. "We have somewhere else we need to be, don't we?"

"Are you that eager to taste my mother's cooking again?"

"You know that's not what I mean."

• • • • •

Outside of Prometheus, outside of home, the sun never felt so tangible as this. Haven basks in its rays. He senses someone coming to stand next to him. He leaves his head tilted back, but he opens his eyes to look sideways.

"Baba," he says with surprise.

"Haven," his father replies, but nothing else.

This stretch of silence between them has been unusual, but Haven thinks his father has been giving him some space. Sometimes when they're eating together, when they're sitting together, Haven's thoughts flit elsewhere and he'll come back to himself to find his father watching him.

"Are you ready, Haven?"

It has been a while since Haven has performed a ritual dance for the vultures to descend. Maybe dancing on that ground again will be what finally makes him feel he's returned. But this question is so like another one from long ago.

"Are you afraid?"

"Baba," he says the word slowly. "Do you think I'm ready?"

He hasn't been gone long, but his father has gotten so old. It hurts his heart to see it. But he recognizes his father's face, his movements, the pauses accompanying his words. But this, this dancing around with their intentions is new. The carefulness of this pains him, but it also aches because it reminds him too much of someone else.

"You have always been such a good pesar," his father says.

Before, Haven might have rebuffed this, might have thought it was some prelude to his father pushing him away. He drapes his hands in his lap, knitting his fingers together. "Why did you want me to join the Alliance?"

"I wanted you to experience the grace of others."

"I thought you wanted me to experience the solar," says Haven. "See it with my own eyes."

"You have always been so loyal to me," his father says. "You were so stubborn, and you wanted to make sure I wasn't rejected." His father touches his shoulder. "But if you chose a different life from mine, Haven, it wouldn't mean you were rejecting me."

Haven examines his hands, the long fingers he laces together and unlaces. "To experience the grace of others," he repeats. "But that required me to be humbled, didn't it?"

The knuckles on his right hand now have scar tissue. These hands tried so hard to hold on to Ocean on top of the scaffolding. This hand touched her face when he first spoke her name. These hands stitched up Cass, gripped Phoenix's legs in the car. They encircled a warm cup Von made for him and held Teo's head.

"We all require grace," his father says.

Haven wants to weep. He even, unfairly, wants to rail against his father, for encouraging him to leave, for not warning him how you can never really come back home. He has changed, and home is somewhere someone else now, but the realization always comes too late.

"I am sorry to you," he says instead. "And I am sorry to Esfir too."

"Ah, Esfir," his father says. "She stayed here for a while, even after your last conversation. I think she was hoping to speak with you in person, maybe to piece together what happened better. I might have tried to convince you to change your mind too."

She hadn't been home when Haven came back though. Neither of them has reached out to the other, and Haven thinks that's for the best for now.

"But not anymore?" Haven asks.

"She left after we saw that broadcast. The one from Seoul," he says. "I think . . . when she saw you with that woman, she finally knew."

"She knew?" Haven repeats. "She could tell?"

His father's sad expression is more yearning, Haven realizes, than mournful. "Haven," he says gently. "I think the whole solar could tell."

Haven's hand goes to his chest, at the sharp throb. When he doesn't speak again, his father touches him on the shoulder. "Haven, I'm happy to have you here. I will always be happy to have you home."

He gently pushes his shoulder toward where a group has already assembled.

Vultures circle overhead; Haven steps into the middle of the clearing to dance for them. Mortemians gather around; Haven dances for them. He doesn't look into the faces of the small group assembled, he doesn't look for his father, but he knows that his father is there.

"Are you afraid?"

Haven dances his answer to that question, his arms outstretched as he imagines wings sprouting from his back. He sweeps his leg around him in a circle, the dust of the dry dirt rising in clouds. Every time he dances, he carries the history of the rituals done before him, he carries his own history inside him. His spine is straight as he balances his weight on his two legs, arms raised and elbows bent in a samabhanga.

Haven spins around, his foot coming down lightly once, before he lifts it and steps farther out. The sun touches his closed eyelids. He stretches his leg backward in an arabesque, lifting on the ball of his left toe as he holds the position in the air, feeling the strength and the solidity of it. He sketches a combination on the ground, and this one is a series of steps he didn't learn from his father or any other Mortemian; it's a combination that Cass taught him, now imprinted into his body. He leaps in the air, and his arms sweep out as he remembers the first time he saw Ocean in the subway, how her dance moved him.

His movements speed up, his steps scuffling up dust as he whirls around with his knees bent, his arms reaching out and in, his chin lifted one way and then the other. His body is subsumed in the steps as he gives himself over to the moksha.

When he opens his eyes, it's to vultures circling, descending from the sky, their dark wings spread wide like his arms, welcoming them back down to the earth. With his eyes open to their wings, his skin soaking in the sun here on Prometheus, the eyes of his father on him, he has his answer.

He stands there, panting, his sweat sliding down his arms. Around him, the others murmur, already moving about, stepping in for the next part of the ritual. He lifts his arm to wipe his brow and turns.

And sees her.

Ocean stands at the edge of the clearing. Her shirt's sleeveless, leaving bare her slender arms with their new scars lancing from where she was shot. He tries to move, tries to think beyond how this isn't possible.

"Ocean," he says. "I was thinking of you."

One corner of Ocean's mouth lifts. "I could tell."

Haven's limbs practically melt. He takes a step before he realizes. Catches himself. His father is several paces away, regarding Haven with his yearning expression from earlier. It mingles with a pained recognition before his face creases into a smile. He motions to Haven. *Go. We'll take it from here.* Haven walks to Ocean, while automatically, helplessly cataloging all the changes in her, all the details he's familiar with.

"How did you . . ." He trails off. His records have to be in the Alliance directory. And even if they aren't, Lupus can likely look up anything. "Why . . ."

"I actually came by your house earlier, but only your father was home. He invited me to the ritual," she says. As they walk, their steps match each other. "Phoenix told us to take some time off. We're not hard up on funds for now. Probably not for a while."

"What does Phoenix have planned for all of you?"

"We're going to figure it out together," Ocean says. "It was always about trying to balance things out, one step, one person at a time. So we'll determine what that means for all of us. But first,

I think we're going to take Lupus's research and try to rectify what Corvus did."

He loves how her mouth shapes the words *us* and *we*, and it makes him ache too. "Do you have a constellation name now too?"

"I do. It's Grus."

"Grus?"

"It's the Crane constellation." She considers. "Although, I've grown to like my given name as is. I might keep it." She tucks her hair behind her ear, unconsciously showing off her tattoo.

"You rode out here?" he asks.

"Phoenix let me borrow a holobike," she says, then adds, "We missed you at Von's wedding."

"I'm sorry I didn't make it," he says. Couldn't make it. It had been too soon for him.

"I think Von was bursting with too much happiness that day to let anything get him down."

Their steps crunch in the dirt and once again, Haven tries to wrap his mind around this, having Ocean next to him as they walk a path he's taken hundreds of times on his own. To have his past now superimposed with an image of her feet next to his, of her shoulder next to his, of her voice.

"Teo threatened to show up at my doorstep," Haven says. "But I guess you beat him to it."

"Well," Ocean says. "We can give him a different doorstep to come to."

Haven stops walking and Ocean faces him. He reaches for her hand. He only means to graze it, but he can't stop himself from taking it. He traces her skin, grazing over the knuckles, marveling at the touch even as he watches Ocean react.

EPILOGUE 395

"I wasn't planning on staying here for much longer," he admits.

He's lain awake at night, thinking what he'd do if he had her before him again. The competing desires to savor, to devour. It trembles in the air as she looks down at their hands, as pink grazes her cheek. He wants her close, he wants to touch, he wants to taste.

"Phoenix has a constellation name for you too."

Ocean's searching his face for his reaction, but her words aren't making enough sense to elicit one.

"For me?"

"It's Lyra," Ocean says. "It's the name of the lyre Orpheus played. But it's commonly depicted on star maps as a vulture carrying a lyre. He thought it would be appropriate."

"What are you saying?" His own voice sounds far away.

"That you have a place with us. With me. If you want."

Haven's breath catches in his throat. With us, with me. Which is it? "If I want?" he repeats. "Is that . . . Is that what you want?"

"Haven."

He's glad she stops because he has to close his eyes against the way she says his name, like it's precious to her. This can't be real. When he opens his eyes again, she's watching him with an openness that threatens to break him. He's come to appreciate that vulnerability as much as his own, to accept it in its broken, imperfect, differing way.

"Haven, do you want to go for a ride?" She tilts her head. She smiles crookedly. "I brought an extra helmet for you."

His own happiness spills forth. "Ocean."

Whatever's in his voice, in his eyes, makes her reach for him. Her hand stops before his face. And he could laugh at the absurdity of it, that she somehow doesn't know that his whole existence hungers for this.

He says, "I told you once that you could lay your hands on me if you were saving my life."

He moves her palm against his cheek, turns his face into it. Her other hand draws a line over his brow, his ear. It curves down the back of his neck, tracing the feathers that dip below his collar. Her touch is like the completion of his self. He opens his mouth to kiss her palm.

Ocean tastes like a blessing, like grace.

ACKNOWLEDGMENTS

The first conversation Sam and I had was about what books we were reading, which seemed auspicious, to say the least. Everything felt natural and good and "of course" with Sam from the beginning. There's never been any doubt that this is my best life with my best person, and how unbelievably fortunate am I to be able to say that? It might be a given then to hear that Sam believed (and kept believing, and still believes) in my writing more than I ever did, and this book (and certainly *Ocean's Godori*) would not exist without him. Not just because of that belief, or because I was able to bounce off ideas and winnow out characters with him, or because of his general cheerleading (I always say that my mom has bought the most copies of my book, but that Sam has definitely sold the most copies)—but because I would not be the writer I am, the person I am, without him. Thank you for coming into my life, Sam, for every conversation we've had since that first one, for supporting and challenging me, and for loving me in all my forms.

My mom rightfully received top billing with my first book, and since the last acknowledgments, she has faithfully taken pictures of my book in stores, come along to events, and was even my +1 at Comic Con, to the delight of all. I love you, umma. I am eternally thankful to be your daughter.

I've always known how lucky I was to have Amy Bishop-Wycisk as an agent, but as time goes on, I keep having to adjust my concept of how lucky I am. The more I work with her, the more I realize "Wow, I am so much luckier than I even realized," and this is a feeling that somehow keeps expanding. Thanks for taking a chance on me, Amy, and thank you for being in my corner.

Editing is a job that obviously requires a lot of expertise, but a good editor is nothing without empathy, and for that I'm so very grateful for Lexy Cassola. It cannot have been easy to take on a book that was a sequel, and she did it with so much care and attention for the story, my intentions, and the characters. Thank you for all that you do, Lexy—for your thoughtfulness, patience, kind communication, and for working with me so painstakingly to make sure that we delivered a story true to what I wanted to put out into the universe. Thanks so much for picking up *Teo's Durumi*, and for taking such good care of it (and me).

And thank you so much to the Zando team. To Molly Stern, who made it possible for my book to make it out to the world. To Nathalie Ramirez, Andrew Rein, and Emily Morris, whom I was able to meet in person and received so much support from!—and a special THANKS to Emily for organizing every conceivable thing I threw at her with such aplomb. To Sara Hayet and Chloe Texier-Rose, who are no longer a part of Zando, but were and are a huge part of *Ocean's Godori* reaching people (and who are also so very kind and cool and have great hair). To Zoey Cole, Natalie

Ullman, and Sierra Stovall for their savvy work and guidance. And a special thank you to Katie Burdett for all her help!

Thank you to Hillman Grad Books—to Lena Waithe, Naomi Funabashi, and Rishi Rajani. I'm so proud to be part of this family. Thank you for allowing me to continue this journey with you. And what a journey it's been! This last year has been full of moments that I will remember and keep close, always, and all because you invited me in. Thanks also to Marquis Phifér and Travis Ing for your kindness, your help, and always being a friendly face at events.

I cannot express enough thanks for Judy Alice Lee, whom I am a fan of forever. It makes me so incredibly happy to think of your voice introducing Ocean to readers, and really it was a dream come true to have you narrate. Thank you so much for your artistry. Thank you thank you to you and Jared Jeffries for all your work for the audiobook recording!

Jee-ook Choi is another dream manifested, and I am ecstatic to have her back for the cover of *Teo's Durumi*. I could ask what I've done to deserve such gorgeous work by Jee-ook and Zando's art director, Christopher King, but the answer is nothing I did could possibly be deserving of such art. Thank you, both.

Thank you to Jesse Oh, beloved 동생 and much respected fellow artist and collaborator. Thanks for letting me use discarded band names for the various clubs used throughout the Alliance series (yes, Psy/Cho and Cool Ranch Norito (놀이터) are from him), for jamming on an 이어도 rendition for the *Ocean's Godori* pre-launch with me, for connecting me to Frederick Park for stick shift driving lessons (Hi, Fred! Thank you!!), and for being an all-around cool and chill human being.

Thank you to Ellis Breunig for our hangouts, for sharing your work with me, and for being someone I could mutually share writing and life with. Thank you for giving me the conviction to hold true to what I wanted for the story and my characters in a time when I was rather uncertain of it all.

Last time, I said Yuki Hayashi's music fueled 95% of my writing/editing, and I'd say that the percentage still holds true. I will continue to express my ardor in the pages of my acknowledgments until the end of (my writing) time. Thank you!!

Thank you again to Whitney Bak for your eagle eyes and razor-sharp copyediting. The Alliance duology is in your debt.

I have so much love for Elliott Bay Book Company and Shelf Awareness, my former and current places of work. I count myself truly blessed to have worked with the coolest, caringest people. I have felt so much love this past year (and before all this book stuff too!). Thank you for always taking care of me.

And on the note of being taken care of, thank you to independent bookstores and their incredibly lovely booksellers. Thank you thank you for reading, for sharing, for inviting me into your stores, and always for talking your latest favorite reads with me. This sequel would not be out now without you.

And finally—a question I got asked often this past year was, who do you write for? And there are a bunch of different ways to answer that, but I really got back into writing because of my favorite reader, Izzy. When people ask me what she's like, I used to answer that we have a lot of similarities, but she's way cooler, funnier, and kinder . . . but that was *vastly* underselling you as the amazing human being you are. Thanks for being my sister. I know you didn't really have a choice in the matter, but that doesn't change how grateful I am to have you. Every day, I count myself lucky (umma should know better than to buy lotto tickets because she got you as a daughter already), but I also think about what an honor it is and how proud I am to be your sister. Thanks.

ABOUT THE AUTHOR

ELAINE U. CHO is the author of *Ocean's Godori* and *Teo's Durumi*. She has an MFA in flute performance and is a kyūdō practitioner.